T0274539

DIVINE MORTALS

DIVINE MORTALS

AMANDA M. HELANDER

HYPERION

Los Angeles   New York

First Edition, October 2024
10 9 8 7 6 5 4 3 2 1
FAC-004510-24206
Printed in the United States of America

This book is set in Adobe Garamond Pro/Adobe.
Designed by Marci Senders

Library of Congress Cataloging-in-Publication Data
Names: Helander, Amanda M, author.
Title: Divine mortals / by Amanda M. Helander.
Description: First edition. • Los Angeles: Hyperion, 2024. • Series: Divine mortals;
book 1 • Audience: Ages 14–18 • Audience: Grades 10–12 • Summary: Soothsayer
Mona Arnett's life changes when the young leader of the royal magicians calls upon
her skill in naming soulmates to help in providing the dying king with an heir, except,
according to Mona's reading, she is the king's soulmate and queen-to-be.
Identifiers: LCCN 2023020674 • ISBN 9781368096171 (hardcover) •
ISBN 9781368096379 (ebook)
Subjects: CYAC: Fantasy. • Magic—Fiction. • Divination—Fiction. • Kings, queens, rulers, etc.—
Fiction. • Love—Fiction. • LCGFT: Fantasy fiction. • Romance fiction. • Novels.
Classification: LCC PZ7.1.H44528 Di 2024 • DDC [Fic]—dc23
LC record available at https://lccn.loc.gov/2023020674

Reinforced binding
Visit www.HyperionTeens.com

For Gma and GP—a true soulmate match

DRAMATIS PERSONAE

MONA ARNETT .... A Soothsayer

TASHA D'MILLIAR .... A Sorceress

ELSIE TANNER .... A Commoner

THE GODS OF THE FLOOD

SEMYANADD .... Wolf God of the Earth

ONYAMARR .... Whale Goddess of the Sea

IRINORR .... Crow God of Love

KORIMARR .... Turtle Goddess of Knowledge

WAYVADD .... Cat God of Self

VERIMALL .... Boar Goddess of Violence

ELEDORR .... Moth Goddess of Death

THE ROYAL FAMILY

KING ISAAC OF HOUSE ANGLINE .... The Last of the Royal Line

THE KING'S COUNCIL

DELMAR WHITMAN .... Master of Practitioners

CELIA RENFIELD .... Master of Whispers

IN GAN .... Master of Ceremonies

LUTHAR PENNA .... Master of Faith

GEORG OVERSEA .... Master of Justice

OLIVIA LANE .... Master of War

TRISTAN SOPH .... Master of Commerce

THE ROYAL PRACTITIONERS COMPANY

BERNADETTE BYERS .... A Soothsayer

ALICE JANIEUX .... A Soothsayer

JOHN HAWKES .... A Soothsayer

FEN TELLERMAN .... A Soothsayer

DANIEL CERVANTEZ .... An Enchanter

JEFFREY TOOMBS .... An Enchanter

PERCY UMBER .... An Alchemist

TALIA'AH AHDUT .... An Alchemist

DIVINE MORTALS

PROLOGUE

The first time I stepped into the Flood, I had just killed my brother. I was eight years old.

We'd been on our evening walk—we took one every night in the summer. Patrick said it was time to go home. I never wanted to do what he told me; he was twelve years my senior and never let me forget it. I ran away, along the bluffs that rose like flat white teeth near the sea. He chased me, caught me by my scarf. We wrestled for it by the cliffside.

He wouldn't let go. He was so much older, and stronger. I asked him, again and again, I *screamed* at him, but he wouldn't let go. So, I did.

And that's when he went over.

I didn't believe my eyes at first. I stood there, my mind pleading with itself, searching for a way out: Maybe the cliff's not as high as you remember, maybe he's only hurt. I knelt on the clifftop, my heart pelting my ribs so hard they might have cracked. How long I stayed like that, I couldn't say. Face slick with tears, I prayed to Eledorr, the moth. I prayed she would deliver me. I *needed* to die like I'd needed few things in my short, charmed life.

After an eternity of stillness, I crawled forward—like I was sneaking up on it, this awful thing I'd done. I forced myself to look. Patrick's body lay contorted at the bottom of the drop. My brother's body. It wasn't the blood that let me know he was dead. It was his limbs—the way they bent at wrong angles, more like a tangled puppet than a person. He still clutched my scarf.

I had killed him. Gods below, I killed my only brother.

Nothing would ever be good again.

There, out of the corner of my eye. A shimmer between two salmonberry bushes. Like a magic spell, the sight drove Patrick's body from my mind. I stood on wobbly legs. Nestled in the bushes was a plane of distortion, hanging at chest height, glimmering like the surface of a pond. I had never seen anything like it.

It seemed perfectly natural to step through.

It felt like nothing, silky as air. I almost thought I'd imagined it. But when I blinked my eyes into focus, the foliage had morphed—no longer sparse, rustling grasses swept by ocean winds, but pillars of alien flora, spongey and moist and glistening like kelp. I gaped and turned in circles, my chapped lips parted.

Everything rippled and swayed. A hundred diamond rings of light reflected off each fir tree whose needles were wispy seaweeds, every colony of eerie orange fungus. The moon above was a pale blue coin, blurry, bobbing like a fisherman's lure in the dusky sky. The smell of brine was overpowering.

My scalp tingled. I lifted my hands to discover that my hair floated upward in a lazy, drifting plume, as if I stood on the bottom of a lake. Yet I could walk without swimming and breathe the water like air.

I could only assume my death prayer had been answered. I'd passed on to the Flood, the realm of the seven gods, and now I would travel to my final resting place in the garden of the dead. Or this was some crafty demon trick, meant to lure me into their enchanted lairs so they could eat my tender heart. Either way, relief coursed through me.

I wouldn't have to tell my mother what I'd done.

The landscape of the Flood stretched flat for a long way. In the distance, I saw a hulking black shape on a hill. A castle, or a fortress. I was too far away to tell. Tirelessly, I hiked along a footpath, through kelp ropes that rose around me like mist, with Patrick's corpse imprinted on my vision. I squeezed my eyes shut, tried to screw them up until all that remained was a wash of dark red, but that didn't help. Nothing helped.

I had been walking for a minute or a day or half a lifetime when a shape appeared in my path. It traveled toward me, cresting a slight hill. The image sharpened as it drew closer.

It was a naked man—mostly. The lower part was human, but above the bare and muscled shoulders sat a giant crow's head, feathers matted and wet, blossoming grotesquely from a fleshy neck. His black eyes glinted as he cocked his head—a twitchy movement, distinctly birdlike yet inquisitive at the same time. He stopped before me. I should have been scared, and part of me was. But a bigger part was ready to face my fate.

"Am I dead?" I asked him.

"No." His beak didn't move, but the words carried through the water clear as a bell.

I looked him straight in his crow eyes and steadied my voice. "Are you here because I killed my brother?"

"No, Mona," he said. "I am here because you loved your brother."

PART I

THE EAST WING

1

I'm lighting Patrick's candle when I hear voices downstairs.

That by itself is not unusual. My parents entertain company often—as do I. But I'm not aware of any appointments today. Hastily, I tidy my sitting room: stacking books of Deveneauxan poetry, tossing errant stockings and ribbons in a heap behind my cabinet, to be trapped against the pink damask walls. Not particularly to my taste, but after ten years of staring at them, I think I would go into shock if they changed.

To me, it seems like yesterday. One long, hazy day since the accident. That's what we call it in the Arnett household: the "accident," nothing more, never mentioning his name in conjunction. Like saying the words aloud, together, would transmute an accident into something much worse.

With an absent frown, I draw the curtain shut around Patrick's altar. It's a modest display: clusters of candles, a dish of sacred seawater. A copper prayer token gleams in the center of the arrangement. The image of a moth scores both sides for Eledorr, goddess of death. I still question that choice of shrine patron. Eledorr ushers souls into the garden of the dead, but I've never gotten the impression she fancies herself a long-term caretaker.

At least, I hope she doesn't. I hope Eledorr stays far, far away from my brother.

Once the sitting room is presentable, I turn my scrutiny on myself. My straw-blond hair falls in neat curls, which I gather at the nape of my neck with a ribbon. I hitch down the baleen corset under my dress until it fits low and snug across my breasts. That tends to help with the tip money.

I've just finished arranging myself on the chaise longue when the door opens. My mother enters, leading a procession of armed men. My facade slips. I've encountered all sorts of customers in my practice, but if any of them carried weapons, they've been more discreet about it. Are they here to arrest me? Perhaps my reputation as a fraud has finally caught up with me. I steady my trembling hands in my lap and put on a mask of amused disinterest.

"Mona, dear, you have visitors," my mother says. I wince at the frailty in her voice. She ought to have sent one of the staff. Two flights of stairs is daunting even for people whose knees don't squeak when they climb.

"Thank you," I say as she closes the door behind her. My muscles relax as soon as it shuts. I hate open doorways. Have since I was eight.

I turn my attention back to the armed men. The leader of the unit is a man in his twenties with a mess of red hair. With him are four bodyguards, standing stiff as boards, clad in King Isaac's black and gold. Mercenaries from the Guild of the Red Boar perhaps, or royal guards on loan from Castle Selledore. A long blade hangs from each of their hips. I try not to stare, not to think about how easily they could cut me to ribbons. But I haven't done anything wrong. Have I?

That's the problem—I always feel like I've done something wrong. Every minute of every day.

"Um. Good day, Ms. Arnett," the leader says in a wavering voice, like he can't decide whether to be imperious or respectful. "My name is Ryan Parsons, um. Yes. I'm assistant to the master of practitioners at Castle Selledore."

My back goes arrow straight. I'm not in trouble—I'm being recruited.

The master of practitioners isn't a magician himself, but a recruiter, manager, and occasional punching bag for elite magical talent. I've wondered if he would come sniffing around eventually. I *have* garnered myself something of a reputation. Of course, how favorably that reputation reflects on me depends on who you ask. I can't blame my detractors and skeptics. I alone have the gift to perform lovers readings, as Irinorr calls them.

It used to bother me. Naively, I thought if I used my magic for good—bringing soulmates together—it might make up for the sins of my past. Instead, I was ridiculed. Only a handful of people visit me with a sincere desire to know their true love. The rest treat me like a circus sideshow. But if I'm going to be a joke, I might as well embrace it.

"And what service may I provide for the master?" I ask with raised brows.

Flustered, Parsons answers, "A—a demonstration is all we seek."

I frown and survey the line of them. Whatever their purpose, they don't mean me harm. That bolsters my confidence; I sharpen the sarcastic edge in my voice. "A daytime diversion, is it? You five were about town and got bored, decided to drop in for a reading?"

One of the guards makes a face, out of amusement or chagrin. I give him a quick once-over. I've seen scant few bodyguards in my time, but a whole lot of society men. I know how they carry themselves. A framework of formal stiffness draped in a superiority complex. This "guard" has it down pat. He's young—very young—but that doesn't fool me.

"Please, miss," Parsons says. His cheeks glow so red it's a marvel he has blood left anywhere else in his body. I take pity on him, because I'm starting to work out what's going on here.

"Fine," I say with a gracious nod. "I'll need an item from you." Parsons begins digging through his pockets, but I stop him. "Not you. Him." I jut my chin at the guard who caught my attention.

My intuition is affirmed when, instead of rushing to comply or looking to his superior officer, the guard stands taller and says, "Why me?"

Coyly, I answer, "Because I've always wanted to do a reading on the master of practitioners."

While the others stand in fragile silence, he fixes me with a long, appraising look. At last, he asks, "How did you know?"

My heart flutters with relief—my guess was right. "Why, you have the bearing of someone who thinks he's important."

My deliberate wording is not lost on him. The faintest of scowls touches his lips.

Delmar Whitman, master of practitioners, is unassumingly handsome, with chestnut-brown hair and dark, dark eyes. He has the pale skin of a scholar or a priest—or a shut-in—and his hair is cropped neatly. Even his guard's costume looks clean and pressed. And he's not much older than my eighteen years. It caused something of a scandal when he was appointed master of practitioners, given his youth and inexperience. But King Isaac selected him personally to serve on the Angline council, over the other masters' objections. It was the hottest gossip at my parents' parties for weeks.

"Anything will do, Master Whitman," I prompt him. "A handkerchief, a lock of hair. But no shoes, please. I don't do shoes."

Hesitant, the master draws his sword and plods over to me. He rests it on my upturned palms. The other men watch, transfixed. I heft the weight of the blade in my hands. Master Whitman backs away, all stern expression and unyielding posture.

I hardly register as the performer in me takes over. With a hum, I bring the hilt of the sword to my face and close one eye to stare down the line of the blade. I know nothing about swords, naturally, but I imagine I look very discerning.

He's probably expecting me to perform my signature lovers reading, but I only do those upon request.

"This is not your sword, Master Whitman," I declare, though I don't need magic to figure that out. "It's a ceremonial blade, and you requisitioned it along with the rest of your disguise. You offered it up because you thought I'd be unable to get your reading from it." I meet his eye. "But you were mistaken."

He stiffens, and a smirk slides onto my lips. I have him. Adrenaline courses through me, the same rush I always feel when giving a reading. The pure thrill of having the upper hand. Just for this moment, I have control of someone's destiny. Not my own—never my own. But this is the next best thing.

Casually, I examine the blade. "Master Whitman, you've employed so many layers of misdirection, it almost makes me wonder if you have something to hide."

He answers in a clipped voice, "Perhaps I'd rather not have my privacy violated."

He's trying to exude an air of authority, but I'm not sure it's working. Beneath that veneer and that youthful face, he must be as nervous as I am. Or maybe that's wishful thinking; maybe I don't want to be the only one in the room who's faking it. My gut feeling is we're locked in a battle of impostors—and the first to show weakness loses.

"So you'd subject your poor assistant instead?" I cross my legs and gesture clumsily with the sword. The thing weighs a ton. Parsons stares bug-eyed at the tip of the blade, his jaw clenched. "Does the master always treat you like this? I hope you're well compensated."

"Just do the reading, please," Whitman snaps. This might be easier than I expected. The fact that he's the prettiest picture I've seen in ages makes it all the more satisfying. He has the kind of face a sculptor could become obsessed with.

Shaking my head clear, I focus on the sword. I test its feel, its balance—not with the acumen of a swordsman, but of a seer. Finally, I set the tip of the blade on my carpet and hold it upright, two fingers on the pommel. The men watch with bated breath. I know what they're waiting for, have known since the moment Parsons asked for a demonstration. They want to see if the rumors are true.

Can Mona Arnett read the future without any tools of the trade? No mirrors, no cards, no runes to throw? Is such a thing even possible?

I let the sword topple to the floor.

It falls to the left. We all stare at it awhile. I frown and pinch my chin, considering my next move. I don't know what comes next any better than my audience. I never know, until I do.

Just one more reason I'm nothing like the rest.

All magic in the mortal realm, so it goes, is built upon runes—the gods' ancient language. Whether painted on stones for divination or etched into copper to imbue enchantments, the magic that sustains our civilization wouldn't be possible without those arcane symbols and the magicians who manipulate them. At least, that's what Irinorr taught me. I don't understand much about runes, but I don't have to. I'm something different.

Other soothsayers can perform obscure readings using runes, but they can't divine names and places and specific events. Half the time, they get back nothing but silence. Those seers are only *sensitive* to magic, like someone who has an ear for music but can't carry a tune. Their magic stems from the Opalvale nexus—the bond that tethers our realm to the Flood. They haven't been favored by the gods, like me.

Irinorr sets me apart from the others. The crow god, patron of love. Protector of the poor, the weak, the disenfranchised. In the fables, he often saves children captured by overzealous demons from being cooked and eaten. Irinorr saved me, too, though not from demons. He saved me from myself. He bonded with me at my lowest point, when my betrayal of Patrick was fresh. He bestowed upon me a magic no one else could claim: the gift of naming soulmates. A magic that required only intuition and my rare, inborn connection to the Flood.

He favored me above all other mortals.

But the truth is, Irinorr didn't choose me because I'm worthy. He chose me because I needed him—and my patron god is nothing if not nurturing.

I stop there. If I dwell on Irinorr, homesickness will crush me. Another week or two, I'd bet, before he deems it safe for me to return to the Flood. Where I belong.

I switch back to the reading, and a feeling niggles at me. It seems appropriate that I crouch down and listen to the sword. I hike up my petticoats, leaning close to the blade. This reading is bound to be challenging, since the sword is not Whitman's. But he carried it on the carriage ride from the castle. Two hours of contact. I ought to be able to glean something.

There it is, barely audible. The sword speaks, whispering in a cold, silky tongue, slipping words into my ear. I lean closer.

And I plunge into the vision.

Through a rippling warp, the sights come to me. I fly through the air across Opalvale. Over marshes and deltas, over the dark-stoned floating bridges that span a speckling of saltwater lakes, their arches topped with green beacons of spellsap shining through the fog. My vision-self swoops over a carriage rolling across cobblestones. I swerve east toward a small village a few miles outside of Selledore—a wetlands town built of stone and stilts, elevated above the miry pools where the goddess Onyamarr's sea-salt demons are said to lurk, stalking children who wander too far. To a cottage with scrubbed wooden walls. I open the door.

The knowledge inhabits me abruptly.

It comes the same way every time—a sudden comprehension, like I always had the answer and needed only to unlock it. My magic is more instinct than art. I follow an impulse, and it shows me the path.

I lift my head. "Channice," I say, "Antony, Michael, and Joanne. Three living, but Joanne died in infancy. Your parents—"

"Enough," Whitman cuts across me, his throat tight. "That's plenty." The rest of them gape at me in moon-faced awe.

"Is it?" I return to my seat and smooth out my skirts, employing every ounce of willpower not to sound smug. "You're a public figure, master. I could have gathered your siblings' names from any number of places."

"Not Joanne." He runs a hand over his stubbly face. Have I rattled him? "Can you give me anything else? A vision of the future?"

"No," I say, perfectly cheerful. In truth, I probably could if I had to. But I'm not so comfortable with the future. It has many paths, branching and weaving, and I never know which to follow. Irinorr says he'll teach me how to tell, one day.

"That's awfully convenient," Whitman says.

"I'm glad you feel that way, sir. I would hate to inconvenience a member of the royal court."

Scowling, Whitman bends over to pick up the sword. He nods in dismissal at Parsons and the guards. They file out the door, leaving me alone with Whitman, and he takes a seat in the wicker chair across from me.

There's one thing of which I'm sure. The master of practitioners didn't come all this way for a show. A sour, acrid taste rises in my throat. I drape my hands over my crossed knees and pretend to listen eagerly.

"It's a nice day," Whitman says, pointing out my sun-soaked window. Reflexively, my eyes dart in its direction. I used to have thick velvet curtains blocking the view, but my mother ordered the staff to remove them. Some sort of exposure therapy. "Why don't we discuss this outside, in the gardens?"

A chill runs down my back. There's something deliberate about his tone, like a test. "If you've got something to say, why not come out and say it?" I reply with a false sweetness so cloying I give myself a toothache.

He studies me in silence, and I stare back, unflinching. I can't let my fear show, or my anger, or the thousand questions running through my head.

"I heard you never leave this house," he says.

He watches my face, searching for some twitch of hysteria, some neurotic glimmer—same as anyone who brings it up. My expression blanks; my limbs go numb. For a split second, I'm back on that clifftop, looking down from a dizzying height, seeing black blood and snapped legs and a broken, lifeless figure that could almost be my brother, if I squint.

Betraying nothing of my thoughts, I shake my head. "I never leave this *wing* of the house."

"For how long?"

"Since I was eight." I glance away, praying he doesn't notice the flicker behind my eyes.

The first time my parents dragged me outside after the accident, I sobbed until I got sick on the grass. So many years have passed since I last strolled the white cliffs of the coast, or visited the port city of Selledore to eat steamed mussels by the bucket, or stood in the misting rain just to feel it on my face. I can't explain it—can't understand it myself. It's not as if I *want* to be this way.

But this is who I am. No point crying about it.

Whitman adjusts the cuffs of his rough-spun tunic. I suspect he's not used to dressing like a common grunt. "If you don't mind me saying so, you seem remarkably well socialized. How is that, if you never go out into the world?"

I smirk. "Surely you've realized the world comes to me."

Whitman's expression remains neutral. I don't think he cares much for me, though he takes pains to hide it. That shouldn't sting, but it does. He must need a big favor from me.

"Have you ever thought about leaving?" he asks.

"No, I really haven't." It's mostly true. I've never been tempted to venture back into the mortal world. On the other hand, I'd run away to the Flood in an instant. The one place I belong, where nothing can touch me.

But Irinorr would never permit it. It isn't safe, he says. Strange, since the Flood is the only place I've felt safe since Patrick died.

Whitman leans forward, hands perched on his knees. "What if you were offered a position in the Royal Practitioners Company?"

The actual offer, spoken aloud, knocks the wind from me. The Royal Practitioners Company. Where the preeminent magicians in the land serve our kingdom and its thirteen provinces, protecting and advancing the interests of Opalvale. No doubt Whitman has plenty of seers in his ranks—and alchemists, and enchanters with their charms and wards—but not anyone like me. I should be tripping over myself to accept.

And maybe I would, in a different life. Maybe I'd have jumped with joy and thanked the seven for the opportunity. But in this life, I am Mona Arnett, the girl who killed her brother, who never leaves the house. That girl doesn't have a future.

"Oh, Master Whitman," I sigh, in what I hope is a dismissive drawl. "If I wanted to be in your stable, I would."

A muscle in his neck tautens. "I would appreciate if you took the offer seriously," he grits out. I'm ruining his well-laid plans. Oh, what a shame. He must have a lot to prove, young and untried as he is. "There are only eight in our ranks at present. Care to guess how many hopefuls I turn away each week?" I don't care to, so he answers himself. "It's in the dozens."

"How nice for you."

He scoffs and sits upright. "Is this a joke to you?"

"Well, yes," I say, placing a musing fingertip to my lips, "though your delivery is all wrong."

We sit at impasse for a few stretching seconds. It doesn't escape me that my callous disregard for the royal magicians might be called blasphemous. Magic is no laughing matter in Opalvale. It's the highest religious duty one can perform, if so able. The gods' gift to humankind, immortalized by the divine runes, to be honored through judicious use.

And perhaps no one has spoken to the master so frankly in a long time. But why should I care about his opinion? I'm no courtier in Selledore, currying favor with the Angline councilors, betting on the victories and downfalls of my peers using reputation as currency. As important as Whitman may be, he can hardly punish me for speaking freely in my own home. What's he going to do—spank me?

Now, there's an idea.

Whitman clears his throat. A flush blooms on my cheeks at the thoughts I've been entertaining. I'm no shrinking violet—not with my parents' glamorous parties and the opportunities they present. Sex is fun, and easy, and completely within my control. But Master Whitman isn't someone I should be fantasizing about. If anything, he's the enemy.

Then again, I'm not above seducing the enemy when called for.

"Let's get down to it," he says. "Come with me to the castle—get the tour, see your accommodations, meet the royal magicians. After that, if you're still not interested, I'll never bother you again." He lowers his chin in a stern look. "But if you refuse, I will send Mr. Parsons to bother you every day until you change your mind."

I scoff. Why does he care so much about recruiting me? The only reason I can think of is my lovers readings. With the power only I possess, I can read the name of a person's true love, their soulmate, the one they're fated to spend their life with. Everything but a home address and a map to get there. But why would Master Whitman believe in my power to name soulmates when far more gullible minds have judged me a fraud?

Maybe he can just tell. He's seen the real deal hundreds of times, after all. A fleeting pulse of elation beats in my chest. What a coup that would be—validation from the Royal Practitioners Company, the highest authority on magic in Opalvale. Still, I can't fathom what use my lovers readings would be to Whitman or the king.

It doesn't matter, anyway. I can never leave this house.

"Master," I say, "I assure you, you're very charming. But I have no interest in your silly magicians' club."

His face turns stony and severe. "Fine. Then I will see you once you decide to stop this foolishness."

"I'm sorry I couldn't be of greater use to you, Master Whitman." I hold out my hand for a parting kiss and give him a significant look.

He ignores my hand, rising to his feet with a razor-thin mouth. "This is important to me, Ms. Arnett. And I'm starting to get a sense of the sort of games you play. Rest assured, I am playing to win. Whatever it takes."

He tosses me one last unhappy glance and sweeps out.

I perform a bit of sighing and slouching on the chaise longue until my mother bustles in. She's wearing her finest semiformal house robe, its lace hem brushing the floor. Must have put it on for the guests. Sitting up, I give her a disapproving pout. "Mother, be careful with all this up and down. It's not good for your knees."

She lowers herself onto the chaise next to me. The tips of her thin, steely hair curl up along her velvet collar. She smells of roses and salt water, like always. "If you'd come downstairs, I wouldn't have to."

Her tone is bland, but I catch the bitterness underneath. I've been nothing but a burden to my parents since I was eight years old. A constant reminder of Patrick's death—a painful memory in human form. If I could make myself useful for something, perhaps that would temper the insult. But I have nothing to offer. My eyes sting; I blink them clear before my mother notices.

"What is it the assistant master wanted?" she asks.

The lie leaps off my tongue. "Oh, he's desperate for a reading. Has some girl he's after."

"I see." My mother frowns, her soft lips wrinkling. "So, when are you going to try for yourself?"

"Try what?"

"Don't be smart. Your soulmate reading." Her tone could beat dye from a rug, it's so firm.

My gaze flat, I kiss her hair and fall back onto the chaise, throwing an arm over my eyes. "I'm fine, thank you," I say, my head hanging upside down.

My mother only wants me to do my own lovers reading so I'll go out and find him. My *soulmate*. Sometimes, I doubt I have one. Surely not every single person in the world is destined for somebody special. Even if I had a soulmate, would I want to know? What would that accomplish? It's not like I would act on it. Yet my mother seems to think knowing would do me some good.

That's if she believes me. Half the time, I wonder if she's humoring me, going along with my claims of unnatural power just to avoid an argument. My father never brings it up at all. I know they'd prefer me to act like other girls my age—attending school, meeting new people, living my life. But my parents are stuck with me. They deal with it the best they can; they try to understand. But everyone reaches the end of their rope eventually.

My mother ran out of slack long ago.

Her hand warms my knee as she stands to leave. "I love you, Mona."

The disapproval is plain in her voice. I squeeze my eyes closed. "I love you, too."

Perhaps my mother just wants me out of the house. Or perhaps she thinks I might achieve some measure of happiness, out there in the world. I don't buy it. Why would I ever leave the east wing? I have everything I need right here.

Everything I deserve.

2

Whitman is good on his word. Assistant Master Parsons shows up at my door the next day and every day that week. On the fifth day, I can tell Whitman has been putting the screws to him. He's sweaty and nervous and more insistent than ever.

"I've been ordered not to go back to the castle without you," he says from my sitting room door.

Reclining on the couch, I stare at the ceiling and sniff in distaste. The oil lamp chandelier, hanging from its gold-painted burst of a medallion, winks down at me. "I can't believe the way that man treats you. It's monstrous. You tell Master Whitman if he wants me so badly, he can come here himself and drag me off by the hair. And use those exact words, if you please."

"But I can't go back—"

"Don't let him intimidate you." I scrape myself off my seat and march up to Parsons, spinning him by his shoulders and shoving him into the hall. "Someone's got to stand up to him."

With that, I slam the door and lie back down, curling up on my side.

This whole ordeal has been a disaster. I long to fill Irinorr in on the annoying details, but I've visited the Flood too often as of late, and he has yet to send me a signal that it's safe. I can't discuss it with my parents, either. I don't bother them with my problems—not since I first told them about the Flood, right after Patrick's death, and they chalked it up to a traumatic hallucination. The Flood is like a story, they said. Real in your heart and head, but not a place you could visit. At least not until you've lived your full life and passed beyond the veil, to be reunited with those who came before you in the garden of the dead.

I doze in fits and starts throughout the afternoon. Around suppertime, someone knocks at my door. I jolt upright, heart thudding, and Agatha, the lady's maid, enters my sitting room.

"You have another visitor," she says, raising her brows. "He looks important."

My pulse quickens, and I ask her to show him in. When Agatha returns, Whitman himself lurks behind her, resentment written all over his face. He's dressed up in his master's uniform—black with a high collar and gold epaulets, a row of gold buttons down the center. My stomach flips with peculiar excitement. Then I remember why he's here, and the excitement snuffs out.

"Master Whitman," I say brightly, like he's an old friend dropping by for a visit. "To what do I owe the pleasure?"

His guise of formality doesn't crack. Or perhaps it's not an act. His smile muscles could have atrophied from years of disuse. "I'm told you wish to speak with me personally."

"Yes, indeed. What took you so long?"

"Believe it or not, I have duties to attend to. And given the state of things, my plate is rather full at the moment, so I'd appreciate if you kept this brief."

I've heard about "the state of things" from my father, a trader with the Guild of Pepperers. There's a botanical disease hitting spellsap orchards across the nations of the Circle Court. No one has lost spellsap lighting or access to alchemical medicine yet, but it's trending in that direction.

And it carries other implications for the superstitious sort: parallels to the myth of the Rising Tide. Withering spellsap orchards are said to be the first sign. Then the resurgence of the seven demon clans, followed by the dead walking among us, and finally, the Flood itself bursting through the veil of the mortal realm like a broken dam, wiping out civilization. Not the most appealing scenario.

"So?" Whitman says, urging me on with a wave. "What is so important that it has to be said to my face?"

Now that he's here, I recognize a flaw in my plan: I don't have one. I didn't really expect him to show. I scramble to make something up.

"Would you like to stay for dinner?" I ask.

He stares at me, unblinking. My face burns hot.

"If I do," he says, "will you agree to come back to Selledore with me?"

No, I will not go with him. I will never go with him. But gears are turning in my head. I like Whitman—well, not as a person. I like his face, and the body attached to it. This may be my last chance to spend time with him. And there goes my mind running off again, imagining all the possibilities that can arise when a young lady is stuck with a handsome, brooding houseguest.

"I might consider it," I hum. "Perhaps. If you stay."

He clenches his jaw. "Very well."

I manage not to grin like an idiot. "Dinner's not until eight. You can stay for the night, if that's more convenient."

"Fine," he grunts.

"Go downstairs and find Deacon. He'll get you situated." I raise my brows and peer at him through my eyelashes. "Unless you'd prefer to sleep in my room?"

He's momentarily speechless, like he's never been propositioned before in his life. Something akin to panic mounts behind his eyes. And with every second that passes, my knotted stomach winds tighter. Have I made a fool of myself?

"No," he says, stilted. "That's not going to happen. Ever."

Well, that answers that. Stuffing down my humiliation, I put on an unruffled air. "Suit yourself. It was just a suggestion." I force a wooden smile. "So, you'll see Deacon about a guest room?"

"I'll do that." He turns to go, but pauses with his hand on the doorknob. His mask of formality is already back in place. "I trust you're not wasting my time, Ms. Arnett."

I blink at him with round, innocent eyes, mostly to keep myself from rolling them. "Of course, master." I might feel bad about lying, if he wasn't such a pain in my ass.

I find next to no peace that afternoon as I wait for dinner. I set out to distract myself. Reading poetry. Napping. Replaying my embarrassing pass at Whitman over and over in my head. Writing a letter to my parents, the same one I've been trying to write for ten years, which begins *Dear Mother and Father, I'm sorry*, and never goes further than that . . .

When I unstick my crusted eyelids, my cheek is pressed against the writing desk. I rub my sore neck, orienting myself; I must have fallen asleep. A sound like a low wind rushes through my ears. I glance around, wincing as my fingers work a muscle knot at the base of my skull.

A man stands by my window.

Screaming, I stumble out of my chair, scrambling back until I hit the wall. How did someone get in here? A sickening dread rolls through me, from the bottom of my stomach up. Whatever this stranger wants from me, I'll hand it over in an instant. I'm not a fighter; I'm a survivor, and I mean to get out of this alive. I hold up my arms as a sign of surrender.

The intruder steps closer. His skin, his clothes, everything about him is washed out, near-translucent white. He glows in the moonlight. Water streams off the fingertips of one hand, puddling on the floor. In the other, he holds a red handkerchief.

No, not a handkerchief. A scarf.

I look up at his face. A pale oval, skin sagging, eyes sunken above crescents of bruised flesh. I recognize him. Couldn't forget him if I tried.

Panic doesn't begin to describe the feeling that constricts my throat, threatens to buckle my knees. When he takes another step, my hands scrabble against the wall as I press back, like I might phase through it.

"Patrick," I croak.

Patrick doesn't reply—doesn't show any sign of recognition. His shambling gait brings him closer and closer. *Run*, screams a voice in my head. But this is my brother, or some version of him. I haven't seen him since I was eight. Ten years of missing him, of praying for his forgiveness. I can't tear my eyes away.

He's a foot in front of me now. I have a decision to make: flee, or stand here and face my fate. Patrick lurches forward, visage blank, arms raised. I shut my eyes and dive to the side.

I'm not fast enough. Patrick moves to block my path, crashing into me with his ghostly body. He feels solid, impossibly real. I twist away, but his limbs are tangled with mine, his grip tight on my forearms. His touch is moist and lukewarm, like the Flood. I chance a peek at him. His wide eyes are disoriented and angrier than I ever saw him in life.

Patrick clutches my chin and forces me to face him. There is no familiarity there, no warmth. He bares his teeth and slides his hand downward, squeezing the tendons of my neck hard enough to crumple my windpipe. Wheezing, I claw at his hand.

With a shove, he sends me sprawling onto the floor. I land on my hip with a thud, coughing. He tried to kill me. My own brother. But I don't have time to dwell on it—I'm busy surviving. As fast as I can, I scramble to my hands and knees, ready to flee.

Patrick towers over me, his anger dissipating. He looks like he doesn't know where he is or how he got there. Still, whether by accident or design, he's blocking the doorway, trapping me inside. I try to think of a way out. Maybe there isn't one.

Maybe it would be better if he killed me.

Then something catches my eye: a glimmer in the air, to Patrick's side. A window to the Flood. On occasion—rarely—one appears of its own accord. Usually when I'm desperate.

My gaze trained on Patrick, I peel myself from the floorboards. His wet eyes follow me.

Hurtling forward, I dive past him into the Flood.

I huddle in the dirt, hugging myself, squeezing my eyes shut.

"What is it, child?" says a voice.

I peek through my eyelids. I'm kneeling on a narrow path through the Flood's lowlands. Above me, the purple sky is webbed with white stars. Gentle currents lap at my dress. Irinorr stands in front of me, his oversized crow's head angled down, concerned.

The sight of him brings immediate relief, but not as much as I'd like. "Something happened," I tell Irinorr between panting breaths. "I saw Patrick, but he—he was . . . dead."

Irinorr considers this without moving a feather. "You saw his mortal spirit?"

"I don't know, I—I suppose." Trembling, I weave my fingers into my curls and grip them.

I've never believed in ghosts. Certain scriptures claim the souls of the unfaithful will be denied access to the afterlife, forced to wander the mortal world. Pure fiction. According to Irinorr, all souls depart to the garden of the dead, regardless of how many prayer tokens they left at altars.

It makes no sense either way. Patrick had been a devout man. He was the one who took me to the chapel in south Seaward twice a week after my parents became too infirm. Who read to me from *Myths of Sun, Moon, and Storm*. Who comforted me at night, promised the shadows outside my window couldn't hurt me if I slept with a prayer token underneath my pillow. A fresh swell of tears presses against the backs of my eyes.

Irinorr sits down beside me, naked as always, but it is an inoffensive nakedness, like an anatomy drawing. I release a breath. His nearness comforts me more than words ever could.

It hasn't always been so. Irinorr scared me at first, with his black eyes and long, blunted beak. He reminded me of living marble, blocked in black and white. But he was kind to me, that first day in the Flood, and so I came back. That's when he took me under his wing as his favored mortal. He told me then, and often in the years to follow, that he would always love me, no matter what I'd done. No matter what I was.

"I am concerned," Irinorr says at last. "If mortal spirits are crossing over to your realm, there are bigger forces at play."

I flinch, my heart plummeting. "Like what?" My thoughts careen back to the dying spellsap orchards, the myth of the Rising Tide. Demon armies are supposed to come before the dead rising from their graves, but maybe the folklore got it backward.

"I cannot say what the cause may be," Irinorr answers. That brings a small measure of comfort. If the apocalypse had started, the gods would be the first to know. "I must consult the rest of the seven."

"Will Patrick come back?" I ask Irinorr in a small voice. For all I know, his ghost is still lurking in my sitting room. "He tried to choke me, Iri. I think he hates me."

Irinorr clicks his beak, troubled. "He may not be fully himself, outside of the Flood. Mortal spirits in the garden of the dead are more self-aware."

While he ponders it, I stare over the seaweed bushes. Above the waving strands of kelp, a school of silvery fish wriggles through the air. Or the water. The Flood often behaves as both. Irinorr once told me it's neither water nor air, but magic.

Somewhere out there, the demons are hunkered down in their burrows. The roads that crisscross the Flood used to be theirs, when the seven demon clans still dwelled in open villages. Then they nearly annihilated each other over their avarice for runes and magic. That doesn't mean they won't raise their scaly heads now and again. I've seen their scouting parties before, but always from a faraway hilltop with Irinorr beside me.

"There may be a way to ensure your safety," Irinorr says. "But you will not like it."

I grip his ice-cold forearm. "I'll do anything. Just tell me what."

"Mortals are creatures of habit, even in death. Patrick's spirit has a connection to your home. Perhaps he cannot travel beyond its walls."

So, Patrick will always be able to find me in the east wing. "What about my parents?" I ask with a lurch in my stomach. "Will he come for them?"

"How would you protect them if he does?"

He has a point. I can only hope Patrick focuses his hatred on me. I clutch my temples, cursing.

"It does you no good to stay there," Irinorr adds. "You will be safer somewhere else—anywhere else. Until we learn more."

"I can't, though," I shoot back, sharper than intended. Irinorr is well aware I don't leave the east wing. "I have nowhere to go."

"Mona." He gives me a look of gentle reproach. "I know you have been invited to stay at Castle Selledore."

Of course he knows. Irinorr watches over me, keeps tabs on my life. I should've known better than to hide something from him. But what he's suggesting is impossible. Isn't it?

Perhaps it wouldn't be *that* bad, going to the castle—just another room in another big house. But then I imagine stepping through my front door, into the fresh air and sunlight. My stomach pinches with pain. No, that isn't an option. I banish the idea from my mind, and my body relaxes. There must be another way.

"Can't I stay with you?" I ask.

Irinorr's black eyes shift. I recognize that look, and I know what gives him pause. My least favorite rule, the one Irinorr enforces with an iron beak: Never stay too long in the Flood. The magic of the Flood can rip a mortal soul in half, in great enough doses. Death follows soon after.

It's beyond unfair. How many nights have I spent praying, crying into my clasped hands, begging to be swept away to the Flood for good? Irinorr insists it's impossible. I've pestered him to explain why so many times I lost count. He's told me, again and again, that the answers would give me no comfort. It doesn't stop me from wondering. What would it be like to disappear into the Flood? To build a shelter of driftwood and kelp ropes, away from any prowling demons, to steal food from coffers and cellars in the mortal world, to read poetry until I wrinkled up and grew old?

"No," Irinorr replies. "You cannot stay in the Flood."

My hopes crumble, though I had no reason to expect another answer. "But—"

"I'm sorry, Mona. It is not safe for you."

"It's not safe to go home!"

"I am suggesting no such thing." He lifts my chin with a finger, forcing me to meet his eye. "There is no better place for you than Castle Selledore. If I am wrong about your brother—if he follows—at least you will have the royal magicians at your disposal. They may be able to protect you until we learn what has caused this."

"How, Iri?" I shout, throwing up my hands. How can anyone protect me against an attacker who can't be wounded—who can't die? I curl in on myself, groaning in frustration.

"Hush," Irinorr soothes, rubbing my back. When I look over, he smiles a sad smile with his big black eyes.

"My child, I am not asking," he says. "I am telling you what must be done."

I sit there numb with disbelief. I've never disobeyed my patron god, not once. But leaving my house for the first time since I was little? It sounds surreal even in my head. As I stare at the gritty sand, I struggle to come to terms with it. Somewhere deep, deep down, I know Irinorr is right. The castle presents a perfect opportunity to run. It would be stupid to ignore it.

And what choice do I have? I can't tell Irinorr no.

"Do you understand me, Mona," he asks, though it doesn't come out like a question.

I nod, stony faced. I hate it with my whole being, but I understand. I have my orders.

He inclines his crow's head and pats my hand. "I will confer with the others. When we have answers, I'll send for you."

I look away, eyes boring into the empty space beside me. Opening a window from this side of the Flood is less uncertain, in terms of destination. Wherever in the mortal realm you entered, the window will send you back there, no matter how far you've traveled in the Flood.

I lift a hand to tease out a portal home, but my heart thuds as I stall. The second I cross over, Patrick will be lying in wait. Ready to strike.

"Wish me luck," I whisper. Irinorr doesn't respond, but I sense his bolstering presence at my back.

A window blooms before me, an inch past my fingers. I hold my breath and crawl through.

The sitting room manifests around me, quiet and dark. I don't pause to check for Patrick. I jump up, bolting for the door—and keep going. I've never run so fast, or so blindly, or in such a direction: out, away, toward the grand staircase.

My pulse pounds in my neck and wrists and gut as I tear across the vast dark landing—a sight I haven't seen in ten years. I don't stop until I reach the west wing. I throw open doors to guest bedrooms, one by one, until I find one locked. Loud and desperate, I pelt it with a clenched fist.

It swings open. Whitman's on the other side, and his eyes widen when he sees me.

"Fine," I pant, hand over my bursting heart. "I'll go."

3

I've never been so nervous in my life.

It's the *waiting* more than anything. Standing around while the staff dashes back and forth, packing my luggage; wondering with a bone-deep chill if Patrick might materialize before me any second. Dreading what comes next. It's not like I'm confronting my fears by choice. I'm simply running from bigger ones.

Not that Irinorr gave me much say in the matter. I wish I had the guts to disobey him. Then I remember Patrick's deathly features, his hand around my throat. I rub the goose bumps that prickle along my arms. I have to face it: I can't stay here.

I wait with my parents in an unused hall in the east wing. Light from the muted oil lamps glints off the dozen framed paintings, the dips and peaks of the gold-leafed frieze that borders the ceiling. The paneled walls, narrow and busy and lined with arcs of clay-colored plaster, add to the claustrophobic effect. I feel the world closing in on me.

Whitman and Parsons enter the room to find the three of us huddled in silence. It's dour as a funeral in here.

My father ruins it by raising his arms in greeting. "There he is! The man who got my daughter out of the house!"

My father jokes like that sometimes. When am I going to get married? When will I get out of their hair? His way of coping with the pain of it—that awkward, pinching discomfort of living with your child's killer. Ha, ha.

"I should make sure my things are ready," I say bleakly. "I'll meet you downstairs." A lump rises in my throat. *Downstairs*. The word makes my muscles burn and clench.

I take off for my bedroom. I just want to get away from my parents. They've been praying for this day for ten years—the day they're free of me. It's an old wound; it shouldn't hurt anymore. So, I act like it doesn't.

When we pass the stairway, Parsons splits off to prepare the carriage. Whitman, with his meddling nature, trails after me.

"You're still here?" I say under my breath as he follows me into my darkened room. Across the way, the curtains of my cracked bay windows flutter like pale, slender ghosts. My mouth goes dry. I can picture Patrick's face so clearly in the dark.

"Can I help?" Whitman asks.

Like he cares. Bracing a hand on my dresser, I pour myself two fingers of whiskey from a crystal decanter and drink it in one swallow. I'm not supposed to have alcohol in here, but I persuaded our housekeeper to sneak it into my room—and by persuaded, I mean whined. Resting beside the forming ring of condensation is my prayer token to Irinorr, a tiny copper disc. The same one I've had since my tenth birthday. Prayer tokens are given out by priests for donations or service, to be left at shrines and chapels to ask the gods for intervention. But those requests aren't heeded. The gods only listen to mortals when the fancy strikes them.

I pick up the token and squeeze until my palm hurts, looking sidelong at Whitman. "Just so we're clear, I'm only going so you'll stop torturing poor Parsons. And you're giving him a month off, I hope you know. With pay."

He gives me an elusive half smile. "Am I?"

"It's one of my conditions." I pour another whiskey. "I suppose you're pleased with yourself."

"Should I be?"

"You won, didn't you?" I mutter. How else can I put it? We were engaged in battle, and I surrendered.

His expression grows strange. Not gloating, like I might have been in his place. Instead, he looks at me like he's never seen me before, like I'm someone else entirely. "What I'm asking of you is difficult. I know that."

I splash more whiskey into the glass. He's speaking in code, but I can translate just fine. Now that he's seen my weakness, he feels sorry for me. I drink the final shot and set down the glass with a clink, squeezing my eyes shut. I feel sicker than ever, but drunk enough, finally, to do what's required.

"Let's go to the castle," I say, brushing past Whitman out the door.

My parents meet us in the entryway. The crystal chandelier sparkles overhead, light gleaming off the polished floorboards and alabaster pilasters. I blink in the sudden brightness. Above the front door, a fresh pine bough hangs from a wooden peg—one of the more superstitious staff's attempt to ward off demons. Whitman stands to the side as my parents say their goodbyes.

My father throws his arms around me, crying and grinning like a fool. When he steps away, my mother takes his place. Her face is soft and loving and terrible. She reaches out to curl my blond hair around her finger.

"This is good," she whispers. "This will be good for you."

I gather her meaning. This will be good for so many people: for her, for my father, for Patrick's memory. I hate that I can't be happy for them.

A touch on my shoulder. I gasp and spin around. Whitman. He gives me a long look—not impatient, but like he can sense my agitation, my need to get this over with.

I glance back at my parents. "Could you go upstairs for this part?"

They don't need convincing. A few muttered *love you*s, and they disappear up the stairs. I can hear my father weeping in the distance. I turn to Whitman, my face beaded with sweat.

"Open the door, please," I order with as much authority as I can muster. He nods, abnormally subservient, and steps toward the door. Places a hand on the knob. Pulls.

A damp, heavy gust of air hits me. There is a smell—an outside smell, wet leaves and petrichor and open space. Before me looms an archway of black.

"Are you all right?" Whitman places a hand on my elbow.

I shudder and shrug him off. "No."

"What can I do?"

My heart is racing so fast, I know it'll explode. What a way to die. Trying to walk through a door.

"I can't do this," I say between wheezing breaths. My chest feels stretched too tight. "I can't do this. I can't."

"Take your time."

I swallow. "Just—just push me."

"I'm not going to push you," he says, offended. "I could carry you."

My stomach heaves, and for the hundredth time tonight, I am ashamed. "No. Put your hand on my back, and—and push me along."

He says nothing. Then I feel the pressure of his hand between my shoulder blades. He guides me forward, toward the threshold.

The portal to another world.

PART II

THE CASTLE

4

I take three steps into the dark before fear crashes over me.

I want to sprint for the carriage, but my limbs are shaking. Glimpses of the grounds harry the edges of my vision. The path ahead is paved with shaved black slate; the gardens around me, choked with moss and angular, manicured rosebushes skulking in the dark; the night sky, full of moon. It shines its hollow light on me.

How do I explain it?

Have you ever failed someone you love? That deep, gut-wrenching shame, the dread, the horror that this—this ignoble, pathetic excuse of a person—is *you*, that within you lurks the capacity to destroy everything you care for, not out of greed or ambition or any evil impulse, but from pure deficiency of character. Out of weakness. No matter how hard you tried, you could never have done them proud. You were never in control.

Everything spins. I throw out my arms for balance, but I drop to one knee, my stomach heaving. Helpless. Useless. I feel my gorge rise and fight against it. I should be embarrassed, but I have no dignity now, no pride left to besmirch. On my hands and knees, I vomit onto the footpath.

Blood roars in my ears. Someone must be talking, shouting at me, or maybe I'm hearing things. My head feels too heavy. I try to stand; I want to more than anything, to prove that I could have left home anytime, that it's always been a choice.

A hand touches my shoulder. The cotton in my ears starts to break apart, and I hear Whitman speak.

"Can you make it to the carriage?" He sounds unnerved, like he wasn't prepared for this. In response, I double over and dry-heave. I don't have the presence of mind to be humiliated. That will have to come later. He touches my shoulder again, and I convulse like his fingers are molten iron. "It's—it's all right," he stutters. "I'm going to pick you up."

I force myself not to gag as he slips one arm behind my back and hooks my knees with the other. I flop like a ragdoll when he stands straight. I'm screaming on the inside, raging, demanding he put me down. But my indignation stays trapped within, my jaw slack, hair damp with sweat.

Parsons holds the carriage door as Whitman rushes inside and lowers me onto the bench. I clamber away from him to press against the far wall, my heart pounding in its cage. Gradually, I become aware of other people in the carriage—castle guards. Whitman sits stiff-backed beside me. I hope he regrets this decision already. With a lurch, the carriage jerks into motion.

I fade in and out from there. Vistas streak past my window: farmhouses silhouetted against the starry night sky, towering tree lines, the north province chapel, stone crumbling along its facade. An hour in, we cross our first floating bridge, the connective tissue between the deltas that carve through Opalvale. I shut my eyes and don't open them until the carriage wheels bump over a threshold of stone. We've reached the city. Selledore.

Memories pour into my mind: the clash of spices, the chatter and laughter and arguments, the clanging of Rynthian prayer bells in the southern quarter jumbled with Ashclaud hymns from the west. I haven't visited since childhood.

I remember the food. While my father saw to business with the Guild of Pepperers, Patrick would take me to the grocers and street vendors and cafés. The sellers stuffed me with candied persimmons and stretched taffy until Patrick cut me off. Most of the time, he acted more like a second father than a brother. Always hanging around at home, telling me off for playing with Mother's oil paints or dropping prayer tokens down the well. It never occurred to me that he helped raise me because my parents could not. I was their late-in-life surprise.

Soon, the walls of the castle ward rise ahead, black and foreboding. Rainbow-sheened spellsap lanterns line the wall on twisted iron posts. We pass under an arched gate and slow to a stop. A dense silence packs the coach as I brace for Whitman to speak.

He holds out a hand. When I shy away, he reaches closer. I smack his arm. I've come to a decision: I will not be leaving this carriage. I won't step outside again.

"No," I say, shaky but firm. "I'm not going."

For a moment, he says nothing. I can feel the cold heat of Parsons' and the guards' stares from the opposite bench.

"Do you want to go home?" It has the cadence of a trick question. Whitman rests his elbow on the back of the bench, twisting toward me. He's steadier now than when I collapsed.

I can't decide, can't act at all. I never should have left the east wing.

"I can't move." The words come cracking out of my throat, followed by the hot tang of shame. All that time spent posturing, playing myself up, undone in moments.

Whitman reaches for me again. I pull away, but with unexpected reflexes, he snares my hands in his. I struggle and thrash like an animal caught in a trap. He holds firm until I fall still.

"Breathe." His eyes glisten in the low light, trained on mine, and his tone is practiced, like he's done this before. It would hurt less if he screamed at me. "Get through this and it'll be over. A few hundred yards to the castle. That's it."

I shrink back, huddling against the carriage wall. I want to curl into myself and disappear. But I'll be leaving this carriage one way or another.

"On one condition," I say, my voice husky. "Never speak of this again."

He pauses, then nods.

I bow my head. My whole body trembles. "You'll need to . . . drag me out, I suppose."

Whitman frowns, but he makes no comment. He glances sideways at Parsons. Dutifully, Parsons jumps out of the carriage, holding the door ajar. A light rain mists outside. The air smells salty and fresh and ancient at the same time. Dread winds around my chest until I can't breathe.

"Go," I hiss at Whitman.

He doesn't need to be told twice. With a tug, he hauls me off the bench. My legs don't want to cooperate, but as I barrel toward the carriage steps, I have no choice but to start walking.

Whitman lowers me onto the soggy lawn. The sky stretches above us for miles like a wide steely bay, mottled with gray clouds and cold patches of stars. Castle Selledore looms like a giant in the dark. Towers and crenellations jut toward the sky along its whole impressive length. By the light of spellsap lanterns, its carriage-sized stone blocks look the color of wet sand.

"Come along," Whitman says, and he guides me forward as my eyes bulge from my head.

The trip across the ward passes in a muddy blur. Dirty water soaks the lawn, seeping into the cloth of my slippers. Whitman and Parsons hustle me through the castle entrance, past the gate guards. Through towering brass doors like giant, hinged ingots, into the main hall. Inside again.

But it's an oppressive, foreign version of inside, a maze of sandstone and slate. Embossed coppery plates line the walls, warm and discolored in the glow of spellsap. The ceilings high overhead are carved elaborately along the joists, painted with glossy frescos of naked, sinewy figures. Demons. From what I can gather, the paintings depict two clans—the boars and the wolves, Verimall and Semyanadd, violence and vitality—fighting to the bloody death.

Overwhelmed, I lock my gaze on the floor, and when we hit a steep staircase, I climb without looking up. Then Whitman takes my elbow and leads me into a dark room. We lost Parsons at some point. I rush to the nearest chair and collapse with my eyes closed, hugging my arms.

"Better?" comes Whitman's voice from nearby.

I open my eyes to tell him off for pretending to care. I freeze.

We're in my sitting room.

Details are off, here and there. The wicker chair is too tall. The leather of the chaise longue, slightly off color. But the pink damask wallpaper is spot-on. The room has a chill, like an underground cellar, but otherwise, it feels like home.

Momentarily too stunned to panic, I stammer, "What—what is this?"

"Your apartments."

"You did all this in a week? After seeing my room *once*?"

"It's my job, isn't it?" He sounds pleased with himself.

I gaze around, lips parted. "You are impressive, Master Whitman."

"Will it help with being away from home?"

"We'll see," I mutter. That all depends on Patrick. Irinorr said I might escape my brother by leaving home. But how did his ghost find me in the first place? Ghosts aren't supposed to do what Patrick did—return to the mortal realm, haunt the living. Try to kill their sisters.

"What will we see?" Whitman prompts.

I recline in the chair and press the heels of my hands into my eyes. "Forget I said anything."

"There's a bell on the nightstand. Ring if you need anything. Staff quarters are down the hall." He circles the room, lighting oil lamps with an alchemical match. They flare to life, bright and cheery. To his credit, he acts like my meltdown in the carriage never happened. He's keeping his word. "We'll be getting an early start in the morning."

I snort wearily. "I look forward to what I'm sure you think will be a persuasive showing."

Shaking out the match, he gives me a bland look. "Can I get a little credit for what I've done so far?"

"I said you were impressive."

"I can be a lot more impressive if need be, Ms. Arnett."

I look at him and raise an eyebrow. He shifts his weight. "In—in my capacity as master of practitioners," he adds.

Sighing, I set my head down. "Right."

41

Whitman hesitates a moment before sitting across from me. With a frown, he asks, "Would it make a difference if I told you why I need you?"

Would it make a difference? Doubtful. But if Whitman wants to tell me, I won't argue. "Perhaps."

"And you understand this can't be repeated to anyone? Not even your family?"

Like I care enough to repeat it. I puff out my cheeks and agree. Whitman nods, sealing our pact, and leans closer. I've noticed he does that when he thinks he's about to say something interesting.

"King Isaac is very ill," he says. "A disease of the bones. The physicians estimate he has a year to live, maybe less."

My brow wrinkles. I knew from party gossip that Isaac was ill, that his line is disappearing, but not how little time he has left. Isaac is the last of House Angline. It started with a rash of accidents, a hundred years ago, and then a plague. A case of infertility here and there. There were whispers of a curse—as there always are with this sort of thing.

"The way things stand," Whitman says, "the line of succession isn't clear. Isaac wants to fix that. He'd like to marry and beget a child."

"Good for him. What does this have to do with me?"

Whitman inhales, deep and slow. Gathering patience. "It's an uncertain time at the castle. A large segment of the company is made up of recent recruits. And I'm . . . new to the position." He looks down to brush something off his knee, hiding his face. "The king wants to use the company to find his bride. It would certainly save time. Last time, when Isaac's parents were wed, marriage negotiations with the Circle Court took fourteen months. But I'm not confident the process will be forthright. I suspect some of the seers have been paid off. I just can't prove it." He bends forward farther. "But you can name Isaac's true love. If we find her, the king's bound to choose her over the false candidates. I need you to swear in as a royal magician and name Isaac's soulmate."

My eyebrow tics up as an irksome thought springs into my mind. "It occurs to me," I say, "you could have brought a pair of the king's pants to my house and had me do the reading there."

"It's not that simple. The council hasn't been receptive to my suggestion. They know your reputation; they don't consider you legitimate. I'm hoping that'll change once they meet you."

Ah, there it is—the condescension I'm accustomed to. Whitman may be young and open-minded, but to the rest of King Isaac's council of masters, I'm nothing but a charlatan.

Cheeks burning, I throw my arm over my face. "I'm very tired, master. I'd like to rest now."

"Of course. Forgive me." He stands up. "You don't have to make up your mind just yet. Think on it."

I ignore him long enough that he gets the message.

"I'll come for you in the morning," he says. My door snaps shut.

It's late, but my mind is restless, beleaguered by memories of the carriage ride. How I acted, what I said. And in the background, the image of Patrick's ghost flickers and flares, refusing to be forgotten. Groaning, I sit upright. I need a distraction.

I spend a minute exploring the apartments—my first lodgings outside the east wing. There are three small rooms: the entry parlor, the bedroom, and a bathroom with its own claw-foot tub.

I stop before a polished chestnut dresser in the parlor. A thick file of papers lies there, conspicuously out of place. Whitman must have forgotten it. Curious, I lift the cover and peek inside. The first page looks like a dossier, with an illustration of a lovely young woman in the corner. The sheet is filled with information: her name, age, and lineage. She's a minor noble from Ashclaud who might, if the stars align, end up a queen one day. According to these notes, she met King Isaac briefly about a year ago. I flip through the other pages; more reports, more eligible noble ladies. Whitman's gathering intel on potential brides for Isaac. He must be putting together a contingency plan in case I don't work out. I bite my cheek, annoyed. Is it too much to ask for somebody to have faith in me for once?

I set the file aside, wishing I hadn't looked, and go investigate the bedroom. A broad feather bed on a carved wooden frame takes up most of the floor, piled with blankets and pillows. On the nightstand, next to a dish of sacred seawater, lies a pile of prayer books and scriptures. My fingers trail over *Myths of Sun, Moon, and Storm.* The yellowing paper crinkles at my touch. *Myths* is the volume of scripture that tells the fable—or the prophecy, depending on who you ask—of the Rising Tide. The seven demon armies, the dead among the living, the eventual tidal wave of Flood magic that will wipe out the mortal realm. It always scared me, as a child.

I decide not to use the bed. I return to the wicker chair, facing the doorway. Doors have always spooked me—like if I turn my back, I'll be sucked out into the world, as if by a riptide. I sit in the dark and glare at the polished doorframe.

Nothing happens. The doorway does not inhale me; Patrick's ghost doesn't appear. After a minute, I shut my eyes and wait, expecting the worst.

A knock at the door.

I blink awake with a start. Light pours through my window.

Rubbing my eyes, I stumble to my feet and yank the door open. There's Whitman, dressed and alert. I glance at my wrinkled skirts, brushing my hair from my face.

He looks me up and down. "Did you sleep in your clothes?"

I frown in wonder. "I suppose I did."

Incredible. I *did* sleep. If Patrick visited, he didn't bother to wake me. I giggle into my curled fist. Whitman stares harder.

I wave him into the room. "I must look a mess," I say, going for my luggage in the corner. One of my stockings has slipped down to my ankle, and my curls are frizzed, my hair ribbon coming undone.

"No," he says too quickly. I glance back. He clasps his hands in front of him, staring at my bare leg. I clear my throat. His eyes snap to mine.

"See something you like, Master Whitman?" I say smartly as I kneel next to my bags, grinning to myself. So, he's not *completely* immune to my charms.

Whitman doesn't dignify that with a response. He backs toward the doorway. "I'll send someone to attend to you. Meet me in the hall when you're ready."

I freeze. "Meet you for what?"

"The practitioners conference." He raises a perfect eyebrow. It reads as a challenge.

I grip one handle of my luggage. Practitioners conference. Of course. That's why he invited me here—to tour the castle, meet the other magicians. But all I can think about is the way I felt in the carriage, and how I never want to feel like that again.

"I'm not well this morning," I say with a defiant lift of my chin. "Tell the magicians I send my regards."

My cheeks sear the longer Whitman goes without responding. "All right," he says. "Thank you, Ms. Arnett." And he closes the door behind him. I frown, skeptical. That was far too easy.

Despite my refusal, a handmaid named Elizabeta arrives to help me dress. She looks even younger than me, maybe sixteen or seventeen. My heart stutters as she does up my laces. I don't feel proud of my behavior, but it's a matter of survival. I can't walk those halls again. Besides, it's in my best interest to drag out my stay at the castle, sidestepping the master's demands, until Irinorr sends word about how to deal with Patrick.

"What part of the castle are we in?" I ask Elizabeta as she yanks my dress tight.

The tiny black-haired girl pauses, leaving me half-laced. "The practitioners' wing, miss. The other magicians' rooms are nearby. They'll be at conference right now, of course."

"Practitioners conference?"

She tugs my laces again, forcing the breath from me. "That's right. They meet thrice a week to discuss the state of affairs."

I glance over my shoulder as she works. She keeps her gaze lowered, her face tense with an emotion I can't identify. Around her neck, a small vial hangs from a thin silver chain. Seawater. So she's devout.

Once I'm dressed, Elizabeta leaves me alone to contemplate the chasm of time ahead of me. I don't know when Whitman will return. I'm itching to go to the Flood, to visit Irinorr, but he has yet to send for me. It'll do no good if he's not ready. What could he and the rest of the seven be discussing? The longer they dally, the more serious the situation must be. Perhaps not the Rising Tide, but something dire, indeed. Something beyond my purview.

Another knock startles me, and I sneer at the doorway. How long can I leave Whitman hanging before he finds a guard to break down my door?

Better not test him. Sighing, I answer it.

Whitman waits on the other side with a messy pile of papers under his arm. He bows his head. "I know, we're late. I'm sorry."

I scrunch my nose. Late for what? Then I notice the posse of well-dressed courtiers behind him. I lean to the side. "What is this?"

"The practitioners conference. We're trying a different venue today." Whitman presses through the doorway, forcing me back. His followers stream in after him. I count nine as they barge into my sitting room, making themselves comfortable on my chaise longue and chairs. A few stand against the walls, arms crossed. These are the magicians, I presume. Assistant Master Parsons is among them, looking squirrelly as ever.

"This is fine," I say, rigid with indignation. Whitman won this round, not that I'm going to admit it. And now I have a gaggle of royal magicians in my sitting room.

Whitman circles the chaise longue and grips the backrest. "Ms. Arnett, meet the Royal Practitioners Company." He holds out a hand toward me. "And this is Mona Arnett."

Abruptly, a young woman stands. I blink at her in surprise.

She's dressed in a rich sapphire gown, contrasting with her ebony skin. Her braided hair coils upward into a knot at the apex of her head. Shock freezes her features in place.

Her reaction bemuses Whitman as much as it does me. "Er, introductions," he says. He points to the standing girl, as if she's volunteered to go first. "This is Bernadette Byers. A soothsayer, like you."

I look at her a little longer. "Bernadette Byers," I echo. A tiny laugh escapes me.

I'm not sure whether to be relieved or alarmed. A familiar face—or familiar name, as it were—ought to be welcome. But this makes not one lick of sense.

Byers and I stare each other down like we're ready to duel. Her round eyes glint. She's scared, and she has a right to be. Maybe we both do.

Master Whitman has proven me wrong. Of his esteemed panel of royal magicians, only *seven* are nothing special.

Bernadette Byers, though, has been favored by the gods.

5

A span of silence passes. A clock ticks somewhere, echoing like footsteps.

"So . . . you know each other?" says a magician against the wall, a brown-skinned woman with a Marshes accent.

Byers and I abruptly end our staring contest, like a spell has lifted. It's too late. The look we exchanged lasted too long, and everyone saw it.

"No," Byers says, smoothing out the signs of recognition on her face. "I've never met this girl before."

All eyes turn on me. I lean against my doorframe and cross my arms. The universal gesture of backing off. Neither of us wants to get into this, especially in front of an audience. "I don't know her," I say with a shrug. "Why?"

No one answers. Warily, Byers sits back down.

Whitman pauses as we settle in. Then he introduces the rest of the royal magicians. There are one or two grizzled veterans, but most of them can't be out of their early twenties, and some, like Bernadette Byers, look as young as my teenaged handmaid. Whitman did say that most of his magicians were new recruits. I just didn't realize *new* meant "barely out of adolescence." Is this entire castle run by a gaggle of infants?

Whitman's company of baby magicians has a little bit of everything: soothsayers, who cast runestones to divine and portend, and enchanters, who craft rune-emblazoned charms. The runes they use—the gods' first written language—are potent, but they have less power on this side of the Flood. Any magician could trace an empowered rune if you dropped them in the middle of the Flood, but only an enchanter can infuse runes with magic in our realm. It's their innate talent, an ability that manifests during childhood, just as it does in seers for divining and foretelling. In simple terms, seers read the runes, and enchanters write them.

The two oldest magicians happen to be the rarest type: alchemists. Students of science, alchemists are uniquely gifted and extraordinary clever. They combine a natural affinity for magic with years of book learning and practical experience manipulating spellsap.

And like Opalvale itself, the company is composed of a medley of skin colors, facial features, and accents. Opalvale has plenty of immigrants, generations of them. Our crown's connection to the seven helps draw people from all Circle Court nations. The majority of citizens are still white-skinned and blond-haired, like King Isaac and me, but it's not uncommon for elite groups like the Royal Practitioners Company or the Angline council to boast a bit more diversity. Whitman selected for talent, not appearance or background.

I struggle not to tune out Whitman's introductions in favor of trying to catch Byers' eye. She's facing resolutely ahead. All the while, I ask the same question in my head: *What is Korimarr's favored mortal doing in the Royal Practitioners Company?*

"To business," Whitman says, drawing me out of my reverie. Hopefully, my participation won't be required. As he shuffles through his stack of disorganized papers, he says, "Now, Mr. Umber, you have a report on the Wetton orchard?"

A magician with long white hair—one of the alchemists—answers Whitman's question. "Aye, sir. My field team met up with the sap harvesters last week. Yields are down across the board. The disease is strangling their orchards. They're recommending rationing soon, within the month."

That must be grim news, because Whitman's face pinches with apprehension. The others around the room don't look too happy, either. I'm not surprised the

Royal Practitioners Company has a vested interest in the spellsap orchards. Beyond the nexus and the runes, nothing confirms the gods' enduring presence like the spellsap trees. Their roots, it's said, penetrate the veil into the Flood itself, soaking up its power and imbuing the plants with qualities not explainable by anything but magic.

"There's been a fair share of rumors as well," Umber adds. "About the cause of the disease. King Isaac's name came up more than once."

If Whitman's expression was pained before, it's in agony now. "What are they saying?"

"People are afraid of what will happen if he dies without an heir. His Majesty's claim to the throne is losing legitimacy. They reckon it's weakening the nexus." Umber regards Whitman sternly. "It's not a theory we should dismiss."

"I'm not dismissing anything," Whitman blurts out, defensive. His cheeks turn red as he reins himself in. If I didn't know better, I'd think Umber was the one in charge and Whitman was being scolded. "We already knew those rumors might start to surface. And we're addressing it."

As I listen, I wonder if "those rumors" could be right. Spellsap trees are nurtured by the Flood's energy, but the trees would stay dormant and the sap inert without the influence of the nexus, the wellspring of magic. If Isaac's leadership has created doubt about his fitness to rule, perhaps his bond with the nexus has suffered as well.

Whitman massages his temple with steepled fingers. "Ms. Byers, can you make it a priority to get intelligence on the Wetton orchards? Anything you can read about the spellsap yields."

Byers stares straight ahead. "Yes, Master Whitman."

The discussion continues, routine matters of shoring up defenses and planning drills and negotiating consultation fees with the Guild of Magicians. Each of the seven gods boasts a handful of guilds to their names. Most magicians have been dealing with their guild—dedicated to the goddess Onyamarr—since childhood, from when they first displayed the aptitude. But I've never had a need for the resources or education the Guild of Magicians can provide.

When the meeting ends, the magicians leap to their feet without any pretense of wishing to stay and mingle. I stand by the doorframe as they stream out. Whitman, last to leave, slows near the doorway, brows raised with expectant smugness. Frowning, I place a firm hand on his elbow, guide him through the door, and slam it shut. I have no interest in hearing him gloat. As I turn away, I notice the folder of bride reports I saw last night has gone missing from the dresser. Whitman must have snatched it on his way out. Strange. I was sure he'd interrogate me about whether I peeked.

I haven't even reached my chaise longue when another knock comes. Growling, I turn around and throw open the door, ready to shoo him away. But it's Bernadette Byers on the other side. I arch my brows. This I can work with.

"Ms. Byers," I say in delight as she slips into my sitting room. I lay myself across the chaise with careful aloofness. Finally, a game I know how to play: social chicken. "How kind of you to call on me."

"Stop." Only a slight quiver of her lips, painted stunning red, betrays any emotion. "We need to talk about this."

"Which part? That you've been concealing your true powers from the master of practitioners? Or that you're hiding your choice of profession from Korimarr?"

She scoffs and looks away, but I'm certain I'm right.

I know of Bernadette Byers the same way all mortals who travel the Flood know each other: the gods gossip. The seven like to exchange boastful stories about the strange, gifted humans they've marked as their own, to mentor and guide and nurture. Unlike other mortals, those of us who see the windows can be trained to perform unique feats of magic. As the favored of Irinorr, god of love in all its forms, I name soulmates.

Bernadette Byers tells the truth.

"What I can't figure out," I say, "is how you're doing it. How does one keep a secret from the goddess of knowledge?" If Korimarr knew about Byers' post as a royal magician, every corporeal being in the Flood would have gotten an earful about it.

She stares at me a long time before replying, "I'd heard a rumor you never left your house."

I ignore the jab, smiling sharp enough to prick a finger. "Master Whitman doesn't know what you can do, does he?" Any part of what she can do, I'd wager—that she can divine without tools, like me, or that she can sniff out the difference between truths and lies.

"So? I use the seer's tools, that's true, but who's it hurting?" Though her words are bold, there's a glimmer of doubt behind her dark eyes. "Throw a few runestones, gaze into a mirror, and no one's the wiser. Better than people questioning how my magic works." Another pointed look.

Though I hate to admit it, she's not wrong. In the minds of most mortals, magic operates by one means only: runes. Of the three canonical rune sets preserved throughout history, only one is used in Opalvale—the Angline standard, comprised of over three hundred runes in total. Passed down by the Guild of Magicians and the priests' Guild, the Guild of the Gray Wolf, for centuries. With those building blocks, seers and enchanters can speak the language of magic. Like any language, the Angline standard runes allow for creativity and ingenuity and personal flair, but only those with an innate connection to magic, through the Opalvale nexus, can manipulate them. Then there are those rare few, like Byers and me, who practice our own brand of magic.

"At least I make good use of my gifts," I shoot back. "What are you doing here, Byers? Aren't you a little young to be playing magician?"

"I'll be eighteen in five months," she snaps.

Almost a year younger than me. That's enough of a gap to rub it in. "Is that so? Did you have to get permission from your nursemaid, or are you old enough for a proper chaperone?"

She sniffs. "I'm not here to bicker with you. I just wanted to say that Korimarr doesn't know I'm in the company yet, so I'd appreciate it if you kept that fact to yourself until I tell her."

"Why haven't you told her already?"

"That's really none of your business." She looks down her nose at me. "Listen, I'm perfectly happy to ignore you until you go back to your gilded palace or wherever. Feel free to do the same. There's no reason we can't stay out of each other's way."

My shoulders droop involuntarily. It's not as though I didn't plan on doing exactly that, but it stings that she can reject *me* just as easily. I've never met anyone like me—a favored mortal. Perhaps I hoped she would warm to me by nature. I feel like a fool for expecting it.

"Fine with me," I say, crossing my arms and leaning back. "Can we start now?"

"Fine with me," she echoes coolly. Then she storms out.

I pull my knees up to my chest and hug them. I cannot wait to go home.

6

The man sitting across from me showed up this afternoon quite by surprise. Master Gan, as he introduced himself—though I could have gathered the "master" part from his uniform, identical to Whitman's. Another member of King Isaac's Angline Council. He's a Diené man, well into middle age, with wiry black-and-silver hair pulled into a short ponytail.

"How can I help you, master?" I ask. In spite of myself, I'm eager to impress Gan—or at least not behave like a child. He has an air of authority I find comforting.

"Actually, I'm here to help you, Ms. Arnett. I'm the master of ceremonies at the castle." He has a gentle, sonorous voice, like a priest. "I hoped to discuss the arrangements for tomorrow night. My staff has measurements for the other magicians, but if I take yours before the modiste arrives, they can bring a few samples to try on."

My brain grinds to a halt, unable to parse his words. "The modiste?" I repeat. "Why?"

Gan fixes me with a questioning stare, his thick brows scrunched together. "For the ceremony tomorrow. When the seers name King Isaac's bride."

I squeeze my fists and splutter, "When— What?"

"I've been planning the ceremony for weeks. I thought you knew."

Composing myself, I try to smile, but sweat beads my upper lip and my rib cage feels too small for my lungs. "Master Whitman neglected to mention how fast things would move."

"Did he? How odd." Maybe I'm imagining it, but Gan sounds cold, like he's no fan of Whitman's. That makes two of us.

I chew the inside of my cheek as Master Gan takes my measurements with a length of knotted twine. There must be a way to stop this ceremony, or at least to disqualify myself. I bet they'd be happy to send me home for bad behavior.

Gan finishes my measurements before I know it. I give him a nod in farewell. His hand hovers over the doorknob before he turns around. "I have to ask," he says. "These soulmate readings you claim to perform. How often do you get it right?"

I tuck a curl of hair behind my ear, thrown by the question. Naming soulmates is a delicate art. On occasion, I have to give an answer someone doesn't want to hear. The lovely news is there's no such thing as a soulmate on the other side of the world you'll never meet. It always turns out to be someone in your life—now, or in the future. The unfortunate counterpoint: You aren't guaranteed to end up together. It's a highly likely outcome, a near-perfect promise. But there's no accounting for human agency, which, every so often, drives us away from our destinies for no good reason, straight into the arms of self-destruction.

"That's hard to answer," I say to Gan. "I could do your reading, if you like?"

"I'm married," he replies with finality. "And I'm already quite certain my husband is my one true love."

He's mocking me, but I'm still charmed by the sentiment. It must be nice to love and be loved with such breezy confidence. I try to imagine what it would be like to have a soulmate: spending all your time together, talking late into the night, laughing at your private jokes, caring for each other when you're sick or upset or in crisis. Actually, it sounds like how Patrick and I used to be.

My chest tightens. Perhaps it's a kind of cosmic justice: I destroyed my brother's life, and now I'll never be that close to anyone again.

I clear my throat so my voice comes out strong and steady. "I'm happy for you, then."

Gan studies me with piercing acumen. It reminds me of Irinorr. That hard, hard stare into my soft, grubby soul. "You strike me as someone with integrity," he says, almost wistfully.

He cuts off there, leaving my rooms with the second half of his question hanging in the air: How could any decent person run a grift like that? Pretending to name soulmates for a cheap thrill and a handful of coins? How do I live with myself?

Whitman must be truly alone in supporting my abilities. Should I feel grateful? Somehow, I can't find it in me. It's his fault I'm here in the first place, being subjected to dirty looks and ridicule. I'm not going to thank him for throwing me scraps of goodwill.

Especially when he only cares about using me.

Whitman comes to check on me that evening. I'm unprepared—reclining on the chaise in my nightgown, squirming into a comfortable position, trying to fall unconscious and put out of my mind the series of increasingly stupid developments since I came to the castle. His knock startles me out of my stupor.

"Master Whitman," I sigh as he enters. I'm tired of fighting, but I can't allow him to run my life from behind the scenes. "I had a visitor this afternoon. Master Gan. He told me a very interesting story about a surprise ceremony you've been planning."

He doesn't even have the decency to look abashed. "That was a logistical decision. Easier to cancel a ceremony at the last minute than to plan one."

"Oh, good," I say. "So cancel it."

"You're still refusing to perform the reading?"

"Yes?" I huff. What have I done to give him hope otherwise? In fact, at this point, it seems unlikely Whitman thinks he can change my mind. What's he really doing here? I shift my legs on the chaise longue, suddenly hyperaware of the bare skin below my hemline, the loose curls of hair cascading over my half-covered collarbones.

It's not outside the realm of possibility. It's what I would do, in his position. Having failed to recruit me to his cause, there's nothing stopping him from crossing the scant few feet between us and lowering his body over mine, burying his hands in my hair and drawing my lips to his for a kiss.

"Can you tell me why you won't do it?"

Flustered out of my daydream, I blurt the first thing that comes to mind. "Why do you need me? Use one of those frauds you have on retainer."

His stare grows sullen. "I'm sure you don't intend to insult me, but I hand-selected each of my magicians. I know how to spot a fake."

"No doubt they are skilled at what they do, Master Whitman, but do not insult *me* by equating me with those hacks."

Whitman crosses his arms. "Perhaps you're not the expert on magic you think you are."

Heat flares in me. So much for avoiding a fight. "Oh? I'm sorry, which kind of magic do you practice again?"

"Maybe I can't use magic, but studying it is my life's work. A person with a bit less hubris might consider that before running their mouth."

We're going in circles. It's exhausting. I am not a fighter by nature; I'm a survivor. And survivors are great at surrendering. "I don't need your permission to run my mouth," I say coolly. "I'll do that freely and when I please. But . . . I suppose I'm sorry."

That throws Whitman off-balance. "I shouldn't have been short with you." He rubs the back of his neck. "It's a stressful time for us both."

"Stress? Is that what's got you so uptight?" I pat the cushion next to me. "Come, I'll give you a massage."

He looks at me flatly. "You can't be serious."

"It's just a joke," I say, turning to hide the traitorous blush that exposes me for a liar. "Besides, you're the one who keeps visiting an unchaperoned young lady in her bedroom. Some might say that's suggestive of something."

"I meet one-on-one with all my magicians. I thought you'd feel more comfortable here."

That much is true. Best not to push him further, in case he revokes those privileges. "Whatever you say. But let's get one thing clear—I'm not changing my mind. Find another seer."

"At least meet King Isaac first."

My mouth flattens into a line. I have no intention of doing what Whitman asks, but if I continue to rebuke him, he'll send me home to Patrick. I need to stall. "Fine. I'll speak with the king, if it's so important to you."

"Thank you." His shoulders sag in relief. "I'll take you to council chambers tomorrow morning."

I seize up. "What? No, I—I'm not going anywhere. Bring him here."

"I'll see what I can do." He considers me in a thoughtful way I don't appreciate at all. "You're doing the right thing, Ms. Arnett."

I glower over the camelback frame of my chaise longue. This will never be my legacy—crowning queens, molding kingdoms. Whitman mocks me by asking. And if I agree, the rest of the world will mock me, too.

7

Morning comes too soon. Elizabeta barges into my room just after dawn to drape me in silk and chiffon. Then I settle on my chaise longue with my back straight, waiting. My hands tremble at my sides. Whitman's knock comes a minute later.

The master of practitioners steps inside, alone. "Where's King Isaac?" I ask, both relieved and agitated. "I thought I was naming his soulmate."

Whitman leans against my wall. "Not yet. We have to convince him of your legitimacy first. If he's persuaded, he'll overrule the council and let you perform your reading."

A sense of dread, an unpinnable foreboding, wells inside me. "Let's get this over with."

"I'll summon the king," Whitman says as he departs.

I remain a fixture on my couch, bracing for another knock. This whole situation is bizarre. Royal marriage negotiations usually go through the Circle Court for its member states. The Court delegates weigh in on all decisions that affect the nations, including royal unions. A counterbalance against a single nation gobbling up others, amassing too much power or land through the exploitation of marriage.

This ceremony would mark a major departure in tradition. Not to mention a liability, if Whitman is right about seers being bribed to influence the contest. But who's going to argue with King Isaac? Opalvale is the most influential nation in the union, whatever the Circle Court's founding articles might claim about the equality of its member states. The nexus is too valuable a resource.

When a knock finally comes, I meet it head on. "Enter," I call.

Whitman comes in, followed by a cadre of three guards in front, two in the back. Between them is a man who must be the king.

King Isaac is adamantly blond, with good-humored, boyish features. He wears a maroon velvet doublet with glittering slashes along the sleeves and a thin gold circlet on his head. Dark streaks bruise the pale skin below his eyes, and he walks with a slight limp. King Isaac is ill, indeed.

I rise to my feet and curtsy. This much I know is expected of me. "Majesty."

He shuffles toward my wicker chair. "Ms. Arnett." His voice is friendly, but it holds a note of unearned authority, the kind that comes from never hearing no. Not quite spoiled, but not *not* spoiled, either. Isaac wasn't raised for the throne; his sister, Queen Aliah, ruled for two years before she passed from a wasting illness. This role was thrust on him quite unexpectedly. But he's still been royalty his entire life. That leaves a mark.

"I hope you don't mind if I sit," Isaac says. "I don't stand for long periods, as a rule."

Who am I to give him permission? "By all means, Your Majesty."

The king of Opalvale inclines his head in thanks and lowers himself into my chair. Whitman and the guards space themselves along the walls.

"Mona Arnett," Isaac begins, like he's announcing me at a party. "Tell me about yourself."

My gaze darts to Whitman. He nods, prompting me.

"You already know my name." I fold my skirts into thin accordions of fabric. "I live in Seaward. I'm the younger of two. What else do you need to know?"

"I'd just like to learn more about you. Your background, interests. Do you have any hobbies? What do you do for fun?"

I give him a smile that verges on mocking. "I like hot baths and long walks on the beach."

I shouldn't heckle the king, but then again, he should learn to ask better questions. Isaac considers me before glancing at Whitman, whose expression is, incredibly, more neutral than ever.

The king twists to address his guards. "Could you give us the room?" They hesitate, but Isaac waves a hand at them. "I'll be fine," he insists. "Master Whitman will protect me."

I can't tell if he's joking. The guards rotate ninety degrees and march out of the room.

Isaac slouches in the chair like it's a throne, crossing his ankles. Any semblance of formality sluices off. "Let's start again."

I smooth out my skirt, the fabric creased where I folded it. "Whatever pleases you, Your Majesty."

"I've heard a lot about you." By his tone, none of it favorable.

Swallowing my apprehension, I attempt a weak smile. "Like what?"

"That you claim to use magic without runes, without any tools of the trade. That you charge people for the names of their true loves, with no guarantees of when or how they'll meet." His eyes flick toward Whitman. "That you're manipulative. And I'd love to hear your explanation for why every soothsayer I've spoken with tells me it's impossible to divine soulmates."

There's no explanation I can offer that he'll believe. If I try telling him my power comes from my bond with Irinorr, I'll end up committed to a sanitarium. I opt for a nonanswer. "Perhaps they're jealous of me."

Whitman cuts in, probably to stop me from talking. "I've interviewed every one of Ms. Arnett's past customers I could find," he says. I shoot him an affronted look. He never bothered to tell me that. "Not all of them were happy with the answers she gave, but none thought she was a fraud. And I've seen her demonstrate her abilities myself. I found her compelling enough."

"I'm sure you did," Isaac says with a look I can't read.

I don't care what he thinks of my act. In fact, Isaac could solve a lot of my problems by rejecting me. But to appease Whitman and remain in the castle, I have to convince him I'm still considering the part.

"Your Majesty," I say, "the easiest way to clear this up is to do a reading on you."

"You think so?" The king's eyebrows shoot up, feigning surprise, but beneath the facade, his eyes sparkle.

"If you give me the chance, I will change your mind. I just need a possession of yours." Lifting a finger, I add, "And Master Whitman is a brick wall of a man, I'll have you know. There's no manipulating that one."

A half grin tugs at Isaac's mouth. "Fine. But I'll not make it easy on you. Whatever you get from your reading, it had better be something I've never told a soul."

I raise my eyebrows. "You're sure?"

His grin widens. He thinks I won't succeed. His mistake.

With his thumb, Isaac hooks a chain necklace that hangs hidden beneath his doublet and pulls it over his head. A signet ring dangles from it like a pendant. "I used to wear this ring everywhere," he says. He holds up a clawed hand and flexes his fingers. "Then my joints decided it would be fun to swell up like grapes. I always carry it with me, though. Will it still work?"

"It should," I say as he drops it into my open palm. It weighs my hand down, heavier than I expected. I squint at it. Something he's never told a soul?

Casually, I slip the ring on my finger, like I'm trying on jewelry at a shop. It's too big. Whitman's mouth tightens, but the king watches with interest. I bring the ring to my lips and blow. Particles of magic like dust issue forth, sprinkling my face. The vision bubbles to the surface of my mind. A dark, velvety, rippling room. Sweat, and screaming. A boy crying.

The knowledge inhabits me abruptly.

I sit up straight. "Your Majesty, do the words 'I'd like to spare you the same fate' mean anything to you?"

The blood drains from Isaac's face. "Yes."

I hand the ring back. Isaac snatches it from me, puts the necklace on with shaking fingers. He tucks the ring under his doublet. I might have gone too far; I wouldn't know. I don't always understand the meaning of my readings. I grasp for a theme—like "something the king has never told anyone"—and regurgitate my impressions.

Whatever the reading meant, it has undone Isaac's easy demeanor.

"That doesn't prove you can name soulmates," he adds. Some color returns to his face. "I'll not overrule the council's decision without a good reason."

"There's a simple way to test it. Let me do your lovers reading. Then we'll find her, and you can be the judge."

Whitman steals a glance at me, and he might be proud; or it's a warning, a firm stare of *That's as much as you need say*. It's hard to tell his emotions apart sometimes. All three of them.

King Isaac scratches the side of his jaw. He bows his head toward Whitman. "Are you sure?" he asks in a low voice. "This won't be a popular decision."

Whitman nods. "Unless you want to call off the contest altogether."

I look between them, feeling like an eavesdropper. This conversation is not for my benefit. But it must have mollified Isaac.

"All right, then," he says, throwing up his hands. He's putting on a show of capitulating, but his tone is light, his shoulders relaxed. He doesn't seem worried. Perhaps he never was. "You've persuaded me. Add Arnett to the roster."

My stomach flips with both pride and defeat. I can't often say I've done *too* good a job. But I never promised to do the reading, even if Isaac agreed. Whitman can't hold me to it.

"I'm honored, Your Majesty," I say. I almost believe myself.

8

Whitman comes knocking minutes before the party.

I stare at the closed door from my chaise longue, a goblet of wine gripped viselike in my hand. He knocks again, then tries the doorknob. I already locked it.

Elizabeta wrangled me into my dress a quarter hour ago. I chose satin, gray, the color of heron feathers and stormy ocean skies. The pale fabric brings out the spangling of freckles across my cheeks and nose. And I let the handmaid dress me without complaint. Easier than railing against it.

But now Whitman is here, and the ceremony will start any minute, and I can't handle it. I'd be hard-pressed to explain why it frightens me so much, even to myself. I just know I can't join the Royal Practitioners Company. If I swear this oath, will I be trapped here at the castle, in a place where no one wants me?

Though, when I put it that way, it doesn't sound so different from home.

"Go away," I growl, loud enough for Whitman to hear. I take another gulp from my goblet. A stream of wine spills down my chin. Drunk already.

"We're starting," he calls, muffled. "Come out. We don't have time for your games."

"I don't play games!" The outrage of my denial is slightly dampened by its slurred delivery. "You play games, Master Whitman. I'm just trying to keep up."

"I'll use your room key if I must."

"Feel free to try," I spit. Slamming my goblet on the side table, I sweep to my feet and grab my wicker chair, dragging it behind me. I wedge it beneath the door handle, wiggling it into position, until it's jammed so tight that the door won't open.

He doesn't answer, but a scrabbling sound comes from the other side of the door. A key slipping into the lock.

"I'm not joining the company!" I yell. I know I'm behaving like a child. I don't care. I'm too far gone, out of my mind with panic.

"I'm coming in." He shoves against the door, but the wicker chair holds fast, barring him. I slink back to the chaise longue, hugging my knees.

He jiggles the doorknob for another minute. Then he starts in on me again. "Ms. Arnett! I can delay the ceremony, if I have to."

I've heard enough. I take my wine goblet and storm into the bedroom. He sounds quieter in there. I climb into bed, steadying myself with my free hand as I burrow beneath the blankets. But as I tuck myself in, the corner of my comforter hits the nightstand and knocks my bedside dish of sacred seawater off the edge. It clatters to the ground with a splash.

"Shit." I search for a handkerchief in the depths of my nightstand drawer and, with a scowl, drop to my hands and knees, scrubbing the stain as I block out Whitman's distant rambling. The scent of ocean tides drifts up from the floor. I pause, savoring it. Then, tentative, I lift the sopping handkerchief to my nose. It smells like the Flood. And my mother, minus the rose water. I bury my face in the cloth.

I can't tell how much time has passed when the hissing starts. I lower the handkerchief, cock my head. A harsh, sibilant noise is coming from the parlor, like a jet of steam from a kettle. Curiosity gets the best of me, and I shuffle on my knees to the bedroom doorway. Across the parlor, steel-blue steam issues from the front door handle—which is no longer a handle but a clump of tacky, near-liquified metal. I arrive in time to watch it plop onto the wicker chair. The hissing fizzles out. With a bang, my door flies open, knocking back the chair so hard it clatters to the floor.

Umber, one of the alchemists, stands on the other side, sporting tinted goggles and thick rubber gloves, his long white hair tied back. Underneath the industrial gear, he wears a fine double-breasted tailcoat and a pair of comically outdated hose. He clenches a spouted, bulbous container in his right hand. Stray curls of steam leak from its mouth.

"She's all yours, master!" Umber shouts into the silence, like he's gone half-deaf from the hissing.

Whitman steps past him, the tips of his ears red. He's not happy he had to go to Umber for help. "Much appreciated."

Umber lifts his goggles to his forehead, leaving red indents around his eyes and nose. He steals a glance at me—skulking like a cowed dog, my resplendent gray gown pooling around my knees. "See you there," Umber mutters to Whitman before taking his leave.

Whitman towers over me as he approaches. Defiant, I meet his eye without rising. His mouth curls down at the corners, but he doesn't look angry, or at least not angry with me.

"Good evening," I say, breathless. "I'm not going."

"Why did you get dressed, then?"

I bite my lip, weighing the answer. I don't want to do Isaac's reading, but I don't want to leave the castle, either. I want not to make any decision at all. I've been standing still, a tree rooted in a riverbed, letting the currents of circumstance flow around my ankles. I let Whitman plan my future; I let Elizabeta gussy me up. But not choosing is a choice in itself, and a risky one. Now I've backed myself into a corner.

"I can't go home," I say, my voice frail. "But I won't join the company, either."

"Why not?" he asks with genuine confusion.

I sniffle. I can't articulate a proper answer. But when I picture myself swearing in as a royal magician, Patrick is there, standing in the crowd and grinning with fierce pride. How can I live that life when Patrick is dead?

I rub a tear from my cheek with the heel of my hand. "I don't deserve it."

Whitman examines my face, gauging my sincerity. Then he sighs. "Come down to the ceremony, Ms. Arnett. Do your reading. You don't have to swear in as a royal magician if you don't want. You'll be a—a contractor. Then you can go home whenever you please."

That option never crossed my mind. "Why would you do that?"

"I told you. I need your reading, whatever it takes."

I laugh without humor. Whitman is offering me an out I can stomach. A brief dip into discomfort, and then it'll be over. I suppose it's the best outcome either of us could hope for.

"How do I know you won't go back on your word?" I ask.

"You'll have to trust me."

I raise a dubious brow, remembering the old adage: *Never broker a deal with a demon.* Maybe Whitman's not a demon, but he's been trying to outmaneuver me since we met. I have a sinking feeling he's won this time. Across the room, my door is open, drawing me out as I've always feared—pulling at me like a current, like a terrible attraction. Like a cliff I want to throw myself off.

"Fine," I whisper. "It's a deal."

Whitman doesn't smile, but it's a close call. He holds out his arm. Quivering, I take it.

He helps me to my feet, guides me to the door of my apartments. I squeeze my eyes shut as we step out of the room. Over the edge.

We walk down the halls without speaking. The pressure of the corridors bears down on me, like the walls are watching us. I ball my hands into fists at my sides and realize, with a swoop in my stomach, I still have the seawater-soaked handkerchief in my hand. I press it to my lips, breathing in. My pulse slows at the scent.

Calmer by a hair, I keep my head down and put one foot in front of the other, handkerchief over my mouth. I don't want to see where we're going, or think about what comes next. How long am I expected to stay? And what's the royal etiquette around throwing up on guests? Aim for the lesser titles?

When we spill out into a vast room, I look up.

High above, near the vaulted ceiling, purple spellsap lanterns float and glow like a network of stars. Pillars carved in intricate relief stand in even, imposing rows. It looks like some underground cave—the kind that sits low by the mouth of the sea and fills up with ocean at night. Garlands of black-and-gold roses hang from the ceiling, swooping up and down like diving sparrows.

More people pack the room than I've ever seen in one place. Jewels drip from wrists and throats, sparkling like fireflies in the low light; satin skirts and bold capes swirl around me. I press the handkerchief harder against my lips.

"What is this?" I ask Whitman.

"The ceremony. It's a big occasion for Opalvale."

I shudder, my stomach packed with ice. Much harder to back out when you're faced with hundreds of guests expecting your cooperation.

"When will I do the reading?" I say as my gaze zooms about, ricocheting off the decor.

"It won't be long. I'll show you where to go when it's time." Whitman seems distracted, staring at something, or someone, over the heads of the crowd. My mood sours. I know what he's going to say before he says it.

"I need to confer with Isaac," he says. "Very briefly. You can join us, if you'd like—"

"I'll be fine." I cross an arm across my stomach. I have no interest in trailing after him, butting in on his conversations, as if I can't take care of myself. Even if it's true.

Whitman gives me a final obnoxious nod and dashes off.

Trembling with adrenaline, I dodge the servers carrying trays of sacred seawater and scan for cocktail glasses instead. I have a glass of champagne in my hand by the time I spot Bernadette Byers across the room. Today, her gown is deep scarlet red. We may not be on speaking terms, but hers is the only prediction I trust other than my own. Her magic is god-given, like mine. It never fails.

Whitman shows back up at that moment, nodding to me. "We're starting."

I glance toward the exit one last time as Whitman drags me away.

We head for a platform up front, bathed in a shock of white light. And there's Isaac, sitting on a gilded, high-backed throne, with a company of guards surrounding him. The seers from Whitman's company are lined up before the king. Master Gan waits in the wings; he must be presenting.

"Are you prepared?" Whitman asks in a low voice as he guides me by the elbow.

I tug my arm from his grasp. "It's a little late for that question, isn't it?" I say icily, and stride up the stairs without waiting for his response. I hear him jog after me.

Whitman takes his place at Isaac's right side while I fall in line with the seers. Byers joins us, completing the lineup. The Royal Practitioners Company has four seers in its ranks: Byers, Janieux, Tellerman, and Hawkes. I glance at the others from the corner of my eye. This is Whitman's company through and through: young, upright, and sober as a panel of judges. Byers is looking particularly austere, unaffected by the jubilant atmosphere. The other three betray a shadow of smugness, their mouths upturned at the corners. The opposite of the confusion and shame I feel standing before the king.

But a strange thing happens as the bright spellsap lights swelter on my forehead and the crowd surges at my back: I grow calmer. This is just another performance, like any of my readings. I lower the handkerchief from my mouth and inhale.

Maybe I can do this.

Master Gan steps forward, and the ceremony commences.

"Today, we have come together to celebrate the divining of the king's new bride!" Master Gan booms. His voice reverberates with energy, so unlike that of the understated man I met in my apartments. He wears a bloodred cape, pierced along the hem with dangling crow feathers. This must be his public persona.

King Isaac grins at the uproarious applause. His eyes sit deeper in his skull tonight, more sunken than before. At his side, Whitman looks on edge, braced for disaster. He's expecting foul play—predictions that have been bought and paid for. It makes me wonder: If one of the seers does get caught taking a bribe, will Whitman face consequences? He recruited the newest members of the company, after all. That kind of blunder won't endear him to the other masters.

The soothsayer Janieux goes before the king first. Her sleek chestnut hair is twisted into a fashionable knot of braids, her lips tinted petal pink. She looks more like a socialite than a magician. I congratulate myself on keeping a sneer from my face as she pulls out a copper tray jangling with runestones. Janieux and the others made their predictions ahead of time—a necessary conceit, as divination tools are spotty, like reading in low light without your glasses. This is for show.

She tosses the runestones a few times, hemming and hawing, then stands to make a pronouncement. "The king's betrothed shall be a woman born in a month with two moons, with a name as fair as flowers and three freckles on her right first finger."

Murmurs erupt from the crowd behind me. I don't know if Janieux is describing a woman they recognize, or if they're astounded by the amount of detail. I exchange a glance with Whitman, his suspicions about bribed seers echoing in my ears. Easy to be specific when you have someone in mind.

Hawkes goes next with a silver rune-engraved mirror, gazing into its depths and speaking of a beauteous woman with a shock of red hair and two parents each with two first names. Tellerman brings out his own set of runestones and prognosticates that the bride-to-be will arrive at the castle on her own business, not knowing of our ceremony today, carrying a message for someone with one too few fingers.

That's interesting. Could the future queen be a commoner?

Then Byers steps forward and bows to the king. Kneeling, she takes out a bag of polished runestones and tosses a handful onto the stage. They scatter with a sound like heavy rain. She pauses, pretending to read them.

"The king's bride will arrive before Gray Mass," Byers proclaims in a loud, clear voice, "and she will be marked by the gods."

I chew on the inside of my cheek. Hers is the only reading I trust with complete confidence, but it doesn't reveal much.

My turn comes. I step forward on light feet, tucking my handkerchief in my pocket. The last of my nerves melt away, running off me like hot wax. The crowd churns with whispers as I approach without a rune or mirror in sight. I bow before the king.

"Hand me your sword," I say from the corner of my mouth.

Isaac reaches for the ceremonial rapier at his hip, but Whitman puts a hand on the king's shoulder. "Nothing flashy," the master says in a low voice. "Use his glove. You're not here to show off, you're here to name the queen."

"What's the problem, Whitman?" I whisper sweetly. "You've seen what I can do with a man's sword." I hold out my hand and beckon to Isaac. "I promise, Your Majesty, it will be fine."

Isaac glances at Whitman, who looks on the ragged edge of murderous. Then Whitman sighs. "Just get this over with."

The king grasps his sword and unsheathes it. His arm shudders to bear the weight, like his muscles have weakened since the last time he wielded it. But his gaze is steady as he gives me the rapier with a firm nod. I take it by the pommel, stepping back.

The room has gone silent and still as a freshly frozen pond. I wave the thin blade above my head in an arc, getting a feel for it, the way it cuts through the air as if through a length of cloth. I'm in my element now—before an audience, shrouded in theatrics. In a burst of movement, I stab downward. The crowd gasps.

I kneel before the sword.

I set my forehead against the hilt, closing my eyes. Feeling the ghost of the king's touch there, on the skin of my brow. Teasing out his threads. I squeeze my eyes tighter, tighter, until clay-red color bleeds into my vision. And I fly.

Up, straight up into the air, with magic blurring everything around me. I hover in the overcast sky. I can see for miles over the gently wooded hills, dotted with spellsap beacons, to the floating bridges crisscrossing the marshes. The Middle Sea to the west gleams gray. Then I dive back down, back into the castle, back into my own body—

The knowledge inhabits me abruptly.

For a heartbeat, maybe two, I do not stir.

No air enters my lungs. They're as stiff as petrified wood. The crowd shuffles, restless. I've been silent for too long.

"Ms. Arnett?" Gan prompts loudly, then softer, just to me, "Mona?"

I jump at the sound of my name. It loops in my head, over and over, morphing from Gan's voice into the silent, mocking tongue of magic that spouted from Isaac's sword to bury itself inside my brain, chanting the words I never—*never*—expected to hear from a lovers reading.

Mona Arnett.

9

Nausea heaves through me as I try not to shriek. It isn't possible. This can't be real. Even if I have a soulmate, it absolutely, unequivocally *cannot* be the king of Opalvale.

And yet I have no other explanation, nowhere to turn. Meanwhile, the entire castle is waiting on me to name Isaac's bride.

I can't give them my name. I'd be laughed out of the castle, or worse. Anyone who doesn't already see me as a fraud surely would after that—and an opportunistic one. Besides, girls who commit fratricide don't deserve fairy-tale endings.

I have only seconds, with an impatient crowd at my back. I need to give them a name. Not a real person, not someone I know. But inventing a name at random also has its perils. Somewhere in the middle, then—a name with plausible deniability.

Clenching my teeth, I finally chisel my voice from my chest.

"Jane Smith," I breathe.

Questioning murmurs break out around me. I spoke too softly. Shaking, I rise to my feet. Gather my wits.

"Her name is Jane Smith," I call out, my chin lifted.

Silence descends over the room like a blanket of snow. Whitman's head falls into his hand.

"Jane Smith?" the king repeats, his mouth slanted in consternation. "How many Jane Smiths are there in Selledore alone? Twenty?"

"I can only give you my honest reading, Your Majesty." My throat constricts, like my own body is trying to shut me up.

More scattered mumbling. Of the five, I've delivered the least impressive showing by far. Master Gan rushes to my rescue. "And there you have it, ladies and gentlemen! Our royal staff will pursue these predictions, and rest assured the king's betrothed will stand on this stage with me soon."

The attendees disperse, grumbling. The other seers nod to me as they walk off the platform. Janieux can't seem to prevent a small smile from nesting on her lips. Pleased, I suppose, that I embarrassed myself. King Isaac gives me a last strange look—disappointed, but not too so, like he never expected much. I don't meet his eye. I stagger off the stage, unsure where to go or what to do. Courtiers jostle me as I fight to escape the main hall.

Whitman catches up and drapes a hand on my shoulder. He's recovered from his initial letdown. "You did fine," he lies, with the air of one soothing a moping child. "You're certain of your reading?"

I dip my head in a feeble nod. I can't say it out loud.

"It's all right," he says, though his cheeks have gone pallid, and he seems to be consoling himself as much as me. "We'll find a way to narrow down the field."

"Whatever you say." I press the handkerchief against my bloodless lips, a hairbreadth from being sick. "Can you do me a favor?"

"What do you need?"

"A possession of King Isaac's." I angle my face away, concealing my half lie in shadow. "If I repeat the reading, I might get more detail." I really do want to try the reading again, just to be sure it's not some kind of fluke, an unprecedented magical mishap. Deep down, I know that's not possible. I still can't stop myself from hoping.

Whitman assesses me from the corner of his eye. For a second, I worry my game is up. But when he answers, there's no suspicion in his tone. "Of course. I'll see to it immediately."

Whitman delivers me to my rooms. The moment I'm alone, I prepare to travel into the Flood. Inching across the dark parlor, I begin my search for a window in the corners of the room. Under the bed next, then along the walls. At last, I find the swath of shimmering air near the chaise.

I step through.

The change is instantaneous. Between heartbeats, my sitting room disappears, and the Flood envelops me.

The purple sky above casts a haze of ethereal light, shading the world in cool tones. There's a rustling in the swaying clumps of seaweed to my side—some small creature, a rabbit or a scuttling crab. Far off, across the lowlands, the gods' fortress looms.

I set off down the path, calling for Irinorr. I need to speak with him, to hear his voice, to process this with him.

But Irinorr is absent—busy tending to his divine works—and I am alone, and King Isaac is going to fall in love with me. In the middle of my stride, I hunch over like my spine's been severed, propping myself up with my hands on my thighs.

Isaac is dying, and the ruler of Opalvale. His soulmate is supposed to be the queen. Once Isaac is gone, his widow will become the sole monarch, responsible for an entire kingdom. I could never fit that bill—and I don't want to. I just want to go home and pretend none of this ever happened.

"Sweet bride of crow," purrs a voice near the ground.

Startled, I look down. Tiny frost-blue eyes like hailstones peer out from between pillars of kelp. I swipe the tears from my cheeks. Here's one entity I'll never let see me cry. "Don't call me that, Wayvadd."

The owner of the eyes slinks out of cover, revealing a tabby cat, his fur sleek and shiny and damp. Wayvadd is the only of the seven who prefers a true animal form.

His pink tongue flicks out to wet his nose. "Since you mention it, I would indeed like to give you a different title. How about consort of cat?" He pauses thoughtfully, his tufted ears twitching. "Patroness of pussy?"

"Hilarious," I say, monotone. "I'm looking for Irinorr. Help or get out of my way."

Wayvadd curls into a lazy ball on the dirt. He rests his head on his paws. "We

73

make these assignments too young, don't you think? How old were you when Irinorr claimed you? Five? Six?"

"Eight," I mutter. Sometimes, the best way to get what you want from Wayvadd is to give him what he wants first. Today, he wants to torment me.

"My, my. Had you gotten your blood cycle?"

"I don't remember," I say. Wayvadd closes his eyes, looking ready to nap. I sigh. "No, I hadn't."

"So, you weren't even a woman yet. Had we waited a few years, no doubt we all would have agreed you were better suited for me, temperamentally." He pries open an eyelid. "And mentally."

I grit my teeth. I learned long ago not to take Wayvadd's comments to heart. Everything the god of self says is crafted to either serve him or entertain him. He can't help it. Ego and hedonism are his domains. And madness.

Wayvadd stretches out a furry arm, flexing his claws. "I suppose I ought to tell you the others are at the fortress. They're having a Serious Discussion. You know how they like to kick me out of those."

Fantastic. The fortress, where the seven's seat of power and the garden of the dead sit behind impassable walls. The one place in the Flood mortals can't tread.

It wasn't always that way; before the demon wars, the fortress was a palace at the center of a metropolis, open to the clans for travel and trade. Then the gods punished the demons for their warlike ways, revoking their runic magics, and slowly, the Flood transformed into an empty wilderness, as it must have been before the gods first coalesced—before the age of demons, and long, long before mortals. Now, centuries later, the demon clans hide in their burrows, biding their time, and the fortress has been shuttered, locked away behind an impassible moat and cyclopean walls. I asked Irinorr once how to get inside, but all he would say is that to enter the fortress, you must already know the way. Typical divine nonsense.

Wayvadd, more than any of the gods, must hate this new age. The Flood has become a peaceful, idyllic place. Wayvadd is loud and shitty. Most of all, he loves to sow chaos. The Flood doesn't suit him anymore.

"What are the gods meeting about?" I ask. *Patrick*, says a hopeful voice in my head. *Banishing his ghost so I can go home.*

"Not your concern. Irinorr will be tied up a while, I'm afraid. Best to return to your mortal coil and try not to think about it. You have a new plaything, don't you?"

I cross my arms with great dignity. "I don't know who's been spreading that rumor, but Whitman is *not* my plaything. In fact, I like him so much we're getting acquainted first."

"First of all, liar. You do not 'like' him. People to you are nothing more than resources and warm bodies." Wayvadd unfurls and sprawls out on his back, exposing a fang. "Second, who's Whitman? Tell me more."

I falter. "What did you mean by 'plaything,' then?"

"Oh, I was just guessing, considering it's you."

I narrow my eyes. "Tell Irinorr I came looking for him. *It's important.*"

"Yes, mistress. Your wish is my command." Wayvadd rolls onto the pads of his paws and trots toward the seaweed bushes. He gives me a brief backward glance. "I've always liked you, Mona." His blue eyes shine as he adds, "I just want you to know, if it were up to me, things would have gone differently."

"What things?" I call after him with a frown.

But Wayvadd struts off into the brush, his tail swishing back and forth. I call out again to no avail. I scoff under my breath, hands propped on my hips. If he knows about my reading, I wouldn't put it past him to taunt me.

As I remember the reading, my chest squeezes, driving the Flood's strange air from my lungs. I can't be queen. There's no role more public, more exposed. I would never be allowed to return to the east wing. My life would be over.

Unless I can think of a way out.

I already set up the scaffolding, in my moment of panic. The seed of a lie. I can walk this tightrope. Still, a part of me wants to drop to my knees and stay here, in the Flood, until whatever fate its essence has in store for me takes over. Perhaps I'd go mad, or transform, gruesomely, into a demon—or perhaps I would just die. There's a whole host of possibilities, each one preferable to taking the throne.

So, there's one option: fade into the Flood, remove myself from the equation. I nod firmly. I don't have to decide now; the choice will always be open to me. That's all I need.

I stand up, dusting off my skirts, and open a window back to the mortal realm.

My apartments are dark and silent. I go straight for the decanter on my side table to wash the night's events away with wine. I don't know my next steps. For now, I only care about escaping into oblivion, forgetting for a time. After I drain the decanter, I hug it to my chest, drowsy and sloshed, sprawled out on my couch as my eyelids droop.

In the darkness, it almost feels like home.

10

When Elizabeta knocks in the morning, I'm vomiting into a basket. I'm not sure of the basket's intended purpose. It was lined with dyed linen and set very deliberately next to my wicker chair. It's a vomit basket now.

Elizabeta's face blanches when I open the door. "Miss, you look awful!"

"Thank you. I'm doing something new with my hair," I murmur.

"Are you ill? Should I fetch a physician?"

"No, but I'd take an ice pack." I collapse onto the chaise and cringe, praying for death. I'm exhausted, hungover—and scared to boot. I still don't know what to do.

Elizabeta returns with an ice pack wrapped in muslin for my head. Somehow, through our combined efforts, we get me bathed and dressed. With careful pats, Elizabeta smooths out my skirts, jostling me as little as possible. She doesn't meet my eye as she says, "Master Whitman asked if he might call on you this morning."

My sour stomach lurches. He'll be wanting to discuss my reading. I grind the ice pack against my temple. "Bring him here."

When the master of practitioners arrives, he has dark circles under his eyes and a look of extreme displeasure on his face. It abates when he catches sight of me.

"Gods below, how much did you drink last night?" he asks, his voice scratchy.

"Not enough," I reply from the relative comfort of my chaise longue. "I should have really gone for it. Death by alcohol poisoning. At least I would have been spared this."

"That's not funny."

"How would you know? You don't have a sense of humor." I risk a peek through my eyelids. The light stabs me. "What do you want?"

Frowning at my brusqueness, he pulls a white linen square out of his pocket. "I brought you this. It's the king's."

My nauseous stomach backflips as I take it from him. The handkerchief is embroidered with threads of shimmering gold and midnight black, bordering the edges and spelling out Isaac's initials in the corner. "Thank you," I say, tucking it away. "Is that all?"

He's careful with his answer. "I want to discuss next steps."

"Right." I study his face, that scheming glint in his eye. Is he going to try and convince me to join the company again? The prospect sends a fresh fissure of pain cracking across my skull. "Speak plainly, master, for once in your life."

"I want your help resolving your reading." A loaded pause. "I want you to stay."

My insides go liquid. "I'm not feeling well," I say as my pulse booms in my ears. "Can we discuss this after I've convalesced?"

Whitman pushes out a breath through his nose. He turns to Elizabeta, who waits by the door. "Can you see to her this morning until she's feeling improved?"

Elizabeta gives a timid shrug. "I do have other duties, sir."

His mouth twists into a scowl. I sink deeper in my seat, moving the ice pack over my eyes. How strange that it still hurts, the way my presence burdens him. I warned him what to expect. It's no one's fault but his own. So why do I feel miserable?

"Fine. I'll send someone to tend to your . . . indisposition." I can hear the frown in his voice.

The instant I'm alone, I whip out Isaac's handkerchief and retry my lovers reading. Eyes closed, I soar above my body, dive back down—and for the second time, I'm ambushed with the unpleasantness of my own name. I scowl and do it again. The result is identical. Spitefully, I ball up the handkerchief and throw it across the room. I've never had a reading so maddeningly consistent. Usually, there's some variance, little details that change each time. I don't know what to make of it. Perhaps the bonds tethering Isaac to me are stronger than those I've read before.

After I give up on that, I have nothing to distract me from the web I've ensnared myself in, like the world's stupidest fly. A wave of cowardice washes over me—a vicious need to retreat back into the Flood. I would be safe there for a while.

Someone knocks on the door. Groaning, I bid them to enter. Whitman comes inside, trailed by none other than Bernadette Byers, who carries a bundle wrapped in cotton. Not the company I prefer while I teeter on the edge of vomiting.

"Good news," Whitman says. "Ms. Byers has volunteered to sit with you until you're feeling recovered."

I hold in a snort. "Doesn't she have something better to do?"

"I have a hundred better things to do," Byers cuts in acerbically.

"I'll leave you to it," Whitman mutters, and he sweeps out of the room like he can't wait to be gone.

I lean back on the chaise longue, squeaking against the shrill, too-loud-for-upholstery suede cushions, as Byers sets her bundle on the vanity. She must be the only one in the castle willing to tend to me—or she's a pawn of Whitman's, sent to bully me into staying. We're silent as she unwraps a strainer and a cast-iron kettle. She clinks about for a few moments, then brings over a whiskey tumbler filled with a swampy liquid.

"What is it?" I ask, eyeing the glass with unease.

"It's feverfew tea. Helps with headaches."

I grab the scalding cup by my fingertips, wincing in pain. Byers plants herself across from me and reclines in the chair.

"That was quite the show yesterday," she says.

"Really? I thought it was a bit of a joke." I take the muslin rag from my ice pack and insulate the glass, protecting my hand as I sip. The tea tastes foul, like burnt vegetables. Miraculously, though, as I drain the cup to the dregs, the piercing pain between my eyes begins to fade.

"Oh, I don't disagree." Byers wets her shockingly red lips. "I'm sure you know how my magic works. I can't sense all lies, all the time. I have to be looking for them. And yesterday, I was."

Chills drip down my neck. She knows.

"What was especially interesting is, of the four magicians besides myself, only one told the truth." Her brows lift. "And it wasn't you."

I unstick my jaw. "It's not what it looks like. The other seers, I don't know why they lied. Whitman thinks they're being paid off. But I—I had to."

"You *had* to lie to your king about his future betrothed?"

"No one would have believed me," I snap. *I* barely believe me.

Her eyes glint like pebbles of amber. "Well, I'll believe you—because you can't lie to me. Tell me what you saw."

I hunch over and groan. The knowledge chafes me. I wish I could wash it away. "You can't tell a soul. Promise me."

Byers rolls her eyes. "Fine, I promise."

I curl inward. "It's me. I'm the king's true love."

There's a lull.

"You are," she says in hushed amazement.

"You see the problem, don't you, Byers?" I toss up my shaking hands. "I couldn't go out there and say, 'Oh, it's me, I'm your true love, make me your bride!' Who's going to buy that?"

Byers is stupefied, processing slowly. Her reading applies to me, too: I am marked by a god, as Byers well knows, and as Gray Mass isn't for weeks, I arrived before it. "But if Isaac's your true love, don't you—"

"I don't care about that!" And if that's what it feels like, meeting your true love—a big nothing, a barely noticeable blip—I don't see what all the fuss is about.

"So, who's Jane Smith?" she asks.

"I don't know. I made it up."

"Arnett, you have to tell—"

"I don't have to tell anybody anything. There's no proving it. Unless you plan on revealing your magic and backing me up?"

Byers doesn't answer. I comb a hand through my hair, puffing out my cheeks. "So, which one of them was telling the truth?"

"Tellerman."

Tellerman, the one who spoke of a girl with a message—a commoner. Shaking my head, I mutter, "That doesn't make sense. How can we both be right?"

"I don't know what to tell you. Perhaps he read the runes wrong."

This conversation is going nowhere. Unless Tellerman's reading somehow gets me out of this conundrum, I'm done talking about it. "I'm feeling much improved, thank you," I say primly. "You can tell Master Whitman you tried your best."

Byers frowns at me with such scrutiny I feel naked. "You might not trust Master Whitman, but he has no interest in antagonizing you. He only cares about the king and the nexus."

"But *why* does he care so much?" I can't remember caring about anything that much in my life. His tenacity is infuriating.

"Besides a sense of honor and duty?" she says with a sanctimonious brow arch. "His position on the council is precarious enough as it is. How do you think it will reflect on him if his first recruits are exposed as traitors? The masters will see it as misconduct or incompetence—I don't know which would be worse. And if some nobleman's puppet marries Isaac and takes the throne after his death, Whitman could be stripped of his master's title and kicked out of the company. Probably out of the castle altogether."

Against my will, my heart twinges for him. "Doesn't he have somewhere else to go?"

"Maybe, but the company is everything to him. He's been studying arcane theory his whole life. He would have joined up himself, if he had the ability."

My mouth forms an involuntary O. Whitman wanted to be a magician? Somehow, I never considered that there were people out there, young people who covet magic, who would realize, as the age of manifestation came and went, that it wasn't their lot. It must be crushing.

"Too bad for him," I say, kicking my feet up onto the armrest. "Now, is that all?"

The judgment resurfaces in her eyes. Without a word, she gathers up her kettle and strainer in the cotton cloth, clanging them together rather louder than necessary. I settle deeper into the cushions. Briefly, I imagine what it might feel like, doing something right—surprising everyone and making myself useful. I haven't helped anyone but me for so long.

Without so much as a goodbye, Byers turns to go. But when she opens my door, she freezes like her feet are stuck to the threshold.

"Ms. Arnett?" she says, her voice shrill. "Can you come here?"

The panicked waver in her words makes me all the more determined to stay right where I am. My fingernails dig into the couch cushions. "Why?"

"It seems you're in receipt of a message."

A message? From her tone, I expected a demon invasion. I creep over to meet her on the far side of the door.

The door, into which a seven-inch serrated dagger has been plunged.

PART III

THE CULTIST

11

T he knife holds my attention for several long seconds. Then I notice the rectangular slip of paper it's pinning in place. Words are scrawled across it in red ink.

> Ms. Arnett,
>   I know what you're hiding. There are consequences for every lie, even yours. Tell the truth.
>   I'll be watching. Wherever you go, I will find you.
>   Remain silent at your own peril.

My stomach lurches with dread. I lift my hand to my throat—a protective impulse. "Oh."

"Gods below," Byers hisses. "Who could have done this?"

I take a step back, like the letter might lunge at me. "It has to be about my reading, right? But no one knows except you." A bolt of shock pierces me. "You didn't tell—"

"I found out two minutes ago, Arnett," she says, exasperated. "Master Whitman needs to see this." She gathers up her skirts to run.

"Wait!" I yell. "Don't leave me alone."

Before I can protest further, Byers splits. I slam the door shut without touching the letter, then freeze with my hand on the doorknob. A thousand fears and questions race through my mind. My forehead slicks with sweat. My thoughts are in tangles, but one thing is clear.

I have to get out of here.

I rush for my luggage beside the chaise longue, stuffing my scattered stockings inside. I can't explain how this note writer knows, but does it matter? They'll hurt me if I don't admit to being Isaac's soulmate, which I'll never do. I'm not safe at the castle.

My door flies open with a bang, startling a scream out of me. I whip around; Byers has returned with Whitman.

"You could have knocked!" I shout.

Whitman enters with the knife in one hand and the note in the other, looking between them with grave concern. His face is wan and blotchy. "Sorry," he says, distracted. I doubt he even knows what he's apologizing for.

"Well?" I say, high-pitched and reedy, gesturing at the note. "What's that supposed to be?"

"A threat, I'd imagine," he mutters.

"Oh, is it? Is it a threat, Whitman? Thank you *so much* for clearing that up!" I join his side and bend over the letter, rereading it. To my despair, its contents haven't changed.

"What does this mean?" he says, pointing at a line. " 'I know what you're hiding'?"

"How should I know?" I snap—convincingly, I hope. "I didn't write it."

Byers stands at Whitman's other side, examining the letter's signature. "That symbol." She swallows, her face waxen with dread and something like veneration. "It's the Guild."

It takes me a second to piece together what she means. The Guild of the Rising

Tide—a doomsday cult from my parents' time, dedicated to ushering in the end of the world. Most of their core membership drowned fifteen years ago in a mass suicide. Their philosophy was simple: The Rising Tide will happen, and nothing can change that, so if the world's going to end, it's wisest to embrace it. Everyone's heard of them, but I'm not familiar with the symbol on the letter.

"The Guild of the Rising Tide?" Whitman asks, incredulous. "How could a cultist sneak into the castle and leave this note without any witnesses?"

Byers flinches at the word *cultist* like it's vulgar. "I didn't say that. I'm just telling you what the symbol means."

"And why would a mostly dead cult be interested in me and my secrets?" I ask.

"I can't explain it," Byers says, her voice cracking. The symbol seems to have scared her worse than the threat. "But that's the Guild's symbol. I'm positive."

"My point is, anyone could have drawn that symbol," Whitman retorts.

I can't listen any longer. I charge back to my luggage and start snapping the clasps. I need to leave this castle immediately, or the next knife might end up in my back.

"What are you doing?" Whitman asks, like it isn't obvious.

"Packing." I close the last clasp forcefully, pounding it with my fist. "I'm going home."

"You can't," Whitman and Byers say together.

I sigh and place my palms on my luggage. "And why would that be?"

"The note says they'll find you wherever you are," Byers says. "You're safer here than at home. At least at the castle, you have the royal guards."

She may be right. My parents' manor has nothing in the way of security. And how safe is home, anyway, with Patrick waiting for me? I squeeze my eyes shut, grasping for ammunition to fight the inevitable. "How would they find me? Maybe they're making that up."

"Even so," Whitman says, "the council must investigate the threat. You won't be permitted to leave until the inquiry's complete."

I scoff. "You're holding me prisoner?"

"Crimes committed within the walls of Castle Selledore are handled with extra care," he explains, though he looks uncomfortable with this development, too. "It's standard procedure. You aren't a prisoner, but if you choose to go, you could face legal consequences for refusing to cooperate with the master of justice."

I rest my forehead in my hands. How can the council strong-arm me into staying when I'm being stalked by a possible killer? If I get murdered, I hope they feel awful about it.

But my only other option is to face my fate and tell Whitman about my soulmate reading—assuming, of course, that's what the letter is referring to. This alleged cultist didn't spell out my secret in detail. Still, a shrewd observer might guess that I'm up to *something* illicit. Who would care enough about exposing me for a liar to resort to threats?

I look between Byers and Whitman. "If I stay—*if*—what happens next?"

The dim spellsap lighting of the hallways casts a pallor of gloom over everything. We climb three sets of twisting stairs to reach council chambers. I keep my head bent until the floor levels out onto a black marble landing. The whole way, I swaddle my handkerchief over my nose, breathing in the seawater scent, thinking about the Flood. On the far end of the entryway, two guards stand beside a pair of heavy metallic doors.

I hold my breath as Whitman pulls on the sparkling brass doorknobs. The doors swing open, exposing a serious room full of serious people, staring at us seriously. And in the center of their somber circle, shining like liquid gemstones, is the key to all magic in the mortal realm.

Now, the Opalvale nexus holds no special place in my heart. Why would it? Yes, it connects our realm to the Flood—so what? I can go to the Flood anytime I like. The nexus means nothing to me.

I am therefore unprepared for the wave of raw emotion that crashes over me, cementing my feet to the floor. I stare transfixed at the column of light. It falls from the ceiling, out of nowhere—a glittering blue-green waterfall of luminescence—and splashes down in the center of the circular table onto a disc of smooth opal.

The faces around the council table are dour, save Master Gan, who smiles with faint recognition, and the king himself. King Isaac, clad in a slitted velvet doublet of green and gold, perks up at the sight of us. His thin blond hair sweeps in a styled wave over the top of his head, but his cheeks are gaunt. The sight of him makes my limbs go numb and leaden. What if he recognizes my secret written all over my face?

Whitman sits in a chair to the king's right side. There are no more empty seats, so I stay standing, hovering over Whitman's shoulder. I try to sort out who is who. Next to Whitman is Gan, the master of ceremonies. Remaining are the masters of faith, commerce, whispers, justice, and war. If Whitman's suspicions are right, one of the councilors in this room could be a briber and a traitor. My palms itch as I observe them indirectly. Could one of them have reason to threaten me? If they did bribe the seers, they could be trying to deflect attention from themselves.

Between each of the seven masters' seats stand marble pillars affixed with basins. Inside, there will be offerings to the gods: stones for Semyanadd, wolf god of the earth; teeth and bones for Verimall, boar goddess of violence; crow feathers and jewelry for Irinorr. The pillars represent the gods' honorary seats on the council.

"Thank you for joining us," says one of the masters, a reedy man with dark brown skin wearing a bulky coat of velvet brocade over his master's uniform. I expected King Isaac to greet us on behalf of the council, but he's sitting silently on his throne, looking awkward. "I am Georg Oversea, master of justice. We've been briefed on the threat you received, Ms. Arnett, and I will be conducting this investigation. The first thing we must discuss is the meaning of the note. Do you have any idea what it refers to?"

"No," I say, keeping my face militantly straight.

"You must have some inkling," says a bleak-looking master, her head shaved near bald. Her tone borders on accusatory.

Master Whitman swoops to my rescue. "It could be based on conjecture, Master Renfield," he says. I recognize the name—Renfield—as belonging to the master of whispers, the king's spymaster. The other masters around the table regard Whitman with staid expressions. "Someone who dislikes Ms. Arnett and assumes she's hiding something. It doesn't mean there's a real secret to be uncovered."

Bless him for that. He's dead wrong, but I appreciate the vote of confidence.

"That's an awfully big leap to make," says Oversea with a skeptical frown. "Ms. Arnett, do you know of anyone who would wish you harm?"

I shake my head. A lot of people wouldn't mind giving me a good slap, but to threaten me with actual violence? No one comes to mind. Certainly no one who'd know about my reading. Yet I can't deny that's what it looks like: I have a bitter enemy out there, someone who's determined to embarrass me or see me punished by the council.

"There's also this symbol at the end of the note," Whitman says, sliding the paper across the table so the masters can see it. "One of my magicians identified it as a symbol used by the Guild of the Rising Tide."

"And how did *your* magician," Renfield the shaven-head spymaster echoes like there's something funny about how he said it, "come to this conclusion?"

Whitman doesn't catch her tone, or pretends not to. "Ms. Byers is an exceptional scholar in addition to being a seer. I trust her."

A wild pang of jealousy sneaks up on me. Whitman must think highly of Byers. He recruited her, after all, and at such a young age. Meanwhile, I'm ruining his contest for queen. What would Whitman say about me, if asked? I'd rather not know.

"Do you think it's authentic?" King Isaac asks Whitman. The masters turn toward him like they don't appreciate the interruption. He may be the one wearing the crown, but it seems to me the council resents Isaac's—and Whitman's—presence.

"The symbol? Unlikely. The Guild barely has a presence in Opalvale. But I wouldn't rule it out entirely."

"We'll keep that in mind," Oversea says so dismissively he might as well have crumpled up Whitman's opinions and threw them in the trash. "For now, our main priority—other than Ms. Arnett's safety, of course—is limiting the spread of information. We can't afford for the public to learn of issues with a seer involved in the contest. The appearance of legitimacy is paramount."

It doesn't feel great to hear Oversea compare the value of my life to curtailing court gossip. At least I earned a footnote in his master plan.

"And I'll try to not make things worse," Isaac adds cheerily. He doesn't quite manage to mask the dejection in his voice. I think of the rumors blaming Isaac and his unsound, heirless rulership for weakening the nexus and causing the spellsap disease. Does Isaac blame himself, too?

"Then we'll keep you apprised as our investigation progresses, Ms. Arnett. I have to be honest—with so little information to go on, there may be nothing we can do. Please do let me know if you think of anything else."

That's it? He can't even pretend to care, for appearances? Before I can respond, Whitman speaks up. "Surely you can station a guard shift outside Ms. Arnett's apartments," he says with a touch of indignation. "You have to do something to protect her."

Well, nice to know *someone* cares. I twine my fingers into a clumsy knot and look down, hiding my flushed face. Of course, Whitman cares about every single soul in Opalvale; I'm not special. It's still exhilarating to hear him say the words.

"That can be arranged," Oversea says in a long-suffering voice. "Now, if there's nothing further?"

With a curt goodbye, Whitman takes my elbow and guides me from the room. Ending it on a high note, before I get another chance to open my mouth. As we exit, Master Renfield gives Whitman a mistrustful glance, almost wounded. What did he do to piss her off?

We don't speak until we vanish down the hall, out of earshot. "What happens now?" I ask, balling the salt-crusted handkerchief in my fist.

Whitman frowns at the floor, hands stuffed in his pockets. "We proceed as planned. We still need to narrow down your reading. Sift through all the Jane Smiths. One of them ought to match up with the king."

"Really?" I swallow. That's not the answer I hoped to hear. "Even after the threat?"

He looks at me intently. "You'll be perfectly safe here. I promise you that."

Safe from danger, perhaps, but not safe from myself. I'll have to maintain my lie for as long as it takes for Isaac to find a queen. My throat seizes up. Every time I think about the soulmate reading, my stomach sinks deeper. I don't want to contemplate any of the possibilities—good or bad, romance or heartbreak. Being the custodian of someone else's heart is too big a responsibility. I can't even take care of my own.

When we reach my rooms, Byers is waiting outside my door like an anxious hawk guarding her nest. "Can we talk?" she says quietly.

I bid Whitman goodnight, and Byers and I go into my sitting room. I'm surprised to see her here; I'd gotten the impression she had no interest in talking to me. Seeing as how she said that to my face.

I flop down on the couch. "Is something wrong?" I ask. Other than the giant knife we found in my door.

"What did the council have to say?" She braces her hands on the back of a chair. Her muscles look tensed. "Do they have any suspects?"

The only person the masters seemed suspicious of was Whitman. "I don't think so. I'm not sure they intend to look, to be honest."

"Why wouldn't they?"

"Master Oversea didn't sound enthusiastic, is all." Perhaps he thinks the threat isn't genuine. Or he's just not too upset at the prospect of me being harmed. If he decides his resources are better spent protecting honest, upstanding citizens, I might be out of luck.

Unless I can catch the culprit myself.

"So, the council's sweeping this under the rug," Byers says with distaste. She sets her hands on her hips like she's about to tell someone off. I hope it's not me. "Protecting the contest by pretending the threat against you never happened. That doesn't seem right." She squints at me. "You know, there's a simple way to resolve this. Have you considered actually telling the truth?"

"Never in my life," I snipe back. I'm not ready to give up—not when there's a still chance to worm my way out of this. I have to figure out who's threatening me so I can make them stop. How I'm going to accomplish that last part is a problem for later. First, I have to track them down.

I frown thoughtfully, turning it over in my head. The person who wrote that threat has to be someone I know, doesn't it? Someone I've met before. Surely no stranger would be so committed to ruining my life? Maybe I would recognize them if I saw them.

"Whoever left me the note could still be in the castle," I say, thinking aloud.

Byers' eyebrows perk up. "That's something. The guards in the gatehouse keep a log of all traffic coming and going."

"They didn't log me when I arrived."

"That's because you were with Master Whitman in a crown carriage. They were expecting you. We could check the log and see if you recognize any of the names from the last few days. Or, if we can somehow rule out every name on the log, it's likely that the note writer never left. They could be someone who belongs in the castle—who doesn't raise any alarms."

I cross my arms and look her up and down. I'm hearing a lot of *we* in there. Not too long ago, she couldn't get away from me fast enough. Now she's inserting herself into my business without being asked? "What's your stake in this, Byers?"

She glances sideways, stalling. "I'm trying to help. Sorry if that offends you."

For a human lie detector, Byers is a terrible liar. "If you don't want to tell me, fine," I say flatly. "But don't feed me some made-up garbage."

"I'm not lying—"

"Save it. You're worse at this than you think."

She shrinks back, chastened, but her judgmental air recovers quickly. "I'm sorry, all right? Is that what you want to hear? I'd rather not share my reasons. It's a private matter."

"Great. I don't care." I want to sound aloof, but real anger radiates as I add, "By the way, you know *my* biggest secret. In case you forgot. I would've liked to keep that private, but I didn't have a choice, did I?"

Byers bites her lip like she's weighing whether to let me guilt-trip her. She stays like that for so long I start to think she might be stuck.

"Forget it," I sigh, waving her off. "Go read a dissertation, or whatever—"

"My parents," she blurts. "They joined the Guild when I was little. My aunt came around and rescued me. I wasn't in for long; I don't even remember it."

Whatever answer I expected, it wasn't that. "So, you thought if the Guild is behind the threat, your parents could be involved?"

"No." Her expression clouds. "My parents are dead. The Guild staged a mass suicide."

"Oh." Patrick's ghostly face flashes in my mind, and I close my eyes to banish him. Losing a brother was bad enough. Byers lost her entire family at once. "I'm . . . I'm sorry that happened."

"It was a long time ago." She pauses as though debating how much more to tell me. "It's how I ended up here, in a way. I was at the same boarding school my parents attended and set to go to Isthen for university—where my parents had been professors. They were second-generation professors, actually. *Their* parents met as scholars in Rynth—engineers, researching new irrigation systems in the grasslands. My parents came by it honestly. That's why I never understood how two intelligent, logical people . . ." Byers shakes her head like she's knocking the cobwebs from her memories. "Anyway, everyone in those circles knows my parents' story. I just wanted to start over. I was thrilled when Master Whitman recruited me. But here I am, looking at that symbol, thinking about the Rising Tide again."

I see how that could be a damper. "Maybe it's like Whitman said. Someone's co-opting the Guild's symbol to scare us."

"I suppose." She sighs cumbersomely. "I don't want to think about the alternative."

I give her a wry smile. "Believe me, I understand what it's like to be haunted by your past."

Byers appraises me. Her eyes shine with simmering magic; it's not a real shine, but I can sense it there. "I do believe you, Arnett," she says.

And she always will, so long as I tell her the truth.

12

After three days without leads, Byers and I move on to phase two: showing up while King Isaac holds court. Just in case I recognize someone in the crowd who I might finger as my note-writing cultist. Byers already checked the gatehouse logs and copied down names for my inspection. I didn't know any of them—unless they used an alias. That idea was a long shot, anyway—though the same could be said of Byers' latest plan. But if the cultist is hiding in plain sight as a courtier, a guard, a servant, or a visiting dignitary, it stands to reason I might spot them at court.

As Whitman and I travel the halls, I ignore my heart's attempts to leap out through my throat, buttressing my handkerchief against my nose and mouth. I convinced Whitman I wanted to hone my soulmate reading by spending more time around the king. Which is nonsense; but Whitman would never agree to me investigating the cultist's threat myself. I'm also not stupid enough to traipse about the castle unaccompanied. I'll never admit it, but leaving my apartments feels a little easier with Whitman watching my back.

"Why does King Isaac make public appearances, anyway?" I say, mostly to distract myself. "If he's our last link to the nexus, shouldn't we keep him under guard in some padded room?"

Whitman's smile is faint. "Some of the masters would agree with you. But I have a different take, and Isaac trusts my opinion."

Isaac does seem to trust Whitman a whole lot. And Whitman seems devoted to Isaac, too. "Then what's your take, O wise one?" I ask.

"The enchantment on the nexus determines the legitimacy of the reigning monarch by the sentiments of Opalvale's subjects. If a majority of the population believes the king illegitimate, the nexus will break. Hiding Isaac away runs the risk of delegitimizing him. People might start asking if he's fit to rule, or if he's even still alive."

I chew on that in silence. The more I learn, the more the situation in Opalvale strikes me as awfully precarious. I try to imagine the dark ages we'd face if the nexus blinked out and took magic with it: No more alchemical medicine. No more floating bridges, whose supports and foundations are fortified by the Guild of Magicians' runic inscriptions. No more indoor plumbing. I scrunch up my nose and resolve not to dwell on it.

Whitman and I walk down the long purple carpet of the throne room, passing between gargantuan pillars of sandstone. High on the walls, above a string of black banners painted with Opalvale's seven-pointed star, angular windows of stained glass offer inlets for the sunshine outside. Guards line the room in a ring—a routine precaution.

A gaggle of courtiers crowds around the throne. Mostly provincials, here on behalf of their Opalvalen houses, but I also see insignias of foreign dignitaries from as far as Rynth and the Sentinel Marshes. Byers told me attending court is fashionable for both residents and visitors at Castle Selledore, making it an ideal place to look for a suspect I recognize. If my cultist is in the castle at all, they're probably here.

A panel of three masters from Isaac's council shadows him off to the side. Oversea—the master of justice—holds a quill, scribbling notes like he's critiquing the king's performance.

Even this late in the afternoon, Isaac is still receiving petitioners. There's a polished wooden cane propped against his throne. I haven't seen him use a cane before. Is he getting sicker? I swallow. That would make it all the more important to find a queen.

Not that I'm much help on that front. Byers has done a quick and dirty reading on my "prediction" to keep up appearances: There are thirty-seven Jane Smiths in the thirteen provinces of Opalvale. Twenty-nine adults. Nineteen who are unmarried. Whitman's plan is simple: Find the women, gather them, and let me do my soulmate readings. We'll whittle them down and be left at long last with Isaac's true love . . . if I were telling the truth. Though, speaking of lies, the women from the other seers' predictions haven't manifested, either. Maybe the councilors who bribed Janieux and Hawkes decided it would be too suspicious if their hand-picked candidates appeared so soon after the contest.

Whitman and I hang in the back of the crowd. A woman stands before the dais, clad in breezy muslin.

"We have been an independent, stable community for many decades now," she reads from a prepared statement. Her voice is stilted but strong. "But the shortages have driven prices to a new high. Our parish farms have always bought fertilizer directly from the local spellsap orchard in Karch. We can no longer afford to. The food that feeds our village has been coming from the cellar stores for over a year. Rationing began two months ago. Already our children are sicker and weaker, but we can't buy the alchemical medicines that would heal them. Without His Majesty's intervention, our settlement will die, and we have nowhere else to go." She takes a long breath and lifts her head to meet Isaac's eye. "Thank you for your graciousness in allowing me to appear before you today."

I worry my lip between my teeth. From the sound of it, this spellsap shortage could lead to famine and illness across the kingdom. I suppose one advantage of shutting myself in the house was that I didn't have to confront all the pain and tragedy and unfairness in the world. But here at Isaac's court, I can't look away. A strange, manic urgency burns in my gut, telling me to do something—shout at the top of my lungs, give away my belongings, I don't know. But my attack of conscience doesn't help anybody. I'm just as useless as the courtiers around me, cooing with false sympathy so they need not feel guilty about their own luck.

"Has the weather been nice, at least?" King Isaac says with a feeble smile.

I shudder with secondhand embarrassment as the Court falls silent. The petitioner before his throne stares at him dubiously.

"I'm sorry," Isaac murmurs, scratching the back of his neck. "Sorry about that. I'm—genuinely, I'm quite distressed by this news." From his flushed face, I can tell he means it. He does care. "There's an edict under review by the council that should afford some relief to those affected by the shortage—"

"We can't wait for an edict, Your Majesty," she interrupts with an edge of frustration. "We need food and medicine now."

Isaac's jaw clenches, his brow drawn with sympathy. He wears every emotion on his face—the opposite of Whitman. "I'll be honest, Ms. Larsen. We aren't prepared for a crisis this widespread. We will be, but we aren't yet. I want to help as much as I can. I'm just not sure how. But I won't send you away without something for your village."

I can't say I've heard many kings address their subjects, but isn't he supposed to pretend he has everything under control? I peek over at the panel of masters off to Isaac's side. Their bulging eyes and furiously thin mouths give me my answer: Isaac is doing this wrong.

"Here's what I propose," Isaac continues. "Our royal stores of alchemical reagents are more than full. Speak with my master of practitioners before you leave, and he'll ensure your village gets whatever it requires for the next month. The edict should be in effect by then."

The masters look more apoplectic than ever, though they remain silent. I glance at Whitman, wondering what he makes of all this; he has the faintest of satisfied smiles on his lips, barely detectable. I probably wouldn't notice if I didn't spend so much time staring at his mouth.

"Thank you, Majesty," says the woman, Ms. Larsen, who sounds both pleased and shocked.

After wishing her well, Isaac opens discussion with the next petitioner, a copper-haired Deveneauxan man. A broad, bold badge of office hangs from the lapel of his jacket, marking him as more than some average foreign citizen.

"I hope my timing is not inconvenient," says the Deveneauxan man, his words clear and sharply enunciated. "Given the challenges your council is facing."

Isaac's skin goes even paler than usual. "Challenges?"

"The spellsap disease. The nexus, your line of succession . . ." He simpers. "Perhaps this conversation is best held in private."

If the observing masters were staring daggers at Isaac before, they're staring entire four-foot longswords at this man. Beside me, Whitman's fingers clench and unclench at his sides, like he'd be happy to wring the diplomat's neck. Whoever he is, he's not popular with the Angline council.

"Those things have nothing to do with one another," Isaac stammers. He's flustered, but he's angry, too. Whispers stir among the crowd.

"Really?" Another punchable smile. "Respectfully, Majesty, why are spellsap orchards dying if not for poor custodianship of the nexus?"

A good question, however snottily phrased. Nothing like this has ever happened before. Spellsap trees have weathered droughts, blights, and wildfires over the centuries, seemingly unaffected while other crops withered. This disease has to be preternatural. My mind harkens back to the Rising Tide myth—blighted orchards, roaming ghosts, and rampaging demon clans—and I shiver. Just a story, I tell myself. But the Guild symbol from my cultist's letter floats into my mind, reminding me it's not "just a story" to some.

"I—I don't think that's fair, Honored Delphin," Isaac answers.

Only then do I realize who this stranger is: an ambassador from the Circle Court's bar, here for policy negotiations. From the copper bracelets he wears, embossed with runes, he's an enchanter to boot. Why would a Circle Court representative treat Isaac with such hostility? Then again, Isaac *did* cut them out of his marriage negotiations. I heard a rumor once about a Lamican prince who tried to elope. As soon as the news broke, there was an urgent closed-door parliament session, and next thing anybody knew, the marriage had been annulled. Perhaps the Court doesn't appreciate Isaac's departure from tradition.

"We can debate the finer points at a later time," Delphin says. "For now, I am simply here to thank you for your generous hospitality in hosting me at Castle Selledore." He bows deeply before sliding back into the crowd.

Isaac closes his black-ringed eyes, like he's erasing the last ten minutes from memory, then looks out over the crowd. "I'm calling a recess before we start in on other matters," he announces.

At his words, the audience begins to shuffle and chat. The three masters put their heads together, whispering conspiratorially. With the attention off him, Isaac sags in his chair, digging the heel of his palm into his temple.

When Isaac notices Whitman at the bottom of the steps, he offers him a weak smile. Then he spots me at Whitman's side. One eyebrow arches. What's that supposed to mean? Is he happy to see me, or aggravated? Or am I obsessing over nonexistent signals now that I know I'm his soulmate? Whatever the case, he beckons us to come closer.

As we approach Isaac on his dais, I'm able to observe the milling crowd. I gaze across the sea of faces. If I met any of these people before—perhaps as guests in our home—would I remember? It's not like I make a lot of friends at my parents' parties. Unless you count a certain, special type of "friend." And *those* might be easier to recognize with their clothes off.

Behind me, Isaac addresses Whitman in a low voice. "That could have been *less* catastrophic, right? Somehow?"

"Don't blame yourself. That jackass was baiting you."

I snort with quiet laughter. I never expected to hear Whitman call somebody a jackass. Giving up on my search, I turn to join them. "I think I have what I need," I whisper to Whitman. "Can we leave now?"

"Don't you want to speak with King Isaac?" he whispers back, confused.

"It was just as good to observe him."

Whitman scowls like he can't see what's so good about it. I told him I came to spend time near Isaac, but I didn't give specifics. Because the whole thing's a big fat lie, obviously.

But instead of challenging me, Whitman looks over his shoulder, into the crowd. I track his line of sight to Ms. Larsen, the petitioner. He's eager to follow through with Isaac's promise of donating to her village. It's funny, this conspiratorial bond between Whitman and Isaac—like they're two boys masterminding a prank right underneath the council's nose, except the prank is saving lives.

"I need a minute with Ms. Larsen. Wait here." Before he leaves, Whitman glowers at me sternly. "Do *not* go anywhere on your own."

"Oh, yes, that sounds like me," I mutter, covering my mouth with my saltwater handkerchief. I hate this castle under the best of circumstances. Why would I wander off by myself with a knife-wielding death cultist on the loose?

"Did you enjoy your first court session?" Isaac says.

I whip around to face his throne. He looks like a feverish orphan with a soup deficiency, as per usual, but he's smiling. It's surreal to be standing next to the king of Opalvale. It's even more surreal that I'm his soulmate. I wince and banish the thought. I have the strangest sense that if I'm not careful, Isaac might reach into my head and pluck it out.

"It was educational," I say, trying for a light tone. "I learned that everyone in Opalvale hates that Circle Court ambassador."

He snickers. "Ah, Delphin's a pain in the ass. The Circle Court parliament has decided to use the spellsap crisis as leverage against Opalvale. Trying to interfere in our affairs because they think we're desperate."

Why do I get the feeling that when he says *we*, he means himself? He confirms those suspicions as he adds, "That's why I need a queen to lend me some legitimacy. Make me a proper king with a family, an heir. You know, before I—" He draws a thumb across his neck with a choking sound.

I can't tell if that's supposed to be funny, so I stifle a laugh. It's shocking to hear him talk about his own death so casually. I'd be scared out of my mind.

"That's also why those three over there are ready to depose me," Isaac says under his breath, pointing at the panel of masters absorbed in conversation. "I keep saying things to 'undermine myself.' According to them, I'm sabotaging my legitimacy every time I open my mouth."

"Perhaps you should stop doing that, then," I say with a small grin.

He feigns surprise. "Now, why didn't I think of that?"

My grin widens. I don't know why he's telling me this, or why I'm listening. Much as I try not to be, I'm curious about the boy who drew me as his soulmate. I should be maintaining a distance between us—my secret is safer that way. But Isaac is easy to talk to. As though I've known him for years.

Oh.

Sudden panic grips my insides and twists. This soulmate match can't happen, destiny or not. I can't be the queen; anyone who's met me could tell you that. More importantly, I can't be Isaac's wife. The strength it takes to love someone, to choose a life with them, only to watch them slowly and cruelly slip away . . . I don't have that in me.

"Really, it's my sister's fault," Isaac says wryly. "Aliah got all the training as a monarch. I was just a brat running wild in the castle."

Then, two years ago, Queen Aliah died shortly after her mother, and Isaac was the last of House Angline. He was fourth in line for the throne, as a child. Then everyone ahead of him died. Isaac had grieved every last one of them.

"I'm sorry about that," I say. "Your family. My brother died when I was young. It's . . . hard."

Why did I just say that? I never talk about Patrick. I got caught up in the moment and forgot to keep my mouth shut. I stare ahead, cursing my idiocy.

"I'm sorry about your brother, too," he says. "It's the worst thing in the world."

I nod, looking over the crowd.

Whitman strides up the dais stairs at that moment. He stops and looks between Isaac and me. Without noticing, I've scooched closer to the throne.

"Everything good here?" Whitman asks.

"Why wouldn't it be?" I lift the handkerchief to my mouth and nudge him forward. "Let's go now, please."

"Goodbye, Ms. Arnett," King Isaac calls out.

I wave over my shoulder as I walk away.

Together, Whitman and I navigate the halls to the practitioners' wing. Halls, I've determined, are a weakness of mine. I shove the handkerchief over my nose.

"You've been behaving yourself well before King Isaac," Whitman states out of nowhere; but from his tone, I gather many sulky implications.

"I always behave myself in front of proper gentlemen," I say curtly.

He lances me with a severe look. "And you'll keep it that way, won't you? Because I can't have you throwing yourself at the king."

I have a second of panic, a flash of fear that Whitman discovered the truth behind the lovers reading. But it passes, and a warmer realization replaces it. "There's no reason to be jealous," I say in an obnoxious, singsong voice.

"Listen to me. Isaac is friendly, but he's still your king. You have to treat him with respect."

"I have been," I snap, getting annoyed. "And you seem perfectly chummy with him yourself. What's the problem?"

"That's different. I've known him a long time. We grew up together."

It takes me a moment to make the logical leap. "You were raised at the castle?"

"Does that surprise you?"

Not really, now that I think about it. Where else would he have picked up that courtly stuffiness? "What were you doing here?"

"My mother was in the company," he mutters.

Now, that's interesting. But I'm not ready to move on from my first point. "The king seems nice, but he's not my type," I say emphatically. Maybe too emphatically. The lovers reading flaps in the back of my head, pestering me. "I prefer brooding men. You know, stern, unsmiling, humorless—"

"Yes, I get it."

Nearing my apartments, we cross paths with the new guards Oversea assigned to the wing, patrolling in pairs. Oversea wouldn't spring for a personal guard escort for me, so this added security was the compromise. We also pass a well-appointed common room I haven't noticed before, not far from the magicians' conference chambers. A fire in the hearth casts cheery light over expensive furniture. I glance inside; Toombs, one of the enchanters, sits in a plush armchair, bent over a clump of wax on the side table. He's carving something with a silver stylus, brow furrowed in concentration. Working on his practice—imbuing materials with the energy of runes. I'm glad he doesn't look up as we pass. Right now, I don't fancy drawing the attention of someone I don't know and trust.

Whitman slows to a stop at my door. "Ms. Arnett, thank you," he says quietly. "I know this hasn't gone as planned, but I appreciate all you're doing to help find Isaac a queen."

I tilt my head back, peering up at him. His face is very near mine; I don't think he meant to stand this close. I could lift my chin an inch and kiss him.

"I suppose you're welcome," I sigh—and before I can stop myself, I set a hand upon his chest, along the line of buttons that runs down his master's jacket. He stares down in surprise, or perhaps disapproval. I can't fault him. I shouldn't have done it, but I'm tired and spent and I want to feel close to someone, if only for one instant. When he doesn't move, or object, or slap my arm away, I curl my fist against him, over his heart. "Now, please leave, Master Whitman, before I change my mind."

He takes a slow step backward, throat bobbing as he swallows. "I want to get an early start tomorrow. I'll send Elizabeta to wake you." He retreats down the hallway, eyes trained on me. "Good evening, Ms. Arnett." He spins on his heel and strides away.

I resist the urge to kick the doorframe as I slip inside my suite.

I retire to my couch and turn the day's events over in my head, thinking, thinking—anything to occupy my mind, so I don't have a spare moment to picture Isaac's face, or wonder what he makes of me. . . .

A loud crash shatters the silence.

Gasping, I jolt upright, instantly alert. Did I fall asleep? How much time has passed? I sit frozen as my heart pounds, listening hard. The chiming and tinkling of broken glass sounds from the bedroom, like shards settling. I hold my breath. Did someone break a window?

"Hello?" I say with a trembling voice.

I wait for an answer, but there is none. I don't hear movement or footsteps. Cautiously, I rise from the chaise longue and tiptoe closer to the room. No shifting shadows in the darkness. I peek around the doorframe.

The magnificent, five-tiered crystal chandelier has fallen from the ceiling and crushed the bed, snapping the sturdy oak bedframe like a twig. Broken crystal glitters over the blankets in shards. I press a hand to my chest, shaking.

There's no intruder, but if I'd been sleeping in that bed, I would have been killed.

13

I stand petrified, debating my next move. I'm not safe here. If the chandelier was tampered with, the saboteur must have broken into my room. How? The practitioners wing is lousy with guards. If someone made it past them once, they could do it again. Unless they're still in my apartments.

I rush to my front door and crack it open. "Help! Somebody help!"

As I strain my ears, doors creak open along the length of the hallway, and overlapping chatter drifts toward me, muffled and confused. I open the door wider and poke my head out. The first thing I see is a pack of armed guards, half a dozen of them, dashing toward my apartments. Oversea's new security measures at work.

A number of royal magicians hang near their apartment doorways, dazed and half-asleep or, like me, wired with adrenaline and searching wide-eyed for some explanation. Byers, wearing a vibrant floral house robe and a silk hair wrap, stares at me from her apartment two doors down. She's one of the bushy-tailed ones.

Whitman bursts from a set of double doors at the end of the hall, his master's jacket pulled on halfway. He follows the train of guards to the source of the commotion. My nerves calm at the sight of him. As he converges on my room, his eyes light up with alarm, and he runs faster.

"Has something happened?" he pants, bracing both hands on my doorframe. His jacket is unfastened, the white button-up underneath half tucked into his slacks. I'll have to save that visual for later. "Were you attacked?"

"I'm not sure." My voice is weak, shaky. I wish I sounded braver. "The chandelier fell. I think it was—I don't know, rigged or something."

"How—" Urgently, Whitman moves me aside and heads for the bedroom. I pad after him on light feet. I'm afraid of making noise, like a murderous cultist might still be listening from the shadows.

"Gods below." Whitman runs a hand over his mouth, surveying the glittering carnage. "Where were you when it fell?"

"On the chaise longue. I don't use the bed very often." In fact, in all the days I've been here, I haven't slept a single night in the bedroom.

"Look, there. Attached to the chain."

I squint, leaning closer. There's a slip of paper tied on with a ribbon. The blood drains from my face. "Another note," I say dismally.

Whitman calls over a guard to walk across the broken shards and retrieve it. I wring my hands as the note is delivered to Whitman, who opens it and scans silently. I hover next to him and read.

> Ms. Arnett,
>   I told you I'd be watching. This is your last warning. Tell the truth. Next time, there will be collateral damage.

A cold lump settles in my stomach, like I swallowed a chunk of ice. It doesn't sound like they intended to kill me—just scare me. Somehow, they know my sleeping habits. They really have been watching. "They were in my room," I whisper. "How is that possible?"

"It's not," Whitman says, gripping the letter too tight. "Guards have been patrolling this wing nonstop." His fingers dent the note as he curls his hand into a fist. He looks at me with a changed expression, stony and unsympathetic. "Ms. Arnett, if there's anything you want to own up to, now would be the time. The council will go easier—"

"I had nothing to do with this!" I shout, slapping his hand away when he moves to pacify me. "What exactly would I accomplish by leaving myself threats calling me a liar? Do you think I'm a lunatic?"

"No." His iciness starts to melt, and he sighs, dropping his head. "No, I don't. But I can't imagine a single alternative explanation."

"That's two of us, then."

My heart palpitates as I stare at the crumpled letter in Whitman's hand. I don't know how this cultist of mine broke into my quarters, but it seems nothing's stopping them from murdering me—or someone else—if they so choose. Again, I feel an almost-unsurmountable urge to run away from the castle, to safety. But where would I go? There's no place in my limited sphere where someone isn't trying to kill me.

All I need to do to protect myself is tell the truth, like Byers encouraged. Just walk up to King Isaac and say, *Sorry for the confusion, Your Majesty, but turns out we're meant to be.*

But whoever my cultist is, the worst they can do is kill me. What I risk by coming clean is worse.

Nauseous, I meet Whitman's eye. "What now?"

He stares back appraisingly. "You're positive you don't know what they're asking of you? What lie they think you're telling?"

"Not a clue," I say without breaking eye contact. "They must think I'm being bribed, like the others. Or they're making it up. They obviously have a vendetta against me."

"In that case, there's not much we can do but increase security. I'll convene the company for an emergency conference tomorrow. Perhaps they can come up with a plan."

I put my hands on my hips. "Shouldn't *you* be telling *them* the plan?"

Whitman scoffs, suddenly preoccupied with buttoning up his master's jacket. "There's nothing wrong with delegating."

I hum noncommittally as I gaze over the sparkling, twisted remnants of the chandelier. Whitman is floundering, clearly at a loss for what to do. Yet I can't feel too much sympathy for him. This is all his fault.

If he hadn't dragged me to the castle, none of this would be happening.

The next morning, Whitman guides me to the practitioners meeting room for the first time. I smother my face in my handkerchief. If someone jumps out to kill me, I don't want to see it coming. Last night, I went to the Flood again to look for Irinorr, hoping to bring him up to speed on the whole threats-on-my-life situation. He was nowhere to be found. Neither were the other gods—not even Wayvadd, the consummate loiterer. It's rare for me to go more than a couple weeks without running into the gods, especially when I'm venturing into the Flood every day. Irinorr hasn't even conjured a sending, a silent illusion, to visit me, as he sometimes does when too many hours in the Flood have rendered me unable to return for a stretch.

I remember how, as a child, I couldn't stand to be apart from him for long. I would sit in my room and wait for hours for his sending to appear. When one arrived, it served as a signal that I was allowed to return—that enough time had passed to make the Flood safe again. The messengers he sent were luminescent, almost solid, nearly real but for flickering lightning beneath their skin. An albino crow, most of the time, or on occasion, a pale man with lustrous blue-black hair, clad in a red vest and jacket. I would break into a grin at the sight, so wide my cheeks hurt, throw down whatever book I was reading, and clamber, pulse thrumming, through a window to the Flood.

And on the other side, we were reunited—in the flesh, where I could jump into Iri's arms for a hug, laughing, like I used to with Patrick. Where he could wander with me down the paths of the Flood and wax poetic about magic as I listened with rapt attention. Sometimes, I talked instead. I opened up to Irinorr about what troubled me. Small things, mostly: the tutors I didn't like or the ones who didn't like me; the months my father spent too much time in Selledore for work, which always put my mother in a foul mood.

Sometimes I told him the big things, too. How I couldn't stand the feeling of my own skin. How I felt like a monster. I hurt everyone who cared about me—Patrick, by killing him; my parents, by being alive. But Irinorr stroked my hair and wiped away my tears with a gentle, icy finger—for he was always cold—and reminded me he loved me, in spite of what I'd done. No matter how wicked I was.

It comforted and wounded me all at once. I had prayed, naively, that he might tell me I was wrong—that I *wasn't* a monster, but a girl who made a mistake. A forgivable one. Some days, in my weaker moments, I still hope to hear him say it.

Whitman stops sooner than I expect him to. I peek over the hem of the handkerchief at a set of mahogany doors, sheening with wood oil, and he pulls them open.

A cozy room spreads before us. Sheets of marble panel the walls above bronze-painted wainscoting, and lines of plaster pilasters segment them. An oval table takes up most of the floor, with dishes of sacred seawater set out along its circumference.

The rest of the magicians have already arrived. The eight of them are subdued as they slump in their seats. Tellerman and Janieux sit on either side of Hawkes, leaning in as he whispers. Byers sits apart from them like she doesn't want to intrude. Those three—Tellerman, Janieux, and Hawkes—were in the company long before Byers and me, and must have formed a bond. I swerve around to find an empty seat as Whitman takes his place up front.

"As you may know by now, there was an attempt on Ms. Arnett's life," he begins. There's a distinct lack of concerned whispering or exclamations of distress from around the room.

"*Was* it an attempt on her life?" asks Umber the alchemist drily. "She's still here, isn't she? What makes you think she was supposed to die?"

"Well, she wasn't, technically. There was another letter left at the scene. If it's to be believed, last night's chandelier accident was more of a warning than a genuine attempt to harm anyone."

"That's what I said," Umber grunts.

"I'm agreeing with you." Whitman tugs on the sleeves of his jacket, perturbed. I have to admit, it does feel backward for smooth-faced Whitman to be up front leading the conference while grizzled, experienced Umber takes notes. A fact that is surely not lost on Whitman.

"Whom do we suspect?" asks the enchanter Toombs. His dark brown skin and closely shorn hair glistens, like he just finished a bath, or an intense moisturizing regimen.

"The council isn't speculating about suspects. That said, there's a symbol on the letters that could be connected to the Guild of the Rising Tide."

My eyes flick to Byers. She stares straight ahead, either deep in thought or pretending not to care. I remember what she told me: that she joined the company to escape her family's history with the Guild. Apparently, she didn't run far enough.

"How did they do it?" Talia'ah Ahdut the alchemist asks, with an undeniable strain of curiosity. "No one saw them come or go."

"Consider that your first assignment. I'd like each of you to examine the chandelier for signs of magical tampering. We'll meet again tomorrow, after I've spoken to the king and council." He squeezes his hands together, gazing around the table like someone might jump in and offer a better plan. He seemed so much surer of himself when we first met. "That's it, then. Dismissed."

Chair legs screech across the floor. I hang back until the room is almost empty, waiting on Whitman. I'd rather be locked away in my room with a personal army of guards at my door, but Whitman extended me kindness when I needed it. He helped me leave my house as I sobbed and dry-heaved and made a spectacle of myself, and he never laughed or sneered once. If I can pay him back, then we're even. And right now, he's experiencing a struggle I understand acutely: feeling like a screwup.

Whitman notices me and asks, "Is something wrong?"

"Other than every single thing that's happened since I came to this damned castle?" I lean against the wall, looking him up and down. "How long have you been a master, anyway?"

He eyes me with reservation. "Six months."

"Do you have anyone to help you?"

"Assistant Master Parsons helps with the administrative side."

"Not that kind of help. Like, a mentor. Someone to ask for advice." Like Irinorr and me. But I can't use my patron god as an example in front of Whitman.

His expression becomes defensive, shuttering his emotions. "Is this your way of insulting the job I've been doing?"

Not the reaction I was hoping for. "Is that what I said? Because I could swear I used totally different words with whole other meanings."

"I can read between the lines."

I cross my arms, not backing down. "What about your mother? You said she was in the company. Can you go to her for advice?"

"She's not around." His voice is dark, grimly sullen. "Why are you asking this?"

I hold in a sigh of defeat. Lesson learned. Never try to be nice; it's just embarrassing.

"I wasn't trying to start a fight." I rub my temples, shaking my head. "I only meant . . . if I were you, I'd feel overwhelmed. I would want someone to lean on who's been there before. And the other masters are useless for that, the way they treat you. I don't know how King Isaac doesn't slap them silly every time they speak to you."

His expression subtly shifts. I can't read it, but at least he doesn't look angry. "You've thought about this a lot."

My cheeks heat up. "I've thought about it a normal amount."

He covers his mouth with a hand, studying me. "Are you worried about me, Ms. Arnett?"

"I'm worried about myself," I shoot back, blushing harder. "I'll worry about you when *you're* being threatened with death by chandelier. How does that sound?"

"It sounds like—"

"Arnett!"

I turn around, thankful for the interruption. Byers hovers in the doorway with a tight, impatient expression. She nods at Whitman as if she just noticed him. "Can I borrow Ms. Arnett?"

He blinks. "She's not mine to lend."

"It's a figure of speech, master," Byers says, giving him a funny look. "Arnett, coming?"

"All right," I say warily as I follow her out. I must not be walking fast enough, for she grabs my elbow and ushers me toward my apartments at a clip. She pulls me into my sitting room, slamming the door behind us.

"What is this about?" I squint at her. "Here to guilt me into coming forward with my reading?"

She screws up her face. "No, I wasn't going to. But now that you mention it . . ." Her eyebrows lift amenably. "Have you considered coming forward?"

"Why, because they threatened 'collateral damage'? You know they're bluffing, right?" I scoff, hugging my arms around my stomach. I have to believe that's true. "Listen, if someone's watching me, they know I don't sleep in the bed. If they really wanted to hurt anyone, they would've crushed me beneath a chandelier by now. It's just a tactic."

"You think so?" She sounds unconvinced. I glower at her, ready to argue, but she switches gears on me. "That's not why I'm here. I might have found something." Her eyes gleam with suppressed excitement. "Some*one*, rather. I think she can help catch your tormentor."

"That's great," I say, though I don't quite believe her. It sounds too good to be true. "Who?"

"Her name is D'Milliar," Byers says, building up to something. "She was Korimarr's favored, before me."

I falter. The gods rarely attach themselves to mortals. I wouldn't expect Korimarr to take on more than one protégé—unless the first was dead. "Where is she?" I ask.

Byers looks me straight in the eye. "I think she lives in the Flood."

14

Tasha D'Milliar, it turns out, is a royal magician. Or she was, twenty years ago—before her disappearance. That's why Byers has hauled me to the library for a royal magicians history lesson.

The high ceilings of the library echo the softest sounds, amplifying the turning of pages and shuffling of boots. Dust clogs the air up to the arcing wooden beams. The room is nearly as large as the main hall, but sliced into sections by crooked rows of shelves. It seems darker here, too, with stone walls the color of charcoal and spiky molding like boars' tusks along the hems of the ceiling. I keep my head down, shrinking away from the spirals of bookshelves that groan under centuries of knowledge. A unit of guards stands at attention near the library doors. After last night's chandelier incident, Master Oversea finally caved and assigned me my own escort. They've been trailing me at a polite distance, which ought to comfort me. But I feel like I'm being watched.

"How did you find out about D'Milliar?" I whisper into the damp linen handkerchief. My breath heats it, wafting scents of salt and seaweed in my face.

Byers has her nose stuck in an old ledger. "From my Wetton orchards research.

Remember when you first came here, Master Whitman asked me to look into the spellsap yields? I finally tracked down the missing spellsap."

"I thought the yields were low because of the orchard disease."

"That's part of it. But Wetton's yields are off by thirty percent, even accounting for effects of the disease. The missing spellsap is draining into the Flood, to a fixed location. That's strange enough by itself. But, Arnett—it's being used for alchemy when it gets there."

I stop cowering and stare at the back of her ledger. Tasha D'Milliar was both an alchemist and a soothsayer, a rare and dynamic combination. No natural law makes it uncommon—it's purely statistics. Few people possess the innate magical knack and analytical mind to do both.

"It's the most likely explanation," Byers says, setting the ledger down. "D'Milliar is there, in the Flood."

"She must have found a way to protect herself from the Flood," I mumble. D'Milliar and I are of the same mind, it seems—except I only dream of doing it.

A filament of hope burns inside me. If the harm done to humans by the Flood can be healed, or warded against, or avoided altogether . . . I'd stay there for good. A little cabin in the Flood, with windows. Something rustic and quaint. A place I can finally be safe.

I tamp down my excitement. Perhaps I'm too eager to believe.

"That's not all," Byers says. "I started looking into D'Milliar's history with the company before she disappeared. She joined as an alchemist, primarily, but her services as a seer were solicited from time to time. There was one case in particular that caught my eye. A string of threats and poisoning attempts against the councilors."

My jaw drops. "You don't think it's the same person? It's been more than twenty years."

"No, the poisoner was apprehended—by D'Milliar. She was able to track down the suspect using the notes he left. She got loaned out to the master of justice a few other times, too. Apparently, she had a reputation for solving crimes where other seers had failed. When she disappeared, the prevailing theory was that she finally got taken out by one of the offenders she crossed. But I'm not so sure she's gone."

It clicks into place. "You think D'Milliar can find the person who threatened me?"

"Perhaps." She jabs a finger at a page in the ledger. "Do you know what this looks like to me? A favored mortal using her god-given magic to perform feats other seers can't. Whatever power D'Milliar has, maybe it's perfectly suited to revealing wrongdoers."

"She's Korimarr's favored. Wouldn't she have the truth-telling, like you?"

"I never asked Korimarr if all her favored mortals have the same magic. Either way, D'Milliar clearly knows how to use it."

I chew on that as Byers shoves the ledger into her knapsack. She put a lot of effort into following this lead, and not just for my benefit. She has her own reason for hunting down the source of these threats—that symbol they left on the notes. "Were any of the criminals apprehended by D'Milliar members of the Guild of the Rising Tide, by chance?"

"A few," she says, nonchalant. Like she isn't desperate to learn if these new threats came from the Guild. "The cult was very active at that time. Attempted assassinations, hostage situations, arson, vandalism. It was a real problem in Selledore."

"I bet." I sigh, kneading my scalp. How did we get here? I never wanted to play detective. If only Master Oversea would do his job. "So, what are you suggesting? That we find D'Milliar and ask her to un-disappear?"

Instead of replying, Byers removes two rolls of parchment paper from her knapsack and spreads one across the table, smoothing it down over divots and chunks gouged out by penknives over the years. It's a map. I place Opalvale, taking up most of the curve of the coast, and the other Circle Court kingdoms surrounding it: Ashclaud to the south, Deveneaux hugging the eastern border, the Sentinel Marshes and Rynth resting on the far side of the Middle Sea's gray-blue splash. Ahn Dien floats by itself in the ocean.

With a brittle rustling, Byers rolls out the second sheet of parchment on top of the first. Another map, one I don't recognize right away, traced on near-translucent paper and overlaying the first like a fitted glove. There are no man-made borders, no dashed lines, no boundaries of kingdoms—just the scraggly twists and angles of islands and deltas. I examine an illustration in the center, penned in dark ink. A massive fortress.

"That's the Flood," I say, surprised to hear the words coming from my mouth. I've never seen it mapped out before.

"I spent a few years exploring the geography after Korimarr found me," Byers says as her eyes rove over the hand-drawn landmarks. "Right there are the Wetton orchards, so here's where we need to go." She taps a small, craggy island on the Flood map.

"But the Flood doesn't line up with our world," I say distantly, overcome with the niggling sense I've wasted my life. Most of my time in the Flood has been spent sulking. Byers is almost a year younger than me and has already accomplished more than I ever will.

"It depends. You have to be intentional about where you're going." She gathers the maps in her arms and tips her head toward the door.

As Byers and I return to my apartments, where we can slip into the Flood unnoticed, I broach a subject that's been on my mind all morning. "I've been meaning to ask. Have you talked to Korimarr lately?"

"Not yet. Why?"

"I went looking for Irinorr last night. I couldn't find him—any of them. I don't think I've ever gone this long without running into the gods."

She gives me a curious look. "Really? Korimarr and I meet once a year, on Tidesfair. How often do you see Irinorr?"

Suddenly, my relationship with Irinorr seems childish—like he dotes on me, or I cling to him. Perhaps that's not far from the truth. "Now and again," I say coolly. "We don't schedule it like an annual review."

Safe inside my rooms, defended by guards at the door, I breathe a little easier. Though it's only the illusion of safety—someone has already broken in once. But by force of habit, I feel slightly more protected when surrounded by pink damask walls.

Byers slings her knapsack over her shoulder. "Are you ready? We'll be going off the footpaths, so don't wear anything nice."

I don't have much to bring, and all my clothes are equally nice, so I shrug. "Do you think we'll run into trouble?" I ask. "The clans?"

"The demons know better than to touch us," she says dismissively. She's probably right. I've been on edge lately, overanalyzing every risk.

With a distant stare, Byers reaches out and flicks the empty air before her. A rippling window to the Flood appears. Figures she would be better at that, too.

"After you," she says, holding out a hand.

A moue on my lips, I fall sideways to plunge into the Flood.

15

The orchards in Wetton are a day's tireless walk from Selledore, but the journey will be shorter through the Flood—so long as, according to Byers, we keep our destination firmly in mind. I try to hold the image of the craggy island in my head as we travel.

We venture deep into the wilderness. Squishy, wet sand covers the ground, swirled with banks of pearlescent shells, the seaweed trees and columns of kelp towering and swaying around us. Clumps of orange and purple coral line our way like common mulberry bushes. And every so often, we pass the dilapidated ruins of an ancient demon settlement, eroded to crumbling foundations by time and liquid magic. A reminder that the clans are out there somewhere.

I glance around. "Do you ever . . . ?" I trail off, unsure how to best string my thoughts together. "Does it ever seem to you the Flood's getting bigger?"

"What?"

"I don't know," I mutter, wiggling my fingers at my sides as the current flows between them. I crane my neck to look at the sky. The daytime moon hangs high and small, like a faded felt button. It was the first thing I noticed when I stepped into the Flood, the day Patrick died. "I remember the moon being closer."

"Of course you do." Her loose braids bob in the watery air as she takes point. "You were a child, everything seemed bigger."

We walk in silence for an hour or two, or three, or four. How odd it feels to travel past these vistas with company. Only the gods have been present during my previous forays into the Flood. It carries an uncomfortable intimacy, letting Byers glimpse this part of my life. But the Flood is as much her secret as mine.

A snap echoes to our right, and I jump sideways. In the periwinkle twilight, shadows swarm behind a veil of kelp.

"Stay calm and shut up," Byers whispers.

A pair of striped, hooked horns pokes through the kelp curtain. A body follows, hooded in robes of what look like woven seaweed, bleached anemic yellow. A clay mask covers its face, with small, circular eyeholes set too wide. My breath comes short. I've seen demons from afar, but always with Irinorr at my side, knowing they wouldn't dare approach us. This one looks more inhuman up close. The way it moves, mostly—almost floating.

Other demons pour out behind the first. I count six total. Each of them carries what looks like a barbed harpoon gun. They wear identical robes and masks, but their horns come in a variety: pronged antlers, curly ram horns, pointed goatlike stubs. All chipped and cracked, like wood swollen from water damage. But what unsettles me most is how nothing about their appearances distinguishes their clan—whether their fealty is owed to Semyanadd the wolf, or Verimall the boar, or any of the seven. They no longer reflect the divine image at all. Have these demons veered that far from the gods?

The one in front with hooked horns scours us with red-rimmed eyes from behind its mask. It says something, raspy and wet. Less like words and more like jets of bubbles. I can't understand its language, but the deep, burbling baritone sounds male.

Byers addresses Hook Horns in a clear voice. "Let us pass."

"Favored mortals," I add, holding up seven fingers and jerking my head to the north, toward the fortress. I point between Byers and me. "*Korimarr* and *Irinorr*. Understand?"

That doesn't help. The demon posse grumbles at the gods' names, a noise like sand grinding into glass, and encroaches on us slowly. I clamp my mouth shut as fear creeps up my spine.

"I thought you said there wouldn't be trouble!" I whisper as we back away.

"I've never seen them act like this," Byers says, her confidence wavering. To the demons, she calls out, "The gods will punish you if we're harmed."

Hook Horns laughs. It echoes behind his mask. He holds up seven pale, pruney fingers, shaking his hooded head. Then he makes a violent motion with his hand across his throat.

The waters of the Flood churn in my ears. Has something happened to the gods? I've feared it, dreaded the slim possibility. But it can't be.

"What are you saying?" I ask with some pantomiming of my own. "The gods are gone?"

The demons close in.

"They're not interested in talking it out," Byers says through gritted teeth. "We should run."

I swallow and nod. Then the demons hiss in guttural tones, pointing six harpoon guns at us, and I reconsider.

"I don't think that's an option," I whisper.

It doesn't take long for the demons to bind our hands in braided kelp ropes. With two demons apiece frog-marching the captives, they start off. I tell myself they only aim to scare us before letting us go. We're favored mortals. The gods would make them suffer for antagonizing us. Then again, demons hate mortals because we stole the gods' attentions, or so Irinorr says. The seven left them to flounder and stagnate while cultivating Opalvale instead.

We come upon their colony some time later, sprawled across bare rock. Trees and coral and clusters of fungus have been slashed or burnt away, leaving an uneven hillside that dives down toward a trench. Squat stone huts, stained black, jut from the slope like dark crystals, and tents of bone-yellow leather cover the flatter ground, stretched over hexagonal frames.

The footpaths are mostly deserted—except, I notice with a jolt of recognition, what looks like a human boy standing beside one dimpled tent. But his eyes are wrong: yellow, with slits for pupils. He watches us indifferently. Behind him, a red bull-like beast, its face slashed with scars, lurks on its hind legs. My instinct is to cry out, to warn the child of danger—but when he turns to walk away, the red beast trails after him, like a pet.

Our captors deposit us in the largest of the leather tents. They shove us down, tie our legs to the benches that line the tent, which seems to be a feasting hall. Hook Horns steps back, eyes gleaming behind his mask like we're prize catches. Beside me, Byers shakes from head to toe, but her expression remains neutral. Maybe she has a plan. Gods below, I hope she has a plan.

A few tense minutes later, more robed demons enter with the human-looking boy and his pet bull. He regards us, unimpressed.

"This is good work." He sounds like nothing so much as a bored child—and unlike with the others, I can understand every word he says. It sends a chill over my shoulders. Only the oldest, foulest demons can speak our language, or morph their appearances. This tiny human package is an illusion.

The boy hums. "We'll keep one and sell the other."

Limbs crackling with panic, I struggle against my bonds. They're secure. Byers' forehead is sweaty and wrinkled. That doesn't look like a forehead with a plan.

"Stop squirming," the boy drawls at me. "Where are you going to run? Moron."

"Let us go," I blurt, trying to buff the desperation out of my voice. "I promise, we won't tell the seven. It'll be like it never happened. What's your name?"

He smirks and answers, in his little kid's voice, "You may call me Kazzath."

"Kazzath. I'm Mona. Can we talk about this?"

Grinning wider, he wrenches a short dagger from his boot. Curiously, like a child tearing the wings off a fly, he reaches out to nick my cheek. I grit my teeth against the pain. A stream of blood flows through the air before my eyes, like ink spilled into a cup of water.

"We'll keep her and sell the quiet one," Kazzath decides. "I want to hear how a mortal begs."

"We beg very well," I rush to supply, my cheek stinging. The words come from my mouth, but it's like someone else is speaking—some smaller, more unhinged person who's lived inside me for so long they've earned squatter's rights. "You don't need to work for it. I'll beg right now, if you'd like."

I'm blathering, nervous. But as I speak, a plan starts to firm up. I keep talking to buy myself time. "I could do a reading on you." I wet my cracked lips. "A lovers' reading. Demons don't have true loves, do they? Who knows what might happen if I try?"

Byers stares at me in baffled horror. Kazzath, though, is intrigued.

"You're scheming something," he says shrewdly.

Damn. I adjust my wrists, chafing from the bindings, and say, "Perhaps. But you're clever enough to catch me at it, aren't you?"

Kazzath frowns in appraisal, considering my point. The expression looks bizarre on his sweet child's visage. "It has potential to entertain me."

He motions to a pale horned demon, who approaches me with a knife. I flinch, but he only kneels and cuts the ropes from my wrists, though I remain bound to the bench by the ankles.

I draw my trembling hands before me, massaging my wrists. "I'll need a possession for the reading," I say in a bleak voice. I have limited experience with pain. I do not appreciate this impromptu education.

Kazzath holds out the knife he cut me with. "I trust you're not stupid enough to try anything."

As I take the knife, hands shaking, I scan the room. Kazzath the child demon, his pet bull monster, Hook Horns, and five robed lackeys surround me. With this tiny blade, restrained by my ankles, the most I could do is take a chunk out of one of them before they kill me. Kazzath is right; I'm not that stupid.

Taking a breath, I clasp the knife in front of my face, staring at it until my eyes burn. But it isn't the lovers reading I perform. Instead, I seek the information I need most: *How can we convince them to let us go?*

Before my eyes swims a mess of lines, bright yellow cuts against a black background. Ancient shapes in the dark.

The knowledge inhabits me abruptly.

And it is not good.

I peek at Byers out of the corner of my eye. She'll object. But what choice do we have, if we want to live? Gripping the knife in my sweaty palms, I look at Kazzath. "You have no true love, but you do have a deepest desire. What if I could grant it?"

Kazzath crosses skinny arms over his red linen tunic. "What would that be?"

"Runes," I answer. "We can teach you how to draw runes of power."

"No!" Byers cries. "Are you mad?"

The child demon's expression goes blank. The idea hadn't occurred to him. But it begins to sink in, very slowly, and a smile creeps onto his thin lips. "Yes," he says, nodding, his smile now wide and dangerous. "Yes, teach me rune magic. Teach me what the gods have seen fit to withhold from our kind."

I don't point out that the gods banned demons from using rune magic for good reason. The gods erased runic knowledge from the clans' minds and souls after the demon wars—and implemented a few other safeguards besides. I pray that Kazzath is ignorant of those.

"If you let us go," I say, "I'll teach you three runes here and two more once you've escorted us to the edge of the village."

"You will teach me all the runes of power you know," Kazzath chuckles, "or we'll take them from you by force."

The blood drains from my face. "That's a bad idea. You'll never break Byers, and I'd do terrible under torture." I swallow, going for broke. "Five runes is still five more than any other demon colony can claim to know. Take the deal."

"No," Byers says through clenched teeth. "We can't." The old adage echoes behind her words: *Never broker a deal with a demon.*

I avoid her gaze. Byers would gladly sacrifice herself before revealing the secret of runes to a demon. But I'm the pragmatic sort. The only unsolvable problem is being dead. Everything else, you deal with as it comes. Because that's what I do: survive, whether I deserve to or not.

"Fine," Kazzath says, and I feel a measure of relief, an easing of the tension wringing my insides. "Let's start."

Kazzath orders Hook Horns to scoop a pile of sand onto the bench. I twist my torso to face it. Byers stares ahead, blocking it out. Straining my memory, I start with two innocuous runes: qalinnad, for finding, and erinom, for light. It's been years since Irinorr taught them to me. I draw the angular shapes in the sand, and when I complete the final stroke, the runes blaze to life, glowing pale orange.

Kazzath's eyes light up with hunger. I trace one more—for foraging—before turning to look at him, imploring.

"I've done as I promised," I say. "Now untie us."

"You have," he says with a gracious nod. "But there's one last piece."

My stomach heaves.

Kazzath catches the look on my face. "You didn't think I would work it out?" he says, grinning. "Runes can only be drawn by a human hand. So, I'll need to take a hand from one of you." Kazzath looks between us. "Do I have a volunteer?"

In a strained voice, Byers cuts in, "Take mine. Just let us go."

My head snaps to the side. Byers' jaw is set in stubborn determination. Damn her.

"You don't need an entire hand, do you?" I eke out. "I drew those runes with one finger."

"Fine. I'm feeling merciful, mortals. I'll take two fingers from each of you."

"I wouldn't, if I were you." I spin a new lie as fast as my fear-logged brain allows. "Humans bleed—a lot. If you cut off too much, we'll die. How will you get the rest of your runes then?"

Kazzath appears to consider that. One of his lieutenants burbles at him, and they exchange strings of wet coos, arguing. The demon points at his wrists and grunts. Another demon chimes in and prods a thumb at his chest, over his heart. One by one, they begin unsheathing weapons from their belts, comparing sizes and heft. None of the weapons look subtle enough to be suited for cutting off fingers. They have a more lethal quality about them. I have a pretty good idea what they're planning.

My mouth tastes metallic—the sour tang of dread. I just want to get out of here alive. I'm past minor details like how many fingers I leave with. I glance at my lap; Kazzath's dagger lies there. A horrible idea crosses my mind. But I've thought it, and now I can't get it out of my head.

I force a shaky breath out through my nose and steel myself for what I have to do.

It happens so fast. I snatch the knife, twist around. Slap my hand on the bench, palm up. I hack the blade down on my pinkie, below the second joint.

The pain unravels me.

Byers screams oddly, with more than one voice. But no—the other voice is mine. I scream and curse as blood spurts from the stump. My pinkie rolls, listless, escaping a few inches before wobbling to a stop.

My hand quaking, I pick up the finger and throw it at Kazzath. "Take it or leave it," I gasp. I shove my hand into my skirts to stem the bleeding. Beside me, Byers wheezes and chokes, breathless with shock. I have the nonsensical impulse to reach out and stroke her head. To comfort her.

The demons are dead silent. Kazzath bends over, retrieving my finger from the sand. "It will do," he says, tilting his head, "for now."

Hook Horns cuts our ankles loose. Dreamlike, we follow the demons as they escort us from the village. I keep my hand wrapped in my bloodied skirt. I have yet to comprehend it, what I've done. Everything I've done.

Kazzath stops at the border of the rocky clearing. "Teach, mortal."

Trembling, I crouch down and draw two final runes in the thin layer of dirt. One for warding. One that plays a pretty tune.

Kazzath stares at them with a covetous smile. "Good. Perhaps I will ask you to teach me more one day." He holds up my severed finger and laughs. Then they retreat, leaving us alone.

A full minute passes.

I gesture at Byers' knapsack, which the demons kindly returned. "The map?" I say, voice shredded from screaming.

She gapes at me. "We're going back to the castle. You need a physician."

"Why waste a trip? We can't be far from D'Milliar." I grip my shaking, blood-splattered hand, trying to ignore the cold feeling creeping up my arm. "That cultist could do a lot worse than cut off my finger if we don't catch them soon."

Shaking her head in bewilderment, she pulls out the map of the Flood. She glances skyward, toward the peaks that stab the horizon. It takes her a minute to triangulate our position. "We're not far."

"Let's go, then," I say, and trudge off in what I hope is the right direction.

We don't speak as we travel. My hand throbs with dizzying pain each time I take a step. I half expect a lecture from Byers, but perhaps that will come later. I do need a physician, but I can't leave until D'Milliar tells me how she survives in the Flood. I'll risk acute blood loss for that.

Then we arrive, so soon it startles me.

A bare-faced cliff rises before us. Too tall to climb, but not vertigo-inducing.

At the top is a house.

We stop short of the cliff and take in the scene. It appears to be an outbuilding—something that started small but received steady additions, tacked on over the years. Turrets stick out of its roof at random like out-of-season tulips poking through the mud. A spire of metal scaffolding, sparking at the apex, juts from the ground on the fortress-facing side.

Byers has already forgotten our earlier torment. "Do you see a way up?" she asks, never ripping her gaze from the house.

I look both directions. The jagged cliff face extends until it curves far out of sight. There are no stairs or ladders.

I cup my good hand around my mouth. "Tasha D'Milliar!" I call out.

Byers groans under her breath, but she makes no comment as we wait. I yell up the bluff once more.

A woman steps onto the balcony.

Her blond hair is cropped short, her skin ghostly pale. She wears a simple purple toga. Following in her wake, two burly green creatures lumber into view, almost man-shaped. Their ever-shifting skin (is it skin?) is pocked with glowing flecks of yellow.

"Go away," D'Milliar shouts down.

As if in punctuation, a fork of lightning unzips the sky, crashing into the metal tower. She doesn't flinch.

"We need to speak with you," Byers calls, her voice reverent. "Please. We're favored mortals—Korimarr's my—"

"Go," D'Milliar says, "away."

Byers is undeterred. "We have a very important—"

D'Milliar flicks something from her fingers. It plummets down the cliffside and impacts the ground before us, opening a crack in the earth. Molten lava, iridescent red, seeps out and floats toward us on the currents of the Flood, its heat drawing beads of sweat to my skin. We leap away.

"That was a warning," D'Milliar says. "The next one lands beneath your feet."

"You haven't even heard what we have to say!" I cry. My vision is blurry—from outrage or blood loss, I can't tell. "I cut off my damned finger to find you!"

"Cut off the rest and see if I care."

Byers' big eyes blink in a lost look. I spit a curse and try to think, but my head is woozy.

"How did you do it?" I call up, my throat constricting. I need to know—just this one thing. "How do you live in the Flood?"

D'Milliar's faint sniff is carried off by the currents high above. She leans over the balcony railing. "You're not ready to hear what I have to say. If the day ever comes that you are, find me again. Until then: *Go. Away.*"

"How should we know when you'll think we're ready?" I scoff.

"If you don't know, then you're not ready."

Growling, I take a wobbly step forward. My balance is off. "What is wrong with you?" I try to shout, but my voice comes out thin. "Where's your sense of—of solidarity . . ."

"Arnett?" Byers says. She sounds worried.

Black lines bleed into my field of vision. My knees tremble.

"Byers," I mumble, right as my legs give out.

Before I faint, I have a split second to hope she guesses what I meant to say, which was *Catch me.*

16

When consciousness graces me again, Byers is hefting me through a shimmering window back to reality. She's more economical than gentle as she deposits me in my sitting room. I can't have been out for more than a few seconds.

"Can you walk?" she says, holding out a hand to help me up.

"I'm not walking anywhere," I murmur. The room is spinning, but that's fine. I might never leave the floor again.

"We're going to the ward. You need a physician."

I lie flat on the carpet. "Bring one here, then."

Byers groans in frustration, but she doesn't fight me on it. She helps me move to the chaise before taking off at a jog. I lie there, sweating and bleeding.

The physician enters alone a minute later, carrying a split-handle leather bag. With steady hands, he administers a spoonful of tonic for the pain. Then he removes from his bag a harsh-looking sponge and an array of thick, oily solutions. I shrink at the sight.

"Do you have to do that?" I ask.

He frowns. "How clean was the implement that made the cut?"

A dagger stored in a demon's boot? "Not immaculately."

He snorts, as if to say, *There's your answer*, and pours a dollop of goopy soap onto the sponge.

Whitman and Byers arrive near the end of my ordeal. I manage not to scream too much. Whatever the physician gave me to dull the pain helps. He finishes scrubbing as Whitman stands behind him with an unreadable expression. I become very aware of how my hair clings to my sweaty forehead.

"What happened?" he asks in a level voice.

"Knife fight with Janieux." I attempt a smile. "Ask how many fingers *she* lost."

Not even a twitch of the lips. He's more humorless than usual. "I need to know if you've been attacked."

"Can the debrief wait until I've stopped bleeding?"

He shifts, abashed. "Well—yes," he says, and glances at Byers. "You can't give me anything?"

Byers hesitates as the physician dabs my wound with herbed honey, then starts packing it with gauze. All is silent but for my teeth-sucking winces.

"I found her like this," she says innocently.

Whitman swears under his breath, rubbing his temples. "Do you think I can't tell when you're lying to me? What exactly did you two get up to?"

"That should stem the bleeding for now," the physician says as he ties off my bandage. He stands with a grunt. "I'll return in half an hour to check."

No one speaks as he leaves. Evening must have fallen while we traveled through the Flood, and little light remains beyond the glow of spellsap lanterns on the grounds filtering through my window. In the lull, Byers takes over the physician's chair. She rests a hand on my elbow.

"Thank you," she whispers. "For saving us."

Oh. That. I shrug as best I can. The pain is abating, but my head's spinning again. I don't think of what I did as "saving" so much as "surviving." But I have to admit, it felt good to help Byers get out of there alive. Better than I expected.

After that, Whitman dismisses Byers with a nod. She smiles at me before she goes. It feels unnatural; I've become so accustomed to her disapproval.

The master moves to my bedside, his eyes glistening in the dim light. "I've placed a lot of trust in you, Ms. Arnett. Why can't you trust me in return?"

I look away. "I do."

"Then tell me what happened."

"It's not about trust." My cheeks feel flushed and feverish, my head cloudy. "You wouldn't believe me."

"Try me."

Sighing, I meet his eye. He leans forward, expectant. There's a perpetual kindness about him that never fails to amaze me. It dismantles my defenses. Or maybe it's this *fantastic* pain medicine.

"I was in the Flood," I say, my mouth askew, "fighting demons."

Whitman nods. He looks . . . *relieved.*

"I thought so," he says.

I blink. I can't have heard him right. Perhaps delirium has set in. "You did?"

"My sister went there once," he says, staring at his lap, "when she was a child."

What little feeling I have left in my body disappears. "Your sister?"

"Channice. My mother never believed her, but I knew it was the truth. Sometimes, she still sees . . ." He motions before him with a flat palm.

My stomach clenches. "Windows?"

"Yes, that's right. Windows in the air."

Outside, in the gray night, a crow lets out a series of staccato caws. I jump, feeling on edge. I hardly know where to begin. "How— What happened?"

"Afterward, when she told our parents . . ." Shadows pass behind his eyes. "Our mother wasn't pleased. She convinced Channice she'd imagined it, that she's just . . . sick. But I was there after it happened, when she came back. She'd seen something."

"Did she . . . run into anyone while she was there?" I ask delicately. I don't want to be the one to bring up the gods.

"I don't think so. She wasn't there for long. It frightened her." He searches my face. I swallow past a lump in my throat. "After you came here, I started to wonder if that's what made you different, too."

"I didn't think you'd believe me," I repeat, sedated and stupid. I can't think of anything else to say. Even Byers and I barely speak about this part of our lives. It's impossible to comprehend that Whitman would just accept it. That he would accept *me.*

The pain medicine snakes through my system, sapping my wits. "Do you know," I say, "you might be the kindest person I've ever met."

Whitman sniffs. "I thought I was stern and unsmiling."

"Well, I didn't say you were *nice*, I said you were *kind*. Two separate things, master."

"That may be the first genuine compliment you've ever given me," he says with a guarded look, as though he's waiting for the part where I ask him for something.

"Really?" I think back for a fuzzy minute. "I ought to do it more often."

He almost smiles. "You know, it shouldn't take losing a finger to start acting like a real person."

"I don't want to be a real person," I sigh, half hearing myself, like a sleep talker. "I want to be . . . I want to be a story people tell at parties. Party stories never hurt anybody."

Whitman frowns. "You look feverish." He stretches his arm toward me, and for an instant, I think he means to lay his hand on my forehead; but he's just fixing his sleeve cuff.

My eyes do feel on fire. "I'm a little warm."

"I'll get the physician." He stands. "We'll talk more when you're feeling up to it."

"I'd like that," I say, my smile drowsy, until I realize he probably doesn't mean a personal chat. My smile dims.

Whitman leaves me alone to stare at the ceiling, with Kazzath's tiny face swimming above me in the dark.

The knife that cut me, it comes to light, fell *far* short of immaculate.

Blood poisoning is an unglamorous experience. I mumble through the fever dreams, babbling at the physicians who cycle through to apply poultices of garlic and tallow and some alchemical emulsion, drawing out the infection little by little. It doesn't help quell my nightmares of blank clay masks and dirty knives, or worse, the ones where Patrick's ghost strangles me in my bed.

With all that time to think, I come to a decision: I have to go back to Tasha D'Milliar. Whether she can track down my cultist is no longer my main concern. She can tell me how to live in the Flood, how to hide there. No more mysterious threats. No risk of my secrets being exposed. And if my first encounter with Patrick's ghost holds true, he can't follow me into the Flood. The only danger in the Flood itself is the demon clans—and D'Milliar must have some way of dealing with them, or she wouldn't have lasted long. I'll finally be safe there.

Elizabeta keeps me company during my first week of convalescence. She helps bathe me and dabs my brow and changes my sweat-soaked clothes. Byers visits, too, but she isn't keen on my preferred topic of conversation: where the gods are. She's not worried. The gods are busy, she insists, and can't come running every time I holler.

And the master of practitioners is in and out, usually to talk about company business. He's engaged in an ongoing battle with the head of the Guild of Magicians—some spat over regulations capping the price of alchemical fertilizers—which takes up huge swaths of his time. The guild leader, I've learned, is no fan of Whitman's, attributing his master's position to nepotism.

"Janieux's candidate arrived," Whitman says from my bedside, eight days after my maiming. My room now smells permanently of honey and a harsh, alchemical tang. "Peony Brenton. She's Master Soph's second cousin, but that doesn't prove anything."

Once I'm back in the Flood, I'll no longer have to care about this political intrigue. My stomach squirms with unexpected nausea. It suddenly occurs to me: Leaving the mortal realm for good means I'll never see Whitman again. But I always knew this was temporary.

I can fake interest, I suppose, for Whitman's sake. Scooting up the bed, I ask, "What would this briber use Ms. Breton for, if she won the throne?"

"Special favors, mostly. The queen will have the tie-breaking vote in council decisions, final approval for funding and grants. Any one of the masters has strong motivation to instill a queen favorable to their interests—any provincial noble as well." In a tight, too-conversational voice, Whitman adds, "Of course, the queen won't have that authority until King Isaac dies."

There it is: an opening to say something sympathetic. I want to, but my tongue trips along the way. "It could be *any* one of the masters?" My brows hop up. "Then why should I trust you? You could be masterminding this whole affair." Whitman does indeed have a vested interest in finding a sympathetic queen: He's clinging to his master's post by a thread. Any queen picked by one of the other councilmembers will be more than happy to give him the axe, once Isaac's gone and can't protect him. My conscience twinges. I regret making the joke already.

Whitman gives me a withering look. "If that were true, it would be very embarrassing for me. None of this has gone the way I wanted."

I can't help myself. "That's not precisely an argument in your defense."

His jaw clenches, and my expression softens. I've antagonized him enough for one day. Not much brings me comfort as of late. Suffice it to say, I like having Whitman around.

A light knock at the door. Whitman jumps to answer it like he's looking for an excuse, and Assistant Master Parsons enters, his face damp with sweat. He must have run here.

"Ms. Arnett," he says, panting for breath. "There's a woman at the gates demanding to see you. Her name is Elsie Tanner. She was rather insistent."

Whitman and Parsons exchange a look of awe, to my bemusement. So, I have a social caller? I don't see the significance.

Then I remember.

My lips part as I reconstruct Tellerman's reading line by line. *She will come to the castle, unaware of this contest, seeking someone with one too few fingers.* I cradle my bandaged hand.

The king's bride has arrived.

17

The throne room has been closed to the public for these proceedings, but it still feels packed. All the masters have come to observe. Byers and the other magicians skulk on the edge of the gallery. Tellerman, whose prediction has now come true, looks somewhere between triumphant and surprised. Whitman and I stand near the dais, to King Isaac's left.

And then there's Elsie Tanner.

Elsie sits stiff-backed in her chair, her posture impeccable. A sheet of tawny hair falls down her back. She wears round, copper-rimmed glasses, like a chapel archivist, resting low on her flat nose bridge. From the quality of her periwinkle satin dress, her station is close to mine—born to a wealthy family but without noble rank or title. A tiny painted hexagon adorns the outer tip of one eye. I've seen the same type of marking on Diené guests at my parents' parties. It's fashionable in Ahn Dien nowadays to use cosmetics as a statement of pride, painting symbols of your clan or profession onto your skin. Elsie's mark has something to do with Korimarr—the pattern is reminiscent of a turtle shell. I remember Byers' reading with a chill. *Marked by the gods.*

Isaac addresses her first. It seems the king has grown thinner in the last week, and he grimaces in pain with every tiny movement. "Thank you for speaking with us, Ms. Tanner."

"Did I have a choice?" Elsie says with a nervous half smile. Isaac smiles back.

Master Oversea cuts in. "Ms. Tanner, why did you come to the castle today?"

"I—I need her help," she says, glancing in my direction. Her voice gains some conviction as she speaks to me directly. "I need your help, Ms. Arnett. My family has arranged a marriage for me, and—and it's not a good match. But if you can name true loves, perhaps I could find my soulmate, and my parents would break the contract. True love is more important than paperwork, isn't it?"

Her optimism jabs into my heart like a splinter. If her parents weren't swayed by her misery and pleas, they won't give *love* the slightest consideration.

"Do you know why you have been brought before the king today?" Oversea asks.

Elsie shakes her head, her mouth clamped shut as though to trap her questions— or, perhaps, her objections to being shuffled around the castle like a sack of potatoes.

"A royal magician predicted a woman matching your description will become the queen," Oversea says. "There were other predictions made, however, and we'll need time to sort through them. Until this has been resolved, you'll have to stay at the castle."

Elsie processes this, her startled doe eyes obscured by the reflection off her glasses. She looks afraid to move an inch. "So, I wouldn't have to marry Lord Severin?"

Isaac's mouth twitches. "No, you wouldn't. That is one of the many privileges afforded to the queen of Opalvale."

She nods slowly. "All right, Your Majesty. I agree to these terms."

"Ms. Tanner must be tired from her journey," Master Gan says, rising. Unlike Oversea, he sounds like he has a genuine interest in Elsie's comfort. "We've taken enough of her time for now. I will see her settled in the guest wing."

Gan and a trio of guards lead Elsie from the hall. She sneaks a last curious glance at King Isaac over her shoulder, sizing him up. As they walk past the magicians, Byers breaks off and trails after the escort party at a safe distance. Performing reconnaissance? I hope so. Byers and I both know that Tellerman is the only seer who didn't lie about his reading—which makes Elsie Tanner the only candidate for Isaac's bride who came by it honestly. Why would Tellerman predict her arrival if she *wasn't* pre-destined to marry the king?

I peek at Isaac out of the corner of my eye. Perhaps Elsie Tanner is the answer to all our prayers. A queen for Isaac, an out for me—and a legitimate, unbiased candidate for Whitman. No one bribed Tellerman to fake a prediction pointing to Elsie. He told the truth. And now that his prediction has manifested, it puts my lovers reading in a whole new perspective. If Tellerman and I are both right, it could be that Elsie is in fact the future queen and my soulmate reading is nothing more than an uncanny—but not impossible—coincidence. Soulmates don't always end up together. In a handful of extraordinary circumstances, it doesn't work out. And I'd say this situation qualifies as extraordinary. I can't deny that I am Isaac's soulmate, but maybe Isaac is Elsie's. They can still be happy together.

Once Elsie and her band turn the corner, Isaac looks around at the masters. "What now?"

"Now we wait, Your Majesty," Master Oversea says. "Once Mr. Hawkes' candidate arrives, we'll have located all the women from the seers' predictions. Then you choose."

Whitman speaks up. "We're still resolving Ms. Arnett's prediction."

"About that," I add, raising a timid hand. No better time than now. "I'd like to try a lovers reading on Ms. Tanner."

A dull susurrus of protest breaks out.

"Your Majesty, I must object," says Renfield, the master of whispers—the woman with the shaved head. She's addressing the king, but she looks at Whitman as she speaks. "It's one thing to give Ms. Arnett a say in this contest, but she mustn't be allowed to interfere with others' predictions."

Whitman's forehead creases with resentment. "What would Ms. Arnett gain by keeping the rightful queen from the throne?"

"Why, she'd be the seer who named the next queen of Opalvale. People have killed for that kind of prestige." She draws a breath and starts again, more civil. "We must avoid the mere *appearance* of impropriety in this process. I understand you're still learning, Delmar. I don't fault you. But Ms. Arnett practices a form of magic unknown to anyone else in the company, and her readings cannot be verified. We must be cognizant of how someone might use her to rig the game in favor of their preferred candidate."

I gawk at Renfield. In just a few sentences, she managed to call me a fraud, patronize Whitman, *and* accuse him of interfering with the contest. I have half a mind to do a reading on all her secrets and wipe that smug look off her face.

Whitman replies, his tone prickly but restrained, "If you'll recall, I was the one who objected to this method of choosing a queen in the first place—for the exact reasons you're mentioning now. And please address me as Master Whitman."

"Of course," Renfield says with a slight smile. "My apologies, master. I haven't yet adjusted. I still remember when you barely reached my hip."

One of the masters chuckles. Whitman stares at the floor like the fight's gone out of him. No one takes him seriously around here. I know from personal experience how disheartening that can be.

"We can revisit this at the next council meeting, if necessary," Oversea says. "Your Majesty, is there anything else on the agenda?"

"Hm?" Isaac lifts his head, like he wasn't paying attention. "Oh, no, nothing here. I'm good if you're good. Are you good?" Definitely not paying attention, then.

The masters around the dais begin to rise and disperse. Isaac stays in his throne, scratching his jaw with a vacant look. I turn to Whitman and whisper, "I need to do Ms. Tanner's lovers reading. It could be important."

Absently, he rubs his palms on his thighs. Still agitated from his spat with Renfield. "What do you think it'll say?"

"If I knew that, it wouldn't be so important, would it?"

"Fine," he concedes. "I'll speak with the masters and arrange a meeting."

"While you're at it, can you arrange a meeting about pulling the sticks out of their asses?"

Whitman snorts with sudden laughter, then straightens his expression. A laugh! I can hardly believe it. I'd have been less surprised if he sprouted wings and flew out of the hall.

I grin at him, pleased with myself. "Let me know what they say, master."

As I leave, he returns an odd quarter smirk. I try to ignore the thousand fireworks igniting inside me—all for what could debatably be called a smile. I never realized there were so many good feelings two people could share without taking their clothes off. It's a bittersweet revelation. Whitman has made it clear he doesn't think of me that way.

I find my guard escort and head back to my apartments, leaving Whitman and Isaac behind. They have a lot to talk about. When I reach my rooms, my hallway guards detach and I'm transferred into the custody of my apartment door guards. I can't spit without hitting a guard in this place. But annoying as they are, I'm grateful for their presence, and the not-getting-murdered that comes with it.

Just as I reach my chaise longue, I hear a knock at the door. I startle and throw a scowl in its direction. Unless Irinorr decided to take the stairs today, I'm not keen on entertaining company. I don't answer it, choosing instead to wait for my guards outside to vet the caller. Apparently, they pass inspection—the door swings open.

I'm caught off guard when King Isaac walks in.

18

Isaac comes in alone, without his customary entourage. It feels wrong, like he forgot to put on pants. I sit up and try to comport myself properly.

"Your Majesty." I incline my head. "Where's your honor guard?"

"In the hall." He lowers himself into a chair, grunting. "Why? Are you planning on assassinating me?"

"Not unless you do something to deserve it."

He flashes a small grin. My heart beats faster now that we're alone. What is he doing here, and why does it require privacy? I wish he'd brought Whitman with him.

"Back in the throne room, with Ms. Tanner," he begins. "You said you wanted to do a reading on her?"

"Yes," I say, cautiously optimistic.

"Why?"

I have to be careful how I explain it, to keep my true motives hidden. "Well, since Tellerman's prediction came true, that means Elsie Tanner could be the future queen. If your name comes up in her lovers reading, that may explain it. You could be her soulmate, but she's not yours. I've seen it happen before."

He frowns, disturbed. I don't blame him. It's an unsettling thought. "And what about this Jane Smith? My soulmate?"

"Soulmates don't always end up together. Ninety-nine percent of the time, but it's not a sure thing. Master Whitman wants to keep looking for Ms. Smith, but who knows how long that will take?" I pick at my fingernails as I talk, stinging with guilt. I can't tell him that I made Jane Smith up. Would he feel better or worse if he knew I was his soulmate, and I have no objection whatsoever to his marrying Elsie Tanner?

He contemplates it for a while, then nods with determination. "Do the reading."

My stomach leaps. Finally, a victory. "Master Whitman's discussing it with the council now."

"No, don't wait for them. Can you do it on your own? Secretly?" He rubs his neck, sheepish about asking me to break the rules. I almost smile. Do the rules even count when you're king? But then I think about the council, how they scrutinize and scold him. Isaac has more constraints on him than most people. Another reason I have no interest in being royalty.

"I'll have to find a pretense to see her," I say.

We're interrupted by a knock. One of the guards in the hallway opens the door. "You have visitors," she calls in. "Shall I tell them to come back later?"

"Who is it?" I ask.

"Bernadette Byers and Elsie Tanner."

Isaac and I share a look of astonishment. If this isn't a case of divine providence, I don't know what is. Elsie and Isaac are destined to marry. I'm certain of it. Someone just needs to make sure it happens.

"Please, invite them in," I call. "My guest was just leaving."

"Yes," Isaac says too loudly. He uses his cane to stand with a wobble. "I was."

Byers and Elsie Tanner slip into my room only to be met by the sight of King Isaac. Elsie freezes in surprise, her lips parting.

"Your Majesty," she says squeakily.

"Ms. Tanner," Isaac replies, still too loud. After an awkward pause, he adds, "We were just talking about you."

I hold in a groan. If I didn't know better, I'd suspect this was his first interaction with a girl.

"Really?" Elsie says, smiling a terrified smile. "I generally don't like people talking about me behind my back, but this seems all right." Her smile tightens, and she glances away, her cheeks pinkening.

"We only said nice things," Isaac reassures her. His voice is more normal now.

Byers cuts in, deadpan. "I'm here as well, Your Majesty."

"Ah, yes. Of course. Good afternoon, Ms. Byers." He promptly turns back to Elsie. "Did Master Gan get you situated? How are your accommodations?"

"Unbelievable," she blurts, eyes wide. "My curtains are made of velvet. *Velvet*. Who does that?"

Isaac laughs, then winces and rubs his chest, like his lungs object to the rough treatment. "The palace decorators aren't known for their restraint."

They smile at each other. Byers and I wait attentively for the moment to pass.

"I'll be leaving now," Isaac says, breaking the stillness. He extends me a significant look. "Good afternoon."

Isaac departs, leaning on his cane with every other step on the way out.

When we're alone, Byers places a hand on Elsie's shoulder and says, "I offered to bring Ms. Tanner to see you while Master Gan sets up her quarters." Byers meets my eye with a wink. "That's why she came to the castle, after all."

I could kiss her for her quick thinking. By bringing Elsie to me before the masters can prevent it, she's ensured the reading will be done whether they like it or not.

"Please, take a seat," I say, gesturing at a chair. I go to my vanity for a decanter of whiskey as Elsie and Byers settle in. I want to create the illusion of a casual chat.

I hand them each a glass of whiskey and sit down, curling my legs underneath me. "So, how did you find me, Ms. Tanner?"

"My second cousin came to you for a reading years ago." She sloshes the whiskey in her glass, staring into the whirlpool. "She met the person you named a few months later. She talked about it so much, I figured I had to try."

I take a drink, hiding my tumultuous feelings. My practice thrives on word of mouth, but it always unsettles me to see it in action. It's a reminder that I have a reputation—and for every customer who raves about my work, there are two more calling me a liar.

"And I've never been to Selledore before," she adds. "I thought I could see the sights."

I smile sympathetically. "Well, I'm sorry your travel plans have been ruined. This must be a bit of a shock."

"More than a bit." Elsie pushes her glasses up the bridge of her nose, a nervous fidget. Yet her smile is still in place. "I hope it's all over quickly. It's too much, being kept in suspense like this."

"Maybe I can help with that." I set my whiskey glass down, heart thumping. "I can do the reading you came here for. If King Isaac is your soulmate, that should move things along."

"Do you know King Isaac's soulmate already?" she asks with big eyes.

Damn. This would be simpler if she'd turned out to be an idiot. "It's complicated," I say, which, in all fairness, it is. "I did an official reading for the contest. But between you and me, it's possible that reading won't be considered by His Majesty. It's too . . . vague."

"I see." She fights to keep up her friendly smile. "All that magic business is over my head."

I feel a pang of guilt—for lying to her, and for the position she's in, even if I can't change it. Eventually, she'll work out that she's not Isaac's soulmate. No one can protect her from that.

"Here," I say, holding out my hand, beckoning. "Your hair ribbon, Ms. Tanner. Let's do it now and put your mind at ease."

With unsteady fingers, Elsie unties the ribbon and shakes her hair loose. I smile at her reassuringly as I take it. Am I looking at the future queen of Opalvale? I can see it so clearly: Elsie on the throne, holding Isaac's hand across the armrests, head held regally high.

An unexpected pang hits me, an emotion I can't identify. Elsie looks so fit for the role, when I picture it. So much more deserving.

I ball the ribbon up in my fist, sinking into the lovers reading.

Thomas Worden.

I open my eyes and glower at the ribbon like it insulted me. Not Isaac. What do I do now? I try the reading again, but it's the same result, a perfect echo. Elsie's sitting across from me, holding her breath. I could lie and say it's Isaac—but is that the best move? Without time to weigh the implications, I stall. Again.

"It seems I've overpromised," I say as I pass her ribbon back. "I can't get a clear reading at the moment. Nothing to worry about; it happens occasionally. It's more to do with me than you." Which is probably what I should've said when I did Isaac's reading. Unfortunately, in the eight seconds I had to make a decision, it didn't occur to me.

"Oh, that's all right." Elsie's understanding tone is sincere, but I catch a thin strain of disappointment underneath. More suspense. "We can try again later, can't we?"

"Of course."

Elsie gives me a last shy smile, then heads out. Byers hangs behind with me.

"I can't believe it," she says when we're alone, gripping the arms of her chair. "King Isaac isn't her soulmate?"

That wasn't hard for Byers to puzzle out. She knows my soulmate readings never fail, and she can tell when I'm lying.

"No, he's not," I confirm grimly. "It's some man I've never heard of."

"I thought for sure Tellerman read the runes wrong. Then I thought King Isaac must be Elsie Tanner's soulmate. Now I don't know what to think."

"Sounds like you should do less thinking in general," I mutter.

"So, what is Elsie's role in all this? Why did Tellerman predict she'd be queen if she has no connection to King Isaac?"

I sigh, abruptly exhausted. "I'm not sure I care anymore." My head droops. "I might be done with all this."

"What does that mean?"

I purse my lips, digging into the frame of the chaise longue with my thumbnail. I don't owe Byers anything—her, or anyone else in this castle. I could leave for the Flood without saying a word. But Byers would probably hunt me down at Tasha's anyway. I might as well come clean.

"I'm going back to Tasha D'Milliar," I say, lifting my chin.

"What?" She gapes at me like I'm mad. "We nearly got killed the last time!"

"If she can tell me how to live in the Flood, none of this matters. The rest of you can deal with Isaac's queen, and my cultist won't be able to harm me."

"Don't call them a cultist," she says with an admonishing look. "We can't prove those threats are from the Guild of the Rising Tide. Anyone could have written that symbol, remember?"

"What else am I supposed to call them?"

Byers sneers and moves on. "D'Milliar won't listen to a word you say. You heard her, she wants nothing to do with us."

"I have to try." I can't let this go. It burns inside me like a kindling fire, spreading farther, blazing hotter each day. Everything here has gotten so out of hand. Patrick's ghost, Isaac's soulmate, Irinorr's long absence, death threats in the night. I want to feel safe again, sheltered. There must be a way to explain that to D'Milliar.

"And what about Opalvale?" she asks, heated, and I feel like a child being scolded. "What about King Isaac's line, the nexus? Your prediction was supposed to help!"

"What does it matter to me who's on the throne?" My voice is harsh, but my eyes burn with the beginning of tears. That only makes me angrier. "Anyone but me, Byers. That's all I care about. Elsie Tanner is a good candidate—a real one. Tellerman didn't lie about his prediction. She's exactly what Whitman was hoping for."

"So, you're using her to ease your guilt about running away?"

"What guilt?" I spit out. But she's not wrong.

Whatever I might profess, I know Whitman would never forgive me for vanishing without resolving Isaac's soulmate reading—if there were only fraudulent candidates in the mix. But now that Elsie Tanner has arrived, everything will turn out fine. Perhaps someday, Whitman and Byers and Isaac will even remember me fondly. A spasm of remorse hits me—a yawning, powerful grief for a life I never lived, but might have. If things had been different.

"You're serious about this, aren't you?" Byers says, her anger somewhat abated.

"I don't have a choice."

She pinches the bridge of her nose. "Fine. I won't argue with you. But wait a day or two, could you? Let me research some protections against the demon clans. At least then you won't be killing yourself."

"Thank you," I say, surprised. I didn't expect her to help me.

"You're welcome," she grumbles. "I still think you're an idiot."

By the time Byers leaves, it's early evening. The day's excitement has drained me to the dregs. I lie down on my chaise longue, a thin blanket covering me. Reminding myself the guards are positioned in the hall helps me close my eyes. For seven restless hours, I sleep.

I blink awake to an amorphous black column, hovering above me in the filmy dawn light. Startled, I fall off the chaise longue and scramble away before taking another look. I half expect to see Patrick's ghost looming there. But I don't.

Assistant Master Parsons hangs from a light fixture on the ceiling, a noose squeezing his crooked purple neck. His face is blotchy with burst veins. His eyes are open.

A note has been pinned to his jacket. The words are large and blocky, big enough to read from the floor.

Tell the truth.

19

Before I can scream, I tip sideways and vomit on the floor.

I hunch over with my head bowed, gasping for breath. I can't get air. I heave again, but this time, nothing comes out but a wet sob. Then I scream like my life depends on it.

It's Patrick all over again.

Another person dead because of me.

The guards in the hall hear the commotion and come running. As soon as they catch a glimpse of Parsons, a loud, frenetic machine of protocol begins to whirl around me. Some guards run out; others run in. They're all shouting. No one seems to notice me on the floor until one guard has the presence of mind to drape a blanket around my shoulders and tell me the council will be here soon. I nod mutely.

One thing I do register: When they unpin the note from Parsons' jacket, there's more writing on the other side. It relays what I suspected—my cultist is changing tactics.

Ms. Arnett,

It seems you place little value on your own life. Perhaps this will get your attention.
Tell the council your secret, or another dies in your place.

It hardly captures my interest that this murder should be impossible. With guards outside my apartments, no one could have hanged Parsons from the ceiling above me as I slept. But it happened. And according to that note, it will happen again. And again.

Unless I come forward.

I cradle my head between my hands, letting out a tearful groan. I can't bear to have another death on my conscience. But it's too late now; I can't take it back.

By the time Oversea and Whitman arrive, the guards have removed Parsons' body. I don't look at either of them. I'm still on the floor next to a pool of vomit, clutching the blanket.

Whitman kneels in front of me. His eyes are red rimmed. "Ms. Arnett, I'm so sorry."

Why is he apologizing? His colleague is dead, and it's my fault.

"We'll need to question you," Master Oversea says, surveying the room somberly.

"I don't remember anything." My voice is scratchy, anemic. "I was sleeping."

"Come, let's move to the common room." Whitman helps me up with a cold glance at Oversea, who seems to be settling in to inspect the crime scene.

I follow Whitman to the practitioners' common room in a daze. As I sit and curl my legs up to my chest, he lights a fire in the fireplace. I listen to it crackle with a distant stare. Whitman sits across from me but doesn't say a word. We lose ourselves in silence.

I feel like I'm going mad, my mind splitting in two. This choice could ruin my life. And yet, it doesn't feel like a choice. There has only been one option from the time I saw Parsons' corpse dangling above me. Broken, strangled. His gaze empty. In my mind, his face blurs and merges with Patrick's. I squeeze my eyes shut, pressing out hot tears.

I can't let anyone else die because of my cowardice. I don't know if I'll survive it.

"It's funny," I say, half to myself. The snapping of firewood is the only other sound in the room. "Naming soulmates isn't always a straightforward practice, you know. I don't think you ever asked about it."

Whitman looks up at me. "How do you mean?"

Sighing, I tip my head back. "I remember a reading I did for a couple once. Two newlyweds who wanted to affirm their eternal devotion. They didn't match up."

He makes a plaintive noise, and I scoff. "It's worse than you think. She got his name, but he didn't get hers. I felt awful, just awful, and I thought, did I make a mistake? But later I learned the woman died in childbirth, a few months into the marriage, and the man—he remarried his soulmate. The name I'd given him. So, I was right after all. He *was* her true love, but she wasn't his. And she had to live with that knowledge."

"Ms. Arnett—"

"That wasn't the worst one." I power ahead, though it hurts. A part of me relishes the pain—feeling all of it, everything I've done, starting with Patrick up until now. "The *worst* was when I told a woman her soulmate's name, and she knew him instantly. He was someone she'd spent time with as a girl, someone she'd fancied. But he became a sailor and he went off and died. Seventeen years old—isn't that terrible? Missed her chance." I rub my eyes with the heel of my hands. "She killed herself, about a month later."

"I'm sorry," Whitman says. "But why bring it up now?"

I gulp a deep breath. "I've been thinking about the contest. There was a flaw in your design."

"What?"

"The other seers asked who the king's future bride will be. But I did a different reading entirely. I named his soulmate."

"I don't understand." He's agitated, like I'm talking nonsense. I suppose I am.

"I'm saying those aren't necessarily the same thing." I press my hands hard into my thighs. "If you want a queen for King Isaac, you already have your girl. Elsie Tanner. Both Tellerman and Byers predicted her—that's confirmation. The king's soulmate doesn't matter."

He bends forward, exasperated. "Where is this coming from? If Isaac has a true love, he ought to have the chance—"

"Does it matter? Is this about Isaac's happiness or the fate of the kingdom?"

Whitman rises to his feet, towering over me. He jabs a finger at the air. "This is important. Now is not the time to make educated guesses."

I breathe through my nose, faster and harder. "I'm telling you this so you'll know that Elsie Tanner is the future queen. There's no doubt about it. And that won't change just because of the other thing I have to tell you."

Whitman's glare frosts over until there's nothing warm left, and for the first time, I'm afraid of him. "Did you lie?" he says. "About your reading?"

I look at the ceiling and blink away tears. "Please, don't make me say it."

"So, you're a fraud after all."

"What?" I shake my head, strands of curly hair flying across my face. "No, of course not. But . . . I did lie. That's why I'm getting the threats." I bow my head, my heart breaking. "That's why the assistant master is dead."

"If you lied, what's the truth?"

His expression is hard, unyielding, and it occurs to me again that he might not believe my answer. Then again, Whitman believed me about the Flood. Maybe I can trust him.

Or I'm about to sign my own death warrant.

I try to speak, but my voice gives out. I swallow and start again. "It's me, Whitman. I'm his soulmate."

I don't dare meet his eye. I stare at the dancing flames in the hearth and pray the truth doesn't blow up in my face.

"Oh," Whitman says drily, sniffing. He tugs at his sleeve cuffs. "You're joking. Not really the time."

I clench my jaw and gather patience. "I've never been more serious in my life."

There's an awful, dragging pause. Whitman sits down with his hands gripping his knees.

"Explain," he says.

I inhale steadily. I'm determined to get through this without shedding a tear. "My reading on King Isaac—it was my name that came back. There was never a Jane Smith."

Whitman says nothing for the longest time. Minutes pass. I can't imagine what's running through his mind—questions, theories, fears. Selfishly, I wonder if he feels sorry for himself, too, for the loss of whatever's burgeoning between us. I'm ahead of him there. I've already mourned our tragic ending.

When he clears his throat, I jump. "Are you sure your reading was correct?" he asks, with a strange warble in his voice.

"Positive. I've done it twenty times." And each time, the vision I received was identical. I've never had such a consistent reading. It's like I'm Isaac's super-soulmate, his even truer love.

Whitman wheezes a laugh, but it's not the heart-melting kind I heard before. He sounds slightly unhinged. "This—this is ludicrous. You understand that, right?"

I frown, hugging my knees closer to my chest. "It's not ludicrous. It's just . . . coincidental."

He runs a hand through his hair, crazy-laughing again. "The council will never believe this."

"Do *you* believe it?"

He finally looks at me. Our eyes lock, and I plead without words for him to be on my side. I can't do this without him. He shakes his head, but it's not a no. More like he's hopelessly bewildered.

"Do you have any proof?" he asks. "Some way to verify it?"

"Yes." I've thought about this, too. My word alone might satisfy Whitman—and that remains to be seen—but the council will want more. Luckily, I have backup. "Bernadette Byers."

His eyebrow raises, but he doesn't look too surprised. Perhaps he's all surprised out. "She knows about this? And she never said anything?"

I open my mouth to answer, then pause. Byers could get in trouble if the council finds out she's been hiding my secret. I'll be doing her a favor if I obscure her role a little.

"Not yet," I say. "But I'm certain she'll tell you I'm not lying."

"That may not be enough."

Apparently, me being Isaac's soulmate is more ludicrous than I realized. "We don't need the council to believe me, anyway. We just need the killer to see I've given up my secret. That's what they've wanted all along."

"But why?" he groans, his head falling into his hands. "Why do they want to reveal this? What could they possibly have to gain? You must have some idea who they are!"

"Slow down," I say, eyeing him with concern. He's not taking this well. "I have no idea who they are. I don't even know how they found out about my reading."

"No one else knows?"

Byers knows, obviously, but I just lied about that. And I have no reason to suspect her. If she wanted my secret out, she could waltz up to Whitman and tell him. He would believe her over me.

"No one knows," I say with confidence, proving I've learned absolutely zero lessons about lying today.

He rubs his eyes, silent again. I can't stand to see him like this, at a loss for what to do. I move over to him, kneeling beside his chair. I place a tentative hand on his knee. I expect him to push me away, but he doesn't, so I stay.

"Whitman, I would never have kept this secret if I knew someone might be killed." I blink back those tears I'm so afraid of, pressing my lips into a quivering line. I need Whitman to believe me, even if I don't believe myself. "I thought I was the only one in danger. I'm so sorry about Parsons."

He nods, a muscle twitching in his jaw. "Don't move," he says suddenly, knocking my hand away as he stands. "I'll be right back."

I remain on the floor beside the fireplace, feeling the heat on my back, staring into space and forcing myself to think of nothing. When Whitman returns with Byers, neither of them looks happy. She sits on the couch where I had been.

"I heard about Assistant Master Parsons," she says anxiously, lacing her fingers together. "This is a nightmare."

"I have something to tell you," I jump in before she can say anything else. My white lie will be useless if she spoils it. "I'm King Isaac's soulmate."

Her eyes widen into stupefied globes. Probably never dreamed I would come clean. "I see," she says slowly. I urge her on with my gaze. "Is that what you've been meeting about in here?"

"Ms. Arnett seems to think you can confirm her reading," Whitman says. He sounds like he hopes she'll say no.

Byers tenses up, like a turtle preparing to retract. "Depends. Are you going to ask me how I confirmed it?"

Even now, she's striving to appear to be a normal magician with no unearthly powers. Does that help me or hurt me? Her magic is stronger than anyone knows—but then again, I might benefit from a supporter who sounds less preposterous than me.

"That's your business, if you want it to be," Whitman says. "For now."

Byers lets out a long sigh, sparing me a troubled glance. "She's not lying. Ms. Arnett is King Isaac's soulmate. But as I'm sure she's already explained at length, that doesn't mean King Isaac should marry her. The other readings all point to Elsie Tanner."

"You're one of them, aren't you?" Whitman murmurs. He shakes his head, reason abandoned. "Like Mona? You've been to the Flood."

"H-how could you—" Immediately, her head snaps toward me. I hold up my hands in surrender. I didn't out her—Whitman just connected the dots.

Byers sighs painfully. "If it helps you understand, then yes. I'm like Mona. But the council will never take that as proof."

"It's good enough for me." His head hangs, and after a long moment, I wonder if he'll ever lift it again. Then he stands. "Let's not wait any longer. I'll gather the council. The sooner we do this, the safer the castle will be."

20

When everything's ready, Whitman sends for more guards to escort us to council chambers. Parsons was just murdered, and his killer hasn't been caught. No one's taking chances. Perhaps I should be leery of a maniac jumping out of the shadows and dealing with me for good, but it's hard to muster any feelings about that. I'm too scared of what awaits me in chambers.

All the masters and King Isaac are present. I don't know how much Whitman told them, but they're staring at me, mistrustful. Byers takes her place beside me. From the corner of my eye, I see her standing neurotically upright, hands trembling at her sides. She's risking a lot, too, by backing me up. I feel a swell of affection for her.

Whitman rests his elbows on the table. His face is gaunt. "Go ahead, Ms. Arnett."

I rock back on my heels, debating where to start. What gives me the most credibility? What makes me look sympathetic? That's not going to help me here. I better stick to the facts.

"When you first asked me about the threats," I say, counting tiles on the ceiling, "I said I wasn't hiding anything. That's not completely true."

My audience waits for me to elaborate. Sucking my teeth, I press on. "I lied about King Isaac's soulmate reading."

Whispers break out among the masters. I take it they weren't expecting something quite so inflammatory. And there's worse to come.

"I didn't want to. But I—I didn't know what would happen if I told the truth." I sigh, closing my eyes. "It's me."

No one makes a sound. Finally, Master Lane asks, "What was you?"

They're not getting it. Clearly, this requires a heavy-handed approach. "My reading said that I'm the king's soulmate."

Gasps arise around the room. I can't look Isaac in the eye.

Master Renfield stands, brimming with ill temper. "You can't proclaim yourself the future queen and expect us to take your word."

"I'm not the future queen," I blurt. "Elsie Tanner is. I may be His Majesty's soulmate, but that's different!"

"Ms. Arnett, what you're admitting to is treason," Master Oversea says in his deep, grave, threatening voice. "Either you were lying then or you're lying now. The result is the same."

It's not as if that thought hasn't occurred to me. But here, in the sublime blue glow of the nexus, surrounded by the bulk of Opalvale's might, the consequences become real. I could be charged with betraying the crown. Then I'd have no *choice* but to retreat to the Flood and beg Tasha D'Milliar to take me in. Living in the Flood is what I've always wanted—in fact, just last evening, I was fully intending to flee there—but now the prospect feels hollow. It would mean leaving before I can repay my debt to Parsons, however I do that. Helping catch his murderer would be a start.

Whitman jumps in. "Ms. Arnett lied because she didn't have any other options. And you haven't asked Ms. Byers a single question." He pauses to calm himself, to regain control. "That might be to your benefit, if you care about the truth."

All eyes turn to Byers. She recoils at the attention.

"Well, Ms. Byers?" says Master Penna. "Did you have something to add?"

Her chest rises as she fills her lungs. "Yes," she replies on the exhalation. She may look nervous, but she sounds confident. "Ms. Arnett is telling the truth. I was able to confirm her reading. I believe she lied at first because, well . . ." Byers shrugs. "She suspected the council would react exactly like this."

"It's true that such a reading would not have been well received at the contest," Master Gan says mildly. "A seer naming themself as a candidate?"

I mask my surprise with a frown. I thought Whitman would be the only master on my side. I send my silent gratitude to Gan for his compassion. I'm not likely to receive the same grace from the rest of the council.

"Then what made you come forward now?" Master Soph asks.

Oversea ventures a guess. "The murder of young Mr. Parsons?"

I nod, staring at the floor. They want contrition from me, but I'm afraid if they see my face it won't meet their standards. I *am* genuinely sorry—but am I sorry enough to appease them? "I never meant for anyone to get hurt. I thought I was the only one in danger."

"And how do you propose we put an end to that danger now?"

I thought it was obvious. "Make sure the killer knows I told you my secret. They said they'd stop killing once I did."

Oversea contemplates it. "This is certainly an unexpected development. Ms. Arnett will have to answer for her behavior. But in my opinion, we can't risk harming the contest's legitimacy by admitting a seer lied. We will stop Mr. Parsons' killer some other way. And what has been discussed in this room need never be repeated in public."

"What?" My fists squeeze, nails digging into my skin. "If the cultist doesn't know I came forward, they're going to kill someone else!"

"I'm sorry, Ms. Arnett. The repercussions for the contest are too great."

"That could be the killer's aim in the first place," Renfield says, running a hand over her close-shorn head. She's moved on from anger to grave concern. "If Ms. Arnett's secret is exposed, the damage to the contest could shut it down entirely."

"Or it could make the contest more exciting," Gan remarks. "The people love drama."

The conversation devolves into the masters bickering among themselves.

"Announce? To the public? It'll make us look like a circus."

"We may have to put an end to this whole contest; it's tainted now."

"What about Gray Mass? Can we hold a festival with a murderer on the loose?"

King Isaac's voice cuts through the chatter. "Please. I want to speak to Ms. Arnett alone."

The masters turn to look at Isaac as though they forgot he was there. I'm trying to forget him on purpose—I don't know what their excuse is. It's his fate they're arguing over, and they don't care a shred about his opinion.

I keep my head down and my shaking hands clasped behind my back as the council and the guards file out without a word.

"Sit, please," Isaac says.

I pick an empty master's seat and face him. His expression is inscrutable. Angry, wounded, shocked, confused—maybe all at once.

When the silence has gone on too long, I ask, "Do you believe me?"

I brace for the answer, but he stares off to the side like he didn't hear me. My apprehension grows as I wait.

"I never expected to marry for love," Isaac says, and incredibly, his voice sounds as warm and inviting as always, if a little fatigued. "Even before the crown fell to me, I knew I'd be matched by the Circle Court with the most fitting candidate. Some woman who's just a dossier to me, who I get to meet once or twice before the wedding. So, when Delmar pitched the idea of a seer who names soulmates, I'll admit I got my hopes up. Maybe it could still happen for me, you know?" He meets my eye, and this time, I see the hurt there plainly. "What I didn't expect was that my soulmate would rather commit treason than be with me."

My blood runs cold. Gods below, I never wanted Isaac to have this knowledge. "Your Majesty—"

"You can call me Isaac. We're soulmates, aren't we?"

I seal my lips, wincing at what feels like a rebuke. "Isaac, it has nothing to do with you. You don't understand what this has been like for me."

"So tell me."

Great. This is somehow worse than admitting I'm his soulmate. I sigh, selecting my words carefully to reveal the exact right amount—not too much, not too little. "I can't be in the world like other people. Every day here is . . . It's like someone is standing next to me and screaming the foulest things in my ear—how worthless and selfish I am, how pathetic, how unlovable—and they won't leave me alone until I'm back home, safe. Being here makes me ill. That probably sounds stupid to you, but it's who I am." I let out a soft, humorless laugh. "Don't you see? I could never be queen. How do you think I'd hold up under that pressure, once you're gone? All that responsibility? Ruling an entire kingdom? I'd start a civil war on my first day."

Isaac covers his mouth, concealing his reaction. Then I hear him chuckling. When he takes his hand away, he's smiling, like this is a joke.

"Sorry," he says, his smile waning. "I'm not laughing at you. It's just that you're perfectly describing how I felt when I found out I was taking the throne."

I falter. "Really?"

"I was terrified. My sister, she'd been ill with the wasting disease for weeks. I knew what might be coming. Dreaded it. And I felt so fucking selfish, because I couldn't tell if I wanted her to live because I loved her or because I *hated* the idea of being king."

I stare at the table, speechless. Isaac and I have more in common than I thought. It doesn't change how I feel about marrying him, or being queen, but perhaps it explains how I could be his soulmate when by all accounts we're nothing alike.

"I have to ask," Isaac says. Now he's the one who won't look at me. "Am I your soulmate, too?"

I trace the table's edge with my fingertips. "I don't know. I haven't done my own reading."

"Why not?"

"It doesn't matter." For most my life, I assumed I didn't have—didn't deserve—a soulmate. But would it be any better if my soulmate was Isaac? He's dying soon. I'm not strong enough to watch my soulmate die.

We each stew in our own thoughts until I ask, "What next?"

Isaac sighs and rubs his stubbled jaw. "We wait for the council's decision. And next week we go to the Gray Mass ball and pretend everything's normal."

"All right." I peek up at him, tugging on my ponytail. "Can I go back to my rooms, or am I under arrest for treason?"

"Don't listen to the masters. They'll calm down in a few days. You can go."

I nod in gratitude and stand up. "I really am sorry, Isaac."

"I know," he says with a crestfallen smirk. "Neither of us asked for this."

Outside in the dim antechamber, I'm met with an unexpected sight: Master Renfield, waiting for me. Whitman and Byers are nowhere to be seen.

"Can I help you, master?" I say cautiously.

Renfield gives me a staid nod. She's dressed in her full master's uniform. Up close, I can see the fine lines around her eyes and mouth that reflect her age. "I was hoping to speak with you," she says. "About the incident. You must be eager to catch the killer of that young man."

I swallow hard. "Of course."

"Perhaps you can help somehow."

My head jerks back in surprise. Given the masters' dismissive attitudes, I didn't expect them to ask me for any more than staying out of their business. "I thought Master Oversea was leading the investigation," I say cautiously, wondering what kind of *help* she's after, and whether it involves me fleeing the castle in disgrace—or worse, attending more council meetings.

"Yes, but the master of justice is overburdened, planning security for the ball on top of everything. He asked my agents to lend aid."

I look Renfield up and down, measuring her intentions. As the master of whispers, she must have an army of spies at her disposal. That could be advantageous in the hunt for an invisible cultist. Still. "Should Master Whitman be here for this?"

"It might be best if he isn't." When I meet that statement with an incredulous frown, she adds, "I know he has your trust, Ms. Arnett, but to be frank, I doubt Master Whitman will approve of this plan. It's not without risk. But I believe it will be to your benefit."

I suppose I can give her a chance to convince me. "What do you want me to do?"

"Merely some light reconnaissance. Keep an eye out, let me know if you notice anything suspicious. Watch those around you for strange behavior. Ask questions of anyone who shows particular interest in your ordeal. Report back to me with your findings. And provide some insight into the killer's thought process, if you can."

"How?"

"You're a smart girl, and personally connected to the investigation. Think it over. If you come up with any ideas about the killer's motive or methods, pass them along."

That doesn't sound so bad—which makes me instantly suspicious. "What's the catch?"

"There's always a risk of further incident when a victim investigates their assailant, though in this case it's minimal. I won't ask you to do anything drastic. I can provide agents for your security, on top of Master Oversea's. And there are benefits to this arrangement, if you fulfill your end." Renfield lifts her eyebrows and scowls in concert, like she's trying to project benevolence but can't make her face work that way. "What reward seems fair to you?"

I have the distinct impression I'm being herded into a trap. Instead of answering, I strike at the heart of the issue. "Why do you need my help so badly?"

Renfield's face wipes blank for a second, then equalizes in a frown. "Your . . . *unique* perspective could reveal information we wouldn't have otherwise."

I narrow my eyes, deconstructing Renfield's guarded expression. Her gaze shifts to the side. It's fleeting, but I think I catch it: a flicker of embarrassment. Maybe even fear.

It finally clicks. This is an act of desperation.

"Parsons' death doesn't reflect well on the council, does it?" I say. A murder in the castle, right under their noses? And no leads? They really *do* need help wherever they can get it.

Renfield's jaw twitches, but her face is otherwise unreadable. "It's an extraordinary crime. We must be creative with our strategy."

Meaning their grand plan is to throw different avenues of investigation at the wall and see what sticks. Renfield's right about one thing—Whitman wouldn't like this. He'd insist I keep a low profile until Parsons' killer is safely in shackles.

But all things considered, Renfield isn't asking much of me. I doubt it'll put me in any more danger than I'm already in. And it comes with a reward. There's nothing the masters can offer me that I want—other than catching my cultist, which, clearly, is beyond their meager capabilities—but I can use this opportunity to pay back a kindness, long overdue.

"Fine. I'll cooperate." I prop a hand on my hip and glare at Renfield. "In return, you protect Master Whitman. Make sure his position on the council is secure for the foreseeable future—during Isaac's reign and beyond. I don't care how you convince the other masters, but this vendetta ends now. If you go back on your word, I will . . ." I struggle to think of a threat I can deliver on. "I'll do everything in my power to delegitimize the crown." No matter how ridiculous a rumor I have to invent.

Renfield squints in confusion, or perhaps disbelief, seemingly caught off guard by my request. "Very well. But I don't have a vendetta against Master Whitman. Quite the opposite. I was always fond of Delmar as a child. His mother and I were together for twelve years."

I blink at her. I had no clue there was so much history between Whitman and Renfield. "Your personal feelings toward Whitman are none of my business," I say, clutching my elbow to the side. It's not easy, drumming up the confidence to make demands of a councilmember. "Just be his advocate from now on. If you can do that, I'm in."

She nods with her thumbs in her belt loops. "Then I expect to receive daily reports from you until further notice. Say, eight in the morning? A standing appointment?"

I grimace. "I don't suppose we could meet at my apartments? I'm doing you the favor."

"If you insist. But you're going to have to spend time outside your rooms if you want to investigate properly."

Turning red, I nod. She saw right through me.

Renfield reaches out to shake on it. Taken aback, I grip her hand, finalizing our deal. She's treating me like a real adult. An equal.

Perhaps I have more friends on the council than I knew.

21

Gray Mass festivities begin outside, in the castle ward. Towering maypoles; big barrels of metheglin, infused with meadowsweet and lavender; joyous fiddling and harping and dancing on the muddy grass. I watch it all from the window of my apartments.

In the evening, the crown holds a splendid formal ball in honor of Semyanadd, wolf god of the earth. I would rather not attend. It's too soon after Parsons' death. But I promised Renfield I would keep an eye out for anything suspicious—which, as she pointed out, is hard to do from the comfort of my couch. Our early morning debriefs have been unproductive so far. Mostly, Renfield quizzes me on aspects of the crime, like she's checking that I did my homework. Just as she asked, I've been going over Parsons' murder in my head, rereading the notes my cultist left a hundred times. I performed readings on the note left with Parsons, too. The only feedback was a faint aura of guilt. Did the killer feel remorse for what they'd done?

With Elizabeta's help, I squeeze myself into a pastel blue gown dotted with silk peonies, my handkerchief tucked in my pocket, and complete the ensemble with lambskin gloves to mask my bandaged hand. I only need two shots of whiskey to make it out the door.

The main hall has been transformed into a celebration of springtime. An arch of woven hyacinth and daffodils covers the entrance. Pages hand out prayer tokens to guests and tip dishes of seawater into our mouths one by one as we enter. In the hall, flecks of light drift through the air like tiny lightning bugs. Wreaths of ivy hang on every wall, along with wolf pelts and, in a few places, mounted wolves' heads. Four long tables are laden with savory pies and roasted pheasant and big blooming artichokes, crocuses tucked between their leaves. Semyanadd is the central figure of the pantheon, so Gray Mass, the first of his two holidays, is always a stupendous affair.

I frown at the bounty on the tables, scratching my arm, uncomfortable. That woman who petitioned Isaac said her village was starving, and yet the royal stores have provided us with a grand, gluttonous feast.

King Isaac sits in his usual spot upon the platform, surrounded by guards and courtiers. Elsie Tanner mingles in the crowd. I concentrate on the pounding of my pulse in my throat as I cross the floor. Is it easier now than it was before, being outside my rooms? I can't tell. There are too many variables, physical and emotional, and new threats to keep track of. I don't think I'm going to vomit, for what it's worth. At least I don't have to be concerned about security. So many of Oversea's sentries pack the room, I don't even need my band of personal bodyguards. I couldn't get assassinated here if I wanted to.

I find Bernadette Byers standing by a ten-foot corn-husk effigy of Semyanadd, depicted as an upright dire wolf. Her eyes fix on me as I walk closer.

"Evening," I say, falsely bright. "How are you enjoying these wildly inappropriate festivities?" News of Parsons' death hasn't been officially released, but it still feels wrong.

Her lip twitches in an abbreviated smile. "I have bad news. Best to get it over with."

"What now?" I ask with exasperation.

"There's been a leak. Word is going around that you're King Isaac's real soulmate."

"What?" My hand goes to my mouth. The news sinks in, and I smile. "That's not bad at all! My cultist will find out I told the truth." I look over my shoulder at the whirling crowd. "Honestly, I thought I'd have to suffer a thousand questions when word got out." I picture hordes of courtiers flocking around me, prying inanely. Normally, I enjoy an audience, but that's just rubbing salt in the wound.

"Arnett," Byers says, like I'm missing an obvious point. When I stare at her, nonplussed, she sighs and sweeps a braid behind her ear. "Nobody actually believes you're the king's soulmate. What did you think would happen after that council meeting? You saw how the masters reacted."

Nobody? That's a bit much. I glance around the room again, paying closer attention to the faces in the crowd. For the first time, I notice people glaring at me, or pointedly ignoring me when I try to make eye contact. Whispering in packs when they think I'm not looking.

"Why is it so unfathomable that anyone could love me?" I say in a low, frustrated hiss. "Am I missing something? Do I have fangs?"

"We're not talking about 'anyone,' we're talking about the king of Opalvale."

"Elsie Tanner is a commoner, too. Nobody bats an eye at her."

Byers tilts her head, like she might find the answer to shutting me up on the ceiling. "I don't know what to tell you, Arnett. You're not Elsie Tanner. You refused to leave your house for ten years and no one knows why. You're not very nice to people. You practice questionable magic that can't be verified and you just proclaimed yourself King Isaac's true love. Are those enough reasons for you?"

"I'm plenty nice," I mumble, crossing my arms.

"My point is, don't obsess over it. People don't like what they can't put in a neat little box. That's not your fault."

Is she defending me? I give her a slanted smile. "I suppose not."

"Now, if you'll excuse me," Byers says, tipping her head, "my date is here."

I look over. Elizabeta, the handmaid, is dressed up for the evening, having traded in her simple dress and apron for a gown of petal pink, skirts layered like a rosebud. I raise my arm to get her attention, and she waves back.

I let out a low whistle. "You and Elizabeta? No wonder you always take so long to get dressed for conferences."

"Shut up," she says amiably as she saunters off.

Instead of standing there by myself, I go get another drink. Guests act like they can't get out of my way fast enough. I grimace and ignore it. A table laden with wines and punch has been blocked from view by a line of folding paper screens painted with spring blossoms and prowling wolves.

Nothing suspicious here—guess my job is done.

I've just filled my glass and stepped away when I collide into someone's shoulder. Elsie Tanner wobbles before me on unsteady feet, wearing a lavender gown of airy tulle. Below her round eyeglasses, she has that hexagonal brown marking painted above her cheekbone.

"Ms. Arnett." She holds out her hands to brace me. "I'm so sorry. I didn't mean to knock you over. I was just coming to say hello."

"Oh?" I wasn't expecting that. Assuming she's heard the rumor that I'm Isaac's soulmate, shouldn't she hate me now? Whether she believes I'm telling the truth or making it up, I'm not doing her any favors. Best to get it out in the open, I decide. "Are you here to challenge me to a duel for King Isaac's hand in marriage?"

She looks mortified. "Oh, no, I'm not— I just saw you were alone, and I felt bad about how everyone's—" Her eyes widen. "Not that I came to talk to you because I feel bad. I also enjoy your company."

If she's trying to heckle me, she's not very good at it. Perhaps she's being genuine. While the other partygoers avoided me and judged me from a safe distance, Elsie was, apparently, the only one who cared that I looked lonely.

I close my eyes, admonishing myself. Not everyone is out to make other people's lives miserable. Elsie chose to be kind—like it's that easy.

"Sorry," I say with a smirk. "That was rude. What I meant was that in your position, I'd have a lot of questions for me."

She blinks, guileless. "Like what?"

"Like if I'm really King Isaac's soulmate."

"I suppose I don't want to know," she says, laughing so quietly I barely hear it.

I feel a surge of guilt. Of course she's not interested in listening to me ramble about Isaac. "Well then, I won't tell you."

Elsie smiles. "Why don't we talk about something else?"

"Fantastic idea." I bounce on my toes, gearing up to be rude again. "Can I ask you a question? Why don't you want to marry this man your parents promised you to?"

"Oh. Lord Severin?" Her eyes cloud over. "It's a generational contract. His great-grandfather loaned mine the capital to start a shipping route, with the loan to be repaid down the family line with interest." She shrugs. "I'm part of the interest."

I've heard of marriage clauses in contracts before. Pledging a family member's hand to another party, in the near or distant future. The contract can be called in at any point where it appears advantageous for the creditor.

Elsie's family has amassed their share of wealth, and Elsie is beautiful.

I grind my teeth. "It's barbaric. The gods frown upon those sorts of arrangements."

"The Guild of Scribes would disagree," she says with a sad smile. "I was training to be a midwife, you know. Before he claimed his right to me."

"Really? For how long?"

"A few months." She points to the ever-present hexagon next to her eye. "See this? It's a Diené marking for healers. My mother taught me how to draw it. It's a respected skill in Ahn Dien—knowledge of the body."

"Perhaps you'll finish the training one day."

"Maybe." She glances away, her neck taut. "My future's up in the air now, though, isn't it?"

"How do you like him, by the way? King Isaac?"

Her cheeks flush a pretty pink beneath their usual light brown. "He asks a lot of questions. He's curious about my midwife training. I always feel I must be boring him, but he keeps asking. He spends so much time around doctors, with his illness." It's minuscule, but her expression changes—a wilting of her lips, a sadness behind her eyes. "I think the medicine interests him."

"Are you sure it's not an excuse to talk to you?"

She grins modestly. "It could be that, too."

Elsie glances toward the king's platform, where he talks with a circle of sycophants, leaning on his cane. He looks her way like he senses eyes on him. His smile brightens. Elsie waves shyly at him, and he waves in return, ignoring the conversation he's in the middle of. When he catches sight of me, though, his smile is quickly replaced by panic. He turns back to the courtiers.

Elsie's gaze doesn't leave the king. "I'd best rejoin His Majesty."

"Of course." I smile and bow my head. "Thank you for not treating me like a leper."

Elsie parts from me with a buoyant goodbye, and I weave into the crowd. Byers has disappeared to who knows where. The courtiers and dignitaries packing the room have been eating and drinking and making merry for hours, and it's starting to show. Tipsy giggles and whoops spout forth from the partygoers, but they're not directed at me. I think the guests have already forgotten they're supposed to be ignoring me—alcohol tends to help with that. Or maybe it's thanks to Elsie breaking the ice. I skirt past an unexpected figure by the fountain, chatting and laughing with courtiers: Honored Delphin, that dignitary from the Circle Court—the one who dressed Isaac down in the throne room. There's a suspicious figure, no doubt. But he's never met me before, so he can't possibly have something against me. His grudge seems to be against Isaac alone.

"Mona!" yells a voice in my ear.

I jump and find Whitman beside me, his jaw set with frustration. My face falls even as my spirits lift at the sight of him. What have I done now?

"I was calling for you." He inclines his head to the side, toward the wall. "We need to talk."

We break off from the crowd of revelers to stand by a blank stretch of stone. For a moment, Whitman says nothing. I jostle my leg. Clearing his throat, he reaches into his pocket and, much too formally, hands me a velvet box. "I got you something."

I hesitate, waiting for further explanation. Then my curiosity wins out and I open it. A pair of silk gloves, buttercream. I glance up, brows lifted.

"They're custom-made," he explains. "The left one doesn't have a pinkie."

I laugh and examine them. Sure enough, the pinkie hole on the left glove is sewn shut. I slip off my old gloves and put on the new ones, testing how it feels to make a fist without a useless bit of fabric flopping around.

"I love them." I peer up at him. "What did I do to deserve this?"

He shifts to the side, rubbing the back of his neck. "Nothing in particular. Truth be told, I ordered them before—well, more than a week ago." Before he knew I was Isaac's soulmate. A bittersweet notion. Was he planning for this gift to mean something more? "I'm not truly sure it's appropriate now. But I—" He lets out a long, thin sigh. "I may have misjudged you, Ms. Arnett. And I'm sorry for that."

I don't know what to say. "I—I suppose I wasn't the easiest person to like when we met."

He sniffs. "No, you're right. I didn't like you much then." He turns away, gazing over the crowd. "But I like you better now."

Something light and warm unfurls inside me like silk ribbon unspooling, jumbling in a pile at the bottom of my stomach. It overpowers me. I'm not sure I enjoy it.

To our side, a harried voice calls out. "Master Whitman!"

A castle guard jogs up to us and catches his breath. He sidles past me to lean toward Whitman. "You're needed in council chambers," he whispers, louder than he probably intended. "There's something you have to see."

If the message alarms Whitman, he doesn't show it. He nods to me in farewell and takes off.

Now, what was *that* about?

Immediately, I search the crowd for Renfield, wondering if this is the sort of development I'm supposed to report. As I scan for her face, I see a guard crouch next to the king on his throne, whispering into his ear. Isaac nods and pushes himself to his feet with his cane, following the guard out of the main hall. The party goes on as if nothing is amiss.

"Arnett!"

I swivel around. Byers barrels toward me, her skirts gathered up.

"A guard pulled out Master Lane," she pants. "Looks like the king, too."

"And Whitman," I say. Perhaps Renfield as well, since I can't find her. "They summoned him to council chambers. The guard said there was something he needed to see."

"What?"

"I haven't the faintest idea."

Byers meets my eye. "But we're going to go find out, aren't we?"

I hesitate for a breath before nodding.

We sneak out of the main hall and begin the winding trip upward to council chambers. The spellsap lights dim the higher we climb. By the time we reach the chambers' entryway, darkness has overtaken us. The only light seeps out from under the chamber doors, an ethereal blue.

A guard at the door holds out his hand. "Off-limits. Get back to the party."

"What's happening in there?" I ask.

He refuses to reply. But just then, Master Renfield charges up the stairs and blows past us, throwing the doors open. Light pours from the room; the nexus is shining bright as the sun.

Around the council table sit seven men and women in towering marble thrones. The men wear red tailcoats accented with black velvet, and the women red taffeta gowns and black lace gloves.

My breath hitches in my chest.

As the doors swing closed, a voice floats out from inside the chambers.

"Who is that in the hallway?" says the voice, smooth and solid, like polished petrified wood.

The doors click shut and the light disappears. Byers and I stand unable to move. Unable even to look at each other. We wait.

The doors open again. Two guards prop them outward, awaiting further instruction. I hear Master Oversea say, "They're royal magicians. This is none of their concern. Master Whitman, did you—"

"I said nothing to anyone," Whitman snaps with a tremor.

"Invite them in," says the smooth voice.

It takes every ounce of resolve to unstick my feet and walk into that room. Byers is worse. Her ragged breathing drowns out all sound in my left ear. We come to a halt before the council table.

A man on the far side draws my eye. He's impossibly handsome, with a chiseled jaw and alabaster skin and the blackest hair I've ever seen, swept to the side. Charcoal markings circle his eyes in angular runic patterns. No one has to tell me who he is.

Irinorr rests his elbows on the table. "It seems we have all been surprised tonight," he says softly.

The chamber doors bang shut behind us.

PART IV

THE GODS

22

Semyanadd, wolf god of the earth.
Onyamarr, whale goddess of the sea.
Irinorr, crow god of love.
Korimarr, turtle goddess of knowledge.
Wayvadd, cat god of self.
Verimall, boar goddess of violence.
Eledorr, moth goddess of death.

These are the seven gods of the Flood.

23

And they all stare directly at me.

For an eternity, no one speaks. I can't remember the last time I went so long without talking.

So, it likely surprises no one when I break the silence.

"Where have you been, Iri?" I say, quiet and reedy. "I looked for you."

Irinorr smiles. It's beyond strange to see a mortal guise stretched over his essence. He wears his faux humanity like an ill-tailored jacket. "We were in the fortress, performing the ritual that brought us here. It is an arduous process."

"And how is it," says the goddess beside him, "that the two of you came to be at the castle?"

I spend a moment studying her, and the rest of the seven. The gods' thrones are spaced between the seven masters' chairs—which, I note, the masters are too afraid to occupy, choosing instead to stand against the walls. Isaac, too, stands off to the side with a desperate, hunted look, like he's an outlaw who's finally been cornered. The offering basins that separate the masters' places at the table have been transformed into carved marble seats engraved with runes.

The goddess who addressed us is brown-skinned, her hair scraped back into a severe bun. Runes adorn her face as well, but her markings are rigid, controlled, a complex pattern I'm not clever enough to recognize. To her left is Irinorr; to her other side sits a woman with tanned skin and a tangle of red hair. That can only be Verimall, the boar. Goddess of violence.

Which makes the one who spoke . . .

"Korimarr," Byers chokes out. She looks on the verge of fainting. "I—I've—"

"Byers and I joined the company around the same time," I say quickly, praying no one corrects me. But who do you pray to when you're trying to slip a lie past the gods? "We looked for you in the Flood, but we couldn't find you to tell you."

If King Isaac or the masters are puzzled by our conversation, they keep it to themselves. Somewhere in the back of my mind, I dread explaining this to Whitman.

"Ah, yes," says a gleefully snide voice. Wayvadd. I give his mortal costume a once-over. Sleek gray-blond hair, pale blue eyes, aquiline nose. "That night we bumped into each other. You were boarding at the castle by then, were you not?"

I hesitate, anticipating a trick. "Yes. The night I went looking for Irinorr. If I'd known how long it would be before we saw you again, I would have told you about the company then."

Wayvadd grins—a clean but visceral slash across his face, like a side of meat sliced open by a butcher's knife. It exposes one glistening tooth.

"Never mind the favored mortals," says the god in the tallest throne. That same glossy, wooden voice from before. Semyanadd, it must be. His hair, styled in a swelling pompadour, is gray, but his face looks ageless. His eyelids and temples are near solid black with runic markings. "We will deal with them later. We must discuss what we came here to do. Where is the king of Opalvale?"

After a pause, Isaac shuffles forward, looking more like a scared boy than a king. I suppose you can be both. "I am Isaac of House Angline, first of my name, Duke of Mayfield and Seaward and overlord of the Ashclaud principality."

To my stupefaction, the seven gods rise to their feet and make deep, sweeping bows, like they owe him allegiance.

"Thank you for your patience, Your Majesty," Semyanadd says as he lowers himself into his throne, "and your hospitality. You may have guessed that we have returned to claim our seats on the king's council, as is our right per the contract."

My heart bounces in my rib cage as I try to make sense of it. I've never heard of the gods' right to claim council seats. The seven must have been planning this move a long time, in complete secrecy. I can't begin to imagine how the other mortals in the room feel.

Isaac swallows. "By my understanding of the oral contract, as passed down my line for generations, the gods may claim their council seats in times of grave peril for Opalvale. Have we fallen upon such times?"

Semyanadd smiles bleakly. "Do you need to ask, Your Majesty? You are the last of your line and you have no clear successor. The mortal realm is in danger of losing magic. Your spellsap orchards are withering from disease. This can only mean the nexus is in peril, and we cannot predict what else may happen if it declines—mortal spirits crossing over, demon clan activity, any number of possibilities. If there is no intervention, many of your people will die."

I press a fist to my mouth. The similarities are too striking to miss. Semyanadd is describing the Rising Tide—the disintegration of reality, the end of the mortal realm. For the first time since we entered the chambers, Byers and I turn our stiff necks to lock eyes. She must be thinking the same thing. Suddenly, a resurgence of Guild cultists doesn't seem so implausible.

"Please, my—lords," says Penna, the master of faith, stumbling over the honorific. Sweat beads his light brown skin. His whole life has been spent in prayer and supplication to the seven, and now they sit before him. "I must ask. Are you telling us that the prophecies of the Guild of the Rising Tide are correct?"

"We cannot answer that," Semyanadd says plainly. I wish he would have laughed at Penna, discredited the suggestion. But it seems he can't rule it out.

"Sounds like it's my fault," King Isaac says forlornly. When the room turns, he remembers himself, and his ears glow red. "I mean, if the nexus is ailing, it's most likely related to my custodianship, yes? My lack of an heir, my inexperience . . ."

Honored Delphin must have really gotten to him. Or the council has been whispering the same in his ear, lambasting him for every tiny misstep. I have a fierce urge to slap them all. Isaac doesn't deserve this.

"We don't know that, either, Your Majesty," Semyanadd says, and to his credit, his words are filled with compassion.

"How will you find answers, my"—Isaac pauses, his lips forming an uncertain O—"sirs?" I don't know their proper title, either. I've always called them by their names.

"We aren't certain yet," Semyanadd says, "but we hope to learn more. That is why we have traveled from the Flood, taken these mortal forms to confer with you. You will need our aid to prevent Opalvale from falling, and the world with it."

Isaac runs a hand through his mussed blond hair. "I see. Then you are welcome to any resources at our disposal. The subjects of Opalvale are your servants."

"And we are yours, Your Majesty," Semyanadd says with a nod. "But at the moment, what we are most in need of is a long rest. Our magic has been exhausted. We will take some time to recover."

"Of course." King Isaac motions toward Master Gan, who goes rigid. "Master, can you please work with the stewards to get the—these seven situated on the fourth floor? And have meals brought up." Isaac glances at Semyanadd. "You—you do eat, don't you?"

"In this form, we do," the wolf god answers with a slight smile.

The gods stand to leave, with a blotchy-faced Master Gan at the head of their procession. They bow to King Isaac as they stride past. Then they come upon Byers and me by the chamber doors.

Each of the seven touches us gently, warmly, on the arm or the brow as they leave. An immense weight dissipates from my shoulders, little by little, with each anointing hand. When it's Irinorr's turn to pass me, he pauses, cups my cheek in his palm with a warm smile. It fills me with light. Eyes watering, I place my hand over his and squeeze.

Irinorr lowers his arm and walks away. My hand clings to his, reaching for him as he disappears through the doors. Then the gods are gone, and we mortals are alone.

A moment crawls past before Master Oversea addresses the room. "Speak of this to no one. There's nothing more to be done tonight. We will summon the council again in the morning."

In a haze, the masters stream from the room. I try to sneak out behind the broad physique of the master of commerce, but I move too slow.

"Ms. Arnett," Isaac calls. "Ms. Byers. Please stay."

Whitman hangs behind, too. I slink next to Byers, affecting my most oblivious expression. Before Isaac says a word, he limps to his throne and sits down gingerly, his face screwed up in pain. I forgot he doesn't usually stand for so long.

For a span, Isaac and Whitman gawk at us like they've never seen our equal before. Which they haven't.

Whitman finally scrapes together a sentence. "Why didn't you tell me?" he says to us both, though his gaze is trained on me.

Guilt prickles the back of my neck, and I go on the offensive. "Oh, let's see." I look up in mock reflection. "Why didn't I tell you I've been receiving magical instruction from the crow god since I was eight? I suppose because I don't like whiling away my time in a sanitarium. No one would have believed us."

"Are there more like you?" Isaac asks with a hand over his mouth. His eyes don't veer from my face. If he had any doubts about my lovers reading, they're gone now. I'm apprenticed to a god; my magic just became far more credible.

"Somewhere out there," I say. "We don't typically meet in person. Byers and I are a fluke."

"So, what does it mean, to be trained by the gods? What do you learn?"

"I learned to do the lovers readings." I turn to Byers, prompting her to make her own disclosure.

But instead, her eyes glassy, she says, "It's been a long day. I need to rest."

I nod in agreement. I feel like I haven't slept in weeks. From the dark circles under Isaac's and Whitman's eyes, they're in the same boat.

"We can discuss it tomorrow," Whitman sighs. "Just . . . don't go anywhere."

By "anywhere," I suspect he means the Flood.

Minus Isaac, we depart for the practitioners' wing, lost in thought. I marvel at Byers' and my luck. The gods didn't question our presence at the castle, nor did they seem aware of our brief and fruitless meeting with Tasha D'Milliar. Is their magic really so weak this side of the Flood?

In my apartments, I unwind by diving into more readings on Parsons' death and the threatening notes. It's hard to concentrate when my mind is preoccupied with Irinorr and what he's doing here. Still, I place my hand on the last threatening note I received and focus on the reading, though I don't expect to learn much more. A subject's intent can obscure the results. When you're scrying something innocuous—names and facts and the like—that's one thing. But divining a secret is different. The mind erects barriers when the subject has their guard up. Surely, my cultist's guard is sky high.

Again, my reading reverberates powerful waves of guilt. It's so close to my own emotions around Patrick, it's hard to separate the two. I shut my eyes with a grimace. My cultist didn't want to kill Parsons—they *had* to. That feeling writhes inside me as I remember Patrick's lifeless body at the bottom of the cliff. I didn't want to kill Patrick, either. I never meant to hurt him. A tear leaks from the corner of my eye, trailing down my cheek. I wipe it away quickly.

A muffled bang startles me. My eyelids fly open to a blurry, dark room. Sweating, I look around.

By my bedroom door, a column of light and texture floats in the air. Held at its side is a blotch of bright red.

24

Patrick's body comes into focus. He stares at me, his ghostly mouth sealed shut. Another shriek builds inside me as I edge away along the chaise longue, tangling my skirts. He shouldn't be at the castle; it's impossible. He's supposed to be locked in his memories at home. I should be safe here.

Patrick walks forward, shedding pools of otherworldly light where he steps. My vanity stool launches into the air as he walks past, though he didn't touch the thing. I scream as it crashes against the wall.

Then my wicker chair hovers off the ground, too, hanging a foot in the air beside his misty form, and when I lock eyes with Patrick, I know he means to hurt me, to hurl the chair at me and break me.

I force myself off the chaise, a shrill noise ringing in my ears, and dive for the door to the hallway. I pull it open, my sweaty hands slipping on the handle.

A dark figure blocks my way. I shriek, covering my head.

"Mona!"

I jerk my head up and bat my eyes clear. It's Whitman.

Gasping for air, I collapse against his chest.

He braces me by the arms as I bury my face, my fists pressed against his sternum. I can't turn around. I can't face Patrick again.

"What is it?" he asks with an edge of panic, guiding me back into the room with shuffling steps.

I curl closer to him. "Is he still here?"

"Who?"

That sounds promising, but I refuse to turn around. "Just answer me, please," I mumble into his master's jacket. "Is anyone there?"

Whitman pulls away, lifting my chin with his fingertips. I blink back my tears as he searches my face with concern. "We're alone."

My brows draw together. "How did you get here before the guards?"

"I was walking down the wing. Thinking."

As my hysteria fades, it sinks in that we're locked in an embrace, my hands trapped against his chest as he holds me with one arm. His other hand lingers near my jaw—no longer touching me, but close, like he might change his mind.

I break away, turning to assess the damage. My wicker chair lies toppled over on the floor. At least Patrick didn't smash that one against a wall. Shivering, I wrap my arms around myself and rush for my chaise longue, sitting with my back to Whitman. The cushions sink as he sits next to me.

"Was someone in here?" he asks.

"I— Well, it's . . ." I stutter, standing at a crossroads. I could tell Whitman the truth and ask for his help, or I could lie and protect my secret. If I'm honest with him, he'll probably think I'm crazy.

But he's believed me about everything else.

"Promise you won't judge me?" I say weakly.

He nods, perfectly attentive. I hate him for that sometimes. I look away. "I saw a ghost."

He's silent for long enough that I get nervous, and I'm running my mouth again. "I've seen him before, once. Back home. I told Irinorr about it. He said I would be safer at the castle, but now the ghost is back, and he still wants to kill me and I don't know what to do, Whitman."

I chance a peek at him. He shakes his head, like he's working something out. "It's odd. I've been getting letters," he says, his brow wrinkling. I rear back; that's not even in the top ten of reactions I was prepared for. "Going on three months now. Reports of sightings. I didn't think much of it—I assumed they were pranks, or . . . troubled people." He gives me an apologetic glance. "All of them came from provinces with high population density or spellsap shortages. I wouldn't have saved them, but the pattern interested me."

Swallowing, I listen as Whitman describes the letters. Ghost sightings from across the kingdom. From what he can gather, the deceased is always someone they know. Someone they watched die. The ghosts appear at night, when the victim is alone.

"So, I'm not the only one?" I say distantly. Irinorr must not have known about this when we spoke last. It's a relief to learn I'm not alone, but this points to a bigger problem.

"Do you know who it is?" Whitman asks. "Your ghost?"

I consider telling him the truth. Instead, I murmur, "Don't want to talk about it."

After a long silence, Whitman clears his throat. "The gods are aware of this?"

"I think so. Irinorr discussed it with them." I hug my arms over my stomach. "Does it bother you? The gods showing up?"

His chin drops to his chest. "The pantheon coming to life? Finding out they've been real all along, truly real? It's . . . It hasn't sunk in yet. I'm more bothered about you."

"Me?"

"Every time I think I've figured you out, I learn some new angle," he says, running a hand through his hair. "And it changes everything."

I wither at the resignation in his voice. He's given up on making sense of me, now that it doesn't matter. Now that I'm Isaac's soulmate. Masking my feelings behind a gruff tone, I say, "I'm the same person I've always been."

He hums. "Are you?"

For whatever reason, that rubs me the wrong way. "Yes, I am. And so are you. People don't change. That's a myth."

"Aren't we living in one?" he mutters.

If only that were so. We may have gods, kings, and true love, but we're lacking the most important ingredient: a hero.

We stare at each other for an awkward second until Whitman asks, "Would you like me to go, or—"

"No," I say quickly. If he leaves, Patrick might come back. I peer at Whitman through wet eyelashes, hugging my arms tighter. "I'd rather not be alone."

His mouth slackens as he fumbles for a response. I realize my mistake. "Not like that," I say glumly. "I haven't forgotten. 'That's not happening, *ever.*'" I mock his words in my dopiest voice.

He relaxes, though not by much. "It has nothing to do with you. And don't act so wounded." He sighs, dragging a hand over his jaw. "I'm sure you have your pick of whoever you like."

I'm flattered, but it's not true. "Not since I met you, I haven't," I say with a casual shrug. It hasn't been an intentional bout of celibacy. I just haven't had the time.

He arches an eyebrow. "Really? You haven't been with anybody?"

"Other than myself? No."

"Yourself? I don't—" His eyes inflate with understanding. "Oh."

I laugh, my cheeks burning. Perhaps I shouldn't have said it, but too late now. I prefer a partner, when I can find one, but since I joined the company, I've been left to my own devices.

"I walked into that one," he says under his breath.

It's almost charming, his reaction. "Does it bother you that much? Talking about sex?"

"It doesn't bother me," he objects too quickly, staring at the ceiling. Calculating how he can possibly respond without making it worse. "You caught me off guard."

I shift in my seat as my body heats up, my center pulsing. I can't discuss this with Whitman without getting excited. I try to wipe the smile from my face. "I'm sorry. I shouldn't say these things to you."

"Probably not." His hands grip into fists, pressing down on his knees. "Sometimes I think you do it just to—" He cuts off, glancing away.

"To what?"

"Frustrate me," he says through his teeth.

Warmth pools between my legs, my encounter with Patrick all but forgotten. In fact, this is just what I need—what I've always used to distract myself. Nothing's going to happen between Whitman and me, especially now that he knows I'm Isaac's soulmate. But I can still ask.

"You could watch me," I say, my pulse thudding. I curl my hands under my thighs. "Touching myself. That doesn't violate your rules, does it?"

His jaw clenches tighter, and he makes a guttural noise that almost unhinges me. "I don't think that would be appropriate," he says with great effort.

"Isn't that the idea?"

He sniffs, his throat bobbing. "And what would I be doing? Standing there like some voyeur in the bushes?"

My eyes go wide. He's actually contemplating it? Maybe he hasn't given up on me completely. I try not to sound too eager as I say, "Or you could touch yourself, too. Whatever feels right."

Whitman's expression remains stoic, but his chest rises and falls with rapid breaths. "This is insane."

"It's just a suggestion." I gather my skirts and pull them up until the hemline hits my knees, showing my lace stockings. He ceases to pretend I don't exist and stares down at my hands, waiting for what they'll do next. "We can talk about something else. Court politics?"

He bares his teeth like he might snarl, his back a rod-straight line. I raise my skirts higher. Testing the waters. "I can stop."

At long last, he lifts his eyes to mine. "No," he says, his expression pained, almost incensed. "Keep going."

A flush spreads over me, to every secret spot on my body. He wants this. He wants it so bad he'll throw caution to the wind, stomp all over his empty appeals to propriety. He wants *me*. Even after everything he's seen of me, all my faults and shortcomings. He trains his gaze on me, refusing to look away, challenging me to call him a hypocrite. I don't say a thing.

I draw my skirts upward until they bunch around my hips. The pale bands of skin between my garters and my hem stand out like moonstone in the low light, smooth and bare. I hold Whitman's stare as I trail my fingers over the garters and then higher. Finally, he gives in, reclining stiff-backed in his seat, head propped to the side as he watches me drag my hands between my legs to stroke my inner thighs.

His own hands perch clawlike on his knees. I reach under my dress and dip into the waistline of my underthings. Whitman lets out a strange, stifled sound that ignites my nerve endings, and I fall still, drinking in the moment.

"Go on," he murmurs, his desperation plain. "Do it."

Three loud knocks shatter the silence.

With a startled jolt, I tug my skirts back down. Whitman staggers to his feet. We exchange a long look, our breathing heavy and labored.

"Answer it," I say with a tremor, though it's the last thing in the world I want him to do.

He wavers for an instant before complying.

On the other side of the door stand two guards. Whitman stares at them like he can't comprehend the interruption. The one in front bows his head. "Good evening, master. We were sent to find you. The council is reconvening."

"What time is it?" Whitman says, swiveling, looking for a clock. He runs a hand through his hair. He turns back to me, his expression unreadable. "I—I have to go. Good night, Ms. Arnett."

"Night," I say quietly as he rushes into the hall. A gulf forms inside me, desire draining out through my fingertips and toes. Tonight will never be repeated. Whitman's too careful, too guarded. Now that he's wise to my tricks, he'll stay away.

I retreat to my bedroom, but sleep eludes me. Patrick could return at any moment. Well past midnight, I give up on sleep. I know what I need to ease my mind. With a shawl draped around my shoulders, a lamp in hand, I venture into the hallway. My assigned guards, posted at either side of the door, attach themselves to me without a word. They don't ask too many questions—I appreciate that.

Master Gan housed the gods on the fourth floor of the castle. I climb the twisting steps to a long corridor, its carpet beet red. The spellsap lights are dimmer here than elsewhere in the castle.

As I approach each door, I press a hand against the sunken mahogany panels, feeling the fine grain of the wood. The fourth door I touch is Irinorr's. How I know, I can't say.

I knock. An instant later, Irinorr answers. He smiles with that absurd human mouth. But his eyes—the smile touches those the same as always.

"Do you sleep in this form?" I ask. He's wearing his dress clothes, a white vest over a stiff golden shirt, embroidered with pearlescent silk threads. The colors should wash out his bone-white skin, but they don't. He glows like the moon. My eyes mist with relief. He's really here.

"We don't need to." He stands aside to welcome me in. "Wayvadd likes to nap away his afternoons, but it's a personal preference."

His room is handsomely decorated, befitting an important foreign statesman. Oil paintings along the walls depict ancient faces I don't recognize. A large bronze globe is installed near the writing desk, ringed with thin, scored loops, like an even more complicated astrolabe.

I sit in an armchair, curling my legs underneath me. "Byers and I were worried," I say as Irinorr sits opposite me. "You were gone so suddenly."

"We are sorry to have caused you alarm. It was important to avoid delay."

"Of course," I say, ducking my head. This is bigger than me or my feelings. "I'm sure you're busy, but I thought you should know—I saw Patrick again."

Irinorr frowns deeply. "When?"

"Just now. He tried to attack me."

"So, you were alone when he manifested?"

"I've been alone every night since I came to the castle, but he didn't show up until now. And Whitman's been getting letters, too. Other people are seeing ghosts."

Irinorr hums in contemplation. "It's unfortunate that these difficulties are occurring in parallel. We are forced to prioritize."

"But if it's all related, couldn't this be, you know . . . the Rising Tide? The dead walking the mortal realm is one of the signs, isn't it? And the spellsap orchards dying?"

Irinorr crosses his legs and glances up, pondering the question. "It's unlikely, my child. Yes, there is a prophecy, nearly as old as the nexus. We witnessed it ourselves. But an event of that scale is difficult to predict. Our bigger concern is that the nexus itself could be the cause. If King Isaac's rulership is lacking, it could create disturbances."

"King Isaac's doing fine," I retort. I don't know if I'm right about that. How do you judge a king, anyway? Isaac hasn't started any wars or executed innocents, and he's trying to feed and clothe his subjects who have little of their own. What else could be expected of him?

Irinorr smiles benevolently. "I'm sure he's done an admirable job. We must explore all avenues, though. Our magic here is weaker than in the Flood, but we can communicate with your realm more easily. We can interview mortals, travel to sites where anomalies have occurred. Inspect the spellsap orchards. If we combine our magics, we will find the source of these happenings."

I sigh, rubbing my eyes. There's one last thing I need to tell Irinorr. "I don't know if the masters mentioned," I say, "but there was a murder recently. Some threats, too."

"And you are at the center." Irinorr nods. "I heard from your master of ceremonies. I'm very sorry I could not be there to protect you, Mona."

I smile tearfully. I wish he had been there, too, but that's in the past. He's here now. "How will I find them? The killer?"

"They will reveal themselves, sooner or later. Their type always does."

I stare into the fireplace. What if this cultist is smart enough to be cautious? How would anyone catch them then?

"Mona." I look up, and his rune-encrusted eyes trap mine. "I also know you are King Isaac's soulmate."

I hold his gaze a scant second longer. Of course. Irinorr must have been aware for years what my lot would be. I ball my good hand into a fist. Some warning might have been nice.

"Do not shy away from this," Irinorr says, soft but admonishing. "I am proud of you for coming forward, but that is not the end. You are aware, I am sure, how important the naming of the next queen will be for Opalvale?"

"Elsie Tanner is the future queen," I declare. "It's the only outcome that makes sense, given the predictions."

Irinorr's mouth bends up at the corner. "The way our futures unfold is not always apparent. But I will tell you this, Mona. Fighting your future out of spite never ends well. You will find yourself in the same position in the end, with a wake of avoidable woes behind you. Best to greet your fate with open arms, in peace."

25

In the morning, I'm summoned to council chambers. Again. Elizabeta helps me dress, all the while chattering about the splendor of last night's ball. How odd that life should go on. As Opalvale rises with the dawn, most of its subjects are ignorant of the gods in their midst. But I have a suspicion that by the time the sun sinks this evening, it will be all anyone can talk about.

When I arrive in the antechamber, Byers is already there, pacing.

"Good afternoon," I say with breezy exuberance. My head is cloudy from lack of sleep.

"They'll call us when they're ready," Byers replies in greeting, without looking up.

"Aren't we cranky," I say under my breath.

She lobs a glare at me. "I'm sorry if I'm not perky enough for your tastes. I had nightmares all night."

"Oh." I feel bad for goading her, but not bad enough to leave her alone. "Nightmares about what?"

"The damned Rising Tide," she grunts. I wince, imagining what those nightmares looked like. Were her parents there, ushering in the end in dark hooded robes?

I wait, my chest tight, while Byers swoops back and forth like a hawk having a conniption fit. She isn't helping my nerves. At long last, a castle guard opens the chamber door and grants us entry.

Fewer attendees than I expected are gathered around the table. Only Semyanadd, Onyamarr, and Korimarr are presiding, without a master or king in sight. Sitting side by side, the wolf god and the whale goddess form a striking contrast: Semyanadd with his coifed hair and pale complexion, and Onyamarr with locs falling past her waist, her skin a dark golden brown—the color of wet sand. So much about them is a contrast to begin with. Semyanadd rules over the harvest, slaughter of livestock, the sun; Onyamarr's domains are the elements, magic, the moon. Korimarr (knowledge, law, and justice) sits apart from them, her nose upturned.

"Where is everyone?" I blurt, before I can process how stupid that sounds. What a way to commence things.

"We had the full council meeting," Semyanadd says. He sits in his chair like it's a throne. "This is just a conversation."

"About what?"

The three gods share a dark look. Korimarr says, "We have learned of the threats against Mona, and of the boy who was killed. In these mortal forms, we are limited. It's clear this killer is a magician, but we cannot identify them yet."

"How do you know they're a magician?" I ask. I assumed the same, given what they've accomplished without being caught, but Korimarr seems so sure.

"The means by which they travel through the castle must be magical. There is rune-based magic that can teleport a person or turn them invisible. It's incredibly advanced but possible. And your chandelier was sabotaged with alchemical components. A magician of any kind would be more familiar with alchemy than a layperson."

"Are they a favored mortal?"

"More likely, it is someone who can pass into the Flood but never received instruction from the gods. It's rare, but these individuals exist, and they can achieve extraordinary power."

Someone who sees windows to the Flood but has gone unnoticed by the gods—like Whitman's sister? What if she has powers like Byers and me, the ability to work magic without runes? There must be others like her out there—even here, in the castle. Still, access to the Flood wouldn't help them move from room to room without being spotted. They can't just be opening windows straight to their destination. All windows on the Flood's side send you back to exactly where you entered in the mortal realm. A neat trick; not particularly useful for traveling between two points. That aside, though, if the Flood is the source of the cultist's magic, it could explain their remarkable talent.

"The letters," Byers jumps in, her voice taut. "Have you seen them? There's a symbol at the bottom, a mark of the Guild."

"We have seen the symbol," says Onyamarr, her smile indulgent, "but I don't think it was left by the Guild of the Rising Tide. It's a very old symbol, adopted by the Guild in its infancy. Its original meaning comes from a Lamican sect of monks who eased the passing of the sick and dying to the garden."

My brows scrunch together. "You think that's why the killer used that symbol?"

"Perhaps. Or they are repurposing it for their cause, like the Guild did before them."

"But it *could* be the Guild," Byers repeats. Judging by the bags under her eyes, those nightmares must have been vicious.

"We can't speculate," Semyanadd says. "But if the killer's motive was to punish Mona, the Guild is not likely a suspect."

"There are no likely suspects," I say, gripping my good hand into a fist. This is the pebble in my shoe that's been digging into my heel from the start. Even if someone found out about my reading, who benefits from making it public?

Semyanadd nods sympathetically. "Trust that we're working with your council to apprehend the killer as swiftly as we can."

With that, it seems we're dismissed. When we reach the door, though, Korimarr calls out. "Bernadette, stay. I want to speak to you."

Byers and I exchange a look. Korimarr doesn't sound cross, so maybe she wants a heart-to-heart with her favored mortal, like I had with Irinorr last night. I mumble my good-lucks to her and leave.

I don't get far before I swerve around a corner and collide with Verimall and Eledorr.

The goddesses of violence and death, respectively, stand in the center of the hallway like permanent fixtures, like pillars side by side. These two tend to stick together. Verimall's red mane of hair is braided in a thick rope down to her waist, her tan skin warm and glowing against her white gown. Eledorr's runes—limned in white instead of black—spread in a moth wing pattern over her eyes and dark brown cheeks. Her short hair curls tight against her skull. I stare at them, my mouth working but making no sound.

Verimall smiles, her teeth glinting like dagger tips. "We meet again, Mona."

"Verimall. Eledorr." I lower my gaze.

"Looking for trouble, are you?" Verimall says with a hungry look. Eledorr stands close to her and watches me in eerie silence. "Venturing out alone? Don't you know there's a killer on the loose?"

"I'm not alone." Not far behind, one of Renfield's agents follows me at a polite distance, dressed in a dark navy uniform that makes no noise when she walks. I've been seeing Renfield's people more and more lately, replacing Oversea's guards as my defenders. I'm not sure what necessitated the change. Perhaps Oversea decided his subordinates have better things to do.

"You're not afraid of the murderer?" Verimall asks. "She seems like a crafty type."

"She?"

"Why, yes," she says, eyes shining. "You do not think a woman capable of that level of violence? Mona, Mona, Mona. You should know better. Men, they give their violence away, like it's nothing. But women hold it inside, close to the heart. Deep, deep inside, festering, until it is needed. Then"—she claps in my face, and I yelp—"it explodes." Verimall reaches out, twining a curl of my hair around her finger. "Pretty, soft Mona. How much violence do you have inside you, I wonder?"

Shaking, I stumble back. Verimall laughs. Eledorr keeps watching me.

I turn on my heel and sprint.

Yes, it makes me look foolish. But in this moment, I want nothing more than to find a place to hide—someplace safe, someplace familiar—and imagine myself an average mortal, to whom the gods are stories.

Once I reach my apartments, I lock the door and run to my bedroom, collapsing face-first onto the mattress. I scream my lungs out, muffled by the comforter. I'm fused to my bed when I hear a knock minutes later.

Reluctant, I rise to answer it. Whitman stands on the other side of the door.

"I wanted to check on you," he says without preamble. "After the gods spoke to you and Ms. Byers."

"It's fine," I mutter, and pull the door wider. Whitman doesn't cross the threshold. "Aren't you going to come in?"

"No," he says.

I scowl at him. "I promise I'll behave myself."

"It's not a good idea." He bows his head, hiding his face.

I slump, though I had no reason to believe this would go differently. "Then why are you here?" I ask dully.

"To make sure you're all right."

"What do you think?" I snap, squeezing the door handle in a death grip. Despite the gods' arrival—or perhaps because of it—running away to the Flood is rising to the top of my to-do list. What do I have to stick around for? We'll never capture Parsons' killer if even the *gods* can't drum up a suspect. Whatever guilt I might feel, however responsible I might be, I'm no help here.

"Please don't take this out on me." The tendons of his hands stand out in relief as he clenches them. "I am sorry about last night, but—"

"Don't flatter yourself." A cruel impulse seizes my tongue, fueled by anger and pent-up fear—and, in some part, mercy. He needs to see the real me. "I have plenty of options besides you, including King Isaac, so don't act like I'm some jilted lover."

Whitman's eyes go blank. "What does Isaac have to do with this?"

"What does my *true love* have to do with this? Really?"

We stare each other down.

"I'll leave you alone, then," he says—but it comes out like a threat. "But I think you understand perfectly well that you and Isaac can't have any kind of relationship unless you marry him."

"Oh, yes, do order the king not to sleep with whom he pleases," I reply coolly. "Let me know how that works out."

I close the door in his face.

Then I go back to my chaise longue, where I drink myself to sleep and pass out for twelve hours straight.

Such is my creeping dread that I find myself visiting a part of the castle I never have before, a place with less value to me than a dusty linen closet: the chapel.

I can't say what draws me to that chilly room on the castle's ground floor. Perhaps because I've always known chapels to be devoid of the gods' influence, and right now, I need a place to avoid them. The gods' appearance feels like a strange, overlong dream.

My guards sweep the chapel for threats, then wait outside the door. It smells like a musty cellar inside. Clean and orderly, but with an ancient, clammy musk about it, the scent of thousands of years of false hope. On the far end of the room, altars to the seven tower beneath stained-glass windows. If it was sunset, rays of tempered light would stream through to fall on the pillars of stone. But it's noon, and the glass is dark.

I crouch before Irinorr's obelisk of an altar, engraved with a crow feather. On the floor before its base weaves a winding pattern of circular depressions in the stone. Already today, three people have left prayer tokens slotted into the holes, offerings to the god of love. One of the tokens bears Verimall's mark. I sneer. People try that, on occasion—leaving a token for one god at the altar of another, when their prayers intersect two domains. Most likely, this supplicant has been crossed by an ex-lover and wishes misfortune upon the poor fool who spurned them. I can relate.

I trace my finger over the carvings on Irinorr's altar and wonder if my cultist has visited the chapel lately. They're guilty, like me. Perhaps they feel compelled to ask for forgiveness.

"Would you like to know something interesting?" says someone behind me.

My head swivels around. Wayvadd leans against a wall in the shadowy depths of the chapel, one hand stuffed in the pocket of his trousers, the other gripping a bejeweled goblet. Gold vines embroider his black jacket and vest, their leaves tipped in diamonds. He must really be as quiet as a cat, to have slunk past my guards.

My shoulders sag. So much for hiding from the gods. Resigned, I fall back on my bottom with a grunt, stretching out my legs. Best make myself comfortable. Wayvadd is not well versed in the art of the quick chat. "What do you want, Wayvadd?"

He stalks toward me. "Why do you assume I want something? I've simply been here relaxing. Observing."

"So, spying on people?" I ask as he slouches against his own altar pillar.

He takes a sip from his goblet. "I like to learn. And I've learned so much already. For instance"—he points to where I sit, in front of Irinorr's altar—"did you know that when mortals come to ask for intervention with a lover, they're as likely to leave a token for me as for Irinorr?"

"What's your point?"

"That you mortals have no idea what love is. You see something you want, and the only thought that goes through your little brains is 'How can I make this *mine*?' It's all about *you*. Delectable."

Well, that strikes me as a classic case of projection. I roll my eyes. "Thank you for your expert opinion on matters of love."

Wayvadd chuckles, sending chills skittering over my skin. "Oh, you don't want to go there."

"What are you talking about?" I sigh, and though my tone is annoyed, I dread his answer.

"You've built a career around advising mortals in matters of the heart, and you don't know the first thing about love." His cruel grin widens. "How could you?"

Clenching my fists, I start to climb to my feet. I don't have to listen to this.

"Oh, by the by—I spoke with your Whitman the other day."

I freeze in place. Wayvadd snickers, gesturing with his goblet. A splash of red wine—or what I hope is wine—sloshes out. "I knew that would get you. Seems your type—*very* good-looking, isn't he? You're nothing if not predictable."

"Look who's talking."

"True, true. You mortals are much more fickle than us gods. Take Master Whitman, for example. Do you know how he got that master's role?"

"Yes, Isaac did him a favor." That was a weak attempt, for Wayvadd. "It's not that scandalous."

"But that's just the end of the story. Have you heard what led up to it?" His unnatural eyes shimmer. "His mother was a royal magician. Young Whitman discovered she was a fake—no abilities whatsoever. So, he turned her in. She had to flee to Rynth to escape imprisonment."

My jaw drops. He has to be making it up. "What do you mean, a fake?"

"She claimed to be a seer, but it was all cleverness and a knack for human nature. Twenty years in the company, and no one caught on but her own son. After she ran, a number of the royal magicians resigned in protest, including the former master of practitioners. They thought she should have received leniency."

My pulse beats in my throat, and I brace my hands and feet underneath me like I might leap up and sprint from the chapel. Why hasn't anyone told me this? It seems so out of character for the Whitman I know—the one who's kind and patient. Even if his mother was a fraud, how could he turn her in, knowing the consequences? An awful idea occurs to me, draining the blood from my face. Did he do it on purpose to create a scandal for the company, and a vacancy on the council—counting on Isaac's influence to secure him the master's position? Byers did say he always wanted to be a royal magician. Without magic of his own, this was his only hope of being part of the company.

"All right." I push myself up the rest of the way. "Nice talk, Wayvadd."

"It's a shame he had to betray you, too."

I pause from brushing off my skirts. "Whitman hasn't betrayed me." I speak the words with authority, like a challenge. I want to believe myself.

"Such devotion, and for a man you haven't even lain with. You've changed, Mona." Wayvadd pulls his hand from his pocket. Pinched between his thumb and forefinger is a burnished silver key. "I suppose you trust him so much, you have no need to verify it."

"I see how it is. There's not enough trouble at the castle for your tastes, so you're stirring some up."

He waggles the key back and forth. "You don't have to take my word. The proof is in his office. Go see for yourself."

My gaze clings to the key. It must be a trick. Wayvadd can say whatever he pleases, but his accusations are insubstantial. Pure hot air.

Then again, why would Wayvadd lie about something so easy to disprove?

I shoot my hand out, plucking the key from his grasp. Wayvadd barks a laugh. He looks at his empty fingers in delighted surprise, like he didn't expect me to do it.

I squeeze the key. "I'm only taking this so you won't have it anymore."

Wayvadd's eyes glint with victory. "You've made the right choice, Mona. Better to face reality than numb your pain with pretty lies."

I frown after him as he heads for the exit, drinking and swerving as he walks. "You're alone, Mona," he calls over his shoulder. "Alone, and always will be. Remember that. It's important to have a solid foundation in these times of turmoil. Helps you keep a grip on your sanity."

Wayvadd laughs his way out of the chapel.

In my defense, I make it two days before I use the key.

The urge comes in waves. What does Wayvadd mean for me to find? There has to be something, or he wouldn't have bothered. Something I might misinterpret, hidden in Whitman's office, something that would implicate him if taken out of context.

As I lie awake that third night searing holes into the ceiling with my stare, I come to a conclusion. The best way to resolve this once and for all is to do as Wayvadd said. I need to search Whitman's office. If I find anything untoward, I'll march up to him and demand clarification. Then we can put the matter behind us, like adults.

In my nightgown, I pad toward the door to the hallway. When I reach the two guards outside, I nod in greeting. I'm starting to get used to their presence. But one of them stretches out his arm, blocking my exit.

I stare at the offending appendage like I can't believe its gall. "Is there a problem?"

The guard spares a quick look at his comrade before addressing me. "We have orders," he says. "You're not to leave your room at night."

"Is that so?" I raise my brows. "Because of the killer?"

"I'd imagine so, miss."

I don't have time for this. I narrow my eyes at the guard. "What's your name?"

"Private Hansen, miss."

"Well, Mr. Hansen, let's engage in a thought exercise together." I pinch my chin as he gives me a puzzled look. "You received your orders from your captain, who no doubt received them from one of the masters. Do you know who I receive my orders from?"

"No," he answers, wary.

"The *gods*, Private. Now, tell me. Whose orders do you think take precedence?"

I almost expect him to challenge me. But, with a nod, he drops his arm. "I can't disrupt the business of the gods," he says, though he sounds a twinge mocking. The guards must be running low on patience—like the rest of us.

"Thank you," I say with exaggerated grace, brushing past him. Then I stop and turn back. "And don't follow me, either. In fact, you're dismissed for the evening. That's an order."

Private Hansen hesitates. "If anything happens to you, we could be court-martialed."

"Don't worry about that." I commit to the only lie I can cook up on short notice. "I'm just going down the hall to Master Whitman's room. We have a private meeting scheduled. If you catch my drift."

If Hansen finds this bit of gossip particularly juicy, he doesn't show it. "I see. In that case, we'll bid you good night." The guards about-face and leave me alone.

That probably shouldn't have been so easy.

Finally free, I slink into the hallway, looking both ways. All clear. Whitman's office is at the far end of the hall. I sneak down the darkened corridor, straining my ears for sounds.

I stop in front of the door and check once more for witnesses. Once I'm sure I'm alone, I stick Wayvadd's key in the silver lock. There's a metallic clunk. I push on the door; it squeaks inward. With a breath of relief, I slip inside.

The office is dark, but my eyes adjust quickly. I tiptoe up to the walnut desk, strewn with parchment and books. Whitman's brain has clearly been scattered lately, and his office matches. How am I supposed to find anything among this mess?

My heart racing, I sift through papers, pick up large leather volumes and check underneath. Obscure rows of figures cover most of the papers—supply ledgers or something of the like. I also spy a few nasty notes from the Guild of Magicians. But nothing unexpected. Frustrated, I start going through the desk.

It's not until I reach the bottom drawer that I see my name. It catches my eye at the top of a short letter, written in a hand I don't recognize.

> *Master Whitman,*
> *I went to see Mona Arnett. I share your concerns. Brought my sister along to get a lovers reading. I can't tell you how she's pulling those "soulmate" names. As for her other readings, they were spot-on. I couldn't get a fix on her method. No cold reading, no hidden runes or mirrors that I spotted. Mayhap you'll have better luck than me.*
> *As for your other question, I did find her a somewhat ridiculous girl, which matches her reputation. I'd not consider her a serious candidate for the company even if she weren't a fraud. She'd make a circus of it.*

The note is signed with a name I vaguely know—a guild magician, someone I did a reading for not long ago. Dated the day before Whitman first came calling.

Whitman receives a report slandering me, and the next day he rushes out to pay me a visit? A pit of unease grows in my stomach.

I keep digging through his desk. Lining the bottom of a drawer, I come across a list scribbled on a scrap of paper. Names of other seers. I recognize a few—renowned frauds, all of them. Whitman has jotted notes next to some, about methods or personalities. *Not flashy enough; too unbelievable.* I scan the list until I reach the bottom. The last name is mine.

He's made no notes, no observations. He's simply scratched a thick, inky circle around it.

I stare at my name in Whitman's script. So, he scoured the kingdom for frauds, and I topped the list? I can only think of one reason he would do such a thing.

Whitman didn't bring me to the castle to help. He never believed I could.

He used me to sabotage the naming of the queen.

26

"**M**ona?"

I tear my eyes from the list. Whitman stands in the doorway, dressed in a crisp white shirt but without his master's jacket. His brows draw together.

I step back. "What are you doing here?" I say, like I'm not the one breaking into his office.

He walks into the room slowly, as though afraid of spooking me. "My apartments are next door. You weren't exactly stealthy."

Cursing myself, I take another step and hit the wall. Whitman keeps encroaching. I slide my hand behind my back to hide the note. He creeps closer, closer, until his face looms above mine. I look up and swallow.

I feel something cold and sharp against the curve of my throat.

I drop my cross-eyed gaze to the dagger at my neck, and the reality of the situation sinks in. Whitman might slit my throat right here.

I lift my chin. "Are you going to kill me, master?" I say, barely above a whisper.

"This is for my protection." He braces his arm against the wall, trapping me. His whole body radiates heat. "It *was* you, wasn't it? Looking for evidence to destroy?"

"What?" I say, wrinkling my brow. "I'm not—"

"Don't bother lying." He sets his jaw and presses closer. "You weren't ransacking my office for fun."

"No," I snarl. "I was searching for proof of your treason."

The pressure of the blade lets up. "What?"

I pull the list from behind me and slap it on his chest. He looks down, startled.

"It's you." My fist curls around the paper, crinkling it. "You're trying to stop Isaac from choosing a queen—you want to break the nexus."

"Mona, no! Where are you getting this?" Whitman wrenches the list from my grasp and scans it. His face falls. "Oh."

"Yes, '*oh.*'"

"You've got it wrong," he mutters, stuffing the paper into his pocket. "I want nothing more than to find the next queen of Opalvale. But this contest is not the way to do it. It's too susceptible to tampering."

"So you brought in a fraud to ruin it?" I say with a wry smile.

Whitman stares at me, his eyes bloodshot, and takes a step back. I breathe easier with the blade off my throat.

"I didn't know how else to stop it," he spits. "My appeals to the other masters were ignored. I thought if I could delegitimize the contest, Isaac would listen to reason and pursue a more—"

"And how did you expect that would work?"

"I knew Isaac would see it my way eventually. By then, it would be too late to cancel the contest. I was giving him an out. If one of the candidates was proven a fraud, it would taint the bunch. Isaac could end it without looking indecisive."

"So you thought you'd accomplish this by proving I'm a fraud," I mock him. "Which I'm not."

"I didn't know that in the beginning!" He tosses his hands up, knife still in his grip. "You had so many of the markers. I thought I could catch you by setting a trap. That's why I left a folder of candidates on your dresser."

"What does that prove?"

"They were fake. The names, the titles, everything. I was sure you'd name one of the invented women, thinking you'd offered up an impressive candidate, and I would have my evidence. I thought you wouldn't be able to resist."

I'm speechless, shaking my head in disgust. All this time, I believed Whitman was championing me. But he never had any faith in my abilities. Should I have seen this betrayal sooner?

"After your reading, though," Whitman mumbles, head hanging, "I didn't know what to think."

I take a step forward, like I might lunge at him. "Why would you do this? Even if you spared Isaac's reputation, what about yours? You're the one who vouched for me."

"You don't understand." Whitman paces around the desk, eyes on the floor, and exhales heavily. "Of course I don't want to be humiliated—who does? The masters already treat me like a child. But this is Isaac's legacy. His—his memory." He stops pacing and goes very still. "That's all that will be left, once he's gone. If he marries some puppet, some briber's pick who'll be controlled from the shadows after Isaac . . . after he's dead . . ."

I want to stay angry, but he's not making it easy. Whitman was just trying to protect his friend. I can accept that. But why me? Why fashion *me* into a fraud?

My eyes swim with furious tears. "Wayvadd told me what you did to your mother."

His face goes as white as a sheet. "Don't talk about that. You don't know anything about it."

"I know that you turned her in. You didn't care what happened to her, did you?" Just like he never cared what happened to me.

"Don't say that," he shoots back, voice thick with resentment. "Don't. I told her what I was going to do before I said a word to the masters. I gave her the chance to run."

"You didn't have to betray her in the first place!"

"People *died*, Mona. They died because she pretended to have a power she didn't. When I found out what she'd done, I begged her to stop. She couldn't face the humiliation. Someone had to make sure she never hurt anybody else." His eyes start to water, and he paws at them with his free hand. "I didn't want to do it. I had to."

For a beat, I put aside my anger and picture Whitman as a young man, taking pride in the fact his mother was a magician, like he always dreamed of being. Not just any magician, either. A *royal* magician. And then that small comfort was shattered.

How had she done it—convinced everyone she possessed the gift of sight? How had she faked reading the runes? I can understand now why Whitman glared so hard at me when we first met, like he could burn down my act with his red stare and sift for something true in the ashes.

We stare each other down, chests heaving. Whitman knows more about spotting frauds than just about anyone. Perhaps he *did* get it right with me. I wince, closing my eyes. I may be an honest magician, but as a person, I'm fake. Cheap. That's what Whitman saw in me.

He watches me as I rub my throat, checking for broken skin. Then he turns his attention to his desk. With deliberate care, he reorders the piles of papers I scattered. "How did you get into my office?" he asks.

"Wayvadd gave me a key. He told me you betrayed me." I look down at my stocking feet. "I'd hoped to prove him wrong."

Now that I've cooled off, though, my greatest suspicions have diminished. If Whitman was plotting against Opalvale, the gods would know. That level of treason would not go ignored—no matter what Irinorr says about staying out of mortal business. Whitman may have lied to *me*, but he's loyal to King Isaac.

"Did you find anything else of interest?"

My head pops up. "Like what?"

"Files on Parsons' murder? It's an open investigation; they're supposed to be confidential."

I snort in derision. "What, a file of blank pages? The council can't name a single suspect."

Whitman stops shuffling papers and stares at me—really stares, like I've sprouted a third arm and he just noticed. "Haven't you figured it out yet?"

I have no idea what he's talking about. "What?"

He lowers his chin, looking down his nose at me. "You're the top suspect, Mona. You're the *only* suspect."

My expression slackens. "H-how . . . ? That makes no sense—"

"Think about it. Somehow, those notes were delivered to you while the hallways were swarming with guards, and no one saw a thing. Parsons' body was in your room, and you were the only person there. The killer's motive is apparently to promote your claim to the crown by 'forcing' you to come forward as Isaac's soulmate. And all the while, you draw suspicion away from yourself by casting yourself as the reluctant victim."

Horrified, I stare into space, piecing it together. Oversea and Renfield didn't assign me guards to protect me—they assigned them to spy on me. Renfield must have approached me to size me up, to fish for incriminating information. She didn't have to interrogate me—she tricked me into doing it myself. The council was so sure I couldn't be Isaac's soulmate that they chased the only alternate theory they had: that in addition to being a fraud and a liar, I'm also a murderer.

I'm nothing but a monster to these people.

"You don't believe that, do you?" I ask Whitman in a hushed voice.

He's silent for long enough it seems he won't answer. Then he sighs. "No. But there's only so much I can do to defend you."

I don't take much comfort in that. "But the gods—"

"Their endorsement helps your case, certainly. But the masters aren't convinced."

I sniffle as I glare at Whitman's desk. Somewhere among those papers are documents that explain everything—the investigative plan, the charges against me, the proposed punishment for my crimes. And Whitman would've let it happen.

I look at him, imploring. "Why are you telling me this?"

"You seemed so interested in the truth," he says coldly. "Now you have it."

The castle walls crumble around me.

This is no place for me—it never was. I was a fool to think I could change, adapt, grow into somebody who might make Whitman and Byers and King Isaac proud. What good does it do to stay here? I'm more likely to get arrested for Parsons' murder than solve it.

I'm done trying to be something I'm not.

"Thank you, Master Whitman," I say, toneless, and stride out of his office.

Back in my bedroom, I work fast. I slip a pair of black leather shoes over my stockings and stuff everything I'll need in a small sack. Then I search my room for a window to the Flood. One appears effortlessly, and I step through.

By the warped, residual light of the Flood's midnight sky, I tear across the lowlands. Through wobbling towers of jelly kelp, filtering the Flood's glow. Past the demon colony where Kazzath lurks. To a high white bluff with a house on top.

"D'Milliar!" I shout. My chest heaves from running.

There is no delay this time. She walks onto her balcony and grabs the railing.

"I'm ready now," I say, my brow set.

D'Milliar scrutinizes me in silence. Then a smile creeps across her face.

"Yes," she calls down. "You are."

PART V

THE SORCERESS

27

I sit on the floor with my eyes closed, legs cramping beneath me. My foot itches. I'm not supposed to move, but I do anyway to scratch it. A listless sigh dribbles out of me.

I'm exquisitely bored.

"Are we done yet?" I ask, peeking through one eyelid.

Tasha sits across from me, her face a peaceful mask. "No," she says without opening her eyes. "And now we're starting over."

I suppress the groan clawing its way up my throat. "What's this supposed to teach me, again?"

"Nothing. I'm just tired of hearing you talk."

I squeeze my eyes shut with a scowl. For the next ten minutes, I try to clear my mind of thoughts, most of which are about how stupid this is. But one week with Tasha D'Milliar is time enough to learn that if she tells you to do something, you do it, immediately and without complaint—or you face the consequences.

I have no intention of suffering through those. Not again.

Time crawls past. I thwack the thoughts out of my brain as they invade. *This is ridiculous. How does this help me? And by the way, Whitman lied.*

I'm ready to topple over when Tasha finally speaks. "That's it," she says.

When I open my eyes, she's already climbing to her feet. I brace to push myself to standing, but before I can, she tosses a wicker basket at me, nailing me in the face. I splutter in protest.

"Go harvest dinner," she orders. "And next time, catch the basket."

I snatch it up and repeat to myself the mantra that has kept me sane this past week: *Whatever it takes to live in the Flood.*

Exiting Tasha's house is almost as much of a puzzle as getting inside. The main parlor, in the center of the maze, has doorways connecting to most every room in the house, except those rooms that have been tacked onto others like links in a growing chain. In place of furniture, piles of blankets and pillows crowd the floor; instead of doors, tapestries hang from the frames.

I pass through three sets of doorways to reach the spiral staircase to the second floor, which leads to the front entryway, shaped in a magnificent beechwood arch. Outside, I lower the rope ladder from the platform and climb down. My arms have already developed a semblance of muscle definition.

I round the house to the north side, to the field of cultivated kelp. It grows thicker here than in the natural forests. At first, I was too afraid to wander Tasha's property alone; after Kazzath, I pictured demons hiding in every shadow, preparing to strike when I turned my back. But Tasha walked me through the security measures she's put in place. Her home and its grounds might as well be protected by Selledore's thick stone walls.

As I snake through the stalks, the evening moon high in the purple sky, I see a spellsap golem kneeling behind a sheet of kelp. Its skin looks crafted from a million green fireflies. With iridescent hands, it folds powdery spellsap into the soil. I skirt around it. Tasha's golems make my skin crawl. I would call them empty behind the eyes, except she neglected to give them any.

After a quarter hour, my arms already sore from pulling kelp ropes by the roots, I hear shouts from the bottom of the cliff. Human shouts. Basket balanced on my hip, I rush to the south side of the house, the cliff-facing side.

Bernadette Byers stands at the bottom of the bluff. A strange warmth fills my chest—a slurry of glee and dread. I'm pleased that she came, and I hate that she's here.

"Arnett!" she cries, half-relieved, half-enraged. "Get down here!"

I shift the basket on my hip. "Welcome to Manor D'Milliar. Is the lady of the house expecting you?"

"Gods below, Arnett—"

"Let her up," comes Tasha's voice from above.

I crane my neck. Tasha leans against the balcony railing, gazing down at Byers with intensity. So *now* she turns into a gracious host.

I sigh and trudge to the east, motioning for Byers to follow. I stop before the flat wooden panel of the supply lift. It nestles in the sandy dirt like a trapdoor.

"See the cliff face in front of you?" I yell down. "It's a secret entrance. Walk through it."

Though she's far below me, I see her face screw up in confusion. "How?"

"It's an illusion—there's nothing there. Just walk through."

Byers bites her lip, staring at the solid rock. Then she steps forward. I hear her squeak as she bumps into the wall of stone.

"Ha!" I peer over the edge, grinning, to find her rubbing her nose and glaring furiously at me. "I can't believe you fell for that."

"Just let her up, Mona!" Tasha barks from the balcony.

My grin fading, I crouch to inspect the runes etched on the lift. I press the combination that retracts the door into the cliffside—which is, in all seriousness, camouflaged by Tasha's illusory enchantments, magic so complicated I have yet to guess how she accomplishes it. Each rune flares to life as my fingertips brush against it. When the grinding of the stone door stops, I push another series of runes to make the lift descend. Tasha has some method of getting up the cliff by herself, without the lift, but I don't know it.

In no time, the lift returns with Byers atop it, clutching her skirts and glancing around the platform in discomfiture. A part of me is glad to see her; but I know she hasn't come for a social visit. Whatever she has to say, I have no interest in hearing it.

I will not be going back to the castle.

"How'd you know I'd be here?" I ask as Byers hops off the lift on her toes like a skittish dancer.

"Where else would you have gone?" she replies caustically.

I shrug in response, unruffled. "This way, please," I say, sweeping my arm toward the house.

When we arrive in the parlor, Tasha has set three steaming copper mugs on the island that cordons off a small kitchenette. She stands behind the counter, resting her elbows on its surface, her short blond hair gleaming in the opalescent spellsap light. Her lanterns are different than the ones at the castle—large and spherical, like swollen soap bubbles, with pearly spellsap that churns and swirls.

Grunting, I throw myself down on a massive cushion. "May I present Bernadette Byers," I say, waving toward her, "royal magician, soothsayer, professional meddler."

Byers loiters near the island and twists her hands together. "It's an honor to meet you, Ms. D'Milliar."

"It's Tasha," she says, holding out her hand. Byers shakes it with disbelieving glee.

"The Flood's resident sorceress," I add, without too much sarcasm.

"Sorceress?" Byers repeats. She hasn't let go of Tasha's hand.

Tasha glares at me before saying, "I do much more than divine and foretell. Seemed insincere to keep calling myself a seer."

"You're younger than I expected," Byers says. She releases Tasha's hostage hand to pick up a mug. I know better than to choke down the steeped seaweed that passes for tea around here.

Tasha blows steam off her own mug. "Usually, the dam is set to throttle time. But Mona complicated that."

Byers stands there, speechless. I step in to explain. "She controls the flow of time around the house," I say, trying to sound unimpressed. Tasha's ego doesn't need the stroking. "The dam's out back, by the lightning rod. Normally, time here passes slower than the mortal realm, but since I showed up, she's made it the opposite. How long have I been gone from the castle?"

Byers is caught off guard, like she didn't expect her participation so soon. "You— you disappeared yesterday."

"Well, there you go. From my perspective, I've been with Tasha for a week." If I'm being honest, it feels more like an eternity. But I hold my tongue.

"I see," Byers says. "Why did she change the time for you?"

Tasha snorts. "Because I may yet convince her to leave my damn house, if she has a life to go back to."

"I *am* going to leave your house," I snipe. "As soon as you tell me how to live in the Flood, I'll go build my own house. I'll even put it *way* across the lowlands from—"

"Your magic won't ever be strong enough," Tasha says, almost taunting, punctuating it with a breezy shrug.

"Isn't that why you're training me? To strengthen my magic?"

"And if you were a decent student, I'd have higher hopes. Gods below, I'd settle for mediocrity."

"Arnett," Byers snaps, shutting down our quarrel. "Stop this. You need to come back."

I recline on the cushion, propping up my head and shooting her a sideways look. "Did Whitman send you?"

"Of course he sent me. But I would have come anyway. You can't just run off like this, there's too much at stake."

"I'd think between the royal magicians and the *literal gods*, you'd have it under control."

Byers looks on the verge of stamping her feet. "You know you have a bigger part to play in this!"

"I've played my part," I shoot back, hugging my stomach, ignoring the feeling of hot, molten shame in the back of my skull. "Whitman knows the truth. And he knows that Elsie Tanner ought to be queen. I have no intention of going back to the castle. I live here now."

"No, you don't," Tasha says under her breath.

Byers glances morosely between us. "What is your arrangement, exactly?"

While Tasha drinks her disgusting tea, I lay it out for Byers. Tasha D'Milliar does know how to survive in the Flood—how to protect herself against its effect on mortals. While we're on her homestead, we fall under that protection. And Tasha agreed to teach me how it's done. First, though, my magic has to be several degrees more powerful. Tasha can train me for that, too. Then I'll be free to live out my days in the Flood, far removed from any thrones or crowns. And also from my family, and from . . . other loved ones, too. But sometimes, sacrifices have to be made.

When I finish, Byers crosses her arms. "I'm not going anywhere without you. I've been ordered to return you to the castle."

"I'd expect nothing less from that man," I mutter. I flop farther back on the cushion, arching my spine so I don't have to look at her anymore. "I'm not leaving, Byers."

With a loud clink, she slams her mug on the counter. "Then I'm staying here until you change your mind."

"Are you, now?" Tasha laughs in derision. "Am I running a shelter for wayward seers?"

Byers seals her lips, chastised. "With your permission, ma'am," she adds.

"If you're here to get Mona out of my hair, you're welcome to stay."

I huff—though in truth, it pleases me. Now I'll have company, someone else to suffer through Tasha's nastiness with me.

Clearing her throat, Byers says, "If you don't mind me asking, Ms.—er, Tasha—if you don't want Arnett here, why did you agree to teach her?"

"I consider it my duty, given what I know."

I sink deeper into the cushion. Here we go with this, again.

"And why is it your duty?" Byers asks.

"Because there's something not right about that girl," Tasha says, tipping her head toward me. I cross my arms and sulk harder. "There's something *off*. I can't put words to it yet, but I can sense it. Mona will doom us all."

Byers looks stricken, avoiding my gaze. I'm not too worked up about it. I've heard it before. Tasha already told me her impressions of my star-crossed destiny, the blurry aura of doom that crowns me like a halo. Real uplifting. Perhaps she's right: If I return to the castle, I might destroy Isaac's bloodline, singlehandedly wiping magic from the world. But we don't need to worry about that scenario. I'm never going back.

How much harm can I do tucked away in the Flood?

214

"Use some elbow grease, Byers," I call over, wiping hair from my sweat-slick forehead.

Byers' lip curls as she scrubs the granite countertop, stained and scored from decades of alchemical experiments. "Focus on your own work."

I shrug and return to ferrying barrels of spellsap into storage. Byers has been cross since her arrival two weeks ago. She claims she came for me, but I'm not fooled. She's burning to learn what Tasha can teach her, too: the secrets of the Flood, how to strengthen her own magic. She just didn't expect our education to involve so much manual labor. Already today, a muscle knot has formed between my shoulder blades.

Despite her brusque answer, Byers speaks up again. "Why make us do the cleaning and cooking?" she says, tossing her wet rag on the counter with a squelch. "She has her spellsap servants. Isn't that their job?"

"Ah, well, Tasha's golems have one major design flaw. They can't feel humiliation."

Byers grumbles and takes up her scrubbing again. If nothing else, chores serve as a break from our taskmaster. And they provide a distraction from other matters, things that might preoccupy our thoughts if we had more free time.

Gritting my teeth, I give the dolly a mighty push and go back to work.

If Byers and I weren't so resentful of our chores, we might marvel at the splendor of Tasha's alchemy lab. Shelves display thousands of ingredients in jars and bottles and vials, boasting colors I've never seen before. Glass tubes and distilling chambers run along the east side of the room and connect through pipes in the walls. There are also two shallow trenches in the floor, lined with copper and smudged with black marks. I suspect Tasha crafts her spellsap golems there.

I've just loaded another barrel onto the wheeled wooden platform when Tasha's distant voice shatters our reprieve.

"Both of you!" she yells. "Get in here!"

Byers and I exchange a look. In the two weeks since Byers arrived, Tasha has never summoned us both at once. Tasha's teachings work better individually—if they work at all.

So far, my education has involved studying histories and memoirs by magicians of no particular note who had nothing interesting to say—except, of course, the ones that spouted deranged theories on demon summoning and human resurrection, likely written in a haze during a night of binge drinking—or sitting in silence with my eyes closed. I never had a formal magical education, but Byers must have gone through the whole guild hall experience—dozens of teenaged magicians, already tired from a day of secular lessons, crammed into one small room as they memorized the Angline standard runes, their childish dreams of power and glamour washed away by the instructor's droning voice. Boring, but effective. Tasha has her own methods, a lesson plan the Guild of Magicians would never sign off on. But if it works, I'll be the first to sing her praises.

We find her in the library tower. Built-in shelves of books line its curved walls up to the ceiling, and rippling Flood light filters through a stained-glass dome above. Tasha waits in an alcove, sitting at a pockmarked table. Her expression is inscrutable. She gestures for us to take a seat.

"Now we come to the cooperative part of your training," she begins. "I want each of you to summarize to the other what you've learned from your readings."

"I'll start," I volunteer, turning to Byers. "Nothing. I've learned nothing."

Tasha waits, but when it's clear I'm done talking, she nods and looks to Byers. "And you, Bernadette?"

I blink in surprise. Where's the scathing reprimand? Or did I give the right answer? Does Tasha *want* me to learn nothing?

Byers, on the other hand, measures her response with care. "I've been reading a philosophical treatise by Emhad," she says to me, but her gaze flicks toward Tasha. "It's on the relationship between faith and worship. I've found it . . . enlightening."

"Give us one tenet from Emhad's philosophy, then," Tasha says.

Byers glances up. "Faith is perfect trust, and it can never be earned, only bestowed."

"Excellent," Tasha replies. It's the first bit of praise I've heard her utter. "You're both progressing as expected. It's time to move on to the next stage of your education."

As I ponder how my nonanswer could be considered progress, Byers asks, "What will that be, ma'am?"

"More reading."

The knot between my shoulder blades tightens. "I don't suppose you might consider teaching us something one day?"

"Oh?" Tasha says, amused. "Like what?"

"What about all those killers you caught back in Selledore? Teach us how to do that." It's what lured us to Tasha in the first place—her knack for finding wrongdoers, a better way to track down my cultist. Not that that's my problem anymore.

"Good old-fashioned detective work," Tasha says, a touch of sarcasm pulling at the corner of her mouth.

"There was a poisoner not long before you disappeared," Byers speaks up. "A suspected member of the Guild. You identified them when no one else could."

"You must be talking about the Northup case." She crosses her arms and sighs, resigning herself to humoring us. "An interesting one. The culprit was a seer who knew how to plant false readings. It stumped the other magicians so badly, I thought they would all resign in disgrace. But once I sorted out which readings were real and which were falsified, it was a simple matter."

"False readings?" I say with disbelief. "You can do that?"

"Sure. It's not possible to block or erase a reading entirely, but you can create a false one to mask the truth. Not very practical, though. It takes a lot of preparation to create a false reading, and if multiple seers repeat it, the discrepancy is obvious."

"Obvious how?"

"The fake reading will be identical every time. None of the natural variations of organic readings, the imperfections."

"So, teach us that," I say. Tasha sniffs in reply, and a bitter suspicion grows in my chest. "Or do you think we're too stupid to learn?" I ask with vitriol that surprises even me. "Is that it? Am I a joke to you? Why bother trying, right?"

When Tasha responds, she sounds entertained. "Get ahold of yourself, Mona. And get studying." With that, she stalks out of the library. I cross my arms and glare at the rows of gilded book spines.

Byers watches me with careful eyes, avoiding sudden movements. "Are you all right?"

"Fine." I grind my knuckles into the grain of the table, thinking of my name on Whitman's list of frauds, circled in fat, bold ink. What an actor he turned out to be. How convincing he made himself—the way he came to me on his knees, eager for my help, begging for assistance. Knowing all the while that my only skill is ruining things. And I believed him, *thanked* him for believing in me. He must have busted a rib to keep himself from laughing.

"You're not a joke," Byers says. I flatten my lips, looking away. "Obviously, you're not."

I almost keep my mouth shut. I shouldn't admit this, especially to perfect Bernadette Byers. "Whitman thinks I am."

"He does not." Self-consciously, she adds, "He told me what he said to you before you left."

My stomach does a swan dive. So much for confidentiality. "Then you've heard I'm a murder suspect, too."

"He knows you haven't done anything wrong," she says staunchly. "He wants you to come back and clear your name."

"My *name*?" I scoff. My name was sullied long before I came to the castle.

"You can pretend you don't care what people think, but I know that's not the truth."

I fold my arms across my chest, glowering. I *want* to not care. But after all that's happened—the feelings I've confronted about myself and those around me—it's pathetically true: I'd love to prove I'm not as bad as everyone thinks. The problem is, I am. I may not have murdered Parsons, but I did kill my brother. And while I'm no fraud, I am a liar and a coward, and I have no defense for that. Perhaps my real fear isn't that I'll be wrongly accused.

I'm afraid that I'll plead guilty.

28

Seaweed ranks among the most nutritious foods in the world—especially when you have a crew of golems fertilizing your kelp fields with magic. Consumed in large enough quantities, it can provide all the vitamins a body needs.

It is also among the easiest foods to get sick of.

After fifty-two days straight, I'm considering a hunger strike. All of this to say, as I sneer down at my bowl of green mush that evening, I feel justified in declaring, "One of you needs to go get us some real food, or I'm resorting to cannibalism."

They both lower their bowls. Tasha, stuffed into the corner of the parlor, says, "Why don't you get it yourself?"

"You know I can't go outside." Though I haven't told her about my condition, the sorceress is prone to regurgitating facts about my life I never mentioned. I doubt any aspect of me is beyond her ken.

"If I call up a window," Byers says, "it'll dump me out in conference chambers."

There's a taut silence. We have no idea what might transpire if Byers returns to the castle. How long have we been missing? What do they think happened to us? Tasha promised to keep us apprised of any major changes in Opalvale, for even Byers' magic isn't strong enough to peer into the mortal realm from the Flood, but Tasha can't—or won't—do any readings of a more personal nature. It's like she wants us kept in the dark.

"I could visit the mortal realm," Tasha interjects. "But I like this food just fine."

Balancing the bowl in my lap, I ask, "You don't miss real food at all? Or *wine?*" I add longingly.

"It's not that bad," Byers chides me. I glare at her. She may not complain about the food, but I've heard her pining more than once for the Rynthian salon in Selledore where she gets her hair braided and styled. We're both struggling to cope this far from civilization. Though I suppose I should be grateful I can just tie up my frizzing curls with a sash and call it a day.

Tasha gives us a small smile. "How about this: I'll make you a wager. If the both of you can work out why you've been studying what you're studying, I'll go out and bring back real food. And wine."

I sit straighter. "How long do we have to solve it?"

"Take the rest of your lives, for all I care. You'll never get it. Not with eighty percent of a brain between you."

With a sniff, I lean toward Byers to mutter, "At least we've got a heart apiece, which is more than I can say for some—"

"You, by the way," Tasha snaps, pointing at me, "don't add toward that percentage. Bernadette has a functioning brain by herself, but I had to adjust for your deadweight. Please, though, feel free to prove me wrong."

"Oh, I will," I say, crossing my ankles and hoping she doesn't notice my cheeks burning with ire. "You're making a classic mistake. Underestimating my intelligence because I'm beautiful." I flip my golden curls over my shoulder. That earns me groans from the both of them.

After dinner, Byers and I convene in the library. We take down the books we've been assigned, poring over them one by one. Byers has been studying philosophy—something called the affective component of faith. As for me, I continue to read from memoirs of dead magicians. And while this round of authors remains just as deceased, the new ones are at least less irrelevant. In spite of myself, I suspect I'm learning something. Hopefully Tasha won't be disappointed.

"I don't get it," Byers says, scanning the title of a thick leather volume. "You get to study magic, and I'm stuck pondering the nature of existence?"

I sigh. "Maybe it's not about the subjects themselves. Maybe there's a common theme, something to do with the authors or the time periods—"

"A puzzle!" Byers flares to life. "And we need both of our books to solve it! Must be some lesson on working together."

"Ugh." I mimic being sick, and Byers snickers. "If that's it, let's hurry up and get this over with."

We dump the books on the table and begin sorting. Alphabetically by author, then by title; in order of date written; by subject, loosely. No pattern emerges. Soon, we're pulling other books off the shelves, researching the authors' lives—where they were born, who reigned while they were alive, how they died. Somehow, I end up halfway through a children's book of demon parables before I remember why we're here.

I don't notice how late we've worked until Byers takes out her pocket watch and says, "Gods below, it's morning."

"Does it matter in the Flood?" I say, yawning.

"You're right," she mutters as she picks up another book. "It's not like I was going to sleep anyway."

"Nightmares again?"

She holds the book closer to her face. "Mm-hmm."

"What about?"

Byers keeps reading, pretending not to hear me. I exhale and survey the stack for my next boring read.

"Last night it was about my parents," Byers says without looking up from her book. I still myself and listen. "We're traveling to see my great-grandmother at her lake house in Rynth. It's way out in the savanna, far from the city—this miniature blue ocean with nothing but grass and baobabs in all directions. Beautiful. I wish you could see it." She sighs. "Then, in the middle of the carriage ride, my parents tell me they have a surprise for me but they can't say what. So I pester them to give it up, but they won't, and I'm starting to get angry. That's when I notice the carriage is driving right past the lake house, toward the water. And we go into the lake."

I frown. "Sounds awful."

"Yup. So, should we read through each other's assignments?" Byers suggests, staring at our teetering mountain of books.

I suppose that's the end of dream talk. "I'd rather eat seaweed the rest of my life," I grumble. "We've got to be missing something."

Byers is silent, turning the problem over in her head. "Well, she broke up our studies into two parts, didn't she? She said we were entering a new stage, or something like that. What's different about your new readings?"

I shrug. "They're of a higher caliber. But I assume she's making our studies harder as we progress."

"Can you show me?"

For the next half hour, I dig through the pile and pluck out books for Byers to compare. She pores over them with focus, arranging them side by side, top to bottom, swiveling back and forth between volumes. After a while, she lifts her head, frowning. "There are a lot of mistakes in here."

I peer up at her without taking my chin off my folded arms. "I told you, she had me reading all sorts of kooks."

"This one's written by a royal magician."

"What? Give me that." I snatch the book from her and scan the page. "This isn't right?"

"Half those runic combinations cancel each other out, when read in parallel. On paper, it looks nice, but in practice it's useless."

I study the strings of runes with turmoil bubbling in my stomach. "Are all the books like this?"

Byers picks samples from the pile at random, looking for mistakes. I worry my lip as she tosses them aside one by one. When she turns back to me, her eyes crinkle in a strange look. "When Tasha asked what you'd learned so far, you said nothing. Why?"

She catches me off guard. "Tasha assigned me a lot of garbage."

"I found fewer errors in that first round of books than in these," she says, prodding a history by a notable alchemist.

"Bullshit. She had me reading about blood magic, resurrecting people from the dead—"

"Those things aren't impossible. The theory is sound. I doubt human resurrection's ever been attempted successfully, but that doesn't make it bullshit."

I blink at the stack of books, trying to make sense of it.

"Arnett," she says, her voice carrying laughter, "she's trying to teach you to stop believing everything you're told."

I open my mouth, groping for a retort. "I don't do that."

"Yes, you do—if someone with authority tells you it's true. When the gods told you not to stay too long in the Flood, you just did it, no questions asked."

"I'm in the Flood now, aren't I?" I counter, but I sound petulant even to myself.

"Because of me." Byers wears a superior smirk I wish I could smack off her face. "You trusted the sources with authority and discounted everything else. You ought to have focused on whether it made sense, not who wrote it."

"A lot of those books were by royal magicians! How should I have known—"

"*You* were almost a royal magician."

That stings, but she has a point. Flustered and sore, I dig through the pile of books. "Then let's see what she's trying to say about you, shall we?"

For Byers, Tasha assigned a smaller number of books, but each is thicker, more obtuse. They all relate to the philosophy of faith.

"Maybe she's telling you to trust the gods," I say under my breath.

"Not Tasha," Byers says, her nose stuck in a book. "She must have had some falling-out with them, to end up in her situation." Her head pops up over the cover. "She's never mentioned anything about it to you, has she?"

"No, and I'm too scared to ask." I hold a book in each hand, squinting at the titles. "So, what changed for you? How are these books different?"

She chews on her lip as she reads. "Lately, most of what she's given me has to do with faith and knowledge. But if she's trying to make a point, it's going over my head. Listen." Byers holds up a crusty, ancient volume. "'Faith is a venture, an action that places outcomes beyond an agent's control. Only perfect knowledge could nullify the risks, and no such ideal exists.'" She shuts the book with a loud clap. "But that's not true, not for us. Tasha and I *can* achieve perfect knowledge."

"Not always." I shift in my seat, teetering on the precipice of an idea. "You can't use your truth-telling on the gods." My spine straightens. "Tasha's saying your powers have ruined you! You're incapable of trusting anyone without the benefit of your magic."

"Because trust is flawed," she says without missing a beat. "Even smart people can put their trust in the wrong places."

"Like your parents?" I say. She glares at me but listens. "They were professors, weren't they? And they still believed the Guild's lies. They trusted wrongly. No wonder you don't want to rely on your own instincts."

Byers sets her jaw. "I have my magic. I don't need instincts."

"Maybe you do, though. Tasha's telling you to have faith in something without knowing whether you're right."

She fumbles for words. I take some satisfaction in that. "Easier said than done," she murmurs.

Byers insists on another hour of checking our answers. Her hands tremble when she sets down the last book in the pile, sighing with finality.

"Are we sure we're right?" she says.

"We'd better be." I can't bear the sneer on Tasha's face if we aren't.

We find Tasha in her lab, elbow-deep in a tank of something foul and oily. Impassively, she listens as we recount our theories. When we finish, she removes her hands from the gunk tank and stares at us for a long moment.

"Do you just *understand* the lessons," she says, her forearms dripping goo on the counter, "or do you *believe* them?"

Both of us mumble that we believe.

"And you will remember them, when the time comes?"

I nod, but Byers asks, "How will we know? What are you training us for?"

Tasha wipes her arms with a filthy rag. "I can't say for certain. The future is a bitch to predict. But I'll tell you this—I feel better about the state of the world now that you two have a little self-awareness." She throws the rag on the counter. "Well, ladies—what are we having for dinner?"

Tasha returns by early evening, arms laden with the most divine-smelling food I've ever encountered, like something from a starving man's dream. Three bottles of Deveneauxan wine as well. She spreads a wool blanket on the parlor floor and lays out our feast. Two roast ducks, dripping with spiced honey, wheels of fragrant cheese, pickled peppers stuffed with rice and ground goat, and loaves of crusty bread—still warm, somehow.

"Where did you get all this?" Byers asks, eyes round as she takes in the spread.

Tasha tosses her a big, firm persimmon. "There's an all-seasons market just outside of the village proper."

"But *how* did you get it?" I say as I pile steamed mussels into my bowl. "Do you have any coin, anything to barter?"

"I don't need money to get what I want," Tasha says with a snort. Byers takes a second look at the food, her mouth tight with disapproval.

We eat in appreciative silence. The wine, dark and sweet, goes straight to my head. I giggle as Byers struggles to scrape a mussel out of its shell with her finger.

"Stop mutilating it," I laugh, crawling over to her. "Use this thing." I show her the hooked sticks Tasha brought back, the kind street vendors hand out with steamed shellfish.

"How do you not know how to eat a mussel?" I ask her as she experiments with the hook, probing inside the shell. "Haven't you lived in Selledore, like, your whole life?"

"Not a lot of seafood served at the boarding school," she says, biting her tongue in concentration. "Headmistress called it 'vermin of the sea.'" With a triumphant grunt, she separates the tender flesh from its casing.

Byers doesn't often talk about boarding school. I don't want to pry, but at this point, we know each other's deepest secrets anyway. "Why did you go to boarding school? Was it after your parents died?"

She twists the stem off a persimmon. "Sort of. Before the, you know . . ." She trails off, but I read between the lines: the mass suicide of the Rising Tide cult her parents belonged to. "I was living with my aunt by then. She rescued me when my mother stopped answering her letters. Thank the seven she did, or I'd be dead now, too. My aunt was the one who enrolled me in boarding school."

I hesitate, pouring myself more wine. When my cup is brimming, I ask, too casually, "So, when did you first go into the Flood?"

Byers lowers the fruit from her mouth. "When I found out my parents were dead. I saw a window in my room, right after my aunt told me."

I nod, eyes burning from too many spicy peppers. "I saw mine right after my brother died." Memories of Patrick rush back to me—how he looked splayed out at the bottom of the cliff, swimming in his own blood.

Wordlessly, we turn to Tasha—too afraid to ask, hoping she'll volunteer anyway. She sets her plate aside, a peculiar look on her face. "I hurt someone. I didn't mean to, but that doesn't change anything."

She doesn't elaborate, and we don't press her.

I open the last of the wine and drink straight from the bottle. As we eat, Tasha's golems lumber through the room, collecting scraps for the compost. We're all full and sleepy when my mouth gets the better of me again.

"So, what happened between you and Korimarr?" I ask Tasha. A pleasant, deceptive warmth creeps across my face. Beneath the haze of alcohol, I know I've asked a dangerous question.

Byers freezes mid-bite. Tasha holds my gaze, unreadable. My skin prickles as I start to wish I hadn't asked.

"Nothing happened," she replies. "It was a slow drift apart over time. I came to realize she would never think of me as an equal."

"But she's a *goddess*," I blurt, then curse myself. I hold my breath, watching Tasha for signs of impending fury.

But she doesn't berate me. She raises her brows and says, "Is that how we should decide who deserves respect and fair treatment? Whoever holds the most power?"

"And the seven just left you alone after that?" Byers says. "They never tried to stop you from living in the Flood?"

"How are they going to stop me? Kill me?"

Would they kill her? The idea chills me. But if the seven meant to harm Tasha, they would have done it by now. An uncomfortable silence pervades the room as we let the question hang in the air.

Tasha sniffs. "The seven would never kill me, or you. They love their favored mortals. I reckon Korimarr loves me to this day. But we're pets to them. Nothing more."

"Did you get to keep your magic?" I ask. "Your truth-telling?"

Tasha's mouth quirks up at the corner. "Oh, yes, I got to keep it. They can't take away what's been taught. But I have different magic than Bernadette. Mine is . . . a prototype of her power."

Byers perks up. "What is it?"

"Let's put it this way. You can tell what is true," Tasha says, nodding to Byers. Her grin widens. "I can tell what's *right*."

"What's the difference?" I ask.

"I think a demonstration is in order. Mona, I am going to ask you a question. You give your honest answer. Bernadette, you confirm that she's telling the truth."

Byers nods her understanding. My shoulders tense in anticipation.

"Mona," Tasha says, "would you let innocents die to keep yourself off the throne?"

The air is suddenly oppressive, like a pile of woolen blankets, heavy on my lungs. Would I let people die so I didn't have to be queen? I chew my lip in thought. I can't envision any situation where I would willingly take the throne, no matter how many lives were at stake. And I already let Parsons die to cover my ass, didn't I? That alone speaks volumes. I stare at the floor, my eyes gritty. No point in lying.

"Yes," I mumble, unable to look at them. My whole head, from scalp to neck, blazes with shame. "Doesn't my happiness matter? Why should I sacrifice myself?"

There's a pause—too long, an eternity of judgment. Byers says, "She's telling the truth." The disappointment in her voice feels like a punch to the stomach.

Tasha hums. "She may be telling the truth, but she's not right."

I look up. "What does that mean?"

"People often say things they believe are true, but that doesn't make them correct. Sometimes they have the wrong information. Or they might think they know someone, but they've made an error in judgment. Happens to the best of us."

Her eyes stick to me, and I can't look away, though I want to. I want to bury my head in my arms and weep.

"You're wrong about yourself, Mona," she says, smiling. "You are stronger than you believe. And when the time comes, you will make yourself proud."

29

I wake with a brutal wine headache. Tasha and Byers are up and eating breakfast by the time I've washed and dressed and applied the alchemical salve Tasha gave me for my finger, which has been doing wonders—the skin is healing well over the stump. I grab two persimmons in one hand and a leftover stuffed pepper in the other and throw myself down on a cushion.

I'm devouring the last of the fruit when Tasha says, "You're ready now. The both of you."

I pause, my juice-sticky thumb halfway to my mouth. "What?"

"I'm going to tell you how to survive in the Flood."

Byers sets her mug on the floor, eyes wide. "I thought you said we were too weak?"

"You aren't anymore."

"But all we've done is read books!" I protest.

A twisted smile seizes Tasha's mouth. "You want proof? Try it out. Divine something at the castle."

My heart hammers. "I can't. I need a focus."

"Try it."

What else can I do? I have to give my best effort, if only to prove her wrong. I close my eyes.

How do I begin?

I don't want to know anything about the castle. Instead, I think of my family. I ask the first question that comes to mind.

Do my parents know I'm missing?

Nothing happens, and my shoulders slump. What did I expect? My magic will never be more than it is now—a parlor trick, compared to Byers' and Tasha's.

But as I wallow, something changes. A colorless string materializes in my mind. It tugs on my consciousness, leading me somewhere. I grasp on to it. It pulls me through the black like a gentle current, nothingness billowing around me. This feels different from my other readings somehow. Before, the knowledge poked above the surface of some deeper well of truth, like a seal breaking through waves, sticking its whiskers in the air. Now I'm diving into truth itself.

Answers snag onto me as I swim downward. My parents don't know about my disappearance; someone's keeping it under wraps. But they miss me all the same. They wonder if I'll ever visit again, or if they'll have to haul their aching bones to the castle. They hope I'm happier now.

I open my eyes with a gasp.

Byers pants beside me, a hand pressed to her chest. She whispers, "How?"

"Your training has been a success," Tasha says with a grin. As we gape at her, she adds, "Would you like to know how the Flood harms mortals?"

We nod.

"It doesn't," she says. "It doesn't hurt us at all. It makes us more powerful."

I hear a strange buzzing in my ears, and nothing else.

"That can't be right." I push the words past a knot in my throat. "The protections around your house—"

"There are no protections. I made that up. You've had two months of exposure to the Flood's raw magic, and you're fine. Better than fine."

I shake my head in disbelief. "But . . . Why?"

Tasha doesn't need me to elaborate. "Because we are their pets, not their equals. And the more powerful we are, the harder it is to keep us in line."

Byers recovers quicker than me. "How did you learn all this?" she says, her voice small and vibrating with wonder.

"When I came here and started this homestead, the answers fell into place. I didn't plan on sharing what I'd learned. I didn't expect to be found." She shoots Byers an odd look, like she would be proud if she wasn't so irritated. "But there's no doubt about it. The Flood is perfectly safe. I'm living proof."

Speechless, I fix my gaze on a point in the distance. All these years, I could have lived in the Flood. Nothing stood in my way but Irinorr's lies. Whenever I felt scared, or hurt, or ashamed, I could have retreated into these waters without consequences. I could have stayed for good. The gods withheld the only thing I ever wanted.

And for what—to stop me from achieving a fraction of their power? What difference does it make to them?

With an intake of breath, Byers sits straighter. "The killer at the castle—could we hunt them down now?"

"The gods couldn't do it," I point out glumly, though I find it hard to care about my cultist right now.

"They said themselves their magic is weakened."

"It doesn't hurt to try," Tasha says.

Trying's hurt me plenty in the past, but Byers and Tasha are set on this. I shrug in defeat.

We close our eyes and attempt the reading. I picture all those threatening notes, stacked up on my dresser. Parsons' body swaying. The shards of brilliant, sparkly crystal covering my bed. Again, there's a whiff of guilt and dread. Nothing more than I've gathered before. Sadly vindicated, I crack my neck and open my eyes.

Byers' eyes are open, too, and directed at me. "Well?"

"Nothing," I sigh. "Same for you?"

"Same," she begins slowly. I have a feeling I won't like what I'm about to hear. "We could always go back to the castle and try again."

Ah, there it is. "Come, now, be serious—"

"I am serious! You have such a connection to this case, Arnett. Much closer than mine. If you went back and performed readings on the notes, the crime scenes—who knows what information you could uncover? You could catch Parsons' killer and clear your name."

Sweat beads along the nape of my neck, and I'm engulfed by a sudden, inexplicable sense of panic, like Byers might send me back with the power of her words alone. "Let me get this straight. You want me to go to a place where I'm the top suspect in a murder that was actually committed by a lunatic who wants to destroy me?" I turn to Tasha, throwing my hands up. "Does exposure to the Flood cause brain damage, too?"

"You're impossible," Byers spits. She storms off to the library tower.

Tasha sits behind the kitchenette's island and sips her tea, impervious to our bickering. I plop back on the cushion and groan. Things were going so well for a while. We had our routines; everyone was happy. Why did Byers have to ruin it by bringing up the castle?

"So, I take it you're not leaving," Tasha says. She sets down her tea with a clink.

"No," I grumble. "I'm not."

"I thought you were here to make your magic stronger? Haven't you accomplished that?"

I roll my eyes. She's twisting my words. "I wanted my magic to be stronger so I could stay in the Flood, remember?"

"Right." She strokes her jawline, her pale skin ethereal in the spellsap light reflecting off the slick wood-paneled walls. "You want to stay in the Flood. Forever. No friends, no parties, no food, no wine. No sex. Not a single customer to impress with your readings. Complete isolation, a total break from the material world. It couldn't be *fear* that drove you here. No, this must be your deepest desire."

My cheeks burn, skin itching with an uncomfortable sensation of nakedness. "You ran away to the Flood, too. Don't be a hypocrite."

Tasha is quiet, as if she's considering. Then she stands up and walks over, crouching next to me with her hands braced on her knees. She stays like that until I straighten my back and look at her face. She's staring at me in that way I loathe—penetrating, familiar, patient.

"I came to the Flood because I wanted to be here," she says plainly. "I want this life. If you can look me in the eye and tell me you want the same—you *really* want it, with all your heart—I won't say another word."

I lace my fingers in my lap and stare at them. Have I ever asked myself what I really want? Mostly, I want to avoid what scares me. I know how to run away, not toward. But Tasha is right—I can't live this austere monk lifestyle of hers.

Where does that leave me?

Tasha snaps her fingers in front of me. My head pops up.

"It's time, Mona. Give yourself permission to live." She peers deep into my eyes. "It's what Patrick would have wanted."

Tears well up until my lashes are wet and my vision blurs. I don't remember telling her Patrick's name, but of course Tasha knows. That doesn't mean she's convinced me to abandon my doubts and charge back to the castle.

"What if I can't do it?" I whisper, voice small with shame.

"Then I'll be wrong, which I have never been before," she says. I snort with laughter, wiping my tearstained cheek. She probably hasn't.

I hope I don't ruin her streak.

We don't have much to pack, nor travel preparations to make. Both Byers and I can call up a window straight to the castle. There's nothing slowing us down. Nevertheless, I spend the morning staring out Tasha's front door at the landscape of the Flood, the beaded curtains floating around me like tentacles.

"Arnett," Byers says from behind me. Her head pokes out around the corner.

"Can't you see I'm busy?" I say. I turn back to the Flood.

"You need to pack."

I pinch my lips together. "I have about three belongings. I'm as ready as I'll ever be."

"Good. Because I can't do this by myself, you know," Byers mumbles. I look at her again. She examines the grain of the wall, running her fingers over it. I duck my head, concealing a grin. Byers actually wants me around?

"All right," I sigh. "But if I get arrested or murdered or executed or whatever else, it's your fault."

Byers glowers at me. "Just go pack, Arnett."

Reluctantly, I go check my knapsack for my meager belongings. When I enter the parlor, bag over my shoulder, Byers stands alone with her stuffed pack clutched before her. Her eyes are wet.

"There's a note on the counter," she says haltingly.

Brow furrowed, I go to investigate. On the island lies a piece of paper, a few lines scribbled near the top.

> I've gone out. Don't wait up for me. Heed what I've taught you—if you haven't forgotten already, Mona.
> I'm proud of the both of you. Please don't ever come here again, even if you need something. Especially if you need something.
>
> Tasha

I snort as I finish, blinking my eyes dry before facing Byers. "Too much of a coward to say goodbye," I mutter. "Good riddance. Let's get out of here."

Byers nods, sniffling. With a quavering hand, she reaches out and conjures a window. My stomach lurches. Our doorway back to Opalvale, back to the life I tried to leave behind forever. Byers gulps a big breath and steps through.

One last time, I glance around Tasha's parlor. I almost expect her to appear in the doorway, smirking. She doesn't.

I squeeze my eyes shut and pass through the window.

Even with my eyes closed, I can tell it's dark. I blink them open. We're in the magicians' conference chambers, its spellsap lamps dimmed. The grandfather clock in the corner tells me it's early morning, just before sunrise.

"What now?" I whisper, though no one's around to overhear. I didn't think this far ahead. No one knows where we've been, and we're clueless about what's happening here. Whitman's quarters would be a good first stop—if I wasn't still furious with him.

"Actually," Byers says, and clears her throat, "I was thinking I would go see Elizabeta."

That's right—she never told her lady friend how long she'd be gone. "Oh, you'd better."

Byers grunts. "You go back to your apartments. I'll meet you there, and we can decide what to do next."

Byers takes off. I jog in the opposite direction, down the practitioners' wing to my quarters. I slip inside, closing the door behind me and slumping against it. I gaze around as I catch my breath. Everything's as I left it, even the silk slipper I dropped on the floor in my haste to get out of here.

I never expected to see this place again. Was coming back the right choice? I suppose I won't know until we catch the killer—or not. Gingerly, I pad across the carpet, like it's an illusion that might shatter if my steps are too heavy. I sit on the chaise longue and relax against its upholstered backrest. Then I close my eyes and wait.

A frantic knocking opens my eyes again. "It's unlocked," I call, expecting Byers. But Elizabeta walks in alone.

"Ms. Arnett," she says with a tearful smile, hand over her heart. "You're all right. I was so worried about both of you."

I flush, embarrassed at this brazen show of affection. "I take it you've spoken to Byers?"

"Yes, she'll be up shortly. She's changing into a clean dress. You know how Bebe is about her dresses."

Bebe? I hold in a snicker. Oh, Byers is never going to live that down. As I fight to control myself, an idea strikes me. "I know you're here as a friend," I say, "but would you be opposed to a bit of business?"

"Not at all. What do you need?"

I cross my legs. "Can you please call on Master Whitman and ask him to join me at his earliest convenience?"

"Oh!" Her eyes widen. "Does he know you've returned?"

"He will soon," I say with a half grin.

As Elizabeta fetches Whitman, I pour myself a whiskey from the decanter on my vanity—a sorely missed luxury. The freshly risen sun filters through my curtains and casts a subtle glow over the room. I get comfortable, sprawl my legs out on the chaise longue. Swirl the whiskey in my glass. Strange, how it almost feels like coming home.

Right on cue, Whitman crashes through the door and breaks my reprieve. He's out of breath, wild-eyed. My heart leaps into the back of my throat.

"Gods below, Whitman," I say, mock scandalized, raising my whiskey like a shield. "Don't you knock before entering a lady's room?"

He stares at me like I might be a hallucination, or a ghost. I'm tempted to feel bad about vanishing on him. Yes, he deserved it. But seeing him here—when I was so sure I'd never see him again—rattles something loose in me, a geyser of messy feelings. I sit straighter and put the whiskey down.

"Well?" I prompt him with a wave. "Do you have something to say?"

"You're alive," he replies in a gravelly voice.

A lump rises in my throat. "Of course I'm alive. How long have we been gone?"

"Two weeks. When Ms. Byers didn't come back . . ."

"We got busy." I look down at my fidgeting hands, fighting off guilt. I'm not quite angry enough to relish his misery.

"Busy?" Gradually, his tone shifts from dazed to incensed. "For *two weeks*? Do you realize what I've done to cover for you? You disappeared in the middle of a murder investigation! I had to invent a fake illness, a fake quarantine—I bribed a physician!"

I stare slack-jawed, lost for words. Whitman went to all that trouble? And after I was so cruel to him?

"I didn't ask you to do any of that," I spit, instead of saying *Thank you* like a well-adjusted person. I regret it immediately.

His face burns scarlet, like his head's about to explode. "Why did you even come back?"

"To clear my name," I say, in Byers' words. I cross my arms with dignity. "I'm going to prove I didn't kill anyone. Byers and I have stronger magic now. We can find my cultist and put them away."

"What?" Whitman appears to shrink in on himself, completely overwhelmed. "How do you plan to accomplish that?"

Sympathy creeps up on me. I stand and take a step toward Whitman, holding up a hand in truce. "I'll figure it out as I go. I . . . I'm sorry, Whitman." I step closer again. "When you told me I was a suspect, I panicked. I didn't know what to do."

"You shouldn't have run away." Tentatively, he reaches out and strokes my arm. I hardly think he knows what he's doing. I wish I could lean in and hold him, but that would break the spell.

Byers chooses this moment to waltz into the room. Whitman backs off, turning around.

Byers looks between us. "I see Arnett has brought you up to speed."

"Welcome back," Whitman says, heavy with sarcasm. "I understand you intend to catch a murderer."

"Not me." She sends a pointed look in my direction.

I rub my forearms as they prickle with goose bumps. Somehow, this feels too fast. I need more time to prepare. But there's nothing stopping me, truly. Inhaling, I step over to the dresser where my cultist's threats are stacked. I pull the top note—the most recent, the one I've had the most luck with. I pinch the corner of the paper, massaging it between my fingers. My stomach lurches with nerves. What if it's no different this time?

Ignoring my doubts, I forge ahead with the reading. Darkness rushes over me in rippling waves. I feel it at once—that sinking dread I've become so familiar with. Nothing new there. I apply pressure until I break through to something deeper, more private. It comes with visions: blurry images of towering black obelisks, shuddering with wrath. A sense of bone-chilling fear bowls me over. I'm guilty, but I'm scared, too. Scared of what awaits me when my day of judgment comes.

I blink my eyes open slowly, like my lashes are gummy with molasses. I frown at the note in my hands. I can't be positive, but I think I know what I saw.

"They're guilty," I say, processing it aloud. "They're afraid of . . . divine retribution. Maybe because the gods are here at the castle?" I tilt my head, puzzling it out. "But it's not the gods they're focused on. It's the chapel. They pray there every night."

A few seconds pass. "That's it?" Byers asks, slightly disappointed.

I scowl at her. "I'd like to see you do better, Bebe."

Her forehead creases in a surly V. "I'm going to pretend I didn't hear that."

"Hear what, *Bebe*?"

"So, the chapel," Whitman interrupts. "The killer spends a lot of time there? Perhaps we should post guards for surveillance."

"It's a start," I say. I hope it'll be enough. I don't know if I can extract more information from the notes or crime scenes. I gaze up at Whitman self-consciously, clocking his mood. Is he pleased with my reading? Is he happy I'm back? I shouldn't care, after how he treated me. How he lied to me.

But when I catch his eye and he looks away too quickly, his throat bobbing, I find it hard to hold a grudge.

30

A pair of guards escorts me to council chambers. I find Isaac inside, sitting alone in his stately chair at the head of the table. He's slumped in his seat, staring at the glittering tower of the nexus in the center of the tabletop. His face is gaunt, cheekbones sharp and pointy, saddlebags dark under his eyes, but his expression is alert.

It took longer than expected for the king to demand an audience with me. Three days have passed, and I've been holed up in my rooms, bothered by no one. Did Whitman tell Isaac where we went for those two weeks, or what we've been doing since we got back? Not that my recent efforts have amounted to much. Further readings on the cultist haven't revealed anything new.

"Did you enjoy your vacation?" King Isaac says without taking his eyes off the nexus.

So, Whitman told him at least enough to confirm I haven't been laid out with a vicious head cold. "I'm feeling much restored, thank you." I sit beside him, in Whitman's chair. "You wanted to speak with me?"

"More like rescue you." He smirks drily. "The council wanted to interrogate you. I convinced them to let me intervene, conduct an interview one-on-one."

Fantastic. The council still has it in for me. I doubt they ever gave me a chance, even before the threats started. Perhaps Byers is right—I *do* want to clear my name. It's suffered enough abuse already.

I'm too scared to ask if the gods want a piece of me, too. They must have deduced where Byers and I disappeared to. We broke their cardinal rule. They must be furious—or worse, disappointed. But I haven't stopped being angry with them for lying about the Flood's effect on mortals. That tempers my fear somewhat.

"What does the council want from me?" I ask Isaac, leaning back with my hands clasped behind my head. The more casual I act, the less worried I feel. "To be regaled with the harrowing tale of my brush with the plague?"

His smirk widens. "Right. Your *illness* didn't help anything, but that's not the masters' main concern. There's a rumor you're investigating Parsons' death yourself?"

My stomach sours. "Did Master Renfield tell you that? Because it was her idea."

"Yes, she mentioned that. But I'm talking about the readings you performed. Delmar tried to pass off your chapel idea as a company lead, but that didn't fool anyone. The masters are apoplectic. Apparently, it's not standard procedure to let a suspect drive the investigation into the crime they're accused of committing."

I snort. It stings to hear confirmation of what Whitman said the night I left. At least King Isaac seems to trust in my innocence, or he wouldn't speak so freely.

"That's not all I wanted to talk about," Isaac says, suddenly nervous. He glances away. "Have you ever been wrong about a soulmate match?"

I wrinkle my nose. Where's this coming from? "No, I haven't. Why?"

He shakes his head absently, tracing a curlicue shape on the council table. "It's nothing. It's just . . . confusing. The situation we're in. When you left for the Flood, I was worried, of course—I wanted you to be safe—but I also . . ." He cringes at what he's about to say. "It was sort of a relief knowing my soulmate was out of the picture. So, if I married someone else, it wouldn't feel so wrong."

That hits me like a slap to the face. I never wanted to be Isaac's soulmate, but it stings to hear him half wish I would disappear forever. I force a grin, trying not to let my self-pity dapple through. "I'm sorry to disappoint, but you're stuck with me."

"You've got it backward. I like you, Mona, I really do. But I've known from the start you aren't interested in me. And . . . there might be someone else who is."

A whole lot of people are interested in marrying Isaac, but I know who he means. "Elsie Tanner?"

Isaac gives a stiff nod. "I'll have to choose a queen soon. The thing is . . . what if I choose wrong?" He eyes me with trepidation. "You're my soulmate. You heard what Semyanadd said about the nexus, how the mortal realm's in danger. How can I risk choosing anyone else?"

I recoil in horrified surprise. "Wh-what? You can't be serious. I—I can't be the queen. The council would never allow it."

"I know," he sighs, and my body floods with instant relief. "It's just my stupid brain going in circles. I don't want to mess this up."

"You won't." Awkwardly, I reach for his hand, but I lose my nerve and stop just short so our pinkies overlap. "It's going to be fine."

Isaac smiles gratefully. Fortunately for me, he doesn't have Byers' truth-telling magic.

The chamber doors clang open. Whitman steps inside, urgency written all over his face. He pauses at the sight of Isaac and me, our hands touching. We pull apart.

"Hello," Whitman greets us woodenly.

"Delmar," Isaac says with a bright smile. Maybe too bright. He pats the seat to his left. "Join us."

"I can't. I just got word," Whitman says, his voice grave. "Master Oversea has a suspect in custody."

I stand up, palms pressed to the table, heat searing down my spine. "Who is it?"

"His name is Simon Hansen. One of Oversea's guards."

Simon Hansen? It doesn't sound the least bit familiar. Who is this menace, and why did he target me?

"How did they catch him?" Isaac asks breathlessly.

"They didn't. Ms. Arnett did." Whitman bows his head to me, and my chest swells with tentative pride. "Her tip on the chapel paid off. He's visited every night since we posted surveillance. We searched his quarters and found the same rope used to hang Mr. Parsons, the symbol drawn on a scrap of paper. That detail was never released to the public."

I can't wrap my mind around it. Catching my cultist had seemed impossible. It still doesn't feel real—because it makes no sense. A crime without motive. "Did he say why he did it?"

"He confessed to killing Mr. Parsons, but other than that, he hasn't said a word. I'd guess he's protecting somebody. Whoever hired him must be the one with a vendetta."

The vagueness is almost worse than knowing nothing. I scratch at the thin skin of my forearm until it's marked with red lines. If this Simon Hansen acted on someone's behalf, my mission isn't over until I find out who.

My blood chills as a possibility enters my mind: the Guild of the Rising Tide. He used their symbol; it's not a stretch to imagine the Guild is pulling his strings. But why? I feel a fierce urge to march to the dungeons and throttle him. After what he's put us through, can't he make this part easy?

"Your Majesty," Whitman continues. It might be my imagination, but he sounds a little sardonic. "I was hoping to speak with you." His eyes flick toward me. "Alone."

I'm curious what he has to say to Isaac in confidence, but I won't squander a chance to retreat to my rooms. I stand and curtsy to Isaac. "Your Majesty." As I walk to the door, I add, "Master Whitman." I pass close enough to brush his sleeve with mine, and I shiver at the contact.

Guards flank me as I return to my quarters—but are they necessary anymore? I suppose they are. Simon Hansen may be in custody, but the mastermind behind the murders is out there somewhere. And perhaps Renfield's spies are still keeping tabs on me. Disgruntled, I slam the door especially hard when I reach my destination, leaving them outside.

I while away the afternoon, ruminating on my cultist. Why would Simon Hansen—or whoever put him up to it—want to interfere with my life? And how did they learn about my soulmate reading in the first place? If the Guild was involved, they might have the resources to pull it off, but what motive did they have to meddle in my affairs? I can't for the life of me come up with an explanation.

Just when I think I'm done obsessing for the evening, Isaac's question pops into my head: Have I ever been wrong about a soulmate reading? A year ago, I would have said it was impossible. Now I'm not so sure. Isaac seems connected to Elsie, a bond I can't compete with. Could I have messed up? A shiver of anxiety scuttles over my skin. Lovers readings are the one talent I'm certain of. I don't know who I'd be without them.

Wound up on what-ifs, I reach for Isaac's handkerchief, the one Whitman brought me after I named the king's soulmate. Perhaps I'll glean some new insight after my time in the Flood. Admittedly, it's unlikely. My previous readings were so consistent they're imprinted on my mind: I fly above myself, then back down, then I'm assaulted by my own name. Exactly the same every time.

Exactly the same.

My stomach swoops as I recall what Tasha said about fabricated readings: easy to spot because they're identical, no matter how many times the reading's repeated. No organic variation. My hands shake and start to sweat. Could Isaac's soulmate reading have been manipulated by someone? Have I had it wrong from the beginning?

Heart pounding, I burst out of the room and run two doors down to Byers' apartments. I bang on the door until she answers in her sleeping bonnet, wearing a frown. In my eagerness, I didn't realize how late it had gotten. Undeterred, I shove my way inside, Isaac's handkerchief balled in my hand.

Byers' entry room is softly lit and tidy, with gauzy white curtains and sky-blue wallpaper. A multihued mural of what I think are baobab trees, tangled in flowering vines—plants I've only seen in books—decorates the southern wall. Did she paint that herself? I didn't know she was an artist. But I remember what she told me about her grandmother's lake house on the savanna, the grasses and baobabs stretching for miles. Maybe Byers created this mural as a reminder of her family's happier memories.

I spin to face her, clasping my hands as if in prayer. "What if I'm not Isaac's soulmate?"

"This is what you wake me up for?" she grumbles, rubbing her drowsy eyes. "You're his soulmate, Arnett. Stop trying to worm out of it."

"Just listen to me," I insist. I tell her my theory.

All traces of sleep disappear from her eyes as they flash with excitement. "It can't be. Can it? How do you find the true reading?"

Perhaps I can use my shiny new magic to separate the false readings from the true. Tension wrenches my muscles tight.

I clutch Isaac's handkerchief and close my eyes.

Who is the true love of King Isaac?

The question flashes like lightning in my mind, cracking the crust of the fake reading; then the answer rolls through me like thunder. My eyes fly open.

And I laugh.

"It's her!" Euphoria surging through me, I spring over to Byers, gripping her shoulders. She grips me back in mild hysteria. "It's Elsie! She's Isaac's soulmate! The reading was wrong before—but it's her, Byers." I whoop at the top of my lungs. "It's her!"

"Elsie's the queen," Byers breathes. "Gods below, it's really her."

I can't calm my shaking hands as I press them to my mouth, or the wild thrumming of my pulse. "This means someone tried to interfere with my reading," I tell Byers. What they hoped to accomplish, I can't begin to guess. But they didn't account for me spending two months in the Flood, gaining the power to see through their misdirection.

"Yes, it does," she says with a distant stare. It hasn't sunk in for her yet. "You heard about Simon Hansen? The suspect?"

I nod. It's unlikely that two separate, unrelated forces at the castle are working against me. And if he or whoever he gets his orders from doctored the reading themselves, that would explain how Hansen knew I lied about my soulmate reading. But what's their end game? What do they hope to gain by making it appear that I'm the king's soulmate? Whoever changed my reading must be a powerful magician, in a class with Tasha herself. I can't imagine what I could have done to earn the enmity of someone like that.

"King Isaac needs to hear this," Byers says quaveringly. "And the council."

"Agreed." I bounce on my toes, giddy, an insuppressible smile spreading across my face. "I'll tell Whitman. You go gather the rest of the masters."

For once, she follows my instructions without complaint.

We head in opposite directions, and I run down the hall to Whitman's apartments to pound on the door.

A minute crawls by before he answers. The door cracks open, and I glimpse his bleary eyes, his chin shadowed with stubble. He's buttoned his shirt halfway. Without preamble, I shove the door wider and let myself in.

"I'm not Isaac's soulmate," I begin, not knowing where else to start. "Elsie Tanner is. Someone interfered with my readings."

Staggered, Whitman shakes his head, running his fingers through his hair. He tries to speak, but a jumble of sounds come out, nothing resembling words. He's close enough to wrap my arms around.

I clench my fists at my sides to stop myself from touching him. "I don't know why, Whitman, but someone rigged my reading. Probably the same person who directed Simon Hansen to kill Parsons. But I can see through their tricks now. Elsie's meant to take the throne, I'm positive."

His brows draw together, forming delicate lines of worry. I want so badly to kiss them away. "Are you certain?" he asks.

"Absolutely." I've never been more certain of anything.

He frowns in thought. "If Elsie is Isaac's soulmate, and she's the woman from Tellerman's prediction . . ." The ridges between his brows smooth. "This ends it. The contest is over."

I beam at him. "Congratulations, master. You found Isaac a queen."

Whitman eyes me furtively. "So, you and Isaac . . ."

"There is no me and Isaac," I laugh. "There never has been."

He looks unconvinced, even angry. "Then what was all that flirtation? Some—some manipulative ploy?"

I back away with an indignant huff. "You're calling *me* manipulative? All your lies, pretending you saw something in me—as if I could actually belong here!" I sniff as hurt takes over for fury. "You made a fool of me."

Whitman's mouth forms a grim line. "Don't put this back on me. From the day we met, you've done nothing but try to manipulate me! The propositions, the—the touching—"

"Gods below," I say, clutching my temples, "how are you this stupid?"

He's stunned into silence. "What?"

I stare at him with furious awe. He really *is* that stupid. Somehow, Whitman's never gotten it through his head that I'm not trying to sway him with sex.

What else can I say to convince him?

I sidle up to him. Whitman looks at me with wide, muddled eyes. Still too dense to understand.

Standing on my tiptoes, I cup a hand behind his head and bring his mouth to mine.

His every muscle stills as I kiss him—gently at first—my lips grazing against his, soft and tender and slow. Then I break away. "I don't need a damn thing from you," I say, and kiss him again, rougher.

He returns it this time, but he's hesitant. Heat pools low in my belly as I deepen the kiss, melting into it, my other hand tangling in his hair. Gripping tight, I pull his head back and give him a stern look. His eyes are alight with lust and questions, but he doesn't interrupt.

"I don't need any favors." I kiss him again and keep going, punctuating each sentence with my mouth on his. "I don't have an agenda." Both hands weave into his hair now, my wet lips brushing his as I speak. He presses urgently against me, fingers digging into my skin.

Words finally fail me. I bury my face in his neck and nip along the curve of his throat. He makes a tiny groaning sound, and something flares in me. I trail kisses up his jaw as his arms close tighter around me, his breath hastening.

I've just reached his ear when he tilts his head back. His eyes gleam brighter than I've ever seen them.

"I need to gather the council," Whitman murmurs, though he stares down at my lips. "We need to set Isaac's wedding at once."

"Can't it wait?" I crane my neck, closing the space between us. I can't bear for him to walk away again.

He inhales. "You're not going to like what I have to say."

"So don't say it."

His jaw clenches tight, but for once, it isn't out of irritation. It's sheer exertion of will. "We can't do this."

"Why not?" Fear and frustration creep into my voice. Every time I cross a line with Whitman, he acts like nothing happened—or if it did, it shouldn't have. He treats me like a scandal. Which, I suppose, is the whole point. The entire reason he brought me here. Ice replaces the warmth that was filling my belly.

I have to ask, though I dread the answer. "Are you ashamed of me?" I whisper, hating how weak I sound—how insecure.

"What? *No*," he says at once, sounding so appalled that I can't help flushing with pleasure. "But the most important thing now is to protect what legitimacy this contest has left. If it gets out you've been sleeping with one of the masters, the council will have grounds to challenge Isaac's marriage. If they can argue rumors around the contest affected the public's perception of Elsie's legitimacy—"

"Then it would be too risky to crown her," I finish. Despite that, I lift my chin. "What difference does it make? We can't undo the rumors."

"But we don't have to make them worse," he says sadly.

So that's it? I stare at him, unsure if I want to slap him or kiss him. Because it's more than unslaked lust that makes me cling to Whitman, desperate not to let go. What if he never holds me again? I can't be alone like Tasha. I can't stand to have nothing but an empty void inside my heart. I just want to be whole.

Or at least pretend, for a while.

Reckless, I take his face between my hands and cover his mouth with mine, coaxing his lips apart. He lets out a stifled moan. My teeth graze his lips, and I run my hands over every inch of him I can reach, my fingers teasing, my only thought to drive him mad with pleasure, to reduce him to a gibbering mess of a man—

Whitman breaks off the kiss, panting hard. His gaze bears down on me; I feel the heavy weight of it. I steel myself for disappointment.

But he doesn't say a word. He kisses me again, hungrily, and pushes me back until I slam against the wall and cry out. His mouth travels down my neck, skimming over my collarbone, as one hand slips under the front of my nightgown and the other grabs my bottom.

"Gods below, Whitman," I gasp, my hands scrabbling over his shoulders.

"What in the name of the seven are you doing?"

Whitman and I stumble apart, spinning toward the door. Byers stands there, silhouetted by the light of the hall, her posture foreboding. It's the least welcome sight I've ever encountered.

"Why didn't you knock?" Whitman snaps, doing up the buttons on his shirt.

"The door wasn't even closed!" she says through her teeth. "I'd expect this from her. She can't help herself"—she flings a finger at me, and I wince—"but you should know better, master! If you care about putting Elsie on the throne, you can't damage the credibility of the contest!"

"Thank you, Ms. Byers," Whitman says. "That's enough." He rubs his hands over his face. "Both of you, get ready. I'm calling an emergency conference."

"Come on," Byers says, grabbing me by the wrist like she doesn't trust me to see myself out.

I glance back at Whitman as Byers guides me to the hallway. "I'm still angry with you," I call. "I haven't forgotten you betrayed me."

I see his faint smile in the dark. "Fair enough."

Byers tugs harder. Reluctantly, I face forward.

"All right, then." I break her grip and bound ahead, grinning. "Let's go make history."

PART VI

THE QUEEN

31

It's three in the morning by the time the meeting convenes. The masters all sit in attendance, as well as the gods. I should have expected them; they're part of the council now. But I still reel at the sight of them in council chambers, their faces impassive as they drink us in.

They lied to us all our lives, Byers and me. Kept us out of the Flood for no reason but to make us controllable. Containable. And then some rogue magician shows up, pulling the strings of a murderer, and we're powerless to stop them. The gods have betrayed our trust and destroyed our chances to fight threats like my cultist.

And yet, as I look at Irinorr through the twinkling light of the nexus, I love him the same. I know then I always will.

"I've made an adjustment to my reading," I announce to the room just as Whitman bade me. "About King Isaac's soulmate."

"An adjustment?" Master Renfield says skeptically. "You held out your first reading as the irrefutable truth."

I give her a dirty look. I haven't forgotten *her* betrayal either. "I've been wrong once or twice in my life. I'm sure you can relate."

"Mona," Irinorr says, gently reproachful.

I hold my tongue and get on with it. "My first reading was false. Someone interfered, a powerful magician. But that's beside the point." In spite of myself, I break out in a grin. "I'm not King Isaac's soulmate. Elsie Tanner is."

Gasps and murmurs erupt. I smile wider, setting my sights on Isaac. He stares ahead and rubs one eyebrow, holding himself up with his elbows on the table. He's thunderstruck.

Isaac clears his throat, pulling himself together. "How did you find this out?"

In broad strokes, I tell them how we strengthened our magic and saw through the false reading. The seven betray nothing by their expressions, but I know they know our secret. Byers and I disappeared for weeks and returned ten times stronger. Where else could we have been but the Flood?

Isaac's smile brightens as I explain, like the more the situation sinks in, the better he likes it. The others seem less convinced. "If you lied before, how can we trust you now?" asks Soph, master of commerce. "Couldn't you be changing your prediction to avoid suspicion in the death of Mr. Parsons?"

"You don't have to trust me." My eyes flick toward the gods. As a group, the masters turn to Semyanadd.

"As I said before, we are still regaining our strength," Semyanadd replies. He sounds a touch cold. "Our magic is weaker now."

Not the glowing testimonial I'd hoped for. Their magic may be weak, but they could have brushed over that to make me look dependable in front of the council.

"But you would know if Ms. Arnett was lying, wouldn't you?" Whitman asks. I brace myself and pray that question doesn't backfire.

"Yes," Irinorr says quietly. "I would know."

Semyanadd says nothing. Nor do the rest of the gods. The masters take that silence as tacit confirmation—I spoke the truth.

"But why Ms. Arnett?" says Master Renfield, her nose scrunched in snide confusion. "Why would this magician change her reading to suggest she's King Isaac's soulmate? What do they hope to achieve?"

"There's a lot we have yet to figure out," Whitman says. "But right now, we need to focus on setting His Majesty's wedding before anyone can interfere further."

"The day before the equinox tournament, then," Isaac peals. Other than a shadow of blond stubble and the perpetual bags under his eyes, you would never have guessed he was dragged out of bed in the wee hours of the morning, or even that he was sick. I press my lips together. Now that the rush has worn off, the fact that I'm not Isaac's soulmate feels . . . odd. Not bad, but not wholly good, either. I can't put my finger on it. "Though that's not much time to plan a wedding. Master Gan?"

Gan looks, if anything, invigorated by the challenge. "My top priority, Your Majesty."

With that, the meeting is done. It went smoother than I could have dreamed. A strange feeling percolates inside me, and it takes me a moment to peg. *Hope.* It's been a long while since I felt that.

As we break off and walk our separate directions, I lean toward Whitman to whisper, "So, are you still angry about me leaving?"

His frown is dour. "I'm not angry. But please never, ever do it again."

I study him as we walk. The spellsap lanterns along the hall cast haunted shadows over his features. How long would he have waited before declaring us missing, or dead? What would he have told my parents? I try to shake those dark thoughts loose. I'm being *hopeful* now.

One week. That's how long we have to prepare for the royal wedding of the century. To say it's all hands on deck at the castle does not do the situation justice. Even the gods pitch in.

The day before, I visit Irinorr. I go alone—no guards. My security detail is no longer necessary, now that Simon Hansen is locked up. Or rather, now that the masters don't have a good reason to spy on me.

When I enter his room, he's standing next to a table, facing away from me. I close the door behind me. "Iri?"

"Come look, Mona."

I approach. Spread out on the circular surface before him is a map, large enough to smother the tabletop. But it's not like any map I've ever seen. Spiderweb-thin lines delineate the Circle Court nations and the Middle Sea, so faint I have to squint to see the borders. Scattered across the map like splashes of paint are glowing green splotches, some bigger and brighter than others. Irinorr smiles at me. That's a relief. We haven't spoken yet of the Flood or how I disobeyed him.

"We're mapping the breaches," he says.

"The what?"

He glances at me in faint surprise, like he forgot I'm an ignorant mortal. "Certain areas where the veil is thinner, where the spellsap orchards have sustained the most damage."

I study the map with a creased forehead. Mere mortal that I am, I can't help but worry. The mood in the castle has been buoyed by the wedding, but once it's over, we'll still be mired in this mess. And we still won't know why Simon Hansen killed Parsons, or if he's the one who altered my soulmate reading—or who he's working for, if not. At this very moment, Hansen's being held in the dungeons, refusing to speak to his interrogators. If I chose to, I could march down there and ask him these questions myself. But something's holding me back—a nebulous, irrational fear. Like if I get close enough to confront him, he might somehow make good on his threats.

With a warm smile, Irinorr waves me toward the armchairs. "But I am sure you didn't come here to discuss breaches in the veil."

"Afraid not," I say, folding my legs beneath me. I haven't readjusted to chairs after Tasha's. "What's a wedding like, Iri?"

He laughs, crinkling his perfect eyes. "Have I been so derelict in your education?"

I shoot him a small grin. Throughout my decade of training, Irinorr taught me magic, not religion. We touched on it here and there—worship and tenets, and the occasional religious ritual. Those more mundane matters that fall under Irinorr's domain—like weddings—didn't often come up. "I just wondered about the basics," I say as I tuck my skirts under my knees. I feel like a child again, asking stupid questions. "You know, what's expected of me. When to sit, when to stand."

"Ah, but tomorrow will be anything but basic. It's a royal wedding." He chuckles as distress wrenches my brows together. "You will be fine, my child. All you need to do is attend. Be there for your kingdom." With a nod, he adds, "For your friends."

I shift in my seat. I am, somehow, even more chary than before. "I wish I'd never come to the castle," I say in a rush. I hardly know where it's coming from. Around Irinorr, all my fears and self-doubt seem to leak out of me. "Everything feels so strange. I can't figure out what I want anymore. I never felt that way at home."

"Change often feels unpleasant," Irinorr says kindly. "That doesn't mean you should avoid it. Some changes can be wonderful. Necessary, even."

I smile at him until, in the comfortable silence, he says, "Perhaps we should discuss your time in the Flood."

My pulse spikes. I have nothing to fear from Irinorr—other than a lecture—but my body refuses to calm.

I incline my head in defiance. "Yes, I was in the Flood. And you lied to me about it. Let's call it even."

"Has it occurred to you there might be good reason we warn our favored mortals away from exposure?"

"Like what?"

"The Flood doesn't only strengthen your magic." His tone draws me closer. "It leaches your humanity, Mona. It turns mortals into monsters."

My mind turns to Tasha. Her social skills are rusty, maybe—but a monster? She threatened to kill us, sure, but she didn't go through with it.

But if Irinorr is right—if Tasha's humanity is forfeit—was she really trying to help me? Or was she manipulating me to her own ends?

"Why not tell us up front?" I ask Irinorr.

"Mortal curiosity is difficult to overcome." His fond but patronizing smile lights a tiny flame of anger in me. "Tell a mortal their soul is at risk, and they'll keep going just to prove you wrong. But they tend to heed you when their survival is on the line."

"You can't be sure what mortals will or won't do. You never gave us a chance to prove it."

"It is inevitable, for your kind."

I keep my head lowered. I have nothing to say that won't lead to more arguing. In my peripheral vision, Irinorr rises and walks over. He leans down to press a cool kiss to my forehead.

"I will always take care of you, Mona," he says against my temple. "Remember that. Everything I do is out of love."

32

The morning of the wedding, the castle is chaos incarnate. I stay in my room for most of it. I can't shake the feeling something will go wrong. Even with Simon Hansen out of commission, there are a million ways this could go south. Including the looming threat posed by Hansen's backer. With each passing day, I feel a mounting dread that the Guild of the Rising Tide is behind it all. But that's a stretch based on what we know. Isn't it?

I fret away the time until the afternoon, then get dressed with Elizabeta's help. She's chatty today. I appreciate the distraction it provides from my churning dread. "Ms. Tanner's perfect for him," Elizabeta gushes as she sweeps my hair off my neck and twists it into braids.

"Mm-hmm," I say, wringing my hands together.

"They'll make such a striking couple."

"Oh, yes." I glance around the room, trying not to fidget. "What do you think of this wallpaper?"

"Wallpaper, miss?"

"Yes, the damask. Pink's not really my color. I'm thinking of changing it up."

"Oh." She contemplates it. "The room would look nice with a soft yellow, yes?"

I hug my arms around myself and try to picture it. I can't hold the image in my head. Not yet. "Maybe," I say with a nervous smile.

Once I'm ready, I meet Byers in the common room. A dying fire in the fireplace casts low, flickering shadows across the near-empty parlor. Byers waits next to the shuttered window, resplendent in a gown of cerulean satin and airy chiffon, her lips coated in a sparkling coral pigment. I'm wearing a buttercream dress, its formless skirt spilling out from a tapered waist. Elizabeta did up my straw-colored hair in a coronet of braids. Next to Byers, I feel like a washed-out painting.

Byers, with her impeccable social graces, doesn't fail to make note of it. "You look like a ghost."

How fitting. "I am trying to fade into the background," I say, looking down my nose, "because this is Elsie's day to shine."

"I see." She narrows her eyes. "Are you doing all right, Arnett?"

"I'm fine," I say too quickly. "Now, let's get to the wedding. I'm copying everything you do, so you know. I'll not make a fool of myself today."

"Oh? That'll be a first."

It doesn't sound like a joke. Exhaling hard, I rush her down the hall so we won't be late.

I've seen the main hall decked out on a number of occasions, but none have compared to this. Garlands of gold and pink foil roses stream across the ceiling and walls, luminescent in the spellsap light. A layer of golden dust coats the king's platform. Altogether, it has the effect of some hazy, blissful afterlife, as if we've been transported to the garden of the dead.

A crowd mills about on their feet—at least a third of them guards, posted around the hall to ensure the wedding goes smoothly. We are so close to having a queen on the throne. A few more hours—barring any last-minute murders—and Opalvale can breathe easier. I see plenty of Circle Court delegates in attendance, too, from all six nations. This must be their way of saying *No hard feelings* to Isaac after he cut them out of the marriage negotiations.

Byers and I shove through the press of bodies, heading for the front. I dodge a trio of servers passing out dishes of sacred seawater; a smell too much like Tasha's seaweed tea wafts from their shallow bowls, and a gust of unexpected nostalgia blows through me. I squeeze my eyes shut and wait for it to pass.

Near the stage, I see something that gives me pause: Elsie Tanner, mingling with the crowd. Then I do a double take. No, it isn't Elsie; this woman's skin is a shade warmer, her hair thicker and blacker. But the resemblance is undeniable. She wears an orange silk wrap skirt with a long-sleeved white blouse, the colors bold and blocky—traditional ceremonial dress in Ahn Dien. Holding her by the elbow is a tall man with white-blond hair and Elsie's exact chin. Her parents. They cling to each other, tearfully ecstatic. Of course they are—their daughter's going to be crowned queen of Opalvale. I wonder if Isaac offered to buy them out of their contract with Lord Severin.

I search the crowd for Whitman. Isaac isn't only his king; he's his friend. Nothing in the mortal realm would keep him away.

That mystery solves itself in another heartbeat.

Lights flare and shine around us, glowing gold, then dim to a low smolder as Master Gan emerges from stage right to step onto the platform. I crane my neck and watch as the rest of the masters follow him, Whitman in the lead. From the other side, the gods ascend. They're dressed in clothing tailored from the blackest fabric I've ever seen, stitched with golden thread that must be spun from starlight.

I try to catch Whitman's eye while Gan starts an archaic speech about the sublime joining we will witness today. He doesn't see me, or else ignores me. I've hardly spoken to Whitman all week. We've been busy, of course, but what if he's come to his senses now that he's considered it—us—in the cold light of day? People make all sorts of crazy decisions at night, in the dark.

I swallow. Elsie and Isaac. That's what should be important today.

As if I summoned them with a thought, the king and future queen appear on opposite sides of the platform. A hush washes over the crowd. Elsie and Isaac climb the polished oak steps in tandem, Isaac moving a little slower but unassisted by his cane. Smiling shyly, faces flushed, they meet in the middle. Gan ties a black silk ribbon around their wrists, joining them as one. The bride and groom smile wider, intertwining their fingers. Byers sniffles beside me.

Not until that moment does it hit me, as Gan's words echo from the ceiling, and Elsie and Isaac step closer to kiss, and Byers reaches for my elbow, weeping: We did this.

I place my hand over Byers', laughing, as a cheer goes up from the crowd.

The ceremony ends. People surge around us, knocking me about. When I get my bearings again, the gods have disappeared, and an honor guard is escorting Elsie and Isaac through the crowd, the masters trailing behind them. Now Elsie will greet her subjects for the first time as their queen. Everyone jostles for position, cramming in close. I escape to the side of the hall. As I linger at the edge of the crowd, I watch Isaac and Elsie smiling, shaking hands with the masses. The masters are no longer with them. I'm standing on my toes, searching for Whitman, when a cry catches my attention.

"Ms. Arnett! Mona!"

Queen Elsie springs on her tiptoes and waves, very un-sovereign-like. "Come this way, Ms. Arnett!" she calls.

I push my way through the crowd to reach Elsie and Isaac. Elsie grabs my hands at once, bringing them to her lips and kissing my fingers. I laugh in surprise.

"Isaac told me what you did," she whispers. Everything about her—her voice, her face, her gold-and-gray gown draped in layers of silk organza—bursts with radiance. "How you saw through the false readings. Mona—thank you." She squeezes my hands. "We owe you everything."

I laugh again, warbly with nerves. "I'm just glad to see the right woman on the throne." I give Isaac a quick wink, and he presses his lips together against a smile. Perhaps I should feel more reticent to give up Isaac as my soulmate. It still rakes me from time to time, a sense of loss I can't define. But it has never been so easy as in this moment, with the two of them standing before me, side by side, flushing with joy.

It almost makes me forget Isaac will be dead within a year, and Elsie a widow.

I clear my throat. "Do you know where the masters went? I want to congratulate Gan. Spectacular ceremony."

Isaac goes ahead and grins now. "Delmar can't have gone far. He should be around."

I huff at him. "Very funny. I'll find Master Gan myself." I draw Elsie into a hug and give Isaac a firmly annoyed handshake.

I meander to a lonely sandstone pillar and sink down beside it, sighing, as joyous music plays somewhere in the room. I hug my knees, staring off and listening to the upbeat song.

"What're you doing down there?"

I look up. Byers hovers over me, judging me inscrutably. She has two drinks in her hands. One must be for Elizabeta.

"Weddings can only be properly appreciated from about floor level," I say. "Come, join me. You'll see."

She crouches next to me, handing me a drink, which I take with mild puzzlement. "Where's Elizabeta?" I ask.

"Dancing," Byers says. "Really, Arnett. Why are you sulking?"

I groan. "I'm not *sulking*."

"You are. Don't think you can get it past me."

I feel an overwhelming urge, welling up from deep inside, to say something empty. Empty and safe, as I've always done. For once, I fight it. "I can't find Master Whitman," I say mopishly.

I can tell she's holding back a laugh. "Why are you so obsessed with him?"

"Have you *seen* him?" I wave my hands up and down to indicate Whitman as a complete specimen. "He's like a beautiful, neurotic monk."

"You know what, forget it. I don't want to know."

"All that repressed emotion, Byers. I just want to spank it out of him."

"You," she says, wrinkling her nose, "are disgusting."

I grin at her mischievously, then look at my lap, turning serious. "Byers, I . . . I don't want to be like Tasha. I don't want to be alone anymore."

She considers that in silence. Then she snorts, like she can't contain her laughter any longer. That drink in her hand is not her first.

"You're not alone, you idiot," she says. "You've got me."

I stare at her. She smiles, her coral lips sparkling.

"All right, fine." I giggle into my glass as I drink. "But I'd still like to find Whitman."

"You will." She raises her champagne. "Here's to the queen. For bringing us together."

Trying to keep a straight face, I clink my glass against hers. "To Queen Elsie."

We drink. All the while, Byers wears a vague grin that doesn't suit her at all. Weddings put her in a very peculiar mood.

"Shall we go dance?" she asks.

We make our way to the east end of the hall, where a swath of floor has been cleared for a partners dance. Couples skate past, weaving and looping around one another like needles sewing a tapestry, the ladies' wide silk bustles brushing as they pass. It hypnotizes me. Byers leaves me to join in; soon I catch sight of her gliding across the floor, smiling at her faceless partner. She's not a bad dancer.

I look past the dancers, to the line of onlookers on the other side, and finally, at long last, I see Whitman. He's standing alone. My limbs prickling, I raise a hand in the air and wave until I catch his attention.

With a faint smile, he skirts around the dance floor toward me. I wait with my hands squeezed together. When he reaches me, he stops short, nodding formally.

Amused, I bend my knees in an ostentatious curtsy. "How are you this evening, Master Whitman?"

He smiles. "My oldest friend was married today. I'm doing well."

We stroll along the edges of the main hall, leaving a gap between us. Beside a pillar, in shadow, we pass Onyamarr in a dress made of streaming strips of cloth. She smirks at me from a distance. The rest of the seven must be around somewhere.

"I'm glad it's over," Whitman says.

"Not yet. There's still *Simon Hansen*." I spit out his name like a curse. After the wedding, I won't have any more excuses to put off meeting with him—though I'm dreading that conversation. It's one thing to wish I had answers, and another to actually go get them.

"But Opalvale has a queen." He glances at me, like he's waiting for me to say something. "Have you decided what you'll do when this is done for good? Will you stay?"

I don't answer right away. I walk on, appreciating the rows of embroidered tapestries, hung especially for the wedding, boasting house crests from around the kingdom.

"Are you asking me to join the company?" I say at last.

"I suppose I am."

"Then I suppose it depends on what incentives I'm given."

He clasps his hands behind him. The corner of his mouth quirks up. "You and Ms. Byers seem to have become close."

I hum but don't confirm it. "What else can you offer me? A salary? Bigger apartments?"

"Are we negotiating now?"

"Well, *I* am. But I must say, if you don't start engaging with my demands, I will suspect you're not taking me seriously."

We slip out into the darkened hallway, abandoned but for a few castle guards. Fleetingly, it occurs to me we ought to return someplace more crowded.

"Where are we going?" I ask quietly, so as not to alert anyone to our presence. My marrow runs hot inside my bones.

"Nowhere." He avoids my eye. "We're just walking."

I look up and down the hallway. Empty. Everyone's at the wedding.

"You should stay," Whitman says, staring at his shoes. "You belong here. In the company."

I try to imagine it: sitting in at conferences, nodding in stodgy agreement, perhaps even contributing once in a while. Would Byers stay, too? Would we meet up in my apartments after each session to debrief? It's absolutely absurd. I can't stop smiling.

I touch Whitman's elbow, and he slows. My hand wraps around his forearm. Cautiously, I close the space between us, bringing my lips to his. Whitman doesn't return the kiss, but he doesn't move away. When I step back, his brows knit together.

"Elsie's on the throne now," I say with a hint of frustration.

"There's still a chance someone could challenge her legitimacy. It's harder to depose a queen than to prevent a marriage, but it's not impossible."

I scoff, hiding the hurt in my voice. "So we'll have this hanging over us forever?"

"Perhaps not forever. In time, Elsie's competency will speak for itself." He takes a deep breath. "But right now, it's a foolish risk to take. It's not worth it."

I don't need him to parse that out. *I'm* not worth it. I hang my head and shake it. "I apologize for my risky behavior," I mumble, and stride off down the hallway. No footsteps follow after me.

I turn a corner, keep going until I reach the communal baths, and duck inside. The connected stone chambers smell of hot steam and perfume. A mosaic of swirled blue ceramic tiles the wall behind three deep basins, drained at the moment. I stop and bend over a stone bench, holding myself up on the heels of my hands.

I don't know what I was expecting. It's not as if Whitman has given me much encouragement these past weeks. It's not as if I ever dared to hope for anything different. Anything more.

A minute passes before someone walks up behind me. I stand, looking over my shoulder. Whitman approaches with his hands in his pockets. He could almost be described as contrite.

He shrugs one shoulder. "Mona—"

"You don't have to explain yourself," I say ruefully. "I understand. I'm not worth the risk—"

"That's not what I said." He cuts me off. "It has nothing to do with you. It's just . . . stupid. We have responsibilities."

"You know how I adore those," I counter, crossing my arms. "We're young still, Whitman. Young people take risks."

"I'm a member of the royal council."

Like that has anything to do with anything. "What are you so afraid of?" I say, searching the grim planes of his face for an answer. "Enjoying yourself? Don't you think you've earned it?"

"I'm afraid of failing in my sworn duties to Opalvale," he says in a quiet, gruff voice. "I can't afford to make mistakes. The minute the other masters sense an opening, they'll push me out. I can't do anything to prove them right about me."

"So you have to be perfect all the time?" Smiling sadly, I reach out to take hold of his hand. "You have to stop punishing yourself eventually."

Whitman rears back, but he doesn't step away. Who can say what crossed his mind—his sister, or his fraud mother, or King Isaac, who's dying a little more each day and he can't stop it—but I see in his eyes that I hit the mark. He doesn't reply, other than to swallow and stare at my forehead like it might reveal the secret to getting him out of this.

"Fine," I concede with a sigh. "You win." I squeeze his hand and turn away.

But Whitman's fingers tighten around mine, and he pulls me back. I stumble until my shoulder collides with his chest. As I straighten, his arms loop around me, drawing me close.

His face hovers next to mine. My heart beats fast as his hands move down my back and hips, bunching and gripping the fabric of my dress—hesitant, like I might object. I'm not sure he knows what he's doing. I'm not sure I care.

"We should know better." His breath tickles my ear. "I haven't . . . I've never done something like this before."

"Stop trying to make good decisions," I mumble, slipping my fingers between the buttons of his master's jacket. "There's no such thing. It all turns out the same in the end."

He sniffs with flat laughter. "That's not true."

But still, he grabs my hips and pushes me toward the wall. I trip backward, hanging off his shirt.

My bottom bumps into the polished marble counter ringing the room. I keep playing with Whitman's buttons, unsure what else to do. I don't want to make a wrong move. He draws a trembling breath through his nose and tightens his grip. In one swift movement, he lifts me onto the counter. I let out a stifled noise of surprise.

My legs swing over the edge to either side of him. Whitman brushes a strand of hair from my eyes. He looks confused. "We should go back to the party," he whispers.

"I was trying to," I say. Neither of us move. When it seems we aren't going anywhere, I lean forward until our mouths meet. His lips quiver under mine.

Then he kisses me back, pressing himself between my legs so they splay out to the sides. My arms hook under his as I grab onto his shoulders, as his tongue swirls around mine. Some rational part of me knows we ought to stop, or go someplace else. But I rarely listen to reason. I'm not about to start now.

Whitman fumbles with the laces on my dress as I nip and lick down his neck. I try to undo his jacket buttons, but they're polished smooth and they slip beneath my fingers. My laces come loose, and he tugs down my bodice to slide over my breasts. I shiver in the chill air until his hands rove around and cup them, coaxing a weak moan from me. I abandon his jacket, go for the button on his trousers instead. My hand slips past his waistband, and he lets out a low, shivering sound and kisses me again, bending me backward toward the wall. If I didn't know better, I'd say he was enjoying himself.

Whitman's hands leave my breasts. I arch toward him in protest, but he touches me again on my thighs, pushing the satin of my skirts up around my hips. I lift my bottom off the counter as he pulls down my underthings, scratching me in his haste. The marble feels freezing against my skin. I tilt back to recline on the counter, and he kisses down my sternum, to my breasts. The counter is too shallow; my head angles to the side, butted against the wall. I barely notice.

One of his hands finds its way between my legs, and with the other he covers my mouth, muffling my cries, and I forget all about my cramped head. He enters me with a sudden thrust, his fingers moving against me. He is unbearably gentle, pacing himself, like he's punishing me. His breathing hastens, and it thrills me to my core, how I can undo him this way. Like he can't help but let his guard down with me.

His brows bunch together as he stares at me. "Gods below, you're beautiful," he murmurs, like he only realized it now. He bends closer until his breath warms my mouth. He smells like champagne. I lift my head to meet him, swiping my tongue across his bottom lip. His fingers tease me again, and I moan against his mouth, trying to moor my hips in place.

And then he moves inside me, pleasure mounting between my legs and deep in my belly. My thighs squeeze him; my nails sink into the sleeves of his jacket, and he holds me by my hips as I wriggle against him, desperate for more of him. He floods my brain, clouding my thoughts, until I gasp and laugh and raise my hips toward his, my back bowing. With a strangled sound, he folds on top of me.

We lie there a while, on the hard, cold counter. I stroke his hair as he rests his head on my chest, catching his breath. I don't want to return to the wedding. I don't want to go back to real life at all.

Then, all in a hurry, Whitman stands upright, like he just realized where he was and in what condition. "That was very stupid," he grunts as he buttons up his jacket.

I sit up, pouting as I check the state of my coronet braids. "Just what every girl wants to hear in the afterglow."

With a softer look, he holds my chin between his thumb and forefinger. I think he might say something then—something charming, romantic—but instead, he leans in and kisses me. A tender kiss, a kiss for someone you want to take care of, not use and throw away. Good enough, for now. I couldn't have done any better. I wouldn't know where to begin, declaring my feelings for Whitman.

We clean up quickly and move to leave, but Whitman catches me by the arm at the archway exit.

"We should go separately," he says, glancing into the hallway. "In case anyone's watching."

I muffle a laugh with my hand. "Gods below, Whitman. I knew you were paranoid, but—"

"It's not so far-fetched. Anyone who'd like to challenge Elsie's legitimacy will be searching for excuses. We're easy pickings."

"Perhaps you shouldn't have done me in the communal baths, then."

Whitman fixes me with a glare, but it warps without warning into blank shock. He stares over my shoulder. I spin around.

Master Renfield stands in the archway. She's dressed in a bloodred suit, her close-shaved hair dusted with gold.

Her eyebrows veer toward her hairline. "I heard voices."

"So?" I shoot back. Despite my flippant tone, my palms are sweaty.

"I came to make sure everything was all right," Renfield says. "What were you doing in here?"

I swallow thickly. Renfield may not be an ally, exactly, but is she an enemy? She knows by now I had nothing to do with Parsons' murder. Still, I can't help but seethe when I remember how she lied about my part in the investigation, how she tricked me into interrogating myself.

"It's really nothing," Whitman says in a low, placating voice.

"Is that so? Because simply being seen here together is enough to shroud Queen Elsie's coronation in scandal."

I wince. "Master Renfield." I smile at her experimentally. "We're on the same side."

"Are we?" She quirks an eyebrow. "I don't know what *side* you're referring to, but I will not cover for the sloppy mistakes of my junior colleagues."

My breath hitches. Is that a warning—or a threat? Has she abandoned all pretense of protecting Whitman's position on the council?

"We're not asking you to cover for anything," Whitman counters, defensive, his face turning an unhealthy shade of gray. "But if you're so concerned about how this looks, perhaps you should keep it private."

Renfield sniffs, shaking her head. "Right. Enjoy your evening." With that, she whirls around and her shoes clack down the hallway.

I look over at Whitman. "You think she'll tell anyone?"

"I don't think so." His complexion tints from gray to green. "But I can't be certain."

"She obviously knows spreading rumors could threaten Elsie's reign. She's not that stupid." I gulp. "Is she?"

"Stupid? No. Treasonous?" He shrugs and musses his hair. "Like I said before, any of the masters had a motive to bribe a seer and install their queen of choice. That hasn't changed."

And we haven't narrowed down that field of suspects. What could Renfield's motive be? A disturbing thought springs to mind. "What about your mother being exiled? After, you know . . ." I gesture at Whitman, like that says everything. He shoots me a slightly offended look. "Renfield told me they used to be lovers. If she bribed a seer, maybe she wants to use that influence to pardon your mother's crimes."

He releases a troubled sigh. "I don't know. It's possible. She still hasn't forgiven me for what I did." A muscle twitches in his jaw. "I don't know if she ever will."

"But would she threaten Elsie's reign over that?"

He waves me toward the exit, and we start back toward the wedding. "I honestly can't say."

I worry at my gloves as we skulk down the dim hallway, silent all the way—finally, and too late, feeling as stupid as Whitman keeps insisting we are.

33

There's one thing I can do to redeem myself: determine if Renfield poses a threat to Elsie. Or to Whitman, for that matter.

Since my return from the Flood, my magic has been strong enough to divine the names of those who paid off seers, but it hasn't been a priority. Our run-in with Renfield changed things. If Renfield is one of the bribers, she's no friend to Elsie, and what she knows is a weapon in her hands.

Immediately after parting ways with Whitman at the wedding, I rush to my apartments to perform a reading. And, to my relief, I come up with names.

Three names. And Renfield isn't one of them.

Soph and Oversea—the masters of commerce and justice—paid off seers to put forth their preferred candidates. And so did Honored Delphin.

Only two seers lied at the contest—three, if you include me. Why three bribers, then? At least Renfield's name is absent. My muscles unclench as I relax into that comforting knowledge.

It doesn't prove she's not a threat. She could be masterminding her own treasonous plan, unrelated to the bribes—but there's no evidence of that. For all I know, her sole motivation is to humiliate Whitman and have him booted out of the council.

All morning before the postnuptial tournament, a sharp pang of worry burns in the center of my sternum. I feel better about Renfield than I did last night, but not by much. Whitman and I endangered Elsie's reign. I knew the risks, but I don't relish facing the consequences. I stare out the window at the robin's-egg sky, grappling with the implications of my reading, until I hear a knock at my door.

Given what happened, I expected Whitman to visit my apartments this morning—and I was right. But I'm surprised to see he's brought along the newlyweds.

The pair of them look out of place in my sitting room, like gold-and-porcelain vases shoved to the back of a dusty bookshelf. They're dressed in full royal regalia. Isaac wears a uniform of white with gold embroidery, a thick black ribbon weaving down the sides of both sleeves. Someone's applied a healthy layer of rouge to his cheeks, masking his wan skin. He has a cane today—his bones must be aching again—but this one is carved of onyx and polished to a shine, not the simple wooden number I saw before.

Elsie's getup is just as elaborate. The bustle of her dress must be reinforced with wire to hold up so much fabric in a wide, arcing bell. A sprinkle of golden feathers trails down toward the hem. The black tiara of her station gleams atop a pouf of tawny hair, and her skin shimmers with coppery powder. Something else about her face looks odd, unnatural, but I can't pinpoint it.

Whitman's smiling, but his eyes are ringed with black circles, worse than I've seen them since the day we met. He missed a spot shaving his neck. Did he tell Isaac what happened between us, or is he ashamed?

Isaac's ever-present guards position themselves in a corner, out of sight. It must be an uncomfortable job—forced to attend meetings that have nothing to do with you, while everyone pretends you aren't there. Suddenly, I feel guilty for treating them like furniture all those times before. I shoot the guards an awkward smile of acknowledgment, but they don't seem to notice.

Isaac and Elsie stay by my doorway, stiff as statues—which must have more to do with their costumes than their moods, for they both are smiling—as Whitman takes a seat across from me.

I look around at the three of them. "Am I in trouble?" I say, forcing a teasing smirk. I have to admit the thought crossed my mind. But their expressions are too carefree for that.

"Not that I'm aware of," Isaac says, though his eyes dart to Whitman. Fair of him to assume I'm in one type of trouble or another with the master of practitioners at any given time. "We're on the way to the ward. Opening ceremonies should be starting soon. But I, uh"—he steals a glance at his wife—"Elsie wanted to—"

"We wanted to thank you again," Elsie says, full of affection. I finally realize what's off about her: the copper-rimmed glasses. I've never seen her without them. "For everything you've done. Oh, I wish you could come with us to the tournament!"

"That would be nice." I suppress a smile. "But they had the audacity to hold it outside."

"Perhaps you could try? Just for today?"

The way she says it—so earnest, and artless, and genuine—like maybe no one's tried asking me kindly before. My heart squeezes. I can't explain it. She doesn't sound frustrated, or coddling. If anything, she sounds sad for me, for what I'm missing.

"Sorry," I say. "I wish I could."

"You can at least walk us to the entry hall," King Isaac says. I can't think of a way to argue with that.

The four of us, with guards trailing behind, make our unhurried way to the castle's entrance. The halls are bustling again, like yesterday morning, before the wedding. So many last-minute changes to put in place. I walk close to Whitman, the body heat radiating from his swinging arm against mine. It feels like torture, not touching him—a well-deserved punishment, and one befitting our crime. I focus on keeping my distance until we reach the bottom of the stairs. At the end of the hallway, the keep's massive, arching doorways, inlaid with runes of bronze, stand open, letting in the heady summer air. Courtiers and castle staff stream in and out. They clog the entryway, carrying banners or garlands or bulky boxes. I freeze on the last step of the stairway.

Whitman glances back. "Is this where you leave us?"

Isaac and Elsie stop, too. They all watch me. I smile fragilely, my gaze migrating toward the front doors. Certainly, it would delight them if I did it, if I said, *What better time than now?* and hiked up my skirts to march out there alongside them, into the sunshine.

They don't understand—not yet. This isn't the same as growing used to a new version of indoors. This is part of me, a part I can't change any more than the color of my eyes or the sound of my voice. They'll see that, with time. I think of Whitman's offer last night: a position among the royal magicians, as they deepen the search for the traitors among us and the cause of the Flood's breaches. A chance to serve King Isaac and Queen Elsie. I believe I can do it—I really do.

As long as I can stay inside.

"Go on," I say. "Have a nice time."

Elsie watches me a moment longer before conceding with a nod. Then, to my bewilderment, she throws herself at me—clumsily, encumbered by layers of linen and satin and taffeta—and wraps me in a hug. I stand statue-still as she holds me, rocking me like a child. Without quite meaning to, I lift my arms and hold her back.

"You're a wonderful person, Mona Arnett," she mumbles into my shoulder.

I blink to dry my eyes, looking toward the ceiling. Stupid, grateful Elsie. What have I ever really done for her? I got some news I didn't like, so I lied about it. And I kept lying, endangering the kingdom, for as long as I could manage, until I got an answer I liked better. That's the great service I provided. I stopped being a liar, eventually. And then, to top it off, I slept with Whitman and threatened her reign before the wedding was even over.

Elsie pries herself away, tears cutting a wet track through her copper makeup. She steps back to Isaac's side. The king nods to me, lifting his hand in a brief, awkward wave. With a few tweaks of fate, it could be us standing together, crowned with twin gold-and-black circlets, in full royal regalia.

Whitman hesitates as Isaac and Elsie head for the doors. He stops on the stairs' landing below me; we stand nearly the same height. If I bent forward an inch, our noses would touch. In a low voice, he says, "How are you?"

"I'm nervous about last night." No point skirting around it, especially after how Elsie gushed at me. "Not the good parts. Just what happened after."

"As am I," he admits. "I don't know if we can trust Master Renfield or not."

"About that. I did a reading. She's not one of the bribers, at least."

Whitman's eyebrows shoot up. "And did you learn who was guilty?"

"Oversea and Soph," I say, and Whitman curses, grabbing a fistful of his hair. "Sorry. I know the timing isn't ideal for making accusations, with the wedding and the gods."

"And we have no other proof of their guilt," Whitman mutters. "Other than what Ms. Byers can corroborate, presumably, but that's not enough. Magical evidence of a crime can only be substantiated if three or more seers can swear to the reading. Those bastards will be sitting on the council until we can find material evidence."

"Sounds like it's time for new laws," I say, only half joking. "Look on the bright side. Renfield's not going to use us to hurt Elsie. Probably. I don't know." I sigh wearily. Renfield could still be planning to go after Whitman, but I don't want to remind him of that now. "I feel awful about this."

"I know."

On its own, my body sways toward his. I clench my fists at my sides. "So why do I still want to kiss you?" I whisper.

"Mona," he says under his breath, glancing around. There's no one within earshot but us. He swallows. "I know."

I'm dangerously on the verge of tears. "Go," I say, forcing a grin. "Watch the tournament. I'll be fine."

Clearing his throat, he nods. Then he turns around and leaves, his stride long and rushed, toward the doors of the keep, toward sun and warm wind and the whole wide world outside.

The castle staff procured me a guest room from which I can see the yard out the western-facing window—the towering stacks of benches, festooned with garlands, and the wide, muddy field, cut down the center by a tilt barrier. I set up there for the morning. The benches outside fill up with merry onlookers, noble and common.

And there are Elsie and Isaac, striding in front of the crowd, led by a legion of guards to their honored seats up front. They're beaming, both of them, and remarkably I find myself smiling, too. I watch the crowd watch them, the king and queen. Elsie is still an unknown quantity, but a dozen or more of the folk in the stands get to their feet and bow to her—her in particular, not the king, not the royal unit. Everyone's relieved to have a queen on the throne.

Then the opening ceremonies begin. A series of horses trots out from both sides of the ward, draped in armored blankets, and as they approach the center, a bright spray of sparks shoots up from the middle of the yard, like embers from a fire, fifty feet into the air. An alchemical trick—Umber's work.

I've never seen a tournament before. Smiling like a schoolgirl, I glance at Elsie again. Her face, too, glows with delight. Neither of us was raised at court; we aren't used to spectacle. Or maybe there are some things you never tire of being awed by. I smile at Queen Elsie, a hand pressed against the cold glass windowpane.

What happens next, I don't comprehend. Not right away.

Elsie slumps sideways in her throne. I blink, unsure what I've seen. She's so far away. My eyes are playing tricks on me.

Something sticks out of her chest. How can that be? My mind won't wrap around it, refuses to.

Then the screaming starts, and the bleeding, all at once.

Isaac pitches toward her as a river of red pours down the front of her dress. A second crossbow bolt—for that's what it is, I realize, that impales Elsie like a stake—thunks into the back of the king's chair, where his body was moments before. The guards swarm before the royal pair, shielding them. One takes a bolt to the shoulder and collapses.

I fight for shallow breaths, each one a battle. I cannot have witnessed this thing. It can't be real.

A blur of thoughts assails me, jumbled and senseless, and then I'm on my feet, running into the hallway, yelling at the top of my lungs.

"Help!" I shout—though who's there to hear me? Everyone is at the tournament. "Somebody help!"

I run and run, and cry out, but no one comes. It's like a nightmare, one where everyone in the world but me has turned to mist and dissipated. I trip down the stairs; my dress snags on a splintered banister and tears. I slow to a stop in the entryway before the arched double doors. The doors to the ward. They're shut now, towering over me, molded in bronze, glinting like bloody sunlight off waves. I hover there, dancing on my toes, before at last I slouch against the doorframe and slide to the ground, my breath tearing in and out of my chest. I stare at my knees.

A guard finally skids around the corner, kneeling before me. He grabs me by the shoulders. "Miss," he says, sharp with alarm. "What's the problem?"

I open my mouth, but the words burrow deeper inside. My body is shaking so hard. "Elsie," I choke out. "Something's happened. She needs a physician, I—I think she's hurt."

"It's all right, miss," he says, and from his tone, calm and reassuring, I almost believe him. "I'll get help."

He takes me upstairs to an empty room—more guest quarters—and guides me into a soft armchair, where I fall back and bury my trembling hands beneath my thighs.

"Stay here, please," he says, kind but firm. Then he leaves me.

Gradually, the haze lifts, a fog burning off from my mind.

And then I understand. I wholly grasp it, that knowledge that some small part of me has cradled since the moment it happened.

The queen is dead.

34

After I killed Patrick, there was a funeral. I didn't go. He was buried in a communal gravesite behind the province chapel, an hour south of Selledore. My father doesn't believe in family cemetery plots. All our souls mingled together in the garden of the dead, he told me, so our bones and flesh and the prayer tokens placed over our unseeing eyes ought to do the same.

I don't know where Elsie's body will be interred. For now, she lies on display in a black marble sarcophagus in the basement chapel. She's been there for three days. At ten o'clock on the third night, the crown will hold a service. There will be the public ceremony first, when anyone can come and listen to Master Gan read scriptures in the main hall.

And I attend. I could wait until midnight, when the private viewing commences, but I want to be there for all of it, to own every second. I don't drink a drop, either, before I descend the stairs from the practitioners wing. I'm sober as I've ever been out in the open pasture of the castle.

The main hall is unrecognizable when I step inside. Its walls, its windows, even the floor are draped with spangled navy fabric, tinged on the edges with celestial purple. Mourners pack the room. I find my place beside a remote column, away from the crowds, and I listen to Gan repeat Eledorr's Dirge by rote, blood pumping in my ears.

Elsie is dead. Elsie, who might have been a midwife, who befriended me when crueler types would've wounded me. Whom Isaac had been bound to. A sob bucks in my chest, and I swallow it, though it fights the whole way down. I deserve this. What I've done this time is worse than any of my sins before. I met Elsie, and I adored her, and then I led her to the slaughter.

I failed to act, and Elsie died because of it. The killer is still among us. Whatever role Simon Hansen played, I knew he didn't act alone. And yet I didn't look further. I should've questioned him before the wedding.

Just after the half-hour mark, Whitman approaches me, standing at my side in silence. I nod to him, but stay facing front. If I permit my body to move any farther, I'll collapse in his arms. We listen to Gan without acknowledging one another.

Then, after a minute, an impulse seizes me, crazed and cruel. "We'll be attending Isaac's service next," I say.

Whitman stares at me, and I see him tuck his pain away behind the iron shield of his expression. "Why would you say that?" he forces out.

"Because it's true." I meet his gaze, bold and hurting, like he is, but in a more honest way. "Have you talked to him?"

The hall is quiet, reverent, except for Gan's booming oration. We have to speak softly, like gossipers at church. Whitman huffs, almost inaudible. "It would be hard to discuss his marriage prospects without addressing the urgency."

"That's not what I mean." And he knows it. "You need to *talk* to him, Whitman. Before it's too late. Isaac needs to hear you say goodbye."

He shakes his head, but the fire has gone out of his glare. Maybe I got through to him. Hugging my arms, I try to listen to Master Gan, but I can't stand it for long. Every word out of his mouth fans my anger.

When I speak again, my voice is brittle ice. "I will find who did this to her."

Whitman says nothing, his jaw set like tempered metal. He knows it as well as I do: Whoever killed Elsie, it's somehow related to me, to my prediction, to the threats and Parsons' death. Elsie is the latest victim of my cultist.

Gan recites prayers for another hour. Then there's a short break before the private viewing. Whitman and I move to the far edge of the hall, away from the others. Between a gap in the shroud cloths on the wall, a beam of starlight falls from a high window.

"Have *you* talked to Isaac?" Whitman asks sullenly.

"I don't know that we're close enough for that conversation."

"You were nearly soulmates."

I give Whitman a funny look. I might accuse him of jealousy, if not for where we are and why. "But Isaac and I aren't soulmates."

"Do you regret that?"

No, he's definitely jealous. I sigh and roll out my neck. I could comfort him with an easy lie. Instead, a strange, impulsive truth leaps from my tongue. "A little."

Whitman narrows his eyes, and I iron out a smile. "It's not what you think." For the first time, I try to articulate it. "I've never—Isaac is . . . noble. I didn't think someone like that could love me. It was a relief. It—it meant something about me." My thoughts come out in a rush. After they leave me, I feel better than I have in days, purged of something painful, like an infected splinter.

"I'm *noble*, too," Whitman says, offended.

I can't help myself. I laugh aloud, at Elsie's funeral. "I didn't think you cared much for me," I admit.

Whatever Whitman's answer would have been, it's lost as a series of reverberating bells chime seven tones in the distance. Midnight—time for Elsie's viewing. We follow the trickle of mourners downstairs to the chapel. A queue forms outside its thick stone doors, propped open. The guards admit people one at a time. When it comes to our turn, I look at Whitman.

"You first," he says in a gritty voice. Either he's being polite, or he's avoiding a painful conversation with the king, who waits inside.

Shivering, I step into the drafty chapel. In front of the gods' pillars, a tall marble sarcophagus, twelve feet long, has been crammed into the room. Isaac stands before it, a magnificent white fur cloak adorning his slumped shoulders. He's using his cane today. He stares off to the side, uninterested in the petitioners who've come to pay respects to his wife.

"Your Majesty," I say, dipping in a shallow, timid curtsy.

"Ms. Arnett," he says with a nod. Everything about him—his tone, his posture, his stare—is hollow, like his spirit has been excavated.

Filled with dread, I sidle up to the edge of the sarcophagus. At the sight of her, lying there—in her royal regalia, and with two prayer tokens, one for Eledorr and one for Irinorr, laid on each of her eyes—my body convulses. She doesn't have her glasses on. How is she supposed to see? More prayer tokens have been scattered within her coffin, left by her loyal subjects.

"May I ask you something, Ms. Arnett?" Isaac says. I nod anxiously, and his red-rimmed eyes meet mine. "Am I cursed?"

I falter. "Of course not."

"Then why?" A bitter laugh cracks out of him. "Why does everyone around me end up dead?"

I shake my head, horrified. "There's nothing wrong with you, Isaac. Your Majesty. It isn't your fault."

"Can you promise me that?"

"The gods would say the same," I tell him. But in truth, I don't know. Is there such a thing as curses? I've never asked.

"Forgive me," Isaac says in a dull voice. "I'm in a morbid mood."

"Of course." I reach for him, to touch his hand, but his entire stance is blocked off. I pull back. "I'm very sorry, Isaac. Elsie didn't deserve this."

He looks up at me, as if seeing me for the first time this evening. "No, she didn't."

I have nothing else to say. Mumbling another apology, I hurry from the chapel. I nod to Whitman as our paths cross, but I don't stay to talk. Numbly, I trudge through the castle back to my apartments.

I'm past the point of exhaustion, too tired to sleep. With clumsy fingers, I unlace the back of my dress and curl up on my chaise longue without taking it off. My mind ticks through each event from the past few days and its implications, taking inventory. I saw through Isaac's soulmate reading. Isaac married Elsie. Elsie was assassinated. If I wanted to, I could keep going, threading this string of incidents to sew a conclusion—from the past, through the needle eye of the present, to the next stitch, the future—but I can't do it. I'm not ready to accept what comes next. I lie there in the dark, muscles throbbing with tension.

After an hour of sleepless tossing, I give up. I know what I need right now—who I need. Who could convince me of a truth that feels too overwhelming to accept.

My big brother.

I lie on my chaise longue, chewing my lip as I say a quiet prayer to Eledorr—though that makes absolutely no sense. Eledorr is at the castle, upstairs. How can the gods listen and heed me now? How can they help me if they couldn't even keep Elsie safe? But prayers aside, I feel in my bones that if I sit here alone in my guilt and shame, Patrick will come. That's how it's always happened before.

A rush of noisy wind blows from my bedroom door, and I place it at once. I turn to look, and Patrick's ghost illuminates the doorway, his face mournfully blank. Trembling, I push past my muscle weakness and force myself to sit upright. He watches me without moving. Silent as ever, so grim, so different from the Patrick I knew in life. I am scared of him—gods below, I'm so scared—but I also need to know.

"Patrick," I whisper. "Talk to me."

He stays silent. My whole body tightens with disappointment, though I had no reason to expect different. Then his ghost steps forward. He walks a foot closer and stops. His sagging brows draw together as he regards me with confusion. Maybe that's what drives him to lash out. He doesn't understand why he's here. But I stay calm, this time, and that calms him, too.

"Please." I peer up at him, tears forming in my eyes. I need this more than anything—more than my fear of the throne, more than my desire to protect myself from pain. "Why won't you talk?"

He stares down at me like an arbiter from on high. This can't be how he hoped I'd turn out—the person he wanted me to grow up to be. He tried to raise me right. If his ghost has been watching me all this time, he must be ashamed. He would expect me to fix this.

There is a way—one way I could make up for my lies, my weakness, my cowardice. I would have to embrace my fate, like Irinorr told me. I want to scream, to cry and rage and laugh in my own face, to tear out my hair. All this heartache and death, and in the end, it meant nothing. I had no choice, from the very start.

281

"Fine," I mumble to Patrick. "I'll do it. I'll speak with the council."

If I expected that would be enough, that he would open his mouth and reply, I was wrong. I watch him as he stands like a blazing, ethereal torch. I watch him for hours, for so long my eyes sting and my head gets woozy. Dawn marks the end of that. Once the beams of morning sunlight crawl across my carpet to touch his ghostly toes, Patrick's body begins to dissolve. Like mist, it grows thinner, insubstantial, slowly, by degrees, until he is nothing more than an impression.

I don't try to stop myself. I cry and cry as my brother fades away.

35

The wide double doors to council chambers swing open, and a guard's head pokes out.

"Your turn," he says sympathetically.

Breathing deep, I gather up my skirts and enter. Bathed in the blue light of the nexus are all seven masters and all seven gods. King Isaac is absent. He hasn't been seen publicly since yesterday, at the funeral. Word is his illness has taken a turn for the worse. With how he looked when I last saw him, I'm not surprised—but I am worried about him, more than I care to admit.

I wrestle with where to cast my gaze. Whitman sits across from me, in his seat beside Isaac's empty throne, and Irinorr off to his side. I settle on Semyanadd. A neutral party.

Semyanadd ensnares my gaze. "Tell us what you saw, Mona."

That is why I've been summoned: my eyewitness account of the queen's assassination. But instead of giving testimony, I say, "You must have an idea who did this."

After a heavy pause, Korimarr speaks. "The bolts were etched with runes of aiming and piercing. A powerful magician, undoubtedly. It's reasonable to suspect the same person who interfered with your readings."

Aiming and piercing. That confirms my suspicions. I take a moment to collect myself, and when I begin again, I avoid Whitman's eye altogether. "So, you know why Elsie was assassinated."

"Of course," Master Soph says, his round face shining in the blue light. "An attempt to kill off the royal line. To end magic in the mortal realm."

"No, it wasn't," I say, my tone infused with spite. Soph is one of the traitors. If there weren't more important matters at hand, I'd accuse him here and now. "The shot that killed Elsie was made from one of the castle towers, wasn't it? Hundreds of yards away? Only a master marksman could do that."

No one corrects me, so I must be right. "And with the benefit of an aiming charm? There's no chance they missed Isaac on accident."

"It was misdirection," Whitman says, his fingers laced under his chin. He already knows what I'm going to say, though we haven't discussed it. My throat tightens. "The killer could have made that shot if they'd wanted. Elsie was the only target. The king was meant to live."

"And remarry," Irinorr finishes. His flawless brow is drawn with sorrow. But he knows it as well as I do—this day is a long time coming.

"It's no secret what this murderer wants." I raise my chin. "They influenced my lovers reading. They killed Isaac's bride. They want to put me on the throne. Maybe it's time to find out why."

The *why* scares me almost as much as the *who*. If it turns out the Guild of the Rising Tide was behind Parsons' and Elsie's murders—and right now, they're my only tangible suspect—what do they hope to gain by making me queen? Whatever their end game, I doubt it aligns with Opalvale's interests, or my own.

Master Renfield gives the tiniest shake of her head. "And how do you propose we do that?" she says, though by her biting tone, she has already guessed my plan. My mouth goes dry. What if she brings up what she knows about Whitman and me? She could ruin everything out of spite. Still, I have to keep going.

"Marry me to Isaac." I almost choke on the words, but I hold the image of Patrick's ghost in my mind, the silent judgment on his face as he towered over me last night. I'm doing everything I can to make it right. To make him proud. "Clearly, this person wants something from me. Crown me, and we might learn what."

"Oh," Renfield says, her grin humorless, "and I'm sure this is unmotivated by self-interest, *Queen* Mona—"

Then Whitman and I are shouting, shouting at her, though I barely know or care what I'm saying. It pours out of me like water through a broken dam. I can't wrap my head around how stupid she is. The last thing I want is power. With power comes scrutiny, and before long, the rest of the world will see that I'm too foolish and cruel and inept to shoulder this responsibility. So long as I am nobody—apart from the world—my shame remains private. Now it will belong to Opalvale.

Semyanadd cuts through our outburst with a sharp whistle, and silence settles over the room.

I breathe through my nose. "You could never know," I say, "what it costs me to propose this. But King Isaac needs a bride, and anyone you put on the throne who isn't me is dead. So, how many women are you willing to sacrifice to prove some kind of point?"

Renfield has nothing to say to that.

When Whitman speaks again, he sounds depleted, scraped thin. "This isn't our decision. It's Isaac's."

"Isaac is ill," says Master Oversea, "as you very well know—and you were the one who had such concerns about the queen's legitimacy in her subject's eyes. How will it look if we put this . . . girl on the throne?"

I snort. I doubt "girl" was Oversea's first choice of descriptor.

"We will endorse her," Semyanadd says.

The masters exchange shocked glances—all except for Whitman. His eyes stay glued to me.

"You will declare Ms. Arnett the rightful ruler?" Master Renfield repeats, disbelieving. "I thought you had no interest in mortal affairs."

"We have an interest in stopping the magician who is murdering mortals," Irinorr says. "And in ending the disturbances in the mortal realm. If Mona must be queen for that to happen, so be it."

"And why would King Isaac agree to this?" says Master Gan, though he sounds less suspicious than the others. Mostly, he sounds scared.

"Because I'll talk to him," I say. "I'll make him understand."

The royal bedchambers are grand, richly decorated but not ostentatious. Velvet hangings cover the windows and the four-poster bed, soaking Isaac in shadows. Carved gargoyle faces, mounted on the walls in a ring, stare down at us, reminding me unnervingly of the masked demons. Spheres of boulder opal stick out from between their slate teeth. Semyanadd's gemstone.

Isaac's bedframe is carved from a warm, rosy stone, inlaid with gold. Logs blaze in the fireplace, heating the room to an uncomfortable warmth. The king must have fever chills.

Whitman and I sit on stools at the side of the bed. The king is hunched over, propped up against the headboard. His pasty skin glistens with sweat and his blond hair sticks to his forehead. But, wonder of wonders, he attempts a grin. "Don't worry," he says. "I'm not contagious."

I don't insult him by asking how he feels. Safe to assume the answer is *bad*. Donning my best bedside manner, I say, "Isaac, this shouldn't have happened. We should have stopped it. I'm so sorry."

He tries to shake his head. "What could you have done?"

"How sick are you?" Perhaps that's rude, but I need to know.

"Physicians say it's psychosomatic. All in my head. Doesn't feel that way."

"But what about the illness in your bones?"

"Same symptoms." He grunts in pain, shifting beneath the blankets. "But it hasn't progressed. The physicians stick these needles in my thigh, draw something out . . ." He shudders. "The values haven't changed."

I nod, wishing there was some measure of comfort I could offer. I give him the best I have. "I want to catch Elsie's killer."

Isaac swallows, shutting his eyes. "Yes. Whatever it takes. You have full dispensation to—"

"You need to marry Mona," Whitman says, very softly.

Isaac falls quiet, but he doesn't look surprised. He must have come to the same conclusion: Elsie's murder ties back to me.

How can he not hate me for that?

"You think Hansen's accomplice will reveal themself, if I do?" Isaac says, staring past us.

"They'll have to," I say. "They're not doing me a favor by making me queen. Whatever their reasons, their plot will be in vain if they don't let me in on it."

Isaac thinks it over in silence. I share a glance with Whitman; his eyes look even darker in the low light, almost black. When I can't take it any longer, I turn away.

"We'll need to move quickly," Isaac speaks up. His sweaty brow furrows. "I don't want to waste any time. A small wedding."

A strange sensation roars through me—relief swirled with dread and dropped into a boiling pot of fear. I've never had a dream that felt half this surreal.

"I'll speak with Master Gan," Whitman says, squeezing his friend on the shoulder as he rises.

I spin on the stool to leave with Whitman, but Isaac's clammy hand touches my wrist. "Stay for a moment," he says.

Wavering, I look back at Whitman, but his face is unreadable. I wish he could stay with me. Part of me dreads speaking to Isaac alone. But how can I say no to a dying, widowed king?

Once Whitman quits the room, the silence grows, expanding into the space he left behind. Isaac clears his throat. "Did we make a mistake?"

My pulse quickens. "What?"

"We could have married sooner. After you came forward as my soulmate. I would never have fallen in love with Elsie, but she'd be . . ."

I can't bear the way his face crumples with pain. If he had never loved her, she would be alive. It's the kind of poison that can taint the best memories.

"Isaac." My voice trembles. "I'm so sorry." And I am sorry, for so much more than what I've done. I'm sorry for the life he was dealt.

"Me too." Wincing, he leans back on his pillow. "So, what are we going to do about it?"

36

My father always wanted to live to see my wedding day. I used to tell him he'd better pray for immortality.

The crown sends a carriage and attendants to my parents' house. They're old; travel is hard on them. But they still come. Of course they come.

When they join me in my apartments, I've already been fitted into my gown. Coppery satin, shimmering with a metallic sheen. I sit on the edge of my bed, turning Irinorr's prayer token between my fingers. They settle on either side of me. My father takes my hand, eyes misty.

"We love you, Mona," he says, voice breaking. My mother's arm wraps around me. She presses her soft cheek against my shoulder.

"I love you, too," I mumble.

We don't talk for a while. Idly, I play with my mother's feathery hair. Then I say something I've been trying to say for a long time.

"I need you to know that I'm sorry about Patrick," I say. "I'd do anything to change what happened."

My mother sniffles. "Mona, we don't—"

"Patrick blames me," I interrupt, quiet but firm. "But I can't apologize to him, so you'll have to do. Can you forgive me?"

"Patrick would never blame you. Never. There's nothing to forgive."

"But he—"

She hushes me. "There's nothing to forgive."

I smile at her, willing myself not to cry.

We go down to the main hall together. There's hardly anyone in attendance this time, except the masters and the gods. They stand on the platform in neat lines, same as before. I nod to Byers as I make to skirt around her toward the stage, but she steps in my path and rests a hand on my shoulder.

"Tasha was right about you," she whispers.

I shake my head, unable to respond. Tasha said I'm stronger than I believe. Yes, I agreed to marry Isaac, but it's temporary, only until we find Elsie's killer. It's not the real thing. I still can't accept that there's a future for me outside of the east wing, and that future will happen whether I like it or not.

I avoid Whitman's eye as I walk up the wide stairs of the platform, across from King Isaac. The king leans on a simple wooden cane, gripped in his white-knuckled hand. Sweat beads his face, and rings of purple surround his sunken eyes. It shocks me that he can stand, even with the cane. He nods, solemn.

The ceremony is efficient, streamlined. Unsentimental. Gan ties our wrists together. Then the master places a thin circlet of black cobalt on my head, the counterpart to Isaac's gold. That completes the transformation.

That's all it takes to change who I am.

"We must go to the east balcony now," Semyanadd says.

His features seem to blur, to ripple, as I stare at him. None of this feels real. "Why?"

"To present you to your subjects."

My stomach seethes as we march, the king and the masters and the gods and I, to the northeast tower, to the balcony overlooking the bailey. Queen Elsie was presented to the public at the tournament, but in my case, a celebration is hardly appropriate. We stop before a wall of glass doors. The sky outside is a powdery blue. My pulse goes wild, pounding against my throat. But when Semyanadd pushes the door open, inviting us onto the balcony, I hesitate only for a moment. I swallow my nausea and step out into the balmy air. King Isaac takes his place beside me.

People pack the lawn around the tower; the gates were opened to the public today. I can't make out faces—just a sea of color and noise, far below. They don't even look human. More like stalks of some strange crop, swaying, a whole field of them. I feel dizzy, like I might tilt and fall over the marble rails and plummet to the ward.

Semyanadd steps up to the balcony's edge. His voice booms unnaturally loud as he addresses the crowd. "People of Opalvale, may I present to you your queen."

A hand presses me forward. I'm not sure who it belongs to.

"Queen Mona," Semyanadd says, "first of her name."

My subjects cheer, because they have to. I stare straight ahead.

Tasha was wrong. In this moment, I don't feel proud. I only feel sorry for myself.

37

My new quarters are attached to the king's royal bedchambers, part of his apartments. His residence takes up most of the eighth floor, a labyrinth of opulence. Lush rugs cover the cold stone floors in all the rooms—the solar, the library, the nursery. That last room is for Isaac's heir, assuming he sires one. It's empty now, but for a wooden cradle in the corner, its white paint peeling off in strips. The other empty rooms were once used for the monarch's extended family. But Isaac doesn't have a family anymore.

There has been so much death in this castle.

The bodies of the recently dead, I've learned, are stored in a chamber adjacent to Master Penna's office within the chapel. That's where Byers asked to meet this morning. Cool beams of light shining from the stained-glass windows that encircle the chamber, hit my face as I enter. The air smells musty but inoffensive—not the stink of decay I expected. A dozen rolling platforms form a crooked row against one wall, and in the center of the room stands Byers, along with our victims.

I approach slowly, like I can put it off just a little longer. Byers hears me coming. She glances over her shoulder with a weary look. "What took you so long, Your Majesty?"

"Don't start with that." I confront the corpses on the platforms before me. Parsons, nude, looking much as I remember him. I swallow a gag and turn to the second corpse. Elsie. She is draped in a long gray shroud that billows around the edges of the table. I squint. No, not gray—the shroud is white, embroidered along every inch with minuscule black runes, hundreds—thousands—of them, so small I didn't notice at first. I wouldn't recognize it, if not for Tasha and the books she forced me to read. Mouth agape, I say, "It's a deathless shroud."

Byers favors me with a nod, like a pleased schoolmarm. "That it is."

I stare at the cloth with round eyes, the runes swimming through my vision. A deathless shroud can delay decomposition for days, even months, depending on conditions. Only a handful exist. Allegedly crafted by the gods and mortals of old together, when the seven first ascended to the mortal realm to form the nexus.

I examine Parsons' body again; it lacks any signs of decay. Byers follows my gaze. "He was under the shroud for a while, before Elsie," Byers says.

"Why hasn't he been buried yet?"

"His murder investigation is still open," she explains. "We have Simon Hansen, but we can't close the case until we know why he did it and who else was involved. But Elsie takes precedence."

I reach out to graze the rough hem of the shroud. "How do we have this?"

"It belongs to the crown. Passed down for generations."

I shake my head in disbelief, focusing on the cloth—the strange and archaic magic, not what it conceals. Elsie, sucked of life. She probably doesn't have her mark of Korimarr anymore—they would've washed that off when they bathed her corpse. Tears choke me, but I push them down and bury them deep. Crying does Elsie no good now.

I turn to Byers, my jaw set. Down to business. "What have you learned?"

"Nothing that makes sense," she says, frowning. Byers has spent the bulk of her time in these chambers lately. A neat stack of papers, wrapped in vellum, rests on the empty platform nearest to her—the company's file on the murders.

"Any leads at all?" I ask.

She looks disturbed as she answers, "I think so. It appears Elsie was not killed by the same person as Parsons."

A jolt shoots down my spine, though it's the only possible explanation—Simon Hansen was behind bars when Elsie was killed. "How can you tell?"

"The shape of intent from the first murder, compared to Elsie's . . . they're like two sizes of the same object. One's just much, much bigger. Does that make sense?"

I gape at her. "Not remotely."

"Here." She guides me by the elbow, closer to the bodies, though I drag my feet and grimace. "Do a reading yourself. You'll see what I mean."

Reluctantly, I shut my eyes, reaching out for the reading, holding the two bodies at the forefront of my mind. Their physical forms dissolve into particulate matter, the essence of themselves. The clouds of their mist glow against the black. I ask what I'm here to find out: *Did the same person kill them?*

The glows fluctuate. Parsons' condenses into a tight, wan light; Elsie's, a brilliant and diffuse spray of orange. The intent, Byers said. Same shapes but different sizes.

Why were they killed?

Sure enough, I glimpse it: how Elsie's mist stretches and swells, like outreaching arms, while Parsons' kicks off smaller tendrils. But they dance the same dance. Killed for the same reason—but the murderers responsible had a gulf of purpose between them. Could the bigger glow be the Guild? If they're the ones backing Hansen, their purpose would surely blaze hotter than his.

That's not all I notice. Parsons' corpse sings with a light and sound so familiar it wrenches at my insides. Elsie's body doesn't have it, this quality. I focus on that bruised-heart feeling, a feeling I know better than my skin. It's the radiance filtering through the dome of Tasha's library. It is Byers' eyes, liquid in dim lamplight. It's a high, small moon in an impossible afternoon sky.

I gasp, and my eyelids fly open. "He's been in the Flood."

Byers has an odd look on her face—grateful, almost, that I can see it, too, that our veins carry the same strain of knowledge and need. "But only Parsons," she says. "Not Elsie. I couldn't place it until I read them both at once."

I rack my brain for how that could be possible, and Byers picks up an object from the platform next to her. A thick wooden stick, snapped off on one end, fletched with trimmed golden feathers. Carved runes run along its length.

I gawk at it in horrified fascination. "That's the bolt that killed her?"

"Most of it. It's from the castle armory, but that doesn't mean much. They could have stolen it."

"But the guards would have easy access."

"True enough."

I scowl down at Parsons' mottled face, trying to make sense of it. Somehow, at some point, his body passed over to the Flood—and came back. "Could Parsons have seen the windows, too?" I muse aloud. "Maybe he never told anyone."

"Perhaps, but . . ." Byers trails off, peering into the distance. I wave a hand in front of her face.

"Verimall," she says pensively.

"What about her?"

"Do you remember much about Verimall's favored?"

My eyes crinkle as I try to recall. "Calvin something. Calvin . . . Meekus?"

"Calvin Meeker. What about his magic?"

I throw my head back, exasperated. "Just tell me what you're getting at."

"Meeker's a combat strategist. He controls the battlefield by manipulating windows to the Flood. He can open a window in one place and come back someplace else."

When it hits me, I cry out, slapping a hand to my forehead. "He could've broken into my apartments without going past the guards."

What a power: traveling freely through the Flood, opening up brand-new windows wherever you please. Meeker could have killed Parsons in a secluded location and moved his body to my room via the Flood, and no one would've seen it happen. It explains every impossible feat my cultist pulled off.

Excitably, I punch Byers on the arm. "Why didn't you think of this sooner?"

She winces and rubs the sore spot. "Because Calvin Meeker is supposed to be dead. I heard the news not long before you arrived. He was in the Ashclaud border patrol; he had a run-in with a gang of poachers."

My shoulders sag. "Thanks for getting my hopes up."

"You're missing my point. What if he's not actually dead? What if he's at the castle right now, going by a different name?"

My eyes widen in comprehension. "Like Simon Hansen?"

"Exactly. There's just one thing I haven't figured out." Her mouth turns down at the corner. "If all of that is true, why's he sitting in that dungeon cell? He could leave anytime."

I match her frown. The rest of the theory weaves together so perfectly. There has to be some explanation for this. "Maybe he did leave," I say suddenly. "To kill Queen Elsie."

"Perhaps, but my readings still suggest two killers."

"Does the crossbow bolt tell you anything?"

She glances at the snapped arrow, discarded on the table. A few droplets of blood stain the wood. "Not yet."

"Then let's go with what we have." I spin around for one last look at Elsie's corpse, at rest beneath the shroud. My blood roars through me. I will make this up to her, whatever it takes. "I'll tell Irinorr our theory."

"No," Byers says firmly, taking me aback. "Let's bring him before the gods and masters without advance warning. What if *Verimall* has been giving him orders? We don't want her to catch wind."

The thought sickens me. I'd desperately like to believe a goddess couldn't be capable of betrayal on that level, even one as bloodthirsty as Verimall. But as I look at Byers, her eyes blazing with conviction, I realize I trust her on this. Probably more than I trust myself.

"Then let's gather the council." I clutch the arrow in my sweaty fist. "Simon Hansen may well give up his accomplice."

In council chambers, I sit on Isaac's throne and survey the room from this strange new angle, shifting uncomfortably in my seat. It's padded with a spongy, molded cushion meant to ease the pressure on Isaac's bones. The king remains bedridden, sicker than ever, but this meeting can't wait. Whitman sits beside me, bathed in the watery light of the nexus. The rest of the masters are interspersed with the seven around the table. Between my fingers, I spin the broken bolt that killed Elsie. No one acknowledges its presence. Perhaps it strikes them as a peculiar token to carry around, but I expect I'll need it.

"First things first." My gaze travels around the table. "Masters Soph and Oversea. You are guilty of conspiring to commit treason. Guards, please remove these men to the dungeons."

A rustle of panic sweeps over the room; even Whitman turns to stare at me. The masters I named sit unmoving, as if waiting for someone to defend them.

"Each of you paid off a royal magician to instill your favored candidate on the throne," I go on. "I have proven it. If you want to avoid execution, you may give your full confession." Still, no one moves. I glance at the guards near the door. "Arrest them."

They spring into action. The other masters shift in their seats as the guards seize Soph and Oversea.

As a guard secures Oversea's wrists behind his back, the master's face swims with vitriol and fear. "This is preposterous. You have no basis for your accusations." Oversea wrenches his arms away, like he's being mishandled. "You will not be queen forever, Ms. Arnett. Remember that."

"That's 'Your Majesty' to you," I say coolly as the guard leads him out of the room.

The air in the room hangs still, tomblike. I turn to Whitman once the traitors are gone. "Master, after this meeting, please ensure that the seers John Hawkes and Alice Janieux are placed under arrest and given the same offer."

"Of course, Your Majesty," he says, eyes shrouded. I doubt he approves of how I'm handling this. But Whitman is not my superior anymore. Renfield, too, gives me a probing look, but for once, she doesn't seem angry. She may even be impressed.

I clasp my hands on the table before me. "Guards," I call to those remaining. "Bring in the prisoner."

No one stirs as the men follow my command.

Two castle guards sweep back through the doorway with Hansen bound between them. His eyes, large and expressive, drink in the scene from behind curtains of lanky hair. It's probably the first time he's seen light in weeks. He makes no attempt to struggle.

He can't be older than sixteen. This boy went to the trouble of murdering Parsons and upending my life. I study the impassive contours of his face, blurred in the nexus's soft light. Where have I seen him before?

Then it hits me—he was one of the guards posted outside my apartments, the fellow who tried to stop me the night I broke into Whitman's office. He looked so much older in his standard-issue leathers and tabard. When I had my run-in with him, he'd already murdered Parsons. I shiver with revulsion.

I grip Elsie's arrow in my fist. "Mr. Hansen. We need to talk."

Hansen says nothing. I take a peek at the gods around me, gauging their reactions. Mostly, their expressions are passive. I start to worry this isn't Calvin Meeker after all. But then my gaze slides over to Verimall, and in a second flat, I have my answer. Verimall's looking at him exactly how Irinorr looks at me—her eyes brimming with love and affection, an unconcealable bond between god and favored mortal. Simon Hansen is Calvin Meeker. So, why do the other gods pretend not to notice? Are they protecting Verimall, or just distancing themselves from a murderer? It's infuriating either way. This is no time to play politics.

I'll have to remind them.

I speak directly to the prisoner. "Am I correct in assuming you have no intention of speaking to me or anyone else, now or in the future?"

He doesn't answer.

"Very well. Then I sentence you to death."

The hush in the chamber crystallizes into something else, a brittle absence of noise—because silence can fill up a room, but this isn't that; this is true negative space, this is a *vacuum*—as all eyes bear down on me.

Master Renfield clears her throat. "Ms. Ar— Your Majesty, it's understandable that you would have some animosity toward the accused, but there is much he can still tell us, and most prisoners are more cooperative without the threat of execution hanging over their head."

I set the broken arrow very deliberately on the table. "There will be no lingering threat. The execution is happening today," I proclaim in a measured voice. "Right now."

38

Calvin Meeker bucks like he might run away, but the guards hold him in place. I scope out the gods again. Most of their expressions have darkened, but Verimall's strains with forced composure.

The guard to Calvin's left sweats under the sudden pressure. "E-execute him how?"

Lazily, I wave a hand. "You have swords. Figure it out."

No one makes a move. I shift on my throne, starting to regret the theatrics. What's the point of being queen if no one listens to you? But I'm too far into the act to drop it now. Inhaling, I slap my hands on the table and stand up.

"Fine," I say, circling around the room to stand before Calvin. I bend over and grab a guard's boot knife before he can protest. Both Calvin and the guard yelp in alarm as I straighten to my full height. "I'll do it myself."

All the masters at the table jump to their feet. Whitman shouts, "Mona, don't!"

I point the knife at Calvin's throat as he quivers, his lips moving like he's trying to beg but can't find his voice. Must be out of practice. "You ruined my life," I hiss under my breath. I pull my hand back to strike.

"Stop!"

I pause and turn around. Verimall staggers toward me, shaking like a child. "Stop, Mona. You won. Bully for you. Just put down the knife."

I lower my arm but don't back away. "Why should I?"

Semyanadd stands, too. "It would be best for the mortals to leave the room now. We have matters to discuss."

His words ring out, the only sound besides Calvin's heavy breathing next to my ear. Surely, no one but the king has ordered the masters to clear the chamber before. But who's going to argue with the gods?

"Let Calvin go," Verimall says in a hollow voice, looking at her favored mortal. "Get him away from her, she's gone fucking mad."

My mouth pulls to the side. A bit dramatic, but I agree with her about ridding the room of Calvin. Kick him out so I can speak to the gods alone.

"Take him to the dungeons," I say to the guards. "And chain him to something." I can't have him escaping through the Flood.

With that, the masters stream out of the room, splitting around me. Calvin and the guards follow. Whitman tosses me a troubled look before the door closes behind him.

As I walk back to the throne, I try to hide my anxious tics, but there's nothing to be done about my shaking limbs and sweaty upper lip. I sit with a straight, disciplined spine.

"That boy is a favored mortal," I say. There's no denying it now. "How long have you known about what he did?"

Semyanadd studies my eyes. Whatever he finds there, his whole bearing changes. He sighs, his mouth a pale line, sitting back down with the resigned look of a prisoner ready to confess. "Perhaps it is the time to tell you. You are the queen now, after all."

"Tell me what?" I try to ignore Verimall's seething in the background. She won't forgive me for threatening Calvin anytime soon.

Semyanadd folds his bone-white hands together, one over the other. The six gods around the table hold their stately poses, unmoving, unblinking. "Mona," he says, "we have learned how the nexus is causing breaches in the mortal realm."

I sit up, my scalp tingling. "You have? When?" I shake myself, remembering what just happened. "What about Simon Hansen, or Calvin, or whoever he is?" I demand. "He killed Parsons, and he helped assassinate the queen!" He also threatened me, but that seems like the least of his crimes.

Semyanadd chooses not to answer. "This may be hard to hear. We need you to be strong."

Cold dread hits the pit of my stomach. "Just tell me."

"Very well," he says gravely, bowing his head. "It is not the nexus itself, but what it represents. The nexus is a tether between the Flood and the mortal realm. For four millennia, it has imbued your world with magic. But the realms have been changing." He purses his lips and inhales, probably working out how to best explain this to an idiot mortal like me. "The Flood is dynamic. The mortal realm is static. Our realm is ever expanding, while yours stays the same. Over a short enough period, cosmically speaking, it causes no issues. But if our realms stay connected, the Flood will tear your world apart. Hence the dying spellsap orchards, the ghosts that you and others saw pass through the breaches."

My brows wrench down. Something about his explanation feels wrong. I can't put my finger on it. "How do we fix it?"

"Only you can, Mona," says Onyamarr. "By the contract, the gods and a monarch of Opalvale must agree for the nexus to be severed. And only a mortal with your connection to the Flood can perform the final act of magic required."

I don't understand. "Why a favored mortal?"

The gods exchange an inscrutable look before Korimarr says, "It was not meant to be that way. The mortal king who formed the contract had your same abilities. Magic can be . . . unpredictable, at times."

Then it hits me, with a sick, lurching sensation. "How long have you known?"

Not one of them answers me. I need them to say this is something new. To prove it's a big, strange coincidence. But they are silent. I look at Irinorr, and he looks back, his eyes glistening.

"How long have you known?" I repeat, louder.

"You must understand, Mona," Semyanadd begins, and the gentleness in his voice makes me double over like I was punched. Gods below, it's true. "If the nexus is not broken soon, your realm will suffer terribly. The orchards are only the beginning.

Next it will be demons, and then the very fabric of your world will tear. The mortal realm will be no more."

"*You* changed the outcomes of my readings." I stare at my lap, unable to face them. "*You* wanted to put me on the throne."

The gods do not respond. I swallow a wave of nausea. So, I'm right.

I have never been so heartbroken, so lost at sea. Everything I ever believed in has been based upon lies.

A droplet of sweat runs behind my ear, down my neck. "Did you kill Elsie and Parsons, too?" I ask quietly. "Has Calvin been working for *you* this whole time?"

"No, he has not." Semyanadd's glance shifts to Verimall. "Unless there is something you would like to disclose, sister?"

Verimall lets out a ragged, empty laugh, so loud I jump. "No killing, you said!" she cackles. "Oh, no, we wouldn't want to add to their suffering! Let her come to the decision on her own—let her *grow* into the role. Ha! And in the end, you did it anyway! You *murderers*."

I look between the gods with my mouth agape. She's not talking sense, but her words inflame me; beneath the gibberish, she's speaking a truth the others are too cowardly to say.

"That's what this was?" Semyanadd utters, watching Verimall with cold anger. "Your attempt to move things along?"

"I told you from the start," she snaps, spittle flying from her lips, "that the girl would never admit to her reading unless we put on the pressure. Yes, I told Calvin to leave the threats. He didn't mean to kill that boy. The little bastard caught Calvin burning the drafts of his letters. There was a struggle—it just happened. So, Calvin put the corpse to good use. It wasn't part of the plan, but I stand by it. It was necessary, to compensate for *her* shortcomings." Verimall flings a finger at me, and I jerk back. "She would never have come forward, the selfish bitch!"

My thoughts pool together sluggishly, but one breaks the surface. If Verimall's telling the truth, she must have ordered Calvin to stay locked in that cell, speaking to no one, to draw suspicion away from me. Hard to sell an accused murderer as the future queen. From the scornful looks on the gods' flawless faces, they weren't in on Verimall's plans.

"Calvin killed an innocent," I say faintly to Verimall. I can't get enough air. "Even if it was an accident, how—how can you justify that?"

"How?" She bares her fangs. "How could I sacrifice a few lives to prevent the suffering of millions? Why don't you ask your beloved Irinorr, or any of the rest?"

I turn to Irinorr, begging him with my eyes to deny it. He only bends his head.

With a shudder, I accept it—the reality I must have already known, somewhere deep inside. Of course the seven assassinated Elsie. Who else could get to the top of the tower and back without being noticed? Who else could make a shot at that distance? It was a feat of godly proportions. Calvin Meeker murdered Parsons, but the gods killed the queen. I grip the broken bolt. Its grain is slippery with my sweat. I meant to do a reading on it, in proximity to Calvin, to learn what new information it might reveal. I don't need to any longer.

I sway on my feet, though I don't remember standing. "You didn't have to kill Elsie. Why would you do that?" Tears swim in my eyes, pooling until they finally spill out. "Why would you kill her? She never did anything to you!"

"She was in the way," Wayvadd says. The cat god leans back in his chair, his feet kicked up on the table. My distress seems to amuse him. "We needed you on the throne. You didn't leave us with many options, my sweet."

"So, why didn't you just *tell* me!" I pace behind my throne. "If you'd just fucking *told* me you wanted to make me queen, I never would have lied! I never would have put Elsie on the throne!"

"What would you have done, then?" Irinorr asks with agonizing patience. I spin on him, holding back a sob. "If we came to you and said you must become the queen? You would have retreated into the Flood, wouldn't you have? We might have lost you for good." He leans forward, beseeching me for forgiveness with his eyes. "This way, you had a choice. It was your decision."

My cheeks blaze. Of course he's right. Verimall is right, too. If they had confronted me with their plans, I would have fought them tooth and nail. I forced their hands.

Elsie is dead because of me.

"Why me?" I stop behind my throne, sagging against it, wiping tears from my cheeks. "Why not another favored mortal?"

Korimarr, her chin raised in flagrant apathy, says, "Yours was the easiest path. We could put you on the throne in the fewest moves."

"How far back does it go? Isaac's line? Did you kill off his family to break the nexus?"

"It was a contingency plan," Semyanadd answers, his long fingers twined together. If I didn't know better, I'd say he sounds nervous. I hope he's ashamed. "Not our first choice. We needed to be in a position where the royal line could be ended, if it came to that. Understand, Mona: If the nexus is broken in this way, there will be some tearing of the veil. It would wreak havoc on your realm, but at least there would *be* a mortal realm. The same will not be true if the nexus remains."

I gaze into the middle distance. The gods say nothing as I process.

If Whitman's betrayal was painful, it has nothing on this. All along, the seven knew how this would turn out. Perhaps from the first day Irinorr found me in the Flood. I was raised as a puppet for the throne, groomed like a prized farm animal. Irinorr encouraged my pliability at every turn. He drove wedges into the cracks left by Patrick's death, prying them open. Because I'm easier to predict this way, to direct. To control. If they went too far and molded me too fragile, too brittle for the role they had planned—well, that's no one's fault but their own.

I steady my voice. "What will happen when I break the nexus?"

"Magic will be gone from the mortal realm," Semyanadd says. "Runes will hold no power; spellsap will remain dormant."

"And my magic?"

"Your abilities are not affected by the nexus. They will remain unchanged."

"Right." It doesn't seem real. Only one more chapter in a days-long dream, this eerie twilight fate has set me adrift in. I meet Semyanadd's eye and ask, "How do I do it?"

"A series of spoken runes."

"Runes?" I frown. "I'm not an enchanter."

"These are not the runes you know. They're much older. I will teach you."

And so he does, quickly and without pomp. Three short, guttural syllables, unlike any runes I've ever heard pronounced. I memorize them as Semyanadd repeats each one—and somehow, they stick in my head, clear and bold, like they're imprinted on my brain. This is no mortal magic I'm tampering with. This is the magic of gods. When I speak the runes aloud in the presence of the nexus, the thing will be done.

My back to the gods, I repeat them in my head. When I have it down, I swivel around.

"I'd like a moment to think," I say.

The seven do not argue. Graciously, they rise one at a time. Verimall sneers at me as she goes. Because of me, her favored mortal's life is ruined. Ten minutes ago, my heart might have bled for her. Now I wonder if the gods care for their favored at all. How could they care and do this anyway?

Alone, I circle the table, studying the nexus's column of light, chanting the runes in my head. The chill air in the room seeps through my gown. Who can I trust? The gods have betrayed me, but that doesn't mean every word out of their mouths is a lie. Tasha would caution me to question their voices of authority. Then again, Irinorr said the Flood has turned Tasha's heart to mush. It would pain me to discover yet another lie my patron god fed me, but Tasha didn't seem like a monster.

Shivering, I spend half an hour winding around that table like a noose drawing tighter. As I pace, I find myself thinking of Bernadette Byers. There's one person I trust with my life. And she can separate truths from lies.

I poke my head out the door. "Bring me Ms. Byers," I say to the guard on my left. She salutes and runs down the hall. I pace the room again until Byers arrives. She snaps the door shut, her eyes trained on me.

"What is it, Your Majesty?" she says.

"Stop calling me that. I need your help."

"With what?" Byers comes closer, but my eyes never move from the nexus.

"I'm not strong enough to do a reading on this." I gesture at the tower of light. "Not without touching it, and I don't know what would happen if I did that." Even after my time in the Flood, I could never read something with this caliber of power— the nexus, or the gods—without a focus. But Byers has always been stronger than me.

"What are you trying to find out?" She approaches the table, leaning closer.

"What will happen if the nexus is broken."

"You know what will happen," she says, perplexed. "Magic will disappear."

"I need to go broader than that. Just . . . give me a general idea. What is the end result of severing our connection to the Flood?"

She searches my face, then shrugs. Letting out a puff of air, she closes her eyes. I wait and wring my hands.

Byers' eyes pop open.

She releases a terrible sound, a pealing cry. Stumbles backward. I jump to intercept her, catching her under the arms.

"What's wrong?" I say, shifting her deadweight in my grip.

Byers' breathing is labored. Her trembling hand covers mine. "Why did you ask me that?"

"Because the gods told me to break the nexus. What is it, Byers? Just tell me!"

A nauseous convulsion racks her body, or maybe it's a sob. My muscles strain as I hold her up. "Arnett, there's nothing. I sense nothing, I—I feel nothing."

I frown. "Someone's blocking the reading?"

"No, it's not that. There's just . . . n-nothing. If you break the nexus, everything will end."

"Everything?" I repeat, my chest thrumming, my pulse beating in my ears. Byers' feet slide over the floor as she tries to stand on her own. "What does that mean, *everything*?"

"The mortal realm," she pants. "The world."

39

We sit on the floor, against the walls, across the room from each other. Byers' loud, slow breathing echoes in the silence. Minutes have passed since her proclamation, and she hasn't recovered.

"Try it again," I say, my chin rested on bent knees.

Her wet eyes reflect the light of the nexus. "My reading's right, Arnett," she replies, her voice hollow. "Stop trying to find a way out."

I nestle my face between my knees. How can she be right? Why did the gods tell me to break the nexus, if what Byers saw is the result? Maybe they can be cruel, sometimes, but not needlessly. They wouldn't destroy our world for fun.

"What will happen if I *don't* break the nexus?" I ask.

After a pause, she shivers aloud. "Pain," she says quietly. "So much pain, and then—and then it's the same. Nothing."

"This is why they chose me," I say, eyes burning like I've been awake for days. "The seven knew I would never ask questions. I'd do whatever they told me, just to get off the damn throne." I cradle my head in my hands, tugging at my hair. They used me. *Irinorr* used me. He raised me for the slaughter.

Pain drills into my sternum, so sharp and strong it takes my breath away. I don't recognize the feeling at first.

Anger. I'm *incensed.* If the gods walked into the room right now, I would fight the whole pantheon with my bare hands.

"I don't understand," Byers mumbles. Her legs splay out on the floor in front of her. "If this is it . . . If this is the Rising Tide . . . My p-parents were right. There was never any point. Nothing matters."

Then, all at once, she's sobbing, her hands forming claws against her face.

I freeze for only an instant before scrambling over. Awkwardly, I put my arm around her shoulders. Her cheek, sopping wet, rests on my chest. I hush her.

I don't know what else to do.

"I wish Tasha were here," she says between hiccups.

I sniff. "Why? So she could tell us what idiots we are for not seeing this coming?"

"I don't know. I just wish I could hear her voice. I think I'd feel better about . . . this."

I snort with laughter—as if this is funny. A big joke. If I break the nexus, the world will be over. If I don't, the world will suffer—and then it'll be over. That's the horrible choice the gods faced—the one they passed along to me. I clench my jaw so hard my teeth ache. How quickly the seven were willing to throw us mortals out with the bathwater. And I would have been their accomplice. No, more than that. Their executioner's axe.

I lace my fingers behind my neck, squeezing my eyes closed. The seven have raised and protected me since I was a child. I want to believe they had no other options. That they wouldn't choose for this to happen, if there was another way.

I lift my head.

"Wayvadd said something, once." I let go of Byers, sitting straighter. "Right after I came to the castle. He said if he had a choice, things would go differently. I didn't know what he meant then."

She stiffens. "You think he was talking about this?"

I scramble to my feet, hiking up my skirts to keep from tripping. "Maybe he knows another way this could end."

Then Byers is up, too, in a hurry, and we bolt out of the room.

The royal guards latch on to our procession, dogging us up the staircases. On the fourth floor, I speed past doors until I come to Wayvadd's and pound on it. When it cracks open, Wayvadd's pale eyes peek through the gap. "Sweet Mona," he croons. He opens the door wider. "And Bernadette. What a pleasant surprise."

"Move," I say flatly. He lets us in without a fight.

"To what do I owe the pleasure?" Wayvadd says, picking up a champagne flute from his end table. He rolls the stem between his fingers.

"Wayvadd, you once told me you were fond of me," I say. He chuckles at that. Gritting my teeth, I go on. "And that things would go differently, if it were up to you. What did you mean by that?"

He glances between the two of us. "And why are you asking, pray tell?"

"I know about the nexus, and what happens if I break it. The mortal realm is destroyed. And if I don't break it, it's still destroyed. Care to explain?"

He goes rigid. Then he laughs again, a soft, charming laugh. "Do I even want to know how you scrounged up that information?"

"What does it mean?" I stare sternly into his eyes. I am the queen of Opalvale. He owes me allegiance, as much as he does the king. "Why did the seven tell me breaking the nexus would stop the breaches in the veil?"

"It will, in a manner of speaking," he says with a shrug. I glare at him. Wayvadd sighs and adds, "Listen, *Queen* Mona—much of what we told you is true. The Flood is dynamic. Your world is static."

His free hand whorls in the air. With a pop, a spring appears between his fingers. He pinches the ends in both hands, holding it horizontal. "This is the Flood. And this"—a small red ball pops into existence between the coils—"is your world. For a while, everything was swell. But as the Flood expands . . ." He stretches out the spring, pulling the coils apart. The red ball drops through and bounces onto the floor. "Your world will fall out of existence. It's tragic, but that is the nature of all mortal things. They come to an end."

I watch the ball roll across the rug. "And that's what will happen when I break the nexus?"

"Yes, *Your Majesty*. And if you neglect to sever that connection, it will be worse. The Flood will expand, but your world will be fixed to it. The force will tear the mortal realm to shreds. You may not believe it, but we have asked you to deal with the nexus as an act of compassion."

"There must be some other way," Byers says. She takes a step forward. "You can't tell me our options are die or die faster."

"I'm sorry, ladies, but life isn't always fair. There's no way to fix this." He chuckles to himself. "You could make it worse, but you can't make it better."

I raise my head. Wayvadd never says anything unpremeditated. "We could make it worse?"

Wayvadd stares at me with slow, unhurried blinks. "Perhaps. But I—"

I charge up to him, and his head rears back. "How could we make it worse, Wayvadd?" I ask. Our noses are almost touching.

A smile stretches across his face. He bursts with clipped laughter. "Oh, *Mona*," he says, delighted. He claps me on the shoulder. "You never fail to surprise me. You want to magnify the suffering of your fellow mortals?"

"Just spit it out."

He hums. "Theoretically, one could forge *additional* connections between the Flood and the mortal realm. The breaches would worsen, and your kind would suffer for much longer. Years, perhaps. Wars, starvation. Much nastier than a quick blinking out or a week of demon rampages. Yes, a truly sadistic person might choose that path."

I look away from Wayvadd's cold eyes. We can stretch the end out? Then why wouldn't we? Better years of suffering than death within minutes. Years means time. Time to find another way.

"How would we do that?" I ask Wayvadd. "Form another connection to the Flood?"

He recoils, eyes bulging. "Mona, I didn't take you for the type. Who knew you could be so cruel?" He laughs again at the look on my face. "Don't bother. I won't teach you how. The rest of the seven would have my head. And you'd need to perform the ritual in the fortress, so good luck finding your way there."

"Well, why don't you tell me how to get inside?"

"Because I can't?" he says in his snottiest voice. "You can only get into the fortress if you know the way."

"That's why I asked you—"

"No," he interrupts. "Being given directions is not the same as knowing."

"Give me *something*, Wayvadd!" I explode, throwing up my hands. He smirks and lifts his eyebrows. "You have to give me something, or we're going to die! You get that, don't you? You understand?"

"Of course I do." He raises the glass to his lips. "But it's not my problem."

Furious, I turn to Byers, like she might rescue me. She shakes her head in little jerks. She has no answers.

I grab Wayvadd by the wrist. He pauses mid-sip. "Please," I say. "You wanted to help me, at one point. I know you did. Now's your chance."

"Sorry, Mona." His sharp grin widens. "Your choice is before you. The world is going to end, darling. All you can control is how."

40

In the cold and near dark, I sit on the hard stone floor of the council chambers. Not very queenly of me, but who cares? I'm alone, and the world is ending. I dismissed Byers, sending her off to be with Elizabeta. No point forcing her to stick around and catastrophize with me.

Should I go home, visit my family one last time? No, they would know something's amiss. I want them to be at peace when things come to a close. Not panicked. Despairing.

I sit there for hours, so long my legs go numb. The stump of my little finger prickles. The nexus glimmers before me, smothering my vision until I can see nothing else.

There is one unsolvable problem in the world. Only one.

And death hasn't conquered me yet.

41

Once I realize what I need to do, I have no more doubts. The conclusion is inevitable—fate, I suppose. For once, it's working in my favor.

I run to the fourth floor, to the gods' wing, and bust through Wayvadd's door. He stands up from his couch, surprised to see me back. I wonder if he expected me to have ended the world by now. What would happen to the gods then? Would their mortal bodies be shredded to bits while their souls bounced back into the Flood?

"Can I help you," he asks, "sweet Mona?"

I inhale, steadying my hands. This all depends on how much Wayvadd suspects. Does he know how long I spent in the Flood? How powerful I've become?

"I wanted to thank you," I say. "You're the only one of the seven who had the guts to tell me the truth. I hate you, but I respect you."

And I hold out my hand.

Wayvadd looks at it, bemused. The corner of his mouth bends up. "Respect, Mona?" He giggles, sounding drunk. "I am worthy of much more than respect. Adoration, maybe. Worship, certainly. But I'll accept it."

Wayvadd grabs my hand and shakes it.

I have seconds to act. My eyes never leave his as I ask the questions in my head.

How to get inside the fortress. How to forge another nexus.

The knowledge inhabits me abruptly.

42

To form another nexus, I'll need a connection on both sides, in the Flood and the mortal realm. I know exactly where to go: the magicians' conference room. The first Opalvale nexus belongs to the crown. The second will belong to the company.

I stride with purpose through the castle, avoiding the eyes of the guards and courtiers I pass. As if they might read in my gaze the unbearable truth I harbor. The spellsap lights in the conference room are dim when I arrive, as always when it isn't in use, but I can still see the milky marble paneling, the bronze-painted wainscoting.

I dash for the conference table, scooting aside the empty seawater dish, and I hoist myself onto the tabletop like a child climbing a tree stump. I have time to figure out what comes next. My royal guards stand at attention outside the door, barring interlopers.

All it will take is a series of spoken runes—just like severing the nexus, except a different incantation. It's not the process that gives me pause. It's the choice. This has to be the right thing, doesn't it? Preserving the mortal world? Or perhaps the gods are right—perhaps I'm fighting the inevitable. All mortal things come to an end. Am I interfering with nature?

Maybe I am interfering, but I don't care. I spent enough of my life frozen in indecision, afraid of taking action. Now I'm ready. I stare at the grain of the table and prepare myself.

The door to the conference room flies open.

With a sharp breath, I look over. Whitman comes rushing inside. My guards have no authority to stop the master of practitioners from entering his own conference room, it seems.

"I saw your retinue out there." He takes in my appearance—hair down, disheveled, huddled on a table. "Mona, the council's in an uproar. What *was* that, with Simon Hansen? What are you doing in here?"

Lips parted, I grapple for an excuse. I don't want to tell him the truth. I can't bear to put that knowledge in his head. And if Whitman knew the stakes, he'd have to involve the council, and the Circle Court, and there would be days, maybe months, of debate.

"Do you trust me, master?" I ask.

Bewildered, he tugs on the cuffs of his sleeves. "Yes. I do."

"I can't tell you what I'm doing, but it will help Opalvale. It . . ." I stumble over the next part. "It won't make Elsie's death right. I don't know if it will get her justice. But—but if I don't do this, her sacrifice will mean nothing."

He shakes his head, like I'm speaking nonsense. Which I am. I wouldn't blame him if he turned around and left. But instead, without argument, he walks over to the table and climbs up, his long limbs bent at odd angles beneath him. It's almost enough to make me laugh, or maybe cry. Straightening his master's jacket, he settles cross-legged in front of me and says, "So, what are we doing up here?"

I grab his hand and place it palm down on the table. Heart pounding, I rest my hand atop his. "We're doing magic."

I squeeze my eyes shut. Then, voice warbling, I speak the runes—a short, blunt set of words, tasting steely on my tongue. A sudden wind blows back my curls, and my eyelids fly open.

The room looks the same.

That's fine. Some runes take time to ignite. I lean back on the heels of my hands and say, uncertainly, "We may have to wait."

Whitman nods, folding his hands in his lap. For all he knows, I've finally lost it and all of this is nonsense. Either he really does trust me, or he cares enough to humor me.

Nerves bubble in my stomach as we wait for the runes to manifest. I have no plan if this doesn't work. "I think I should tell you something," I blurt out.

"What?"

"I don't know. I—I don't know how to say it." I'm not even sure what I want to say.

He's silent, reaching across the table to stroke my arms. Am I scaring him? I hope not. I want him to be at peace, too.

"I'm not good at these things." To my eternal embarrassment, I'm teary-eyed. Over this? When the whole of existence is done for? "All I want to say is, with enough time, I'd find a way to tell you. . . . I'd get better at it, I think. Being a real person. And there's so much I wish I could say to you now, but I don't even know how to properly—"

"Mona." He lifts my chin with a finger. I sniffle, staring into his dark eyes. "You won't be queen forever. We have time."

An invisible hand crushes my heart. I swallow the sob that threatens to escape me, turn it into a wet laugh. "You're right," I say, brushing a strand of hair from his forehead. "Of course you're right."

"What's this?" comes a voice from behind us.

Byers stands in the doorway with a dubious frown. Whitman and I must look a sight, sitting on the conference room table. I open my mouth to explain.

A flash of light interrupts me.

With a start, I swivel toward its source. From the table's center, a glimmering tunnel of teal light sprouts up toward the ceiling. The mortal end of the second nexus.

"It worked," I breathe. My voice swells with excitement. "It worked!" I turn back to Byers. "This is it. We can fix this."

Her eyes widen. She grasps my meaning. We can delay the mortal realm's end.

"What can I do?" she says, striding forward. "Can I help?"

"What is this?" Whitman cuts in. I almost forgot he was there. His face is warped with shocked wonder. "Is this the nexus?"

"Almost," I say. "I can't tell you everything yet. We just need you to keep this quiet for a bit, until Byers and I can finish it."

He grips his knees, unable to take his eyes from the pillar of light. I wish I could hold him, hush him, tell him this will all work out. "What are you going to do?" he asks.

I look to Byers. "We have to go to the Flood," I say. "We need Tasha."

43

With the knowledge I stole from Wayvadd, I have my way in, and my way how. I'm only missing the who.

The voyage to Tasha's passes quickly. Byers and I know the path well by now. When we reach the cliffs and I call her name, she walks out on the balcony right away, like she expected us. Her nose wrinkles.

"You're stupider than I thought," she says, "coming back here."

I grin sadly. "You were right about me, Tasha. I am dangerous."

That catches her attention.

Despite her lukewarm greeting, she lowers the lift and guides us to the house, into her parlor. Brews us mugs of steaming tea. An impulse to rush her screams within me; this is too important to wait for tea to steep. But I know how Tasha responds to being rushed.

When the tea is done, we sit on cushions across from each other, like old times. "What do you want?" Tasha asks bluntly.

"Byers missed you," I say. "You should let her visit sometimes." Byers twists toward me, staring daggers.

Tasha harrumphs. "If that's why you're here, you—"

"Please. I wouldn't have come back if I had any choice."

I tell her everything that's happened. I tell her what must be done.

Her tea remains untouched as she listens. "And you want me to—"

"It has to be you," I say. "There's no one else." I reach out, laying my hand over hers. Tasha twitches like she wants to pull away. "You took me in for a reason. You knew what I was up against. Now I need your help to finish it."

She stares between me and Byers. I have no backup plan if she refuses. No one else has her unique qualifications. I need her help to form the second nexus.

Her mouth flat, Tasha nods.

I release a sigh of relief through my nose. One problem down. Now I only have to stop the world from ending. Far less daunting than convincing Tasha of anything.

"We'll need to go to the fortress," I say.

Tasha's brow creases, like maybe she thinks she agreed too soon, now that she knows how stupid the plan is. "Mortals can't enter the fortress."

"Unless they know the way."

"What's that supposed to mean?"

I smirk. "Come with me. I'll show you."

I lead the two of them—Korimarr's two favored mortals—to an inlet near the isle. I concentrate my intent; I choose the way purposefully. We stop at a bay covered in broken, pearlescent shells, waves of mercury-thick water lapping on the shore. The Flood's ocean within an ocean. Byers and Tasha stare across the bay to the isle on the other side. The water is impassible, deep and unyielding, nothing like the liquid magic surrounding us. Under normal circumstances, we wouldn't dare to cross it.

I crouch near the waterline. On the surface layer of the sea, I trace a rune with my fingertip: mohelo, for knowing.

Where my finger touches, the ocean crystallizes.

I stand up and watch as a solid crust of silver-blue glass spreads out from the rune, across the bay. It forms a narrow path. The glass stretches in a line, growing, cascading, until it reaches the other side, planting its far end on the isle's beach.

"It's a riddle," I say, turning to Tasha and Byers. "You have to *know* the way."

"So, this is it?" Byers swallows. Sweat beads her forehead. "We're breaking into the fortress?"

"What choice do we have?" Tasha says.

I nod in solid agreement. No more debate to be had on the matter. The gods left me no choice but to defy them.

I take the first step onto the path.

PART VII

THE ISLE IN THE FLOOD

44

I've dreamed about this place since I was eight: the isle in the Flood, where the seat of the seven gods and the garden of the dead lie hidden behind fortress walls. To enter, you must already know the way.

Beyond the walls, there's the fortress, grand and gargantuan. Ceilings that a whale could swim beneath, dipping and peaking with limestone arches, supported by pillars three arm spans wide. Pale halls, inlaid with gems and precious metals. A throne room big enough to fit all of Castle Selledore inside. At the front of the room, there's a seat carved of ancient stone. Semyanadd's throne.

I rush us through the empty, cavernous halls. No time to stop and gape, though I want to, badly. I don't know how long we have until the gods catch up. We press onward, through twisted gates that scrape the mottled sky. The backmost gates, the gates that lead to the isle's most sacred site.

The garden of the dead.

A blanket of murky green stretches for miles beneath the roiling purple sky. Weeping willows the size of houses line neat paths that weave together like spiderwebs. Crystal pools dot the ground. Between the trees, wispy forms glide past. My pulse speeds up at the sight of them. The souls of departed mortals.

Tasha and I stand across from each other at the base of the grand staircase. Byers, twining her hands together, stays back. The garden sprawls to our side.

"What now?" Tasha says. She doesn't look scared. She doesn't look anything at all.

I kneel, pulling Elsie's broken crossbow bolt from the pockets of my gown. I plant it in the loamy earth. A marker. "We come to an agreement," I say, standing. "Then you speak the runes. I've done it on the mortal end already."

She nods, but I'm distracted by a pearly wall accumulating at our side. I glance over, and my breath hitches. Ghosts—hundreds of them, forming a crowd. They're gathering. Watching.

Heart stammering, I address them. "I know we're trespassing. But we're here to help the mortal realm. Do we have your permission?"

They stare vacantly.

I speak again, tripping over my words. "Is . . . Is Patrick Arnett here?"

None of them move. Tasha pinches me on the arm. My eyes snap back to hers.

"You don't have time for a family reunion," she says. "Let's get this over with."

She's right. I give her the runes to repeat. The new connection will form right there, between us.

"Mona?"

I know that voice. I search the crowd of ghosts, my sight sharpened by hope.

One ghost steps forward.

Patrick scowls at me, his pale form rippling. My red scarf is wrapped around his wrist.

"There you are!" he says, holding out his arms. "You can't run away like that, I thought I'd lost you! Do you know how angry Mother would be?"

I cover my mouth as a whimper rushes out of me. I step toward him. "Patrick?"

"Obviously." He waves me over. "Come, it's getting late. We need to be home by sunset."

He's speaking to me. This ghost is nothing like the one that haunted me—the silent, vengeful one. Even his face has been restored to its former handsome warmth. I remember what Irinorr told me: *He may not be fully himself, outside of the Flood.*

But here in the garden, Patrick is himself again.

Patrick knows me now. He spoke to me as if no time has passed, like I'm the same eight-year-old brat he dragged home every night.

I wipe my wet cheek with the back of my hand. "You don't hate me?"

Patrick snorts a laugh. "What are you talking about?" He floats closer, sets his hand on my shoulder. I don't feel a thing. "I could never hate you, Mona."

I reach out to touch his cheek, but my fingers pass through it. I suck a breath through my teeth. "I'll be ready to go in a minute. I just need to take care of something."

Patrick shoots me an exasperated frown but nods. He steps back to blend in with the crowd of ghosts.

I turn to Tasha. Her stony expression bolsters me. I nod once, and she opens her mouth. Speaks the runes.

They sound beautiful, falling from her lips.

Nothing happens right away. I'm expecting it this time. Just like on the mortal side, these runes will need a few minutes to cement. To my side, Byers' shoulders are bunched up to her ears. She looks like she's been crying. I wonder fleetingly if she saw her parents out there. Did they speak to her, too?

A booming thud shakes the ground beneath us, like a giant door being slammed. Could the nexus have formed that quickly? I whirl around, but there's no beam of light.

"Someone else is here," Tasha says. "On the isle."

A jolt of fear shoots through me. The gods have arrived to stop us. Could they reverse the runes Tasha has spoken? I glance between her and Byers.

"Stay here," I say. "Guard this spot. I'll hold them off."

Byers steps toward me. "One of us should come with—"

"No. I don't want them suspecting I had help." I need them to underestimate me, as they have all along. The Mona they know never depended on others, or let others depend on her.

That Mona would not have gotten far on her own.

Tasha nods. "We've got you. Go."

I turn on my heel and run.

I reach the main hall of the fortress without a second to spare. As I jog for the dais, a series of loud, furious footsteps thuds up the entryway stairs. Their source will be within sight any moment. I dive for Semyanadd's throne.

When Irinorr finds me, I'm slouched in the throne, my legs crossed, chin propped up on my knuckles. I will myself not to pant for breath.

"Not so fun from the other side of the throne, is it?" I call as he crosses the endless room. No one follows after him. I expected their full force, but perhaps the gods believed Irinorr alone would best be able to negotiate with me.

He's wearing the guise of a god again. His crow head tilts in worry—it seems genuine—as he appraises me, taking in my dress scuffed with mud, my black tiara askew. He approaches with caution, skirting the column of light that bursts from the floor. The original Opalvale nexus—the Flood's end of the connection. It bathes the tile around it in a puddle of aqueous blue light.

Irinorr walks closer. "Why did you come here, Mona?"

"Isn't the better question *how* I came here?"

"How does not concern me. I want to know that you are not hurt. That you have not done anything rash."

I clench my fists until my knuckles blanch. "Why'd you have to do it this way, Iri? Why couldn't you have told us what was happening, let *us* make the choice?"

"Because there is no choice to be made." A creeping urgency sneaks into his voice. "There is the way of mercy or the way of suffering. I love you, and all my mortal children. I would never choose for you to suffer."

"But it's not your choice," I reply, harsher than I intended. "It's ours, and you tried to steal it from us."

"It is not only mortals—"

"You used me, Iri. All those years, were you even mentoring me? Or were you honing a tool?"

"You must believe that I love you. You do not know how it has pained me to set you on this course. But I could not stand to see you suffer, Mona. I could not bear it."

My eyes sting as I look away. He steps closer.

"It's over now," he says softly. "Whatever you set out to do here, it will not work. Let me take you to the castle. We'll do it together. What do you say?" He stretches out his hand.

I stare down at it, disdainful. "How did you find me? Wayvadd told you?"

"He guessed what you had done, after your last meeting. Semyanadd is . . . not pleased he allowed you to pull that trick."

I smirk. That, at least, brings me some measure of satisfaction.

"Mona." Irinorr sighs, his crow beak clicking. "It is no use. To form another connection between the Flood and the mortal realm, you would need a resident of the Flood to agree to the pact. You knew the gods were unwilling. Did you think the demon clans would comply?"

I shrug. He needs to believe I'm foolish, full of hubris. Like I usually am. "I've dealt with demons before."

"Even so, it is too late. The connection takes time to form. If you started the process now, I would interrupt it. There is nothing left for you to try. Come home, Mona. Say goodbye. It is time."

I lean back in the throne, humming. The Mona he knows wouldn't let him sway her so easily. Best to keep playing hard to get. "You need me to sever this connection, yes? What do I get out of it? Can we negotiate?"

Irinorr's black eyes are wet, like liquid obsidian. "Mona, when the nexus is broken, you will die."

"What if I don't want to die? You're a god, Iri. Can't you make that happen?"

"You wish to become a denizen of the Flood? To live here once the mortal realm ceases to exist?"

"Yes," I say, nodding in slow approval. "Could you make it so, if I asked?"

Something like disgust shimmers in the black pools of his eyes. "I would have to consult the others."

A deep-earth tremble shakes the walls of the fortress, loosing dust from the ceiling. Particles float down through the soupy air. Irinorr glances up, spins around in confusion.

It's finished.

"Never mind." Giddiness wells inside me, hysterical and overpowering. I giggle into my fist. "It's over now."

Irinorr circles back to me as the shaking dies down. "What have you done?"

I stand from the throne. "I can show you, if you'd like."

Like something from a dream, I guide Irinorr down the halls of the fortress, to the garden of the dead. In the foreground of the garden, at the bottom of the stair-case, shines a beam of light. It sprouts from the ground around Elsie's broken bolt like a clear blue tree trunk. The light glitters, drifting downward in a shower.

Irinorr's breath comes fast through his beak. He doesn't rip his gaze from the column of light. "How?"

I smile at him. "Gods and demons aren't the only ones who live in the Flood."

"Hello, Irinorr," Tasha says. Right on cue.

She wanders into view from her hiding spot beside a glassy pool and stops on the other side of the shaft of light we've built together.

Byers comes out, too, her face lined with determination. "Irinorr," she says with a respectful nod.

He glances between us, bare shoulders tensed. "What have you done?" he says, the weight of his despair dragging the words down. "You have put the Flood at risk. You've joined the two realms so tightly, *both* will be torn apart."

"Good. That should give you plenty of incentive to solve the problem."

"There is no solution. There is no way to stop this."

"You'd better get creative, then."

Irinorr stands stock-still, emotions masked behind his animal expression. "The breaches will get worse, much faster. Demon armies will take your lands. The carnage—"

"Spare me," I say, holding up my hand. I have no desire to hear it. Not yet. In time, I'll have to face what I've done. But not today. "All I want is for you to gather the seven and figure out how you're going to make this right."

Irinorr shakes his head. "The best and quickest way is to revoke the contract—to sever this connection."

"Not going to happen," Tasha cuts in. "I agree with Mona. The world may be a shithole, but it deserves a chance to be saved."

In the corner of my eye, ghosts meander through the garden, gleaming between trees. Patrick is out there, somewhere. At peace. I can't say if he's truly forgiven me, or if I might forgive myself someday. But my brother loves me, even after I killed him.

When Irinorr speaks again, it is with a deep, fragile sadness. "You will come to regret what you have done today, Mona. It pains me, the suffering you have guaranteed yourself. And others." He lifts a hand in the air. "When that time comes and you wish to take back what you've done, I will be there for you."

Irinorr snaps, and my vision blurs gray.

45

He's transported us to council chambers, Byers and me.

The masters, and even the king, are gathered. A meeting about our sudden disappearance, I would wager. The seven have returned to the Flood for good. The old marble basins stand in place of their thrones, as though nothing ever happened.

Every face turns toward us as we materialize in the room, all wide eyes and frozen expressions.

I touch my tiara, adjusting it. Perfect center.

"There are some things you need to know," I begin.

46

In my royal quarters, I wait for news. I expected to hear *something* before now, three days since we forged the second nexus. Reports of invasions, disasters. Evidence of the breaches stretching wider. But there's been nothing yet.

By the time Whitman comes to see me, late-afternoon sunshine is streaming through my window. He pauses at the doorway to glance behind; a guard's foot sticks through the crack in the door, propping it open. Now that I'm queen, strange men are not allowed in my bedchambers—not without a chaperone. Whitman doesn't comment on it. He sets his jaw and moves on.

"You have news?" I ask.

He nods, rubbing the back of his neck. "The first invasion. A small band of demons in Essen. Casualties in the dozens."

"What clan?"

"The report doesn't mention, but they wore red uniforms."

"The boar clan." I wrinkle my nose. Verimall's demons have always been the most brutal of the seven clans. I let that reality flow through my veins, icy cold. My fault. Every moment of pain and cruelty from here on out.

But every moment of hope, too, and joy and life.

I can't help myself. I have to ask. "Did I do the right thing?"

Whitman bows his head, and my stomach sinks. "The right thing?" he says. "I imagine the right thing would have been to take this to the Circle Court. Then it could truly be a decision made by mortals. Not just one of us, but all of us." As I cringe, he adds, "But in your shoes, I would have done the same."

Incredibly, that means a lot to me. If Whitman would've made the same choice, it can't be all bad.

I give him a weak smile and change the subject. "What of Honored Delphin?" I ask. The third traitor. The patrolmen of the master of justice's order—who've been temporarily assigned to Lane, master of war, until a replacement can be found for Oversea—spread out across the kingdom to search for Delphin, in the unlikely case he is still within our borders. Chances are he headed straight back to Deveneaux.

Yet in his absence, Delphin answered another mystery through the dossiers he left behind: the three bribes, when only two seers lied. Delphin paid off Tellerman, but the seer got cold feet at the last minute. He gave his real reading instead. The gods didn't rig Tellerman's reading; they shouldn't have needed to. By all rights, he should have lied and delivered a false prediction. The gods' glimpses into the future surely foretold it that way. But Tellerman, as humans are wont to do, acted unpredictably. He went off and divined the rightful queen.

Technically, Tellerman committed a crime by accepting a bribe in the first place, but I'm in no hurry to bring charges.

Everyone deserves a second chance, right?

"Delphin's safe in Deveneaux by now, likely," Whitman answers, echoing my thoughts. "You could request the Circle Court extradite him to face trial here."

"Sounds like trouble we can't afford at the moment."

He nods, his face grim. "I have to tell you," he says in a rush. "I've been removed as master of practitioners."

"What?" In my lap, my hands squeeze fistfuls of skirt. "The council can't do that!"

He attempts a pained smile. "Yes, they can. Isaac cosigned it. I . . . I think he blames me for Elsie's death."

"That's stupid," I spit. "It was my fault, if anyone's."

"And I'm the one who brought you here." Shrugging, he shoves his hands in his pockets. Resigned but not defeated. "I don't regret it. The council was always going to push me out. This just gave them an excuse."

My bottom lip quivers. All Whitman ever wanted was to be part of the Royal Practitioners Company. It defined him, gave him purpose. But maybe this injustice is a blessing in disguise—a chance for him to step out of his mother's shadow. "What will you do instead?" I ask.

"I'll be touring Opalvale with a company of soldiers. To learn what we're facing."

"What?" I shoot to my feet. "For how long?"

"As long as I'm needed, at His Majesty's discretion."

I wet my lips, at a loss. We have no clue how dangerous the world is about get. Why would Isaac send Whitman into that mess?

He can't do this. I won't let him.

I surge up to Whitman, clutching his jacket. "What do you know about fighting demons?" I hiss, shaking him. "You're going to get yourself killed!" I shake him again for good measure.

"I'll be careful." He grabs my hips, drawing me closer. "This is how I can help, Mona. This is my part to play. It's no more dangerous than what you did in taking the throne."

My fists tighten around his starched jacket. I fumble through my thoughts, desperate for a way out. Nothing comes to me. Just another shred of suffering I've brought into the world.

He sweeps a curl out of my eyes. "It won't be forever."

"Oh? Just like how I won't be queen forever?" I say with a pout. Now that we know how dire the breaches will become, and how much depends on the nexus, it would be foolhardy for me to step down. Especially considering Isaac's poor health.

"Yes," he says, "like that. There's a light at the end of the tunnel. I promise." He bends his head and presses his lips against mine. I shut my eyes, try to store away this warm, safe feeling inside me.

I feel him pull away, headed for the door, and suddenly, it's too much. He can't leave me—not like this. I rack my brain for something to say.

"I know you're in love with me, Whitman," I call out, holding my breath. I chance a peek through my eyelids. He pauses halfway to the door.

"I thought we should get that out in the open, before you go," I say.

He smiles over his shoulder. "And I know you're in love with me. But I don't think that's how these declarations work."

I smile back, and Whitman disappears through the doorway.

The moment the door snaps shut, I rush toward the hall that joins my room to the king's quarters. I knock before barging in.

Isaac is sitting up in bed, looking better than he has in days. He swings his legs over the side and rises.

"Why are you firing Whitman?" I say, arms knotted across my chest.

He grunts as he stretches to his full height. "I'm reassigning him. Master Whitman is the best man to assess this threat."

"That's bullshit." I jab a finger at him. "You're punishing him. Don't do this, Isaac. Don't take your pain out on your best friend."

Isaac shuffles over to his floor-to-ceiling windows, staring outside. "Del has to go on a little road trip, and you're comparing that to what I've been through?"

"That's not what I'm saying. I . . . I just wish you wouldn't send him away."

Isaac glances sidelong at me, arms crossed. "There's also the matter of what Master Renfield told me."

The blood drains from my face. "She— What?"

"About you and Delmar. How she caught you."

"Isaac, I—"

"Don't worry, she came directly to me. The rest of the council doesn't know. Renfield is smart enough to realize that discrediting you publicly isn't in anyone's best interest. But if word does get out, somebody will eventually put together that you could bear a child who isn't mine. A contested heir. So, you see, Delmar can't stay here."

Despair winds around my windpipe. I can't bear to contemplate any scenario where *I'm* the one giving birth to a baby princeling. I always assumed I'd get out of that somehow. Now the thought seems naive. Worst of all, it's my fault Whitman is being sent away. He kept saying we should be careful, and I pushed him, brought him down to my level. I can't even be angry with Renfield. She probably did the right thing.

Isaac turns toward me, takes a step in my direction. "You saw the garden of the dead, didn't you?"

My head whirls at the sudden shift in conversation. "Well—yes, but—"

"Can you take me there?"

My mouth falls open. I didn't expect the question, nor do I know how to answer. I can't tell him what he wants to hear. "No, Isaac," I say as gently as I can. "There isn't a way."

He strides closer still, until he looms in my face. His bloodshot eyes burn. "Please, Mona. Do this for me, and I swear, I'll make Delmar a master again—you can have your own apartments together, for all I care. Just let me see Elsie."

"I can't, though— There isn't—"

"Please!" he cries, and tears spill onto his cheeks. He falls forward, his face pressed against my shoulder, like he could burrow inside me. "Please let me see her."

He weeps, shuddering. I don't know what to say. I stare ahead and bring up my hands to rub his back, and I shush him—my husband, the king—as he sobs into my dress.

The magicians' common room has an unusual guest.

Technically, it has two. The first is me, sprawled on the couch with a bottle of wine swinging from my hand. The second is a gorgeous tabby cat, its fur sleek and shiny. It slinks through the doorway and jumps up on the cushion beside me, curling into a ball. I've never seen a cat in the castle before.

"Where'd you come from, kitty?" I say, reaching out to pet it.

It lifts its head. "From your mother's house."

I gape as the pieces clunk into place. "Wayvadd?"

"Aren't you clever," he drawls. He rests his head back down on his paws.

"What are you doing here? And like *that*?"

"Oh, you know," he sighs. "When you pulled that stunt on me, Semyanadd wasn't thrilled. Not thrilled at all. So he stripped me of my godhood, turned me into a mortal. These things happen."

My eyes bulge. "He can do that?"

"He hasn't had the need, for the past billion years or so, but he can."

"Did he do the same to Verimall?"

"The boar? Oh, she was much cleverer than I. She knew how livid Semyanadd would be at her disobedience, so she ran."

"Ran? To where?"

"Who knows? Personally, I hope never to find out."

I eye him warily. "And you're not angry with me?"

He chuckles, revealing pointed, gleaming teeth. "Now, when did I say that? No, Mona. I revile you. And you'd better get used to me, because I plan to stick around. I want to witness every delicious moment of your downfall."

I swallow past the lump in my throat. "What does that mean, my downfall?"

He chuckles again. "You have no idea, do you? What you've done? All those holes in the fabric of reality? When the veil tears in the mortal realm, demons pour through. But what about in the Flood? When the veil tears there, what pours through then?" He rolls onto his back and stretches out a paw. "You have no conception of what you've unleashed. Your mind can't begin to comprehend it."

My forehead breaks out in a cold sweat. "This really is the Rising Tide, isn't it?"

"The Rising bloody Tide again!" He rolls his eyes, a skill I didn't realize cats possessed. Perhaps it's just him. "Haven't you figured out that's nothing more than a mortal ghost story? The gods only played along because we needed you scared. If anything, *you* created the Rising Tide. Stop trying to blame some apocalyptic prophecy. It's just your bad luck."

I calm my shaking limbs. He's playing games. Messing with my head—his favorite hobby. "Well, I think you wanted me to do it," I declare.

His whiskers pull back in a mewling laugh. "Oh, *of course*. You caught me, you clever thing. It was all part of my grand plan to destroy the universe. Listen to yourself, woman."

I squint at him. Whatever Wayvadd claims, he wouldn't have brought up a second nexus unless he hoped, in some recess of his soul, that I would forge one. Why mention it at all, if not for that? He counted on me doing what mortals do best: finding some way, however improbable, to ruin the gods' divine plans.

It makes perfect sense. For Wayvadd, the end of the mortal realm must have seemed unendurable. An infinite lifespan with no one around to worship you, no puny human minds to mess with? Worse than death. Perhaps he didn't mean to lose his godhood in the process, but plans are rarely executed without a setback or two.

"I don't believe you," I say.

"I don't care," he replies with a yawn. "Your doom is nigh, all the same."

I've had enough. "Shoo, cat," I say, shoving him out of the seat. Wayvadd yowls and darts from the room, slipping out just as someone else walks in.

It's Bernadette Byers, wearing a starched black-and-gold master's uniform. I stifle a giggle of surprise.

"Why do I find you irresistibly attractive all of a sudden?" I say, tapping my chin reflectively.

Scowling, she plops onto the couch and sighs, "It's only temporary, until they fill the master of practitioners's seat."

"You mean until Master Whitman returns," I say aggressively. I haven't given up hope that he'll be reinstated.

She makes no comment on that. "Why are you drinking in here?"

"I'm the queen. I can drink wherever I damn please." In truth, I'm not sure what I'm doing here. Better this than sulking in my royal quarters. And perhaps it's a stepping stone, of sorts, to other parts of the castle. Other parts of the world.

You have to start somewhere.

Byers crosses her legs and slouches. Her eyes are puffy and dark from lack of sleep—nightmares again. "Look at us, Arnett. The two most powerful women in the world."

"Hey, now." I pass her the wine bottle. "Don't qualify it. We're the two most powerful *people* in the world."

"Hear, hear." She takes a swig from the bottle and hands it back.

Byers has the right of it. She and I—the queen and the master of practitioners—have powerful magic and positions to match. There's not anything beyond us, any wrong we can't reverse. We can drive back demon armies. Protect the people of Opalvale, preserve their hope in the bleak days to come.

Restore rightful rulers to the throne.

"Hypothetically, Byers," I say, drumming my fingers against the bottle, "if you wanted to bring someone back from the dead, how would you go about it?"

ACKNOWLEDGMENTS

I would like to extend my sincere thanks to the following:

To my inexhaustible agent, Laura Rennert, for sticking with it even when we thought hope was lost; your tenacity and indomitable spirit got us here today. To my editor, Rachel Stark, and editorial assistant, Elanna Heda, for seeing through to the heart of this book and helping me craft the perfect YA version. My deepest thanks and gratitude to the authenticity readers who offered their perspectives and insight. To the entire team at Hyperion, including the people I haven't met yet, for bringing this story to life.

To my mentors, Rachel Morris and Ava Reid, for all the support and guidance, and for picking my book in the first place—I still feel incredibly lucky. An extra special thanks to WF/FW/NDZ/whatever we're calling ourselves these days, who are quite literally the other half of my brain cell; each and every one of you is on this list, so don't make me type it out. An even specialer thanks to Vaishnavi Patel for holding my hand during the showcase and to Sami B. Ellis for the webtoon recaps.

Huge thanks, bear hugs, and windmill high fives to my early readers for their invaluable input and encouragement: Lore Austin, Catherine Bakewell, Cate Baumer, Connie Chang, A. Y. Chao, Micah Clarke, Kate Dylan, Chandra Fisher, Lani Frank,

Gigi Griffis, R. K. Justice, Mary Li, Victor Manibo, Erik Mercer, Briana Miano, Shelley Parker-Chan, Sarah Mughal Rana, Allison Saft, Bee Shabbir, E. J. Sidle, Jen St. Jude, Lauri Starling, Emily Varga, and anyone else I'm forgetting.

To the team at Fox Ballard for all your support over the long, grueling years of failure (and the somewhat shorter years of success). Special thanks and credit to Taliah Ahdut for letting me straight-up steal your whole name. To the Overlake BHU for lending me that pencil and paper. To my therapist, for obvious reasons.

To my parents: There are no words to describe how grateful I am for the idyllic childhood you provided us and the pretty okay adulthoods you continue to be involved in. To the Helander, Jones, Smail, and Correia extended families for your contributions to my happy memories. To Allison and Emily, my first friends and earliest readers: You are my actual soulmates.

And to Mikey, my biggest supporter—emotionally, nutritionally, psychiatrically, and otherwise: Eighteen years later and I still haven't met anybody else like you. I'm starting to suspect I never will. Thank you for seeing why other people might like this book.